Enjoy

More than a Job,
An Adventure

By

Meredith "Ike" Anderson

Mill Creek Press

Salt Lake City, Utah

The events and characters in this book are fictitious. Certain real locations and public figures are mentioned, but all other characters and events described in this book are totally imaginary.

Published in the United States by Mill Creek Press, LLC

Library of Congress Control Number: 2007926720

ISBN: 978-0-9740158-6-6

Printed in the United States of America on acid-free paper

Mill Creek Press web site address: www.millcreekpress.com

pfb32975
First Edition

Cover Design: Kristi Publications

Dedication

To Linda Anderson, my lovely wife, whose love, patience and encouragement has made this book possible.

To Nikki Hansen, the college Dean who told Meredith he had talent.

To my niece, Brenda Mae Kinghorn Welch, without whose love and nagging, some of the characters would not have come to life.

To Meredith's brother, Levor Oldham, the true and loyal friend who is always there.

To Ceil DeYoung, Vicki Wheeler, June Barrus, Christy Petrie, Shamayne Mason and the other members of the League of Utah Writers who have critiqued this book.

To my friend Mike Eldredge who inspired me to get this project into print.

To the men and officers who served aboard the USS CURRITUCK SOUND (AV7), and the USS PRINCETON (LPH5).

Navy & Marine Corps Rank and Rate Chart

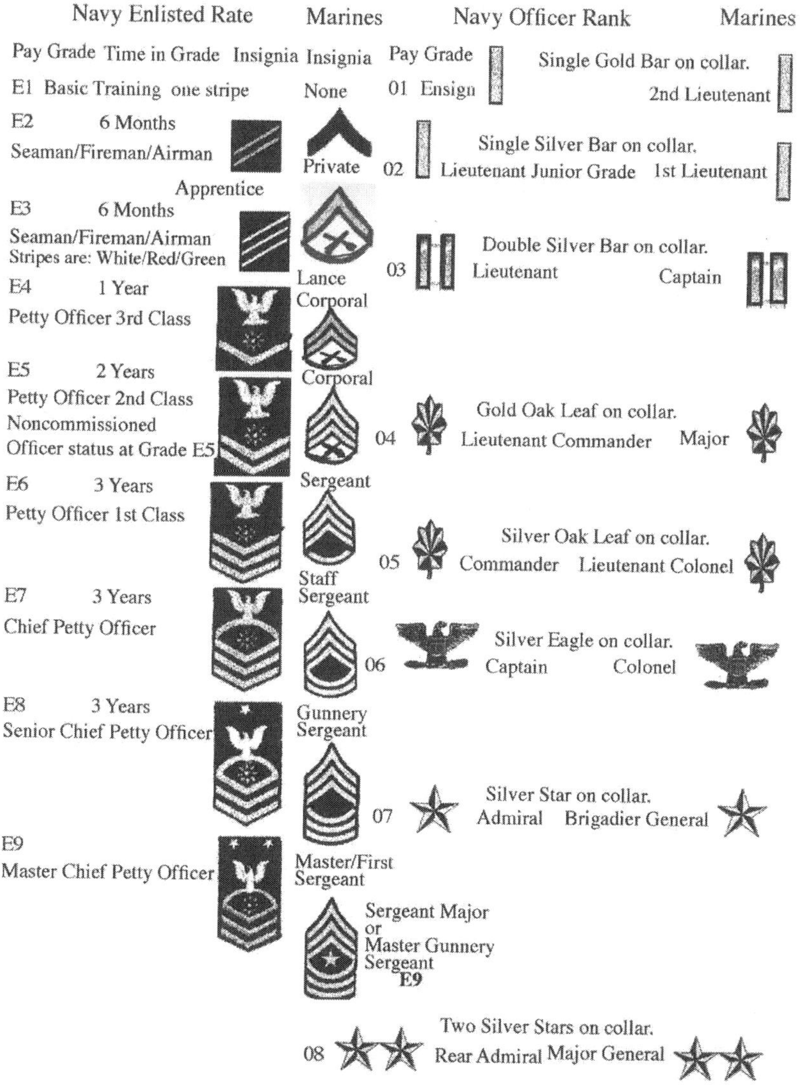

More than a Job,
An Adventure

Chapter 1

Running Away

Pete lathered soap over his lean wiry body. Shampoo bubbles caused his hair to stand high on his head. He felt the tremor under his feet. The building shook. The whole crew rushed from their showers to the windows to look at the head frame of the mine shaft. Seventeen naked men, dripping suds and water, held their breath as they watched.

An explosion! Fire, fed by gas, raced through the tunnel of the mine like an angry dragon chasing its prey. A yellow-brown ball of fire, dust and rocks blew high into the sky as the fire serpent's head sprang from the mine entrance into the open and gasped for air. Like a great dying beast, it shook its head violently and fell forward to die near the shower house. Debris rained onto the roof.

Next, came a ball of smoke, like someone might exhale from a cigar. Great billows of white, gray and black rolled from the tunnel entrance and ebbed away at the surface. Emergency alarms blared in the compound. Miners and engineers ran everywhere.

Pete grabbed a towel and began to brush water from his body, ignoring the soap in his hair. Men dripping with water moved quickly through the shower house in various stages of nudity. Pete dropped his towel and began climbing back into his mining gear.

The door to the shower building burst open. It was Pete's shift foreman, Art Hause. He was pale and breathless. "Get your gear on men! We have a job to do!" Without another word, he went to his locker and started changing back into his mining clothes.

Within five minutes the entire first shift of eighteen men were dressed in oxygen breathing gear, descending into the mine as the cable paid out from the machinery house.

A gas and engineering team had gone down already. Lighting had been restored the full length of the main tunnel. When first shift got to the bottom, the engineers had already attached portable air pumps to the venting system that had not been crushed by the explosion or the cave-in. The air had cleared. It was breathable.

Pete pulled off his breathing gear and looked around, hoping no one could see the fear in his eyes.

There was no sign of caving in the south drift as the men stood at the intersection of the three tunnels. The entrance of the north drift on the other hand had caved badly. The steel rock bolts strained precariously but held. The chain link fence fabric against the ceiling swelled downward like a balloon about to burst.

Art was yelling orders. "Pete, you go with Ransom and Casey. Bring power equipment from the south drift."

Instead of mucking the fallen rock into bucket cars and taking it to the surface as usual, the miners diverted the overburden into the south drift as fast as they could. In an hour, they discovered there was only spot caving. The air smelled nasty, like spoiled cooked cabbage, a smell that made Pete think of the swamp lands next to the Colorado River where he used to hunt ducks.

Shortly after breaking through the cave-in at the entrance to the drift, the miners found the first body. It was the second shift gas man. He had not reached the work site in time to prevent the accident.

Damn, Max! For your own sake, you weren't late enough, thought Pete.

Doctor Newell arrived from town and the medical team carried the body away to the surface.

The team was feverishly filling a mucking bucket at the third caving when Art came up behind Pete. "You guys take five and get a drink of water." His deep voice crackled. He banged his fist on the side of the mucking car they were filling. "The medical team says we're not going to find any survivors." His face was grave and he was almost sobbing. He turned slightly, hiding the tears swelling his lower eyelids. "When the gas exploded, the fire drained all the oxygen from the drift. The air was sucked right out of the gas man's lungs. They would've all died of instant suffocation if they weren't caved on."

Pete always told himself he would never work underground, but here he was. After graduating high school in the spring of '63, a friend of his deceased father had hired him. He had spent the last two months working as a powder man's helper. It was dirty, dangerous work, but he had been raised around hard rock mines. His mother said that drilling and blasting were in his blood, but he was frightened of being underground. It was all he could do to sit on the shuttle when his shift group started down into the mine every working day.

The mine was over a thousand feet deep with two main drifts. His shift, the first shift, worked on the south drift and the second shift worked on the north drift. At this mine, the two tunnels, or drifts, coming off the main shaft were rich in uranium ore. The north drift was afflicted with all sorts of problems. It had to have extra water pumps, vent fans and air pumps because they hit so many small pockets of gas and so much water. In spite of the problems, the uranium ore being taken from the north drift was much richer than the ore Pete's shift was taking from the south drift. The company was paying a bonus of a hundred dollars per drift foot mined and the second shift was getting out almost ten drift feet per shift.

The shuttle, for all its modern mining methodology, looked much like a string of roller coaster cars strung together. Each section contained four open seats on a platform mounted above small steel railroad car type wheels. There were five sections coupled together, front to back, like regular train cars. A large horseshoe coupling attached the last car to the heavy steel cable that lead down from the machinery house. A huge winch in the machinery house raised and lowered mining cars as the rich ore was brought to the surface.

The men of first shift resumed work. Adrenaline failed, the work became heavy and tedious. The anguish, the sense of urgency was gone. It was four in the morning when the last body was brought to the surface. Big Mike Simmons boss for the second shift. Like most of the men, he didn't have a bruise on him, just a startled, wide-eyed look on his face, his unlit cigar clinched between his teeth.

Pete leaned back against the mucking car and remembered the scene as second shift had boarded the shuttle the previous evening. All had been laughing and talking, each as eager as a brand new bride, but now, ten hours later, all eighteen had died.

The earlier scene flashed in his head as he looked away from the passing stretcher. Ten short hours earlier, the southern Utah sun was going down as Pete stepped from the shuttle car. It was good to be back on the surface again.

Big Mike was stepping onto the shuttle to descend with his crew as Pete picked up his lunch pail and backed clear of the shuttle. "How many feet did you guys blow today, Pete?" Big Mike asked as he sat on the wooden seat.

"We got out about four feet today." Pete felt pleased. "But, hey, we did smell gas this afternoon. Where's your gas detection man? I think you'd better check before you start blasting. Maybe you should call Engineering. You might have an air pump out or something."

Pete had felt uneasy since several men from his gang reported smelling something like swamp gas.

Art, an old timer, said "It's nothing -- a small gas rupture in the hard rock up in the north drift most likely."

"Don't you worry about us, sonny." Big Mike winked, putting a stubby cigar in his mouth. He always chewed, but never lit. "We've been around this hard rock mining a lot of years, and by the time this shift's over, every man here'll be able to buy a brand new car with this month's pay." He removed the cigar and pointed it at the youngster in front of him. "Just so you won't worry, I did talk to Engineering. There is an air pump out and the pump man and the gas man will both be down on the next shuttle, and," he stuffed the cigar in his reddened face, "we'll move two drift feet before this shift's an hour old!"

The shuttle creaked and began to move down the track into the tunnel, fading out of sight. Pete shook his head and walked on toward the shower house and changing room.

Outside the shower house he hosed off his boots, took off his slicker and helmet, and washed them down. He noticed the gas man from the second shift go into the shower house in his street clothes. He was obviously late.

The mine was new, so all of the surface accommodations were modern and quite comfortable. The shower building was red brick with a red tile roof. The interior was tiled in white and gray stone. There were twenty five individual stalls and always plenty of hot water. Pete went to his locker, stripped off his clothes and hurried to the shower. The hot soapy water really felt great after a day of slogging around in the damp, dusty, mine. Even the particles floating in the air were wet and stuck to him after every blasting. He felt he could stay in the shower for hours, the warmth of the hot water soothing every muscle of his body. **Then the explosion**.

* * *

Shaking his head to clear the nagging memory, Pete joined A very unhappy crew in the showers. Pete didn't remember taking a shower. He was crying so hard he had trouble tying his shoes.

Art sat next to Pete and put his hand on his shoulder. "I know it's hard kid, but it does happen. It's one of the risks we take, and we've lost a few good men," he said. "You take some time off, and when you get to feeling better, we'll talk about it."

Pete looked up into the soft grey eyes in Art's hardened face. "A few good men..." He felt the salt from his tears burning his throat.

"Art," he gathered his composure. "I told Big Mike we smelled something. I told him to wait for his gas man." He could feel bitterness and fear overwhelming him. "No!" He stood, gathering his personal gear. "You tell personnel to send my check to my mother. I'll never go down in a mine again. I quit! When I die, they won't have to dig me up to bury me!"

* * *

The next thing Pete remembered was waking up in his own bed. His mother stood at the foot. "Are you feeling all right, dear?" she asked. "You've slept for more than twenty-four hours. I have some nice bacon and eggs for you if you'd like. After breakfast, I'm going over to Mrs. Thompson's. She's having a very hard time of it - her Bill being lost in the accident and all."

That's my mom, Marie Peterson, he thought as he dressed. *Mom is always helping other folks. Why can't she help me? Since Dad died, she's quit listening to my fears of going underground.*

When breakfast was over, Marie turned to Pete. "Ricky is at the public swimming pool. The Johnson's pool is being repaired. Are you going to be all right until I get home?"

"Mom," he said in a kind, convincing tone, "when you get home, Rick will be your only son at home. I'm leaving this place. I'm going up to Salt Lake to find a job. A job where I don't have to go underground."

Pete knew his mother recognized the resolution in his voice. She did not try to dissuade him. She picked up her purse and covered basket, kissed Pete softly on the cheek and walked out the door.

After his mother left the house, Pete packed a few things in a small athletic bag and tossed in his shave kit. He would run as far and as fast as he could. He could not stand being in a town where the whole place was in mourning. He wanted to be in a place where he could walk the streets without some prying face asking, "What happened at the mine? How did eighteen good men die?"

The two-hundred dollars in his dresser he had been saving to buy new wheels for his car stared up at him. He took it out and left one hundred on the kitchen table with a short note for his mother.

Dear Mom, I'm going to Salt Lake to stay with Alice and Ken for a while. Maybe Ken knows a job I can get. I promise I'll write. I Love you, Pete.

He trudged out to his car, a well-used '56 Ford. As he opened the door and slid under the wheel, Rick, and two of his high school buddies walked up.

"Hey Pete!" Rick was smiling. "Where you off to? We're going over to the Thompson house to see if there's anything we can do to help out. Why don't you come along?"

Pete turned and looked at his brother, a youngster with reddish brown hair. He loved this little guy that was already as tall as he. Rick was the one who nicknamed him Pete, and helped him realize that he didn't have to be called Beauford for the rest of his life.

"No. I don't think so, Ricky. I've got to get out of here. I won't talk to the families of dead men."

He smiled up at the young man leaning against his car. "Just promise me one thing, Ricky." His voice became a whisper. "Don't ever go underground."

Rick leaned back, his hands on his hips, as Pete started his car. "Okay. I promise," he said as Pete drove away.

It was sundown when he reached Alice's house, a nice little red brick cottage with a big yard in the suburbs. His mother had called ahead, and Alice and Ken waited supper for him. Their welcome was warm and generous, and there were no questions about the mine or the disaster.

Pete started looking for work right away, but there was none to be found for a nineteen-year-old with little or no experience at anything but mining or driving a twenty-six ton ore truck.

During the evening meal, his third week at Alice and Ken's house, Ken asked, "How's the job hunt coming, Pete?"

"I'm afraid I didn't find anything again today," said Pete. "Pass the peaches, please."

Alice handed Pete the bowl of sliced peaches. "You know, there's more work than civilian jobs."

"I know sis, but I filled out applications at both Hill Air Force Base and Defense Depot Ogden. They're just not hiring right now," Pete said.

"You might talk to the Navy recruiter." She smiled. "You know, our family has a proud tradition of every man from every generation serving at least one hitch and every generation providing at least one career man, usually an officer graduate of the Naval Academy."

"Wasn't your Uncle Bill the last one?" Ken asked. "Didn't he retire as a Captain just before your dad died?"

"That's right, honey," said Alice, dabbing her lips with her napkin. "Our brother, Bill, who is ten years older than Pete, followed up on that part of the family tradition a long time ago. He joined the Navy as soon as he finished his senior year of high school. He's now a Second Class Storekeeper, not an officer. Remember, he did go to the US Naval College for just over three years."

"It strikes me," Pete said, "that there's some shame or disgrace there somewhere. Anybody going to school for three years should have stuck with it and become an officer."

Alice sighed. "He's on his third tour of active duty and Mom is always a little extra proud of him."

"Maybe she knows something we don't," Ken said.

"Or maybe she doesn't understand exactly how the US Navy does things," Pete said.

Pete realized his welcome was wearing thin. He felt as dependent on others as he had been as a ten-year old. *Yep. All grown up, graduated from high school and still Mamma's little boy, or sister's little brother.* Pete decided to talk to the recruiter.

Early Monday morning Pete went to the recruiting station in downtown Salt Lake City. He stopped to look at the poster in front of the office. It depicted a broad shouldered young man about his age in full dress blues standing on the deck of a battleship, huge guns bristling over his head and flags waving in the background. The caption at the top read 'Go Navy.' The banner along the bottom read 'More than a job, an adventure.'

As he pushed the door open, he noticed three desks. Two men close to the door were dressed in blues. A man in a khaki uniform sat far in the back. Pete recognized the anchor emblem on the collar of the khaki shirt. He was a Chief Petty Officer.

The man at the first desk looked up as Pete came through the door. "Hi there. What can we do for you today?" he asked with a broad smile. The atmosphere of the recruiting station was warm and friendly. Pete looked around at a neat, clean, well arranged, modern office. The Petty Officer at the next desk stopped typing and smiled, acknowledging Pete.

"My name's Beauford Peterson. My friends call me Pete," he answered. "I have an older brother in the Navy, and he seems to like it pretty well, so I thought I'd come down and see what it's all about."

The Petty Officer shook Pete's hand. "Well, have a seat . What's your brother's name and where's he stationed?"

After they talked for a few minutes, the Petty Officer took Pete back to meet the Chief.

"Hey, Chief," the Second Class said as they approached, "you served with Bill Peterson in Washington, didn't you? Look who's here. This is his younger brother, Beauford."

The Chief rose to his feet, his hand outstretched in welcome. "So this is Pete!" His long narrow face beamed. "I'd recognize that Nordic swagger anywhere. Just look at you! You're a carbon copy of your brother ten years ago." Pete felt like he was being welcomed home after a long trip.

The Chief went on. "Bill's a good man. One of the best under cover men the Naval Intelligence Corps has. What do you hear from him?"

Pete looked up at the big man. "I'm afraid Bill doesn't write much. All I know is, he's on sea duty somewhere in the Pacific."

The Chief motioned him to sit in the chair across from his desk. "One thing's for sure, wherever he is, there'll soon be a decrease in the criminal element. He and I worked some terrific cases in the Atlantic Fleet, and he was always easy to work for. You knew just what was going on." The Chief lit a cigarette as the Second Class returned to his desk. "Enough of this old home week stuff! Let's talk about you and your plans. What kind of work would you like to do? Is there any particular field you're really interested in?"

Pete squirmed uneasily in his chair. He suddenly felt uncomfortable having this man be so friendly and know him so well when he had never seen nor heard of him before.

"Well," Pete said, "I'm not really sure. I'd kind of like to get into something that would be in demand when I return from active duty."

The Chief smiled. "We have just the thing for you. Your Navy is currently in need of electronics technicians, we call 'em ETs. With the world turning to more than just television, there will be a high demand for your skills when you get out. But wait. For you, something special - nuclear electronics technician. How does that sound? The enlistment is a six year contract instead of four, but the schooling is very extensive.

"If you don't mind," he said, pulling open a drawer and removing some papers. "I'll make arrangements for your physical and mental testing at Fort Douglas today, and if you pass, you'll be sworn in this evening."

He removed the cigarette from his mouth and scratched at his forehead with his thumb. "All you have to do is be there and do the best you can on all the tests. You'll want to take your car home. Stay there until you get a bus ticket in the mail. You'll come back up here and board a plane for San Diego and boot camp. After that you'll be on your way, a regular Navy sailor."

Pete took a deep breath as he left the recruiting station. The world of mining and all its misery was behind him.

Chapter 2

The Adventure Begins

The Chief was right. The following Monday, at 10:30 PM, Pete was aboard an airliner setting down in San Diego. There were five men in his group. When he got off the plane, he saw a soldier, a sailor and a marine, each directing traffic. "Navy this way!" The sailor was shouting as he pointed to a large gray bus.

It was well past midnight when the lumbering bus came to its final destination. The driver hit the door release with his boot like he was dismounting a familiar horse. He was out the door. Just as quickly, a tall, thin Petty Officer appeared in the aisle at the front of the bus.

"Listen up, people!" he barked. "There are troops asleep here, and you are not going to wake them up! You will listen to what I have to say and then get off the bus, quickly and quietly. Outside the bus, you will find yellow circles painted on the pavement. On those circles are painted numbers. Stand on one of those circles. That number will be your billet number for the entire time you're in boot camp. Remember that number. When you're asked your billet number, that's your number. Move!"

Departure from the bus was anything but quiet. The large group of recruits sounded like a herd of wild pigs. As they walked toward the dimly lighted assembly area, Pete paused to look up and read the brightly lit sign, twelve feet over his head.

'Welcome aboard. You are now men of the UNITED STATES NAVY. The tradition of the service demands your utmost effort. Give it cheerfully and willingly.'

The big sign formed an archway over a wide sidewalk in front of a two-story barracks building, a small sign on the front that read, 'Receiving and Orientation.' The assembly area was right in front of a set of large double doors.

After being pushed here and there by any number of his fellow recruits, Pete was standing on billet number 56. A black recruit on his right spoke to him. "My name is Washington, Dion Washington."

The young man, a head taller than Pete's six feet, with a deep baritone voice extended his right hand in greeting. "What's a billet?"

Pete looked up at the smiling face, white teeth clearly visible in the dim light, and shook the offered hand. "I think it means 'bed' or 'assigned space,' but I'm not positive."

A short stocky sailor passed through the ranks picking up the manila envelopes the recruits had all been given at their home town recruiting stations. These envelopes contained their original enlistment contracts, their pre-enlistment test results and physical examination reports.

They were marched inside where each man was given a mattress cover and blanket. The group was then led up some stairs to the barracks on the second floor where they were to sleep for the night.

Having grown up in a house where Mom made all the beds, and being used to sheets, Pete had no idea what a mattress cover was. Pete turned to Merric, one of the men that had accompanied him from Utah, and held out the mattress cover like an open pillow case. "Merric, how do you use this sheet? You got any idea?"

The giant farm boy placed his mattress cover neatly on top of a bunk and spread his blanket over it. "It's easy, Pete," he explained as he crawled into the mattress cover. "All you do, is pretend it's a sleeping bag."

At one in the morning, Pete was too tired to press the point, so he followed suit.

He had just fallen into a fitful sleep when he was startled awake by the ringing of a broom handle banging inside a metal garbage can. A Chief Petty Officer was stirring the stick. Pete watched the people around him jumping from their bunks, putting their clothes on. He looked at his watch. Four-thirty in the morning!

In minutes, the entire group was outside standing on their billet numbers. "Now!" the Chief barked. "We're going to march to chow."

The march to the chow hall took about five minutes. "Fall out, you've got ten minutes!" the Chief ordered. There was a large assortment of food from which to choose. It was well prepared and there was plenty of fresh milk, Pete's favorite.

"This food is great," Pete said to Washington as he took a bite of toast and speared a bite of scrambled eggs with his fork.

"Gentlemen," the Chief said as he rose, picking up his tray.

The rest of the recruits began to rise and follow the Chief to the scullery to drop off their trays.

What? What? thought Pete as he stood by reflex and followed the line to the scullery. *I just started to eat! What kind of breakfast is this?*

He watched as his breakfast slid from the tray into a trash can. He pushed the tray, along with his silverware and cup, through the scullery window.

A mess cook in dungarees smiled at him through the window. "You'll get used to a ten minute meal, Boot!"

The sun was beginning to break over the horizon as the formation approached building 214. The morning air seemed damp and cool, but it had a salty, crisp, clean odor.

"Halt!" The Chief's command came down like a clap of thunder. "This is the first day of an interesting career, I can promise you that. I want you to line up in front of this door by billet number and go in for your hair cut. When you come out, you'll form up on your billet number. Fall out!"

It was not long before Pete found out about Navy barbers. His long, curly, blonde locks were on the floor in less than fifteen seconds.

Bald, I'm bald! He marveled, *It's funny how much the white kid from Texas looks like the black kid from Michigan.*

After his hair cut, he returned to stand on his billet number in company formation. He noticed a Petty Officer in dress blues watching the group from a porch on the next building. The smallish man watched with more than average interest and seemed to be analyzing every person in the ranks. Noticing the intensity with which the first Class Petty Officer was watching, Pete looked around for the Chief who had taken them to breakfast. He was not to be seen.

The small figure placed one hand on the top of the porch handrail and hopped over onto the tarmac. The Chief reappeared. "Attention!" he bellowed, pointing to the approaching First Class. "I've enjoyed working with you boys here at Receiving and Orientation. Now, it's time for you to go with your own Company Commander. This is Mr. D. L. Worley, Signalman First Class. Mr. Worley will see you through the next nine weeks, which will be the basis for your entire military service. Mr. Worley," he saluted the approaching Petty Officer, "I give you Company 449."

"Gentlemen," said the new Company Commander. "This is to be a nine-week training period. Each day of each week has a number consisting of two digits, the first number being the week of training you're in and the second number being the day of the week. Each week will have five days. Weekends don't count. This day is your One-One Day. Graduation from basic training will be on your Nine-Five Day."

Company Commander Worley now moved the company over to uniform issue. As each man entered the door he was handed an empty sea bag. As he passed down the line between two long counters, shirts, hats, shoes, raincoat, sweater, watch cap, neckerchief, socks, underwear and pea coat were thrown into the bag. Regrouping on their billet numbers, outside, the men were ordered to pour the clothing onto the tarmac in front of them and a Petty Officer with a clipboard went through a list to make sure that every man had a complete issue of clothing.

"When you get your first two month's pay checks, you might wonder why it's only thirty-five dollars instead of seventy, like you signed up for. These uniforms are the reason," the Petty Officer growled, holding up his clipboard, "you have to pay for them."

The Petty Officer moved to a point at the center front of the company. "At this time, I'd like you to choose a complete uniform of dungarees. Strip - completely, and put on your new uniform with white deck shoes. You may call them low-cut tennis shoes, whatever." The company stood for a moment, looking around. The company was standing in an open area, outside, between two buildings. "Move! Get naked! Change your clothes!" shouted the Petty Officer. "Don't be trying to keep your civilian skivvies. Peel off those jockey shorts and put on your Navy issue boxer shorts."

Pete began to pull off his clothes, looking around to see black and white bare butts scrambling to put on Navy issue clothing. He felt his temperature rise in the chill morning air and his face flush. *This is not happening,* he thought. Who would have you get naked with all these people around, and in the middle of the street? He dropped his underwear on the tarmac and dressed as quickly as he could.

"You were issued a heavy manila envelope with your home address on it," continued the Petty Officer. "Put your civilian clothes into that envelope and give it to the sailor passing through your ranks with a large mail bag. Your clothes will be mailed back to your home."

"Put everything else into your sea bag, put the carry strap on your shoulder and prepare to move out."

Company Commander Worley now took over and marched the company across a bridge to a new section of buildings called Camp Nimitz.

As the company faced the large new concrete building they were assigned, Pete could see his barracks in the upper right hand section of the building overlooking the courtyard where he now stood. There were white lines painted on the concrete surface of the courtyard. It was sort of like being a kid again.

"This is your yard," the Company Commander cautioned. "You will not leave it without permission. You will not talk to, nor associate with any other recruits in any of the adjacent yards. There have been cases of spinal meningitis here. It seems to spread through association. Each company must be isolated for three weeks before they are safe to move across the bridge, back to the main base. Don't interfere with anyone else's isolation, and don't let anyone mess you up."

In his yard, Pete noticed that there was room to assemble the company, that left room for a clothesline and a long cement table with lots of metal buckets under it. The two story barracks buildings on either side and the ones across the courtyard were set up the same way.

"Gentlemen!" Company Commander Worley belted out. He smiled as he pointed to the concrete tables. "This will be your washing machine while you are in basic training. You will use the buckets under the tables for water, and scrub your dungarees and whites with the brushes in those buckets. You will get the smell of mothballs out of all of your clothing. You will get a new washing machine on your Four-One Day, when we move across the bridge."

Immediately outside of the double entrance doors to his company's barracks on the right was the Company Commander's office and bunk room. On the other side of the hall was the head, or bathroom. What a bathroom! It had more urinals than a bus station and forty feet of commodes. The shower was a gigantic communal room with at least forty hot and cold running water spigots, but only one drain in the center of the shower room floor.

After becoming familiar with their barracks, the company marched back to the main base where they drew their bedding issue and their shower and shaving kit which they learned to lovingly call a 'douche kit.' Douche is the French word used by Napoleon's army for shower or bath. They were also issued a combination lock for the little drawer in their lockers to keep their personal things like letters from sweethearts and their snacks or geedunks. Geedunks were those unauthorized sweets, gums and candies that were smuggled through the mail from home. These were definitely items that everyone wanted to keep locked up.

The recruits had put in a full day by the time the company returned to the barracks from dinner on the main base. The sun was going down.

"Company. Halt!" Ordered Company Commander Worley. "Before I dismiss you, I want to draw your attention to the stationery kit and ball point pen that you were issued. You will write a letter home tonight before you turn in. Company. Dismissed!"

The next day at the testing facility, the men were tested and classified for the job assignment they would get in the fleet. Pete did very well on the tests, and his slot in the Electronics Technician "A" School in San Francisco was guaranteed.

Pete stood his first sentry watch that same night. He had the "Midwatch," a four-hour stint from midnight to four AM. The watch consisted of walking around the barracks watching for fires or any other disturbances that might come up.

Fire watch is very important. In the event of a fire, it was his responsibility to get all hands out of the building. Fire was not too much of a danger in this new barracks, but across the bridge, one of the world war two vintage barracks had burned to the ground in six minutes.

Pete cruised around the barracks through the large bathroom area and back through the barracks again. He spent the time trying to commit to memory the first eleven "General Orders," which every member of the company was expected to know by the next morning.

Suddenly, the main doors to the barracks burst open. There, in the red night light shining from the hallway, stood the Duty Chief Petty Officer. A Seaman in dress blues that accompanied him yelled out, "Watch! Watch!"

The Chief was now growling. "Watch! Where are you? Get yourself up here!"

Pete overcame his startled emotion and approached the Chief with a salute. "Seaman Recruit Peterson here, sir!"

The Chief towered over him and growled down into his face. "Who left the head lights on, boy?"

Half frightened out of his wits, Pete sprang to the nearest window. Looking down into the courtyard below, Pete heard the words from his lips. "I don't know, sir. I didn't even see a car drive up."

The way the Chief grabbed Pete's arm made it obvious that he did not appreciate Pete's sincerity. He dragged Pete into the bathroom and pointed up at the ceiling. His face flushed with rage.

"This is the head!" The large vein in his neck throbbed and his complexion grew red. Waving his left arm about, he pointed up with his index finger. "Those are the head lights, you idiot! Now, who left them on?"

"I guess I'm responsible, sir." Pete managed. The words catching in his throat. "I've been on watch since midnight and they've been on the whole time."

"Jumping jacks! Begin!" The Chief screeched and went out the door.

Being no dummy, Pete immediately started doing jumping jacks. After about ten minutes of rigorous exercise, Pete realized that the Chief had left the building.

* * *

Time began to pass quickly as he learned to spit shine his shoes, shine his brass buckles and to wash his dungarees in a small bucket and hang them on a clothesline using a piece of twine. He learned that rank was for officers and rate was for enlisted men. The proper way to fold his uniforms and tie his neckerchief did not come so easy. The knot always seemed to be upside down.

Sitting in the patio, polishing his shoes with the rest of the company, Pete had a conversation with Ryan Owens, a brawny, blonde fellow from Arizona. Owens was a Naval Reservist. He had been in the Navy almost a year, but had not been to basic training. In Pete's mind, Owens was the 'Encyclopedia 'de Navy.'

"In a standard four year enlistment, how much rate can you make if you stay out of trouble and study hard?" Pete asked.

Owens stopped buffing the shoe he was working on and set it down. "I think you can make E5, that's the Second Class Petty Officer grade," Owens said.

"That's my goal then. I'll be a Second Class Petty Officer at the end of my first four years of service."

When Pete turned in that night, he thought about his conversation with Owens. *My only goal in life was to escape the underground world of mining. I now have a real goal in my life. To be a Second Class Petty Officer.*

The following day, after class, Pete stopped by the official Rank and Rate chart to get a complete picture of his goal.

Navy & Marine Corps Rank and Rate Chart

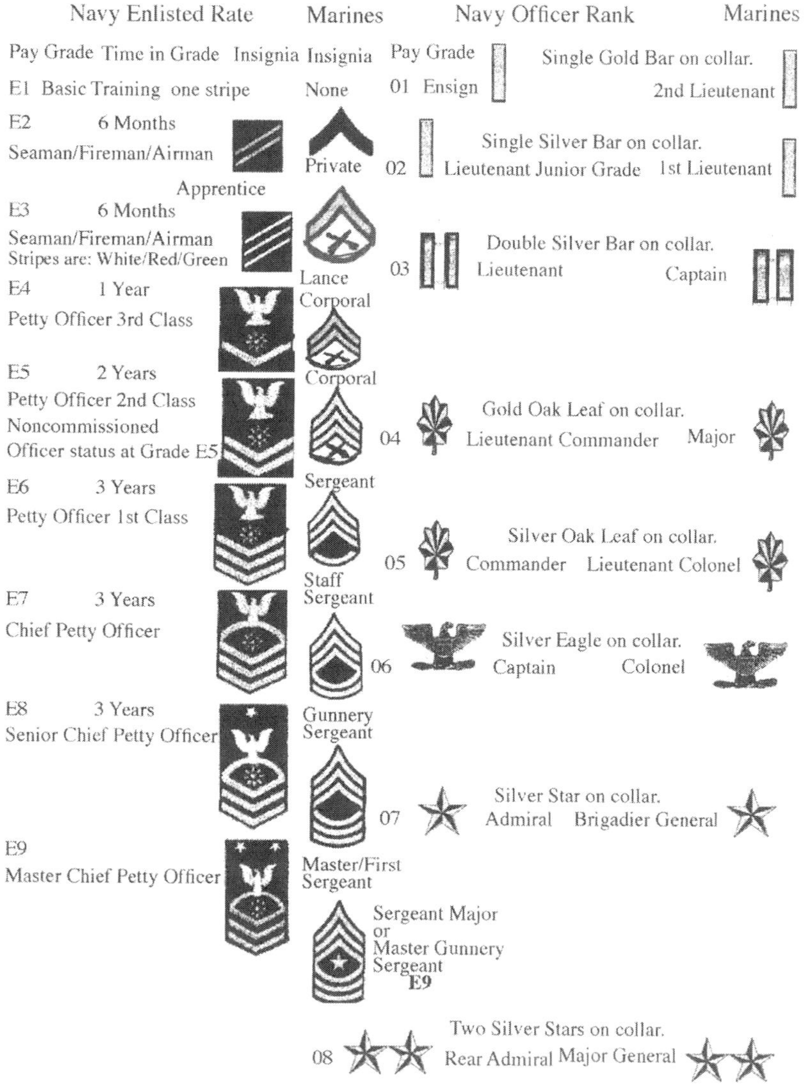

Between the marching, exercise, and military study, Pete found time to go through battery after battery of physicals and shots. The Navy had a new method of giving shots. The old needle was not used. There was an air-powered gun that just shot a burst of air along with the vaccine right into the arm muscle. Five to eight different shots could be given in one single burst of air. Initially, these didn't hurt as bad as the old-fashioned needle. The shots created a bruised lump under the skin that had to be rubbed to disperse the medication and after awhile, they stung just as bad if not worse.

On his seven-three day of training, Pete was in fire fighting school. The sky was overcast with a light drizzle. The oil fires, set in the open area by the Fire Instructors burned hot and every face was coated in black soot. Florescent orange armbands were the only separation of student and instructor.

A siren sounded over the entire base P.A. system, and everything came to a halt. The instructors and the Company Commanders ordered all the training companies into the observation bleachers while they went into a small nearby office. After about ten minutes, they returned with the news of President Kennedy's death.

Pete looked at the bowed heads and tear streaked dark faces in the bleachers as the rain came down. Warm tears washed the soot from the cheeks of practically every recruit. Many were visibly shaken. Many were angry. Pete was very sad.

What a horrible thing to happen, Pete thought. As rain washed his face, he looked toward heaven. *Seems like the right kind of day for this kind of news.*

All training was suspended for the balance of the day and Pete had ample time to brood over his country's misfortune.

Pete had joined Kennedy's Navy. A Navy with a powerful, warlike stance and armor that rattled fiercely, but there was little likelihood of a war.

It takes a real statesman to instill respect without response from an enemy. Now, it's President Johnson's Navy. The nation might be in trouble, he brooded.

As the country mourned, the Navy had recruits to train. Normal routine marched on.

Eight-Two Day was a visit to the dental corps. The company was lined up, by billet number, and run through x-ray, cleaning, polishing and pulling. Pete had one bad tooth the dentist said had to be removed.

Pete was sent down the passageway to "extractions." Pete entered the room, which resembled a large barber shop, with six other recruits. They had already been given novocaine, a true overdose by Pete's estimation, administered by a Seaman Dental Technician in the room before. There were two Dental Technicians by each chair. The technicians were thumbing through papers as Pete entered.

As Pete sat down a Petty Officer, a Third Class Dental Technician and a Seaman were in his face. A bib was placed around his neck. The Seaman held him back against the headrest while the DT3 went into his mouth with a pair of dental pliers. Pete expected to hear the metal pan beside him ring with one "plink" as the corpsman dropped his tooth, but there were five!

The DT3 was speaking to him as the Seaman stood him up, stuffing gauze in his mouth and removing the bib. "Now," said the DT3 with a smile. "Harris, we want you to go over to the dental barracks for the night so you can be observed for loss of blood and shock. You don't want to smoke or you'll create a dry socket and we'll have to cut your gums open."

"Hair..luris?!" Pete tried to speak, but there was too much gauze in his mouth. Pete grabbed the Third Class by the arm and pointed to the name on his shirt frantically.

The DT3 looked around the room. "Smith!" he roared, to a Petty Officer across the room. "Don't let that recruit up yet." He went across to the other Dental Technician. Papers were exchanged.

The recruit in Smith's chair was shoved down again. Pete's Dental Technician pulled out his pen and circled and scribbled things on Pete's chart as he returned to where Pete stood.

"Sorry about this kid," he said with a sheepish grin. "The charts got a little mixed up. Don't worry. Uncle Sam will buy you a brand new bridge, and besides, you would've lost those teeth in forty or fifty years anyway. Go over to dental barracks and spend the night."

The next afternoon, all dental patients were allowed to return to their own barracks. They had "no duty" passes, so they could spend the rest of the day in their bunks.

When Pete reached his bunk, he noticed that the barracks cleanup crew had finished their "field day" of the barracks. The highly waxed and buffed floor was shining brightly. The "field day" crew was the company's Cajun trio, Breaux, Reaux and Benwah. They seemed to always be together.

Pete thought the most memorable thing about these three was that Breaux didn't have a watch and he was always yelling across the barracks at all hours of the night. "What time it tiz, Benwah?" Benwah would answer back with the time. For two weeks Pete thought that asking the hour was the only communication of which Breaux was capable.

Removing his boots and dropping onto his rack, Pete noticed that the "trio" had a bunk torn apart about three bunks away from him. It was Dumbowski's bunk, an upper.

Dumbowski was a very muscular, athletic little Pole that performed a ritual when getting into bed every night. Right at 'Tattoo,' the bugle call that is sounded five minutes before 'Taps,' he would stand in the aisle between the two sets of bunks and scream out like Tarzan, swing himself high into the air over his top bunk and settle with a thud, causing the bunks to squeak and groan. If anyone in the entire barracks had gone to sleep a little before Tattoo, he would certainly be startled to his senses by Dumbowski's maneuver. As a result, more than one member of the company had asked Dumbowski to knock it off. He would not. There was a lot of talk about what should be done to get Dumbowski's attention. It had to be something that would make him respect the people that were already asleep.

The Cajun threesome had removed all of the support springs from around the edge of Dumbowski's bunk frame and replaced them with thread from their sewing kits. The bunk was then remade in the sharpest military fashion. That night when Dumbowski performed his going to bed trick, the thread holding up his mattress gave way and down he went to the bottom bunk. The entire barracks roared with laughter at the "WHOAAAA!" scream that followed his Tarzan call. That was the last time Dumbowski sprang into bed.

For days after Dumbowski's "great fall," all Pete had to do was think about it and he would get the giggles, giving him relief from his toothless ordeal.

The following night, Pete had the Midwatch. Before taps Benwah asked to be awakened at zero one-hundred hours. At one in the morning, Pete woke Benwah, who went to the head. Pete turned off the lights as he left and continued on his tour of the barracks.

When Pete finished his round and was back at the main entrance again, he found the terrible 'trio' standing beside the bunk of the company Recruit Chief Petty Officer, Dave Merric. "What are you doing?" Pete demanded in a harsh whisper.

"Quiet," said Reaux. "This guy thinks he's immune to all practical jokes. He makes fun of everyone else. Nobody would dare play a joke on him, or so he thinks. We're going to give him one."

They had filled his outstretched left hand with shaving cream. Breaux took a tear strip off of a pack of cigarettes and ran it over Merric's left cheek. The reflex action was that of a cow's tail swatting at flies, and Merric ended up with shaving cream all over his face.

The culprits could not bar their laughter as they scurried back to their bunks. Merric woke up to find himself covered with shaving cream. The darkness of the bunk room vibrated with laughter. Pete, of course, hadn't seen anything. Pete was making sure that the head lights were off.

The company's training intensified as the weeks wore on. Each man was issued a 1908 Springfield rifle so the company could learn to march with them and do the "sixteen count manual of arms." For everyone, the first mistake was to call the weapons "guns." Naval jargon called them a "piece," and the recruits had to make sure they used the term. Anyone who didn't, got to write home and tell their mother they had to sleep with their piece.

After calling his piece a gun, Seaman Recruit Benwah had to march up and down, from one end of the bunk room to the other in his underwear. He held his piece out vertically in front of him with his right hand and gestured to the front of his boxer shorts with his left as he sounded off in a loud voice. "This is my piece," he raised the rifle. "This is my gun," he pointed with his left hand. "This one's for fightin' and this one's for fun!"

Pete learned about reporting aboard a ship. The Ensign (American Flag), is always saluted first and then the Officer of the Deck. The person boarding then says, "Request permission to come aboard, sir."

They were trained to use sound-powered telephones, a super headset telephone that worked entirely without the benefit of electricity. There was new vocabulary to learn: "port" for left, "starboard" for right, "forward," and "bow," for the ship's front, "aft," "stern" and "fantail," for the rear and "athwart ships" for across in the middle. "Passageway" for hall, "bulkhead" for wall, "ladder" for staircase or any other vertical climbing device. There was "deck" for floor, "overhead" for ceiling and catch phrases like "belay that" for cancel that, but "belay" also meant to tie something off. The word "chit" was introduced. It was a catch-all word for "form." You didn't fill out a "request," you filled out a chit. "Turn to" was also a big one, meaning 'go to work.'

There were classes about how ships are laid out. Decks are counted downward from the main deck, first, second and so forth. Counting upward is said oh-one, oh-two, and so forth all the way up to the signal bridge, which is located at the base of the mast.

A week before graduation, Pete was assigned to one of the normal courtyard sentry watches. It was the midwatch of course. Pete seemed to have all the luck when it came to the midwatch and had a midwatch about once a week. He began to enjoy the loneliness and solitude of walking a post in the stillness of the night. He took advantage of the time to memorize and review in his mind the classes he had during the day.

First General Order: 'To walk my post in a military manner, keeping always on the alert, being especially watchful at night...'

Pete dressed in the darkness beside his bunk and removed his piece, the old Springfield training rifle, from its thongs under his bunk. He put on his peacoat and reported to the Officer Of the Guard, whose office was in the next barracks over. Pete relieved the sentry from his company and began to walk his post. It felt good to know that he wouldn't have many more of these chores to do, at least not on this base.

On the base, there were two commands, the Base Command, or real Navy, and the Recruit Command. Therefore, there were two types of sentries and patrols. The recruits were training. The real sentries and patrols were manned by Marines in jeeps with loaded weapons.

He was half way into his watch, zero two-hundred hours, when Pete saw through the fog, a figure approaching the sentry post next to his. The figure was slightly hunched and weaving a little as if intoxicated.

"Halt!" commanded the sentry thirty feet from Pete. The figure stopped. The wisps of fog washed around him as the flood lights shown down from the barracks roofs, casting the courtyard in a dim shadowy light. "Advance and be recognized!" came the next command from the sentry.

Pete began to move down the perimeter of his post until he could make out a Chief Petty Officer's uniform. Pete was within ten feet of the confrontation with the intruder. The Chief's face was familiar. It was the Chief Petty Officer that had him doing jumping jacks on his first fire watch. He had apparently been off the base or at the CPO Club having a few drinks and now he was on his way back to his barracks.

"Thank you, sir!" sounded off the sentry. "You may pass." The Chief began to move slowly past the sentry, but at that moment, a Marine Corps patrol jeep turned the corner of the next barracks and entered the courtyard area. The jeep flashed a spotlight ahead of it onto their position. Suddenly, the Chief jerked himself erect yelling something that sounded like Chinese, and then, in a terrified voice, said, "You're not taking me back! You're not taking me back, you little yellow devils!"

The Chief lunged at the sentry, knocking him off balance and jerking his piece from his hands. In a flash, the rifle butt caught the surprised sentry across the chest and the barrel struck his forehead. The sentry went down without a sound. Pete moved toward the fray. The Chief was now in front of him, ready for locked hand-to-hand battle. He dove, pushed and lunged, but Pete managed to fend each blow with his piece.

The Chief continued ranting and raving that Pete was a little yellow devil. Finally, his rifle butt grazed Pete's face and the force was so intense that Pete felt the blood burning his cheek in the cool night air.

Pete yelled. "No! No! Chief, we're Americans! We're Americans, you stupid jerk!" Pete was wearing down and losing his composure. The Chief's attack was relentless, as he drove on. Pete swung his piece up into the Chief's ribs as hard as he could. The Chief's face was bleeding, but he only staggered a little and attacked Pete with more fury.

The butt of the Chief's piece caught the bolt on Pete's weapon and sent it flying from his hands across the dark concrete courtyard. The Chief drew back slightly, for the kill. His face snarled with vengeance. It was a hate Pete had never seen before. Pete drew back a pace. The Chief's face became expressionless, he fell forward at Pete's feet. A Marine Sergeant was standing where the Chief had stood, with a heavy oak night stick in his right hand. Another Marine was administering first aid to the downed sentry.

"Looks like we arrived just in time," said the Sergeant, turning the Chief's body over. "Or we caused it! This is Chief Parker of Training Command. He was a Korean War POW. He escaped five times and was recaptured four. *I bet when we hit him with our spot light, being drunk and disoriented,* he thought it was a searchlight and the Reds were coming to take him back again. I've heard about things like this happening, but I've never seen it."

The second Marine came to Pete's position. "I've got an ambulance on the way for both of these guys. From what I know of this Chief's record, you're very lucky to be alive."

The Marine Sergeant holstered his night stick. "Call your Duty Officer Of the Day and come with us."

Pete spent the rest of the night explaining to the Base Officer of the Day what had happened. Pete felt bad for the sentry, but he felt a deep remorseful sorrow for the Chief and what he must have gone through to make him so terrified that he would kill to escape.

Who knows? If that spotlight had not hit him in the face, he might have just gone on back to his barracks and gone to bed like he had every night since he last escaped from that Korean prisoner of war camp.

* * *

It was now the week before graduation. Orders came through. Pete had been assigned to the *USS Kingston* (LPH 15). The Kingston was a Landing Platform, Helicopter.

It had been an attack aircraft carrier during World War II, but had been refitted to carry twelve-hundred Marines and one-hundred helicopters. Each chopper could carry eight men and their equipment. The job of these airborne Marines was to "vertically envelop" the enemy. Fly in behind a retreating enemy as a ground force made a frontal assault.

Graduation day was a day for the memory. It was a bright sunny day without a cloud in the sky. The morning fog that normally plagued the early hours of the day was not present. By mid-morning, thirty-six companies were formed up, ranging in size from forty men to a hundred.

Prebble Field was a sea of white hats atop blue uniforms as Company 449 marched into its brigade formation. As the company approached the reviewing stand, they heard the command, "Company! Eyes right!" The company marched by to the applause of the entire reviewing stand. As the Navy band played *Anchors Away,* Pete's heart pumped like a kite dipping through the air, pausing as if to fall and then catching a warm breeze again and flying to new heights. Tears welled up in his eyes and he blinked to catch his breath. He had made it. Another step away from mining. Pete was now an E2, a Seaman Apprentice with another stripe to be added to his left sleeve and a little money to be added to his pay check. He now had two stripes and was looking forward to picking up the third. Looking forward to the day when he would be a Seaman.

My new job, my adventure, has begun.

Chapter 3

The Alligator Navy

After a two week leave at home with family and friends, Pete boarded a plane in Salt Lake City and flew to Los Angeles, where he shared a cab to Long Beach Naval Station with four other sailors. The ride was quiet. Each man lost in his thoughts of home, the past, and the future. Upon arrival, each sailor paid his portion of the fare and left the cab at the head of Pier Echo.

One sailor went to the submarine tie ups, two went toward the destroyers which were tied together in a row, and the last sailor and Pete started down the pier toward the *USS Kingston* (LPH15). The other sailor was shorter than Pete by a foot, a sturdy little man with red hair, he had no trouble hoisting his sixty-pound sea bag onto his husky left shoulder.

"My name is Brent 'Red Dog' Aimes," he said. "I'm going aboard the Kingston for preschool indoctrination. PSI they call it. I'm going to be an ET. ET is the abbreviation for electronics technician. What's your story?"

"I'm Pete Peterson. My story is the same as yours," Pete said as he shifted his sea bag from his right to his left shoulder and grinned.

Half turning, walking sideways, Red Dog went on. "Hey, maybe we could do this on the buddy system. Do and learn things together. I think you can get things done a lot faster and better if you have someone to go through it with, don't you?" The young man extended his right hand. "Pete, old boy," he said with a slow drawl, "when you have a friend from Texas, you have a friend for life."

Pete had been sizing up Red Dog since the minute he saw him, he already felt as comfortable as an old pair of slippers. He shook the outstretched hand.

They wound their way up the great wooden staircase which crisscrossed back and forth thirty feet above the pier to the gangway stationed on the platform at its top. They crossed the gangway to the aft Quarterdeck located on the hangar deck of the old aircraft carrier, saluted the National Ensign and then the Chief Petty Officer on watch.

"Request permission to come aboard, sir," Pete said.

"Permission granted," said the Chief, returning their salute. They gave the Chief their order packets.

"Messenger Of The Watch," said the Chief. "Take these men to the ET Office."

At the Operations Electronics office, a Third Class ET took over and showed them to the division berthing compartment on the second deck.

"This is where you guys will be living for the next few months, so make yourselves at home. Don't forget. My name is Beers. I'm a communications technician. This is my bunk here." He pointed to a lower in a vertical row of five bunks hanging by chains from the ten-foot ceiling. "You can have the one above me, Pete, and you can take the one above him, Red." He pointed to some shiny aluminum lockers. "There are plenty of empty lockers. Take your pick and stow your gear. When you finish, come up to the ET shack on the 02 level. If you have problems finding the place, just ask anyone. They'll point you in the right direction." He turned and disappeared up the ladder.

As they were stowing their gear and changing from their dress blues into their dungaree uniforms, a Seaman came down the sharply angled staircase. "My name is Joe Krammer. I'm the division's leading Seaman," he said, as he handed them each a pillow, pillow case, mattress cover and blanket. He also handed them a canvas belt with a buckle on each end.

"My name is Pete and this is Red," Pete announced as he shook the offered hand. Pete held up the strap Krammer had given him. "What's this for?"

Krammer chuckled. "You guys really are boots, aren't you? Those are bedding straps. We don't use them in port, but when we're underway and the Boatswain blows reveille, you get out of bed, fold up your blanket, lay your pillow on top of your blanket, and secure it all down with that strap."

Krammer tapped the matching strap clip that was welded onto Pete's bed frame. "This strap over your bedding will ensure that nothing floats around in the compartment in the event that water gets in here. You see, if a space floods, we just drop in a submersible pump and clear the water to keep the ship afloat. That strap is called a 'trice.' You'll hear the Boatswain say, 'Now, all hands heave out and trice up.' That means it's time for you to get up, make your bunk, and trice it up, or strap it down, which ever you prefer. There is one more feature to these bunks. Once they're all triced up, you start at the top bunk and push them up against the bulkhead where they will lock into place. Then, you see, nothing can float around and get into the pumps when you're trying to clear the water. Pretty simple, isn't it?"

Krammer turned and started for the ladder. "I'm going up to the head. When I get back, have your bunks made and be ready to go topside."

When the new arrivals reached the ET shack with Krammer, they found a spacious modern electronics workshop. A large caged-in space at the back of the compartment had shelves piled high with portable testing equipment. The brightly lit main room had many comfortable stools along a workbench running the full length of the compartment. There were tables and chairs, and in one corner, a large color television bolted to the bulkhead.

Fifteen men, counting themselves, were in the large compartment. When they came through the door, everything seemed to stop, and a tall lanky Marine Sergeant walked up.

"Welcome to the amphibious forces, fellows. You're in the alligator Navy now. My name is Sergeant Hana." He extended his right hand to Pete. "I'm the division Chief Petty Officer. In the alligator navy some of the jobs you might be used to seeing sailors do, may be filled by marines. There are three marines in this, Operations Electronics or OE Division. I was a swab jockey like you, but I switched over for the money."

The Sergeant turned slightly and pointed to two young men in Marine greens. "These two corporals are learning to be ETs because, like the Corpsman program, the Marine Corps doesn't have enough of their own or they don't have any at all, as in the case of Hospital Corpsmen. If you men would be interested, there are openings in the combat electronics school starting up next month. You'd go to special Marine Corps training for combat and after a couple of radio schools be assigned to a combat ready unit."

A broad smile covered his face as he shook hands with each new man. "Of course, we're not at war right now, so it's pretty good duty if you can get through the combat school."

He turned and pointed to a large plastic board on the wall which was filled with grease-penciled names. "This is our division's Billet Board. You'll note that your names are already on the board, as well as your sleeping and work assignments. This board will also show when you are due for leave or to be assigned to the mess decks for a month. We're supposed to provide one Seaman per month on a rotating basis to the mess deck, as does every other division aboard the ship, to ensure the ship is entirely self sufficient. The only thing wrong is, we must have division strength of eight Seaman before we can do that. With you two added to the roster, we're up to five."

Sergeant Hana paused to light a cigar and resumed. "Peterson. I've decided to put you with Beers to learn the ship's entertainment system. You'll also have TACAN and IFF gear responsibilities when we're underway, but for the moment you'll learn radios, televisions and phonographs.

"Aimes," the Sergeant gestured with his newly lit cigar as he tucked his Zippo into a shirt pocket. "You'll have radar and radar repeaters on the bridge and in the Combat Information Center. You'll be assigned to the CIC with Hansen and Wiley. They're our best radar techs."

He dusted the ash from his cigar into a butt can hung on the side of the work bench. "We'll get underway next month for operational readiness inspection or ORI. I'll be expecting you guys to shine for the visiting brass when you go to General Quarters. Look on the Billet Board and find your Battle Stations. I'll have Krammer take you around and help you learn your responsibilities at GQ. I won't stand being embarrassed by my men at 'Battle Stations'."

Beers and Krammer both accompanied the pair to their battle stations.

"I'm sorry for the 'used car' presentation your first hour in the division," Beers said. "Sergeant Hana doesn't usually ramble on like that, but lately, he's really been trying to sell the Combat Technician program."

Pete's General Quarters station was on the bridge as a sound-powered phone talker to the ET shack two decks below. Krammer would be on the other end of the phone so he felt comfortable. Aimes would be on sound powered phones in CIC to the ET shop.

"The OE Division has a Third Class Storekeeper named Platereau assigned," Krammer said. "A Cajun from Louisiana. He clowns or pulls practical jokes all the time." Pete recalled the Cajuns in his boot camp company. Pete quickly discovered Platereau had a similar sense of humor.

Pete's second morning on the Kingston, Platereau was turning out of his top bunk, about eight feet off the deck. The rest of the division were nearly dressed and ready to go to breakfast, while Platereau was just sitting up. "Hey Pete!" he called down, appearing only half awake. "Would you please move my socks?"

Pete looked down on the deck to see a lone pair of socks lying on the highly polished tile floor. "Why?" He felt a little perplexed.

Platereau raised his right hand and turned his head slightly. "Because, you dummy!" he moaned in a half audible tone. "I don't want to jump on 'em and break 'em."

Pete kicked the socks aside as Platereau jumped down. The entire berthing compartment roared with laughter. Pete had just fallen for a joke.

Beers piped up, "Look out, Pete. That boy will get water on you when he jumps. He's a swamp rabbit." Beers went on to expand on the joke. "He's still got watermarks on his legs from spending his life in the swamp."

Platereau was now nearly dressed except for his socks. He stopped dressing and pulled up his trouser leg to expose his calf and ankle. "See my watermarks!" He smiled, like someone showing a trophy.

"Water marks, my ass!" Pete said. "Your socks are too tight!"

Pete had been aboard ship for a month and was enjoying his new life. He had checked out the Seaman and Basic Military Requirements courses from the Personnel Office. He studied and prepared for his advancement-in-rate test he would be eligible to take in four months.

One morning, Red and Pete were standing in the chow line, waiting their turn to pick up their trays for breakfast when he heard unfamiliar words.

"Prison'ah! Make a hole!"

Both men looked up the line to see where the sound was coming from. Two brig prisoners with clean shaven heads, wearing bright orange coveralls, were marching smartly in close order, in front of a Marine brig chaser. "Prison'ah! Make a hole!" the lead prisoner barked. They had been to breakfast and were now crossing the chow line through the athwart ships passageway on their way back to the brig.

Red and Pete stood at the passageway threshold. As the prisoners came to a halt, the first prisoner spoke loudly in cadence to the brig chaser, "Request permission to cross the threshold, sir!"

Red punched Pete in the ribs. "You hear that, Pete?" he whispered. "Pizza on ya! Make a hole," he rhymed with a chuckle.

"No!" Pete cautioned, just above a whisper. "It's serious. 'Prisoner. Make a hole' is just so we'll move."

At that instant, the prisoners went by, and the huge brig chaser's hand caught under the back of Pete's collar. "Making fun of the prisoners, uh, mothball? You can join them!" He snatched Pete into the line behind the second inmate and Pete found himself marching along in a robot like manner, chanting along with them, "Prison'ah! Make a hole!"

Pete didn't fare too well when they got to the threshold of the door leading to the brig. The prisoners stopped, and Pete didn't. Pete went on chanting and crashed right into the back of the prisoner in front of him, knocking himself and both prisoners sprawling across the passageway to the snickering delight of the entire chow line.

"Okay! You dummy!" shouted the brig chaser. "Now, you can go first and listen for my command." He grabbed Pete's arm, jerked him to his feet and into the front of the line.

The rest of the jaunt to the Brig Commander's Office was uninterrupted. Once the little procession reached the office, Pete was placed at parade rest, his feet apart, his hands behind him about eighteen inches from the bulkhead beside the office door. The brig chaser then pushed him forward to rest on the balls of his feet with his forehead against the wall. The inmates were then marched off to their cells. Pete was left balancing against the bulkhead, his forehead holding his body weight.

A few minutes later, the brig chaser, a Lance Corporal, returned and entered the office. The pressure on Pete's forehead was almost unbearable, and his ankles began to burn. He thought he was going to pass out.

The office door opened. "Inside, idiot!" The brig chaser ran his nightstick against Pete's ribs as he passed in the narrow doorway. "Stand at attention in front of the desk, you impudent slob!"

Pete came to attention, every muscle rigid. Fear gripped him -- the same fear that had taken over on his first fire watch when another authority figure was overwhelmingly dehumanizing.

The man on the swivel chair behind the desk was the Brig Sergeant. The huge man had his back to Pete like he was in deep thought, but his body was sharply erect. He had short blonde hair with grey temples. The back of his khaki uniform shirt had sharp military creases in it that ran at angles to his waist from his broad shoulders.

In one motion, he spun around placing his arms on the desk in front of him. A small curled pipe hung from his lips. Pete had only been aboard ship for a month, but he had heard stories about this old boy. He was tough. Real tough. He could whip any five men on the ship at the same time.

"Who the hell do you think you are, making fun of my prisoners?" His face was in a snarl. "You don't think these people have enough trouble? You like to persecute them?"

He took the pipe from his mouth and laid it in an ashtray. "You know, I can arrange for you to get to know them just a little better. Well, speak up dimwit! What do you have to say for yourself?"

Pete felt a hard spot thickening in his throat and struggled to find his voice. His stomach churned and his heart raced. "It was an accident. I mean - I was talking to someone else. I mean - I didn't mean it. I mean - I wasn't making fun of anyone."

His eyes trailed down the front of his uniform. His mind screaming to his body to settle down and quit shaking, but his body was not responding. Pete could feel his legs getting weaker.

The Sergeant spoke again. "These people are your shipmates and mine, and nobody, but nobody, makes fun of one of my shipmates!" He picked up his pipe and took a long draw. As the smoke escaped, he continued. "I'm going to let you go this time, but don't you ever pull this sort of thing again or you'll answer to me." He raised his hand and motioned toward the door. "You're dismissed! Get out of my sight!"

Pete didn't go to chow that morning. Instead, he went up onto the weather decks under the flight deck and sat down in the warm sunlight. He stared out into the harbor toward the other ships, but he wasn't really looking at them. He was trying to figure out how he managed to always find trouble. How does it happen that a person can get himself into a situation of which he is neither a part nor wants to be a part? How can it be that a person loses the most basic communication skills under stress?

Later that morning, Sergeant Hana explained to Pete, "What happened to you has happened before, sometimes with more violent results. The Brig Boss, Sergeant O'Hare, has the capacity to be a real monster. The bad part is that when the brig chasers pull someone in, if they try to complain to the Legal Officer, the case is dismissed because O'Hare never uses physical force, just a personalized form of intimidation."

"Intimidation," Pete said. "I gather that's what was done to me."

"There is one more thing I might mention to you," said Sergeant Hana. "I'd keep an eye on that red headed buddy of yours. He seems to have a knack for getting you into bad situations."

* * *

It was just before noon when the ship got underway for sea trials and Operational Readiness Inspection. The Kingston had been in dry-dock for a major upkeep refit, and some work had been done by the sand crabs (civilian workers) in almost every area of the ship. It was finally time to put all of the repairs and new equipment through the paces before the ship actually got underway for the Western Pacific or WESTPAC as it was called by the old hands.

OE Division didn't have anything to do with the line handling parties of the "Special Sea and Anchor Detail," which helped the ship get underway. Red Dog and Pete stood against the rail of the 02 level catwalk watching the activities and listening to the various commands issued by the Captain and the harbor pilot as the tugs moved the ship away from the pier and righted it in the direction of the open sea.

The athwart ships passageway door to the catwalk opened and Krammer stepped outside. "Which one of you guys has the duty today?" he asked.

"I do," Pete replied, leaning back on the wire rope hand rail. "What's up?"

"Petty Officer Third Brown wants to see you in the ET shack," Krammer said.

Pete reported to Brown. He was filling in the duty roster of underway assignments. A section on the plastic panel had always been blank before. The "Special Sea and Anchor Detail" section, which Pete had been told OE had nothing to do with, now had a name in it, Peterson.

Pete turned away from the board and looked at Brown, who wore a black arm band with white letters that read, Duty Petty Officer of the Day. "Holy cow!" Pete exclaimed, "I've got the special sea and anchor detail for our division, and I don't know what I'm supposed to do. I'll probably get into trouble over this."

"Don't worry about it," mused Brown, taking a sip from his cup of coffee. "It's real simple. All you've got to do is go to the bridge and sign the 'Underway Log' indicating that the entire division is aboard and ready for sea." He leaned on one elbow and pointed a finger. "You'd best get right to the bridge and see the Quartermaster of the Watch before we cross the breakwater. If you don't get that log signed, you'll get Sergeant Hana into a lot of trouble, and I can assure you he wouldn't like that."

Pete raced from the ET shack, up the two flights of ladders to the bridge. He stopped short of the doorway. The Captain was on the bridge with the harbor pilot. The ship was just about to the break water. He saluted. "Request permission to come onto the bridge, sir," he sounded off.

Following protocol, a young officer of the line lowered his binoculars and turned toward him. "What's your business?"

"Special sea and anchor detail, sir," Pete answered.

"Permission granted," said the officer, passing a salute and turning back to his view of the harbor entrance and the approaching open sea.

Pete dashed onto the bridge and found the Quartermaster completing an entry in the ship's log. "I'm here to sign the Underway Log for the OE Division," he wheezed, exhausted from his race against the clock.

"You're Peterson? I've been looking for you," said the lanky First Class QM. He began to shuffle some papers around on his small desk. "Rats! The Messenger of the Watch must've already taken the log sheets down to the Operations Office on the main deck. You'd better get down there on the double and get them signed before they get to the Executive Officer or your whole division will be doing military punishment on the flight deck."

"Oh, spit!" Pete moaned. He rushed off the bridge and flew down the four sets of ladders to the main deck. *What a screwed up Navy this must be,* he thought, as he scurried along the main passageway toward the Operations Office - *giving a man an important assignment and not telling him until after the ship is underway.*

In four minutes, Pete was standing at the half door of the Operations Office. He was greeted by a Third Class Petty Officer, as if he had been waiting for him. "You, Peterson? You're too late! The log's been sent over to the Personnel Office for verification. Their office is on the first deck, forward of the crew's mess. If you know where it is, you might still have a chance to sign it."

The Petty Officer smiled in a very unconcerned manner as he eyed the sweat appearing on Pete's nose and cheeks. "You'd better hustle, or the XO will have your whole division doing military drill with the Brig Sergeant on the flight deck. I wouldn't want to be in your shoes if you make Sergeant Hana walk punishment."

Pete didn't want to be in his shoes either, but he was. He spun away from the door, his feet already moving. The sense of urgency overwhelming.

The main deck passageway was long and wide. He ran past people in the busy hallway. He had to make the turn at the end of the passage, go down one deck, and he would be there.

As he made the turn at the end of the passageway, two officers appeared from the other direction. Pete flew right into one of them, and they both went sprawling. Pete slid a few feet down the passageway and came to rest against an athwart ships bulkhead. He tried to gather his senses and get to his feet. The younger officer was helping the other officer up. Pete's reflexes were shot, he was slow getting up.

Before he knew it, there was an officer on either side of him, lifting him up by the arms. The older officer's voice boomed in his ears. "What's going on here? Are you okay, son?"

Pete's vision focused. The man speaking wore silver oak leaves on his collar. He was a full Commander. The single encircled gold star on his left breast pocket told Pete that he had just flattened the Executive Officer himself, Commander Clay.

"It's my fault, sir. I had the duty and I didn't look at the roster. I thought I did, but I guess didn't. It's my responsibility. My division shouldn't have to suffer because I screwed up." Pete put his hat on and stood a little taller. "I'll do the military detail for all of the men in my division because it's not their fault. I should've checked the roster before I went out on the weather deck. I tried to catch up to the Underway Log, but everywhere I went, a courier had just left to take it somewhere else." Pete pulled off his sea going ball cap and clutched it in front of him. "I know I'll never catch up to it before it gets to your desk now, and everyone in my division will be in trouble. It's not their fault. I'll take full responsibility for it."

The Commander's voice was soft and soothing. "First time at sea?"

Pete relaxed a little. "Yes sir."

"Just be cool, son. It's all right. Why don't we step into the Legal Office, right here, and you can explain what you're talking about." He made a tilting motion with his head, and the younger officer opened the door to the nearby office.

The Ensign, with Legal Department acorns on his collar, now spoke. "Do you think I should get a Corpsman up here, sir? This sailor sounds like he's gone off the deep end."

"No," said the Commander, squinting his right eye and opening the left one very wide. "I think what we have here, is a practical joke we can all enjoy."

Pete accompanied the two officers into the Legal Department Office, and they all sat down. "You're a boot aren't you, son?" asked the Exec, with a smile.

"Yes, sir," Pete replied, feeling quite at ease. "I'm an ET striker from OE Division, and this is my first time at sea.

"An ET, huh?" His smile broadened. "They usually send you boots after a fallopian tube for the radar as your baptism into the fleet. Do you know what that is?"

"No, sir. I don't," Pete answered. He could feel a sheepish redness creeping across his face as he ducked a little.

The Commander laughed. "Well, when they send you after one, no matter where they tell you to go, head for sick bay first."

The Executive Officer leaned over the desk. "You see this?" He pointed at the telephone on the desk. "This is the key to making a practical joke work. You send a new person, whether he's enlisted or officer, somewhere and before he gets there, you call ahead and let other people in on the joke. They think it's funny and just keep sending him on from here to there until he's worn out. When he goes back to his own division, everybody sits around and has a good laugh."

Pete hung his head. He'd been had. Not only was Pete had, but he was probably in deep yoghurt for knocking the XO on his can.

"Now," said Commander Clay, pushing back in his chair. "You go back to the ET shop and tell them the truth. Tell them that you weren't able to catch up to the 'Underway Log.' You take the heat and be very calm about the whole thing. I think you'll enjoy how this joke turns out."

Pete went back to the ET shack and caught holy HEE HAW. Laughter rocked the ET shop for most of the afternoon. Everybody thought it was really terrific that he was a super guppy, the biggest sucker in the sea. He did notice that Sergeant Hana did not come by the office all day. Their division officer, Lieutenant Morten, didn't come by the ET shop for his usual visit either.

The next morning, right after breakfast, the bugle call for 'Quarters for Muster' sounded, and the entire division went to its assigned section of the hangar deck to answer muster. After roll call, Sergeant Hana saluted Lieutenant Morten and reported that all hands were present or accounted for.

There was a long veer of the boatswain's pipe. "Now. Officer's Call. All officers lay before the mast!" Lieutenant Morten marched to the center of the hangar deck where he was joined by the Gunnery Division Officer from the other side of the hangar bay. The officers marched toward the far end of the hangar deck, being joined as they marched along, by all the other Division Officers of the ship. Soon, all the ship's Division Officers were assembled at the far end of the hangar bay in front of the Captain; the Executive Officer stood at his side. Each officer saluted, gave his morning report and waited to hear any special orders or changes in the ship's 'Plan of the Day.'

After Officer's Call, all of the Division Officers marched back to their division, passed the word from the XO to their men, and dismissed their divisions. This was not the case for OE Division.

"Gentlemen," Lt. Morten looked a little drawn as he spoke. "It seems that we didn't get the 'Underway Log' signed yesterday. Therefore, the brig Sergeant is waiting on the flight deck for us. It seems we're scheduled for two hours of military drill this morning. The brig division will supply the arms and Sergeant Hana will instruct. Those who pass the military as well as the physical part of the drill will be dismissed immediately. The rest will drill until they get it right. Take over, Sergeant."

Sergeant Hana saluted, and the division officer departed. "Division. Attention." commanded Sergeant Hana. "We will regroup on the flight deck in five minutes. Division dismissed."

The division returned his salute and began to file up the two ladders to the flight deck. As the division reached the first stairwell, Pete could hear Brown's voice. "What's this bull? There's no such thing as an Underway Log. I made that up. How'd the XO get involved?"

When the division reached the flight deck, Brig Sergeant O'Hare was handing out M1 rifles for drilling purposes. Sergeant Hana was pacing up and down as the men were issued their pieces.

Pete watched his Sergeant for a moment and a sudden realization came over him. Sergeant Hana was wearing his combat boots instead of his flight deck safety shoes like the rest of the division. That was a dead give away that the Sergeant was in on the XO's joke.

"Company. Attention!" barked Hana. "We'll return to the basics for these drills. First, give me fifty pushups. Go!"

Red Dog, Michael and Pete were all boots, and their condition after basic training gave them a distinct edge over their softer shipmates. They quickly completed their pushups and returned to attention.

"Okay, you boots, you're done. Get over here." Sergeant Hana smiled at Pete. "Now, you three guys. Give me the sixteen-count manual of arms. Begin!" Picking up their M1 carbines, the youngsters whipped out the sixteen-count manual of arms and came to parade rest, while they waited for the Petty Officers to finish their pushups.

Hana turned with a little sparkle in his eye. "Having you guys do this is a waste of time. You haven't been away from it long enough for it to be punishment. You guys go up there on the 01 level cat walk and watch the rest the men work on their basics."

After forty-five minutes, there was only ET3 Brown and Sergeant Hana working out on the flight deck.

"That ought to be enough to give him the idea, Sergeant." A strong voice came from the wing of the bridge to the flight deck. It was Commander Clay!

Brown turned his head up toward the bridge. His face turned bright red. His practical joke had backfired.

The division was dismissed and told by Sergeant Hana to 'Turn to. Commence ship's work.'

Pete went back to work feeling that he had been initiated into the alligator Navy.

Chapter 4

Mud Marines

Pete spent the rest of the morning with Seaman Krammer going from radio room to radio room checking and rechecking the new, upgraded, replaced and repaired radio equipment throughout the ship.

Pete was finishing the sweeping of Radio Room 3 when his buddy Red walked in. Pete thought of Red as a good kid. Just a little boastful. According to Red, there was nothing that the US had ever been involved with that had not included a Texan. If there was a fight, the Texan won it single handed. Red was about five foot six, well muscled with dominating features. He had an excellent personality, and was well liked by all the men in the division.

"Hey, Pete, look at this!" he said in a cheery voice as he entered Radio Room 3. "Look at the brochure Sergeant Hana just gave me. It's an opportunity for us lowly sailors to participate with the US Marine Corps in some real action if there is any. You know President Kennedy was sending advisors to South Vietnam. Well, there might be a fight over there, and we might as well go with the

Marines. We don't need to sit around on some stupid ship. What do you say, Pete?"

Pete took the brochure, opened it, closed it, then handed it back. "Not really interested Red."

Aimes would not be slowed. "You know the Marine Corps doesn't have enough electronics technicians. We can get in on the ground floor of this operation. Look at this list. We'd pick up at least ten more good schools." He held the list in front of Pete. "At least look!"

Pete took the list, opened and closed it again. "This is really great all right, Red. We get ten schools and only two deal with electronics. The rest are Marine Corps and special forces schools. A person could get hurt going to that kind of school. They have Marine Drill Instructors and those DI's specialize in pounding sailors into pulp. If I wanted to be a jarhead, I'd have joined the Marines." Pete handed the list back to Red and began pushing his sweepings into a dust pan.

Red grabbed Pete's arm. "Come on, Pete. Be a bud. It's our chance to be Mud Marines. The real deal! I ran away from college to join the Navy. My folks are counting on me to amount to something, and this is a terrific chance for me. It wouldn't hurt you either. It's just a lot of schooling and then getting stationed with a bunch of jarhead Marines, and that's not so bad, is it?"

He knelt beside Pete who was filling his dust pan and continued, "We could go though school together. We'll have 'head of the chow line' privileges when we get back aboard ship."

He leaned his round face close to Pete's, his green eyes pleading. "My old man has been pulling strings and pushing me around for as long as I can remember. He's got lots of dough and political influence, but he can't push me around while I'm in the Navy. You'll think about it, won't you, Pete? You'll have until tomorrow at three in the afternoon. You'll think about it, won't you?"

Pete slumped back against the a large radio console. He didn't know whether to laugh or cry. Red just discovered he joined the wrong branch of the service and now he has a chance to rectify the mistake, but he's afraid to go alone.

"Okay, Okay!" Pete pushed himself upright. "I don't have anything planned for the next few years. I'll go play mud Marine with you."

Red's reaction was that of a youngster at a birthday party, a visible display of joy. He jumped into the air and shook both fists in jubilation. "Yahoo!"

"Well," snarled Pete. "What are you waiting for? Get down to the ET shack and tell Sergeant Hana you have a recruit to add to his Marine Corps roster."

Two weeks later Pete stood on another billet number on another parade ground. They were training with the elite Marine Special Forces Group at Coronado. The southern California sun beat down on his face and the sweltering tarmac burned through the bottom of his new combat boots.

The Drill Instructor strutted up and down, his campaign hat pulled low on his forehead, swearing insults and giving his opinion of all the bottom-feeding sailors in Uncle Sam's Navy.

"Sailors are lower than whale poop," Sergeant Walters railed, "and that's on the bottom of the ocean! You are all bubble-heads as far as I'm concerned! You have no business being here! You are all stupid. You could get a good Marine killed! If I have anything to say about it, you're not going to get a good Marine killed!" He pounded his right fist into his left hand. "You will be properly trained, or you won't be in this outfit. Remember! If the training is too tough for you, all you have to do to quit is take off your helmet and throw it on the ground. Just pull off that tin pot and throw it down. No one will say a thing.

You'll go back to the command you came from. No hard feelings."

The training was arduous. A combination of Marine Corps basic training and all the tricks the corps had learned in all the wars it had fought. The stress was overwhelming at times, but something made the men stick it out. In a very short time, a company of one hundred and twenty had only sixty-four left.

Pete watched the company dwindle as the training progressed and tried to control his temper, do his job and stay quietly in the background. Staying in the background was getting harder. At six feet, he was nearly a head taller than the majority of the trainees. He had pursued track and basketball in high school and he generally condidered his long wiry frame as an advantage.

* * *

At four hundred yards ahead of the company, Pete eased his stride.

"Why you slowing down?" came a voice from behind. "My coach always taught me not to give anyone a chance to catch up," he said as he came alongside Pete.

Looking down at the muscular little man keeping pace next to him, Pete said, "I'm not letting anyone catch up. I just want to set a pace I can finish this course with."

The smaller man's heavy field pack rested easy on his shoulders as he began to extend his gait. Pete pressed his stride slightly to keep up.

"I like you. You can run," said the smaller man, extending his right hand. My name is Gomez. Isidro Onisimo Gomez. I'm going through this school so I can go to Beach Master 'A' School. They won't even consider you, unless you pass this school."

Pete and Isidro became fast friends. Pete and Red also found a friend in the young man that bunked next to them, Skippy Winters. Skippy was having a hard time of it. The emotional strain of the training seemed to be wearing on him more than the physical. Pete and Red had both counseled him to drop out and go back to the fleet, but he felt he had to stay. He was the high school football hero, he got a lot of letters from home, everyone was counting on him. He couldn't quit.

If he left, he felt he would be a total disgrace to his family. His dad had been a hero in the second world war, so now he had to prove something to the folks back home, as well as to himself. With this kind of mind set, it was no wonder he would not take off his helmet and give up. He told Pete that his father had a little saying he used every time there was a football game to be won. "Come home with your shield in victory, or come home on your shield."

Sergeant Walters could see that Skippy was near the breaking point, and threatened to bust him out of training and send him back to his boat if his attitude didn't improve.

When the company got to the machine gun live fire obstacle course, Pete could see that Skippy's determination to complete the course had weakened.

Sergeant Walters explained. "The fire will be twenty-four to thirty inches above the ground, so keep low. If someone does get hit, stay down! The live fire will last five full minutes once it starts. Just get through and get it done."

Pete nudged Red as they approached the course. "Let's stay close to Skippy just in case he decides to do something that isn't too bright."

"Okay," Red said. "You go first and we'll keep him between us. If he tries to stand up, I'll break both his legs."

As the company entered the mud holes and barb wire entanglements, Skippy began to moan, "Nobody cares! I can't take this life anymore!"

Pete and Red were both under wire entanglements and Skippy was in a muddy depression between them. Pete spun over on his back, pushing the wire entanglement away from his face with his piece.

Pete was too late. Skippy rose on his knees and Pete could see the raking thirty caliber machine gun fire sewing a line across the front of Skippy's fatigue jacket just below the breast pockets. Pete stared in terror at the blank look on Skippy's face as his body shook from each round hammering home. Finally, his knees buckled. He rolled over backward and fell in a heap on the wire over Red. Pete gasped and froze. He had seen death, but never this close. He could not breathe. He fought for breath as he struggled back to help Red Dog.

Later that day, the Chaplain told the company that Skippy had received a 'Dear John' letter a few days before. Three days and the training would have been over. Just three short days!

Sergeant Walters lectured at morning muster. "You men, if you survive the next three days, will be assigned to various Marine, Beach Master and SEAL special forces units around the world. You will be the best the US Navy has to offer."

Red was doing an outstanding job. He was a born hand-to-hand expert and everything else just came to him. He was mentally and physically tough.

The company stood on a strand of lonely white beach at the hand to hand combat course. The men were in a long straight line, tallest to shortest. Pete was second from the end on the tall end of the line, Red was at the other end of the line.

"Peterson!" It was Sergeant Walters' grinding voice. "You wormy-eyed slug! Is your mind off in never-never-land? Your daydreaming could get a good Marine killed, you idiot! Are you hearing me, slug?" His voice rang loud and sharp as he came to stand in front of Pete. Pete flinched as the hard brim of Sergeant Walters' campaign hat pecked against his forehead just under the edge of his helmet. He was in Pete's face. "You think I ain't watchin' you, don't ya, slug?

"Are you hearing me, pea brain?" Sergeant Walters bellowed. His face close. The black coffee he had for breakfast burned Pete's nostrils. "In case you ain't been here, pea brain, I was talking to your mates here, about never losing your temper when you're in a hand-to-hand situation."

Just as quickly as he had appeared in Pete's face, he wheeled on his heel and went down the beach to continue his hand-to-hand lecture. He was going over the finer points of the bayonet as a tool of the special forces trade.

For some reason, Pete felt the lecture take on a humorous tone. He nudged the man beside him and whispered, "I'd like to stick my bayonet in him."

His lips had hardly moved, and he was sure he had not made any motion, but suddenly Sergeant Walters spun around and marched back to face him. It was as though he had heard Pete or read his mind.

"Is that so, lily lips?" the Sergeant bellowed. "Have you got a bayonet, fish bait?"

"Yes Sir," Pete stammered. Surprise gripped him. Fear and shock made his voice drag and change pitch. He felt the words lock in his throat.

"I can't hear you, you chicken liver!" The Sergeant's demeanor had not changed.

Pete suddenly felt a surge of fire race through his veins and his face flushed. "Yes, sir! I have a bayonet, sir!" he screamed in a tone of anger that he did not recognize as himself.

"Sooo-- Fix your bayonet, you yellow dog!" yelled the Sergeant, stepping back to see Pete's response.

Pete was out of control. He seemed to watch from outside himself as his emotions took over. In one motion, he pulled his bayonet from his backpack scabbard and locked it into place on his piece. The next thing he knew, he was on the attack. Sergeant Walters was his prey and he would have him! Walters would taste the steel that he praised so highly. Pete attacked!

Suddenly, Sergeant Walters' hand was on the barrel of Pete's rifle. Pete could feel his body in motion and he marveled at how beautiful the sky was as he passed over the Sergeant's head and came crashing down on his back. The lights went out as his head snapped back over his heavy field pack.

When Pete opened his eyes, he could see the gleaming steel of his own bayonet flashing in the sun as it traveled downward toward his face. He knew at that exact moment, this would be another of Sergeant Walters' training accidents. He heard the sing of the blade as it swished by him and buried to the hilt in the sand next to his throat.

As quickly as he had called his anger, Sergeant Walters regained total composure and was once again lecturing, walking up and down in front of the troop. "Remember, above all else! Never lose your temper in a combat situation. You've all seen Peterson work out with weapons and you know he's very good. If I hadn't gotten him angry, he probably would've killed me." The Sergeant moved to stand over Pete, grasping Pete's right hand with his. "Get up, Pete," he said in a low tone. "We have a course to finish, partner."

Chapter 5

The Real Thing

The final two days of Special Forces School passed quickly, and the men were back aboard the Kingston after seven weeks of special schooling.

Sergeant Hana came into the ET Shop carrying two envelopes. One he handed to Pete, the other to Red. "Looks like you boys have your assignments. Tear 'em open. Let's hear where you're goin'."

"My dad is going to be proud of me this time," said Red Dog as he slid his finger across the back of the envelope, breaking the seal. "I wrote him just before we left for school." He quickly read the enclosed orders, jumped to his feet and dropped the papers to the floor. "He's still screwing with my life!" He stormed from the ET shack.

"I've been assigned to Company L, Third Marine Division, right here aboard the Kingston," said Pete, pulling his orders down from in front of his face.

Sergeant Hana knelt and picked up Red's orders.

"Where'd Red get assigned, Sarge?" Pete asked.

Sergeant Hana stood, laying Red's orders on a nearby work bench. "Pete, you have to remember, Red's dad is wealthy and has a lot of pull in Washington. I can see why Red's disappointed. He's been assigned to the Naval Attache' at the United States embassy in Paris. He really wanted a combat unit."

The next day Red Dog was gone, and along with him, Pete's first friend in the fleet.

Pete enjoyed being assigned to the Third Marine Division. He had 'head of the chow line' privileges. There was always plenty of hot water for showers, and as far as the peacetime seagoing corps goes, this was the duty to have. Red had wanted sea duty with a fighting unit, and here Pete was, getting it.

For all intents and purposes, little about Pete's status aboard the *USS Kingston* (LPH 15) had changed. As an Electronics Technician striker, he stood underway watches with the ETs. Except for a couple of Marines in Company L, the ET's were his only friends. The one true difference was when the Marine company had air drills, Pete changed into his Marine greens and filed to the flight deck with the Marines of his company.

Stationed aboard an LPH, they were a ready vertical envelopment group. There were ten Marine companies and their choppers, all waiting patiently for their orders to act.

The old Kingston had completed all of her sea trials, and the civilian sand crabs had been put ashore. The crew had all taken their leaves and completed all of their special schools. The ship was tied up at pier Echo in Long Beach.

It was spring, but there was a chill in the air. President Johnson had pledged to the South Vietnamese he would send more U. S. troops to help push back the northern threat. None of the people on the Kingston even knew what Vietnam was. The ship began to buzz with rumors, scuttlebutt of a specific nature. 'We're going to Vietnam.' Pete's only question was, "Where is Vietnam?"

It was the twelfth of May when the ship got underway out of Long Beach. They were told they were on their way to Japan, and would arrive there about the twenty-eighth of May.

During the trip across the Pacific, Pete moved into the Marine berthing space and spent all of his free time with the men of his company. Sergeant Millen, the company honcho, held classes explaining Vietnam and the necessity of employing American troops. He told Pete it would be vital to his own well-being to know each member of the rifle company and how each one thought.

It wasn't too hard to get to know Lonie Johnson, the company Hospital Corpsman. He was the only other sailor in the company, and naturally they hit it off right away. There were some other real great guys though, Anderson from Idaho, Haynes from Montana and Borgie from Arizona. Pete had a lot in common with them, since they were from the West and familiar with his beloved desert of southern Utah.

The twelve guys flying the choppers for Pete's company were old dudes. Jackson, the oldest, was going to be twenty-four in June. At nineteen Pete was classified as being middle-aged.

When the pilots went to flight briefings, they were given orders cut by antique typewriters on old mimeograph mats and run off on ancient mimeograph machines by very young Yeomen in the ship's Air Operations Office.

Pete looked at one set of orders.

The pilot had to help the Marine radioman recognize a map plot. Pete could hardly read the washed out blue lines against the very low quality paper. The paper was so bad, Pete thought he might get a splinter from handling it.

The only thing the pilots knew was, they were indeed going into combat.

What had happened to the trip to Japan?

The pilots went to their flight briefing and picked up their orders as a group from Air Operations.

It was zero four-hundred hours when the Boatswain's pipe rattled the berthing compartment to life. "Now reveille, reveille! All hands heave out and trice up. The smoking lamp is lighted in all authorized spaces. Breakfast will begin on the forward mess deck in ten minutes for all Marines and flight crew personnel. Flight stations will go down in two hours."

Pete turned face out in his bunk and looked across the aisle at Borgie, a very sharp lance corporal. "Hey Borgie. Why did you leave such an early wake-up call?"

He sprung out of his rack and put his foot on Pete's bunk giving it a shake. "I don't know, Pete, but from what I hear, this could be the real thing." He slid on his trousers and continued, "from what I heard on watch last night, there is supposed to be a whole fleet of troop transports ahead of us, getting ready to dump ten-thousand dogfaces on the beach at zero eight hundred, and at the same time, we," he said, gesturing to himself with his thumb, "are going to cut off the retreating enemy from the air and give the folks back home some good news to read about their newest Asian war." He pulled a shirt from his locker and disappeared up the stairwell out of the berthing compartment.

"Now flight stations! All Marines to flight stations!" barked the Boatswain's Mate of the Watch over the 1MC.

It was an unnecessary announcement. Almost all of the Marines were already at their stations, standing inside the island superstructure of the ship on the stairwells awaiting the command to board their aircraft.

A corpsman in whites appeared in the lower deck hatchway. "Lieutenant Page, sir!" He waved, trying to get the Company Commander's attention. "Sir. Sergeant Millen won't be going with you. He's in sickbay right now. We took out his appendix about two hours ago. Flight operations told me to tell you a replacement is being flown in from Saigon, and he'll be here shortly. He's coming in on one of those new jet powered choppers."

The night was extra dark. The sea was silent, and the air was heavy with moisture.

There was so much humidity Pete felt wet from head to foot. He stood near the doorway watching the Airedales on the flight deck as they scurried here and there. The sputtering of the helicopter engines cranking up was the only break in the silent darkness.

A flood of light splashed on the flight deck as the conning tower lights came on for the landing of an incoming chopper. There was little or no noise as the sleek green helo came smoothly to rest outside the main superstructure tower where the assembled troops stood. Pete could see a form in combat gear disembarking in the shadow-ridden spot lights. The figure stooped low, picked up his pack and weapon and moved quickly to the shelter of the superstructure as the chopper became airborne and disappeared into the darkness.

The figure stood inside the tower, rendering a right hand salute to Lt. Page. "Sergeant Walters reporting, sir!"

Pete's tongue thickened in his mouth and his eyes squinted down as his ears tested the air once again for a familiar voice. *Holy cow! It's him! My combat school Drill Instructor*. Before he knew it, Sergeant Walters stood before him, his arms outreached, embracing him.

"Pete, you son of a gun! You're still alive! By golly, just goes to show you I'm a good trainer of men." He began to laugh and introduce himself to the other men down the ladder. The tension in the compartment was quickly broken by his presence and everyone felt at ease.

The ship's Chaplain began to pass down the stairwell, through the ranks, giving his blessing as he went. Pete didn't feel too religious at the moment, but it was reassuring to see the Sky Pilot anyway.

Pete heard the coughing and choking of the last helo as it began to start. The sputter broke into a smooth whirring throb as the rotor blades dipped and raised over the dark flight deck. The kerosene smell of aviation gasoline was heavy in the morning air.

"Now Flight Quarters! Flight Quarters!" piped the Boatswain's Mate of the Watch.

Pete started to move down the line. Sergeant Walters was directly in front of him and the company radioman was in back as they crouched and half ran the sixty-odd yards through the darkness to their waiting helicopter. All eight men took their seats, watching the crew chief pull the large metal door closed behind them.

The chopper leaned and lurched, as the engine cranked up tight for departure. Pete looked up at the pilot seated well above his head and wondered, *How can the Army have all kinds of brand new equipment while the Marine Corps sets here in a heavy metal mix-master?*

The helicopter had been in flight an hour when sunlight began to find its way down from the cockpit above the marines. Pete knew this chopper could fly an easy one-hundred miles an hour. They hadn't done any maneuvering to speak of, except to join fourteen other choppers in formation.

Even though they sat shoulder to shoulder, the noise of the engine directly overhead made it impossible to speak with one another. It would be even harder to get the attention of the crew chief who wore a flight helmet.

The crew chief stood and shoved the side panel door open.

What a sight! Tall grass, like wheat, and rice paddies stretching away for miles on one side. High hills rolled out on the other, covered by all kinds of foliage and trees. The huge leaves on the trees blew away from the rotor backwash of the choppers as they came down.

The company landed on a flat area slightly above the rice fields. High hills covered with jungle rose to their left. A large outcropping of rocks behind them created an easy area to protect. A half-mile away, at the next plateau level above them was a road, where a long column of troops marched westward. The helicopters were coming in from the east, flying west.

The troops were moving casually, and in good military manner. Their column never broke stride as the choppers hovered and the Marines began to disembark. The troops moving on the road were not on the run as the company had been led to believe they would be.

Pete sat in the doorway of the chopper about to jump. "Let's get 'em, Pete," called out the company radioman as his boot found the small of Pete's back. Pete rolled sideways from the surging doorway and vaulted through the tall grass to the unseen ground below. As he landed, a sharp pain stabbed through his left ankle and he nearly doubled over. It was sprained. Marines were running everywhere.

Sergeant Walters yelled. "V formation! Automatic heavies at the corners! Dig in! Get under cover on the double!" His entrenching tool was already swinging wet dirt over his shoulder.

We're vertical envelopment, thought Pete. *Why are we digging in? Oh, what the hey, Sarge always knows what he's doing.*

The troops on the road continued on their unobstructed sojourn. The choppers had pulled out, and the company was pretty well dug in when Pete began to look for the radioman. Pete couldn't lose him, or he'd be out of a job. He was two foxholes away with the Company Commander. Pete hopped in the hole and sat beside the radioman who was trying to raise the ship on his radio. "Ulcer, Ulcer. This is Valuable, over."

Pete looked from the radioman to Lieutenant Page whose face was pale and drawn like something was radically wrong. Lieutenant Page spoke to Sergeant Walters. "Dad gum it! I knew it! We're in the wrong place. Do you see twelve-hundred Marines here? No, you don't!" His finger was near the center of the chart he had between himself and the Sergeant. "Those idiots set us down in the wrong place." Calm now came into Lieutenant Page's voice. He understood the problem and was ready to cope.

The sector assignment on their orders was messed up. Something had caused the orders to be printed as sector 3-8, instead of the correct sector, 8-8.

Lieutenant Page turned to the radioman. "Sparks," his voice took on a smooth, controlled tone. "Get the ship on the horn and tell'em we're in sector thirty-eight, not in eighty-eight like we're supposed to be. Tell'em we're company strength and have, what appears to be, a complete enemy infantry division on our left flank at about one-quarter of a mile." Lieutenant Page pushed his helmet back on his head slightly and clinched his fist. "Hurry up, Sparks! I think we're in for a fight if those folks out there figure out we're not with them."

"There's a red communist star on the side of that six-by truck, sir," one of the riflemen on the left flank called.

The mere sound of his voice, carried by the breeze, was like a command to the soldiers moving slowly down the dirt road. There was a rush of communist troops, and the road was completely clear except for the large truck and a half-track which was turning into position to bring it's machine gun to bear on the company's position.

Privates Hellman and Cook, the Marine mortar team, watching the maneuver, fired a salvo. The half-track, carrying ammunition, exploded in several volleys. Pete's company was engaged in a fire fight.

The enemy took cover, firing their weapons from where they were. Most of them were armed with bolt action single fire, rather than automatic weapons.

The lieutenant cupped his hands to his face and gave a loud command to the company. "Give 'em everything we've got, boys! Let 'em know the Marines have landed!"

Sparks handed the field telephone transceiver of the radio to the officer. "I've got Ulcer on the line, sir," he said, as the Company Commander took the telephone hand set.

Bullets skipped the dirt and cut the grass around the foxhole. Pete shrank down closer to the Sergeant. Sergeant Walters was raking the hillside with his M-14.

"You know the story, Ulcer," said Lieutenant Page. "There are so many of 'em, they can come and get us at will. We can't hold out long in this position. We'll have to have help and have it real soon." He hesitated and listened to the voice from the ship. "Listen, Gar-Rammit! These people are not throwing rocks. This enemy force is moving in fast. We're throwing everything at them and they're still coming down the hill. The hill?" He spun the chart in front of him as he replied to a question from the ship. "That would be point niner, two, seven, able on the grid, sir. Okay, you send planes off of the Bonnie Dick, but you'd better get some support over here on the..."

He slumped forward. He had been hit. He was dead.

Holy shit! This is the real thing! thought Pete.

Tangible proof of war that ravaged lands and destroyed entire peoples lay slumped against Pete's knee. The hair on the back of his neck stood up, he felt a pang of terror when he saw where the silent round had spent itself at the base of his Company Commander's skull.

Sergeant Walters was already talking with the ship on the radio. His voice was loud and clear and angry. He didn't care who heard him.

"The lieutenant's dead! We don't have time to chat with you people! You'd better get hot, and I mean right now!" He handed the phone to the radioman.

"They're going to open up with the guns from a couple of destroyers and a cruiser. When the shells start splashin', you guide 'em in." He picked up his M-14 and started firing at the front line of the column of troops advancing down the hill.

Pete had been schooled in amphibious assault for beach attack. Ironically, he was landed by helicopter in the middle of jungle-ridden farmland. In combat school, he had been well trained in the use of the M-1 rifle. The M-1 had been substituted for a sidearm, a bulky .45 caliber pistol. It seemed all of his training had been scrapped leaving Pete totally unprepared.

If Pete had to be in this position, he was glad to know he was here with Sergeant Walters, the Marine Corps' answer to Superman. Pete wasn't worried about going anywhere with him. Pete knew he was as tough as nails, and he was not going to lose his composure. He was banging away, knocking the enemy down like rows of wheat before a combine.

A heavy low-toned whistle began to vibrate the air. Within the tone was a *thump thump thump* like someone pounding a wet cardboard box with a baseball bat.

Pete had never heard it before, but he knew what it was - the shells from Naval guns off the coast. The first round poured in. It hit the top of the hill near the burning truck. There was an explosion as mud and debris flew in all directions.

"Tell 'em to drop their sights two degrees and pour it in here, Sparks!" yelled Walters from his forward corner of the foxhole.

The bodies of Lt. Page and another Marine had been removed. When Pete heard Walters' voice he looked at Sparks. It was too late. An enemy round had found its way to the collar button of Sparks' shirt and his Adam's apple exploded without a sound.

"Corpsman!" Pete screamed, pulling the radio hand set out from under Sparks' body. "Sarge! I'll take over for Sparks, you keep after those gooks."

The corpsman, undaunted by the goings on around him, slid into the foxhole with them. He took one look at Sparks and dragged him out of the hole toward the rear. It was as though there were angels around the young Hospitalman Third Class. Shells struck the ground all around him, but they went totally ignored as he toured from hole to hole patching men up.

The ships off shore had their own spotter aircraft in the air. The firepower was being directed at the enemy with utmost furor. The enemy did not know they were in a world of trouble. The human wave continued.

Three US Navy propeller driven fighter planes arrived on the scene. "Valuable, Valuable. This is Fire Hook. Come in Valuable," the lead pilot's voice crackled in Pete's ear.

"Hello, Fire Hook!" Pete answered excitedly. "Have you got some bombs to lay on this position?"

"We've got napalm, buddy. Where would you like us to dump the load? Throw yellow smoke grenades from your position so we can see you and dump on the enemy and not on you." The pilot's message was crisp and clear as the fighters zipped overhead.

Pete turned to Sergeant Walters. "Sarge. Fire Hook wants us to throw yellow smoke to identify our position so they don't dump their napalm on us."

The sergeant handed Pete a smoke canister with a blue top and said, "Throw this!"

Pete hesitated.

"Throw this!" he repeated, "and then tell the pilots what you threw, but be quick about it!"

The heavy ring dug into Pete's finger as he jerked it from the canister with his right hand. He could hear the hiss of the burning fuse when he lobbed it out to their left as far as he could. As he did, he looked up to see the hills above them were alive with YELLOW SMOKE. The enemy had been monitoring the radio and had thrown yellow smoke grenades. He could already hear the fighters approaching from the east, making another run from their rear. Pete screamed into the radio handset. "Fire Hook! Hold your fire! Fire

Hook, We are the blue smoke. I repeat! Fire Hook, this is Valuable. We are the blue smoke!"

The fighters veered off just as they reached the last Marine entrenchment, and the lead pilot's voice crackled the radio again. "You'd better be glad someone's thinking down there, son. We just about burned you up."

The aircraft turned, approaching along the road on a north to south run. They were low - so low they caused the brush to rustle with a heavy wind.

Sergeant Walters cupped his hands to his mouth and called to the machine gun emplacement on the left flank. "Napalm! Come home! Napalm!"

The gunner from the rice paddy position jumped to his feet and started through the mud in a crouched run toward Pete. His powder man, apparently dead, stayed at the gun.

The Marine stopped his flight and ran back to his gun. Pete now understood what the gunner was doing. He had left two open cans of ammunition at the gun. If the fire from the napalm hit the cans, many of the men in the forward foxholes, including Pete, could be killed. The Marine flipped the lids shut on the cans and grabbing one under each arm, started to make the run for home.

Pete didn't know what napalm was. He had heard of it as a flame thrower propellant, but this was his first encounter with it in bomb form.

The aircraft broke its descent and leveled off as a shinny silver cylinder, pointed on both ends, fell away from under the wing. The cylinder struck the ground and bounced in a very high arc. As it reached the top of the arch, it broke open like a giant water balloon in slow motion, but it wasn't water. It was fire!

Pete saw the gunner's face. It was Borgie. He was within twenty-five yards of Pete's position.

Walters screamed and waved both arms down violently.

"Hit the deck!"

Borgie dropped the ammo cans and sprang into the air. His knees splashed down on the can tops and his whole body submerged in the mud of the rice field as the flames swept over him. Pete lept from his foxhole and headed for Borgie. Haynes was at his elbow. Pete swept the burning gel away from the surface where Borgie's helmet lay and found him in the muddy water. Haynes and Pete each hooked a hand under an arm, and ran for cover.

When they got to Haynes' foxhole, the corpsman was waiting for them. A couple of slaps and a little smelling salts and Borgie was almost as good as new - he had broken both knees burying the ammo cans and had a slight burn on the back of his neck.

Pete raced for his own foxhole while Sergeant Walters gave him covering fire.

"That was a pretty good trick," Sergeant Walters said as Pete dropped in beside him. "You know, a fellow could get his south end shot off if he made a habit of that kind of activity."

Pete picked up the radio handset and put it to his ear. "Thanks, Navy! You just about burned us up as it was!" Pete said, trying to regain his breath.

The ear piece crackled as a new voice came on line. "Valuable, Valuable, this is Army Two Niner Romeo. We're coming in to take you home, Valuable."

Pete laid the phone down and looked to the east. There were three Army big banana troop helicopters coming over the horizon. Pete felt a tremendous surge of relief race through him as he slapped Walters on the shoulder. "The Army's coming. They'll be here in five minutes."

Walters kept banging away. It seemed as though the human wave assault was getting heavier.

Pete thought, *There might not be anything left for the Army to pick up when they get here.*

Walters turned to Pete, his hands covering his face. Blood was pouring between his fingers. His voice was a painful, yet soft, screech. "Pete! I'm hit!"

When he fell, so did Pete! *Not Sergeant Walters! Every Marine in the Corps can die. I can die, but not Sergeant Walters.*

Pete lost control of himself. He screamed for a corpsman and cursed Walters. At the same time, he jerked the sergeant up by the collar and slapped his face repeatedly. "Don't you die, you slug! You can't get out of this that easily, you slime!"

Pete didn't feel the rifle butt that separated his hands from Walters.

He realized Haynes and Anderson were both on his chest. Haynes was yelling, "Get the radio, Pete!" Pete's awareness finally came into focus and he dragged the radio hand set to his ear.

"Valuable, Valuable, this is Puff the Magic Dragon," said the voice on the other end. Pete searched the sky for what he could see. "Anderson, is there an aircraft up there?" he asked.

The human wave assault was on top of them. Enemy soldiers charged past on their way to the rear. Bodies were falling everywhere. One had fallen with a leg or arm shot off and the stub was hanging over the edge of the hole directly above Pete. Blood was dripping down onto his face. Pete struggled to get up, but Haynes and Anderson would have no part of it. Haynes handed him one of his grenades. "They're so close you can hit them in any direction," he said as he resumed firing into the onslaught.

Pete pulled the pin on the grenade and threw it sidearm into the air with a prayer that it wouldn't hit his own guys.

"Right on, Pete!" shouted Anderson as he handed him three more grenades.

Pete threw his eighth grenade when he heard Puff The Magic Dragon attack with his twenty millimeter cannons. Just a few rounds and the enemy was retreating. Haynes moved off Pete's chest and allowed him up to see the action.

The army choppers landed and their guys scurried to load the dead and wounded Marines. Army stretcher bearers jumped from the choppers to help their medics.

Through the dust and smoke, Pete saw their amazing savior. Puff The Magic Dragon as it was called, was an old silver DC-3 with twin fifty-caliber machine guns and twenty millimeter cannons in the doorway. What a sight! When Puff spoke, the enemy ran for cover. He flew in a tight circle cutting down everything in sight. Trees fell from a single hit, grass was on fire and enemy troops ran in all directions. They had finally had enough of the Marine rifle company and its helpers.

It was four in the afternoon the next day when Pete rolled out of his bunk and headed for the showers. After he dressed he went to sick bay to see Sergeant Walters.

He sat on the bunk across from Sergeant Walters. A large bandage covered his left shoulder and part of his back. The bullet had entered his helmet, parted his scalp and swirled around inside his helmet before entering his back. He was waking up. His eyes blinked and traveled up to meet Pete's.

"Hey, Pete," he said. "It's good to see you, pal. What's the story on the unit? Can you tell me?"

Pete leaned over, swallowed hard, and spoke softly. "I probably shouldn't be the one to tell you and maybe this isn't the place for it, Sarge, but of the one hundred and twenty guys we went in there with, there's just seventeen left. There's you, me and fifteen others that are either up in the berthing compartment getting some sleep or right here in one of these sick bay bunks." Pete felt the lump harden in his throat as he finished.

Walters blinked a couple of times, a tear visible on his cheek. "Did they get all of our guys out, Pete?" he asked.

Pete could feel the tears dancing in his own eyes as he tried to force the words out. "Yes. Our entire company came home. The ones that will go stateside soon are in the coolers down by the galley." He could not bear to carry on the conversation further. He put his hat on, turned his head away and left for the weather deck. That same strange emotion of fear, anger and disgust that had gripped him at the time of the mine disaster swept over him and wrapped him like a shroud. He wanted to run away.

I can't run, he thought. *I'm on a ship. Where could I go? There must be a reason I'm here. Maybe there's a reason for me being here.*

He found a quiet place in the sun below the flight deck on the port side of the ship. He felt numb all over, as if he had just left a giant dental chair. The war was the real thing, all right! He had seen it and so had many others who would not be able to think about it any more.

A month later, Borgie would receive the Congressional Medal of Honor for the act of heroism that saved many of his comrades from exploding ammunition.

Chapter 6

Tiger

Pete looked down into the water. It was clear blue as it was most of the time on the South China Sea. He sat in the well deck just below the flight deck with his legs crossed, his head and shoulders over the side, his chest against the steel life line and his hands around the line on either side of his body.

He peered down as far as he could. Where the ship had anchored, the water wasn't very deep, maybe forty feet. He could see the brightly colored coral bottom below. The surface of the sea was dead quiet. Many times Pete had sat here and pretended he was looking through the clear glass of a giant aquarium.

Now he was seeking the solitude of the spot, hoping to forget what had happened. Thank God for the beauty of the sea. The ugliness of the previous day ebbed and washed away right before his eyes. He could see only the movement of tropical fish in the space below.

He realized the tiny ringlets breaking into bigger circles were tears falling from his eyes. He didn't know how long he had been there, but he was beginning to feel better. It still didn't make sense, but at least it didn't hurt so bad.

Pete heard footsteps on the flight deck above him, and a voice calling his name softly. "Pete. Sarge would like to see you up at the ET shack." It was Pepsi, a Second Class Communications Technician. He was a large friendly fellow with a true personal warmth. He was liked by everyone in the division.

He was always handy if there was a problem - the next best thing to having a chaplain in your own division. He listened to everyone's problems and gave good counsel.

Pete wiped his face on his sleeve and kept his face turned away from the Petty Officer above him. Pete saw Pepsi's shadow on the water as he stood against the flight deck life line above him.

"Pepsi," he said, mustering his best composure, "would you tell the Sergeant I'll be right there?"

The big man's shadow turned from the rail and hesitated. "You take all the time you need, Pete. I'll tell him you'll be along."

Twenty minutes later, Pete found Sergeant Hana sitting alone in the ET shop having a cup of coffee.

"How you doin', Pete?" He poured a cup and set it in front of Pete as he sat down. "Hey, pal. This hasn't been the same division without your antics."

He took a cigarette from a pack on the table and offered Pete one. As they lit up from his shiny brass Zippo, he went on. "Pete, I've been asked to talk to you by the field commander over at Third Marine on the beach. The *USS Charlestown* has just put twenty-two infantry companies on the beach under his command, and they don't have any ETs. Oh yeah, two thirds of their companies have com techs, but the rest would be up the creek if they got into combat and something happened to their radio or radioman.

"The place on the beach is called DaNang, and the commander is a personal friend. I promised I'd talk to you to see if you'd consider being assigned to K Company until your orders for

Stateside rotation came through. All the men who survived 'Death Row Hill' - that's what they're calling the engagement you were in - are being rotated out to other overseas stations. The rest are going home in body bags on Pan Am out of Saigon."

Pete thought about it for a few seconds as he sipped his coffee. He would just as soon go with a live company of jarheads as stay aboard and sleep in a berthing compartment full of empty bunks, the occasional ghost and nightmares.

Two days later, Pete stepped from the door of the Sikorsky UH-32 Sea Horse to be met by Sergeant Perkins, a Korean War veteran, from K Company. He took Pete to the barracks.

It was a 2 X 4 frame building with plywood walls built up 2 feet high. The rest of the structure was open plastic window screen to the ceilings. The roof was draped green canvas nailed to 2 X 4 roof joists. It was a nice barracks building with the company close to everything, bar, PX, and shower trucks. The shower trucks were 40 foot semi truck trailers parked near the barracks, hooked to compressors and water heaters. He entered the back door of the trailer and found a modern bathroom. The drains drained into pumper trucks.

"Real showers!" he said, giving Sergeant Perkins a smile as they continued the tour.

"There are sentries at the entrance to the trailers. You have to have permission to enter and shower," Sergeant Perkins said.

Perkins showed Pete to an empty top bunk. The bunks were steel, with metal frames and two-inch cotton tick mattresses. The guy below Pete was Hospital Corpsman Davis from Chicago, and beside him was Lance Corporal Decker, a short wiry guy from Montana. Pete acknowledged the introductions as he stowed his gear. Another marine, PFC Palmer joined the group as Pete finished filling his locker.

The men, all new to the base, exchanged brief histories and discussed how to best spend their free evening.

Lance Corporal Decker, being a real honest-to-goodness marine, made a suggestion. "Let's go over to the Army's version of an Enlisted Men's Club for a few beers. Doc Davis and I were there a few days ago and it's not a bad place, considering."

As the group entered the club, another screened 2X4 structure, Decker pointed to the bar. "To get a drink, you have to go to the bar and pay the bartender in Military Pay Certificate. A dollar certificate buys 20 tickets, one ticket buys a beer. The waitresses only handle the tickets to make sure the real money, the MPC, doesn't get funneled to the Viet Cong." The bar was large, filled with a couple hundred small round tables and petite Vietnamese waitresses. The room was busy, already filled to two thirds of its capacity.

"I don't care what the system is," Pete grinned, slapping the table with an open hand, "as long as you can get a cold beer."

"I'm afraid the beer is warm," said Decker. "They keep it outside, stacked on pallets covered with canvas, just like C-rations or ammo. Cases and cases of Budwiser, Hamms, Pabst, Oly, Coors, Buckhorn and other brands at a nickel a can." Decker pushed his chair back and held up his right hand. "I'll bet their beer stack is twenty feet high and covers half an acre."

The four men settled at a small round table in a corner and began to drink up the two dollars worth of tickets Pete had purchased.

"I think we've drunk plenty for tonight," Pete slurred. "One thing about the military, at least you can drink legally, even if you're only 17."

"Maybe they figure if you're old enough to die for your country, you're old enough to drink," said Decker.

The men rose from their table in unison and stumbled or crawled the 100 yards to their barracks and tumbled awkwardly into their bunks.

The next morning, Sergeant Perkins was walking through the barracks, calling people by name and tapping the bottom of their feet with a sheathed bayonet. It was 7 A.M.! The longest he had ever been allowed to sleep on a normal day in the military.

"Smith, Harmon, Decker, Palmer, Peterson, Willows, Sparemont..." Sergeant Perkins recited until he had his squad picked out. Being the communications technician, Pete was picked, and Willlows was the radioman.

The selected men dressed hurriedly and gathered their gear together. Pete was glad there was no time for breakfast. The warm beer from the night before had left his stomach feeling like it would not hold up to even the smell of food.

The squad went into the briefing room and met Lieutenant Baxter, an Annapolis graduate, reportedly an excellent leader. Sgt. Perkins and the brigade commander were also there. The lieutenant would lead the squad on this special assignment.

The men were briefed as a group, three squads from three different companies, going to different objectives.

"Men," the commander cleared his throat. "The Marine Corps has been called on to try out some new tactical procedures here in this area of the war zone. We want to make ourselves effective as counterinsurgency squads to curtail the activity of the Viet Cong and infiltration by the North Vietnamese Army. These new programs are called Search and Destroy Missions, a new concept straight from the Pentagon. You men are to be sent out in squad strength units in individual helicopter drops." His hand swung toward a large map of South Vietnam, Laos, Cambodia and Thailand. "Naturally, you men will try to be as invisible as possible, so surprise will be on our side. Your objectives will be to disrupt, destroy or put out of use, targets useful to the enemy. Each squad will have a specific objective. Your squad leader will brief you all on your specific targets."

Holy cripe! Pete thought. *Here I am, getting even farther from the amphibious assaults I was trained for - unless you call jumping into armpit-deep elephant grass and rice paddies, amphibious assaults.*

Pete's mind wandered. He wondered what the families of the casualties from L Company were being told about how and where their sons had died. It was an election year and President Johnson might not like it well known that ground troops were being used extensively in more than an advisory role in South Vietnam. Evidently, he was hoping a popular mandate at the polls would allow him free rein. Too bad most of us are too young to vote.

Lieutenant Baxter would lead this patrol. A twelve man infantry squad which included Sergeant Perkins, Willlows the radioman, Pete as communications technician and Hospital Corpsman Third Class Davis at the head of the squad. Corporal Sparemont, the demolitions expert and an automatic weapons team, Private Smith and Lance Corporal Harmon were in the middle. Lance Corporal Decker, Private Palmer and Private Havers who were sharpshooters would be the scouts for the squad. An ARVN officer, Colonel Tsin accompanied the squad as interpreter. The squad boarded a Bell 205/UH-1, a new helicopter delivered to the Marine Corps the year before.

The plan for the mission was simple. The patrol, with an interpreter, would land at a certain point in the interior of the country. Their objective was to take out a bicycle bridge on the Ho Chi Minh trail.

The bridge was over a deep ravine filled with thick cover and a flowing stream. Its destruction would temporarily halt the flow of weapons on the trail.

The squad would be picked up at a designated pickup point on the second day of the mission. The squad had to be able to arrive before the pickup chopper. They were warned if they did not show up by the pickup time at point B, they would be declared missing in action. No effort would be made to search for them.

"There should be no resistance - a piece of cake. Have a nice ride in-country," the commander said. He smiled as he dismissed the squad.

Pete was uneasy. The last time he had been on a mission that was a "piece of cake," 103 Marines ended up in body bags. Pete was not going to be caught with just a .45 pistol and a bayonet on this mission. Sgt. Perkins issued him an M-14.

Pete looked out of the chopper window at the beautiful jungle below. It was so peaceful and quiet. There were no signs of hostile movement.

After an hour of flying, the crew chief consulted with the pilot, came back and put his head down and spoke to Lt. Baxter. The chopper began to descend. It was different from what Pete had experienced before. The pilot put the chopper on the ground to let them disembark, not hovering 6 feet off the ground as in the last landing.

The squad moved quickly, passing peasants working in rice paddies. The peasants looked up momentarily and just as quickly, turned back to their work. Either they were used to the constant fighting or it was not healthy to pay attention to troop movements, no matter the color of the uniform.

The squad found the four foot wide trail easily, as indicated on the map. The black dirt was packed hard, marked by bicycle tracks, prints of bare feet, tennis shoes and thong sandals. The trail was bordered on each side with thick jungle. Hundred foot trees towered overhead, making it shaded and dim. Pete felt like he was walking in a tunnel. Birds and monkeys called to each other in the canopy above. The thick foliage absorbed much of the sound. Pete worried if using the trail was a wise idea, even if there was supposedly no resistance in the area.

Lieutenant Baxter put Private Palmer out thirty yards ahead of the squad as a scout, equipped with a whistle that made a sound like the chirping of a jungle bird. He would blow it, warning the squad of approaching danger. The column fell in behind, with the drag man twenty yards in the rear. They did not expect to meet anyone, and being confident of the briefing's "piece of cake" tone, they walked along at a leisurely pace.

Two hours into their walk, they were startled by the shrill double chirps of the scout's whistle. Sergeant Perkins signaled, an open hand above his head, closed as a fist, which was jerked down quickly. The squad slipped into the thick underbrush along either side of the trail.

The jungle became deathly quiet. The calm feelings of a moment before were now replaced with bunching, tightened muscles as perspiration popped from every pore as Pete slid down under the foliage at the edge of the trail. The screaming memories of 'Death-row Hill' raced through his mind like wild horses.

This is bullshit, he thought. *I've got to get a hold of myself. Got to focus on something else.* Pete decided his mom would really love the large "potted plant" he was crouching under. *Yep, Marie Peterson always fell in love with the biggest, greenest plant in the store. No room in our tiny trailer house.* He could hear his mother's voice. *We could put this in your room, honey...*

As Pete watched, three men came into view, moving down the trail. Two of the men carried a third man on a stretcher. Their clothing was identical: brown pants, white shirts, brown tie belts in the traditional baggy pajamas style, no weapons visible.

The Sergeant blew his whistle and the entire squad jumped out onto the trail, half in back and half in front of the men.

The marines were facing each other with weapons at the ready. The two men on the trail froze in their tracks. The squad's Vietnamese officer, Colonel Tsin approached and spoke to the stretcher bearers. The men said they were with a Cambodian businessman on vacation, hunting tigers. A cornered tiger had attacked and killed one of their party. The injured man on the stretcher was being taken to a nearby village for medical treatment.

Before letting the men pass, the officers and Doc Davis inspected the man's wounds. Doc Davis applied some sulfa powder to the wounds.

When they had left, Lt. Baxter called the squad together. "Guys, we'd better get our plans straight. It was real stupid to jump out on the trail facing off against each other. If those people had been the enemy, all they would've had to do was duck and watch us kill ourselves in a crossfire. Henceforth, you'll all take cover on the same side of the trail according to Sergeant Perkins' signal."

"Sergeant," Lt. Baxter said. "Have the men take ten." The squad knocked off for a can of C-rations and a rest.

When they continued, they were confident they were still alone. After another three hours of steady walking, they found their objective.

The Bridge over the River Kwia, it wasn't! The bridge Pete had been led to believe was so important to the enemy, allowing men and materiel to flow into the area, looked to Pete to be just four strands of hemp woven with 5-foot strips of bamboo. The bottom was supported by two thick hemp ropes and two more heavy ropes made handrails going up the ravine sides. Pete knew a heavily-laden bicycle could cross it with ease.

The rope bridge was over a chasm, 30 feet deep and 70 feet wide, with a stream running in the bottom. Pete had expected the bridge over the Colorado River and all he saw was a little creek in the bottom of a deep ravine. Apparently the bridge worked for the purpose of getting supplies across.

The squad crossed and set up sentry posts while their explosives expert, Lance Corporal Sparemont from New Haven, Connecticut, went to work. He planted multiple C-2 plastic explosive charges. He even placed charges in some trees near the vertical edges. He hooked everything up to a battery-operated electrical detonator to make a "simultaneous implosion."

"That way," he said, "all the debris will go into the ravine and not make a mess in this beautiful jungle. OK, guys! Duck!" The charges blew up with an overwhelming roar, turning the demolition into a bridge launching. The sound echoed down the trail like a bullet report down a tunnel. The men standing too close were blown over. Those lying down had their helmets knocked off.

"Hey, that's bad stuff," Willows muttered as he picked himself up. Pete thought of a few other words as he crawled over to his helmet and emptied the dirt out of it before placing it back on his head.

Sgt. Perkins grabbed the Lance Corporal by the shirt. "Sparebrains!"

"How come you used so much explosive?" he demanded.

"Well, I looked in my handbook under suspension bridges for the correct amount. See?" The entire squad looked over his shoulder and saw the picture of a steel suspension bridge resembling a span of the Golden Gate.

Pete realized Sparemont was really under-trained. "A hand grenade probably would have done the job," he said.

With the objective completed, the company started up the trail with Havers on scout. Havers was a stubby kid, only 1/2 inch over the minimum height requirement to get into the corps. Decker, only an inch or two taller, was on the drag.

"It's so dark in this jungle at night, you can't see your hand in front of your face," said Sergeant Perkins. "When the sun goes down, to prevent becoming separated or lost, we have to stop."

"It'll be nice to rest after travelling all day with these packs and weapons," said Pete.

The mellow conversation of the squad was broken by the scout's signal from around a sharp bend in the trail ahead. Sergeant

Perkins pointed to the left side of the trail and the squad dropped out of sight.

As a boy punching cows in Utah, Pete could tell when horses or cows were moving along a trail by putting his ear to the ground. He decided to try it.

Pete's ear told him there were "many" men moving down the path at a quick pace. The rattle and clatter of guns and slings was soon heard, along with the padding of sandals and bare feet. Pete laid on the ground watching and listening until the space in front of him was filled with about forty fast moving bodies stretching along the trail.

The Viet Cong came down the trail, straight into Decker's position. His weapon fired just as the Sergeant gave the squad the order to fire. "Click-click" went the M-14's.

"Get 'em, boys!" Baxter shouted.

"Damn safety," growled one of the riflemen.

The Viet Cong in front of the squad were more heavily armed than the average infantryman, all carrying double weapons, extra strings of ammo and grenades. The Viet Cong began to fall in a jumble of bodies and flying equipment. Cries and shouts came from their mouths as the M-14s continued their merciless fire. The firing ceased in seconds.

One VC managed to throw a hand grenade, and Decker instinctively jumped from his cover to get away from it. Pete saw bullets tear into Decker's shirt as he fell over onto his back in the brush. The unfortunate VC that hit Decker was chewed to pieces by bullets from four marines before he hit the ground. The rest of the enemy fire had gone harmlessly into the jungle.

Perkins jumped onto the trail and ordered, "Check all the bodies and finish them off if they're not dead!"

The squad quickly dragged the bodies into the brush. The group they had just fought was probably the lead group of a convoy. The rest would be along shortly.

Willows found a kid about 15 who was still alive and moaned when he moved him. Sgt. Perkins looked at the youngster's wounds.

"Just put him in the brush. He'll be dead in a few minutes."

Sparemont and Harmon scooped intestines off the trail to remove all traces of the ambush. The blood already had started to dry and turn black. The smell nauseated Pete. Luckily, even this odor would dissipate momentarily in the brush.

Pete noticed Doc Davis was tending Decker, dressing his wounds. An IV was running in his arm and a shot of pain killer, morphine, had been inserted into his thigh. The pain killer looked like a green tube of travel-size toothpaste with a needle on it. Everyone carried three vials of the valuable medicine.

Decker was shot up pretty bad, and the light was fading fast. Doc Davis opened an aluminum framed folding stretcher, so Decker could be carried in some comfort. Decker was stripped of his equipment. The corpsman applied a battle compress to his chest and back. Pete gently took off his friend's helmet. Decker drifted in and out of consciousness, arousing occasionally to jabber incoherently. He was losing a lot of blood, even with the pressure dressings. Decker was just a slight kid - 18 years old, 130 pounds - Willows and Harrison carried him between them. The corpsman slung the IV over Harrison's shoulder.

Sergeant Perkins and Lt. Baxter held a powwow with the interpreter. "There's no way the squad can use this trail now. We must cut through the jungle. These guys were probably the escort for a convoy. We can expect to meet double this number from the main body if we stick around," Perkins explained.

Luckily, the jungle could be traversed with machetes. The soft plants could be brushed through quietly. The squad paralleled the Ho Chi Mihn trail following compass headings. They walked and hacked their way along.

"Once the sun goes down, the day is over, completely dark, no twilight. The scout found us a nice little clearing about 35 feet across," Sergeant Perkins said.

In their packs, the men had small flashlights: small, one C-cell lights, with a round dome shaped lens. The small lamps were quite bright. Sparemont put one in the center of the circle and one by Decker whom Doc Davis and Willows had propped up against a large tree. The tree was backed by the jungle.

"How's Decker, Doc?" Pete asked as HM3 Davis sat down next to him.

"I don't know," said Davis. "I'm afraid we're going to lose him."

The squad gathered on the opposite side of the clearing from Decker. Being near a comrade so close to death was hard on the entire squad. The men opened C-rations and began to discuss their situation with the sergeant and the lieutenant.

Lieutenant Baxter thought well-informed troops who knew where they were and what was going on worked best.

"I estimate we're about 3 kilometers west of the Ho Chi Minh trail. By going directly north in the morning, we'll come out near noon about five klicks from our pickup point."

"If we're 3 klicks from the trail, how about a smoke, Lieutenant?" Havers asked.

"Oh, yeah. Go ahead and give Decker one too," he answered.

Doc Davis lit a cigarette and took it across to Decker, placing it in his lips. Pete watched as Decker took a drag, coughed and sputtered. Smoke began to drift out the top of Decker's shirt pocket. *He must be hurt pretty bad,* thought Pete. The corpsman rejoined the group around the map.

The conversation slowed and the camp became quiet. Pete looked over at Decker, remembering he was the first person in L company to befriend him. Pete's heart was breaking.

Decker's head suddenly jerked back. His jaw went slack, and the cigarette hung limp, stuck to his lip by saliva. The fingers on his right hand twitched and lay motionless. He was dead.

Pete did not hear the soft voices of the other men anymore. He stared at Decker's face. Pete felt the look on his own face mirrored the look on Decker's, total shock and surprise!

As Pete sat thinking about Decker, a large shadowy apparition silently appeared, half hidden by the tree next to Decker. In the glow from the flashlight lying by Decker, it appeared to be a 30 gallon trash can lid with ears. At first, there was no discernible color except for two large piercing eyes, cast back to Pete by the weak light, like two burning embers in the dark. There was a low grunt and growl as the head came into full view.

It was a tiger, a big tiger! Pete froze. The great gaping mouth opened above Decker's shoulder. Two huge fangs hung down like daggers.

Pete turned and grabbed Sgt. Perkins by the arm. "Tiger!" he whispered. Everyone turned and looked. As if in slow motion, the tiger grabbed Decker's body by the upper torso, shoulder first. Decker's head canted sideways as he was lifted like a doll in the mouth of a puppy. Pete grabbed his piece. He pulled the bolt of his M-14 and let it slide forward, but his weapon would not move.

Pete realized a strong hand was gripping his wrist. The Lieutenant's voice came to him in a commanding but soft tone. "I can't let you fire that weapon, Pete. If you want that tiger, you'll have to go after him with your knife."

Decker's body disappeared behind the brush. A wave of nausea washed over Pete. He wanted to puke.

Sergeant Perkins pulled Pete by the arm into the center of the group. "Something like this must've happened to the tiger hunters we let by us," he explained.

The men spent the rest of the night in a circle, back to back, their weapons tucked between their knees. No one was sleeping. The men shivered, and silently wept for the loss of their friend. Pete tried to assure them that Decker was already dead when the tiger took him away. He had not flinched when the jaws descended into his shoulder.

When daylight broke, the men looked for signs of the tiger or Decker. All they found were a few tracks, no drag marks on the ground from the body. Decker's body had been carried away.

How will it be explained to Decker's parents? Pete wondered. *Missing in action? Killed in action, body not recovered.* Perhaps it would be best if they didn't hear the whole story.

Chapter 7

A ROK (Rock) Encounter

The squad had only a few hours to make it to the rendezvous point - the 'LZ' or landing zone as it was called.

They started out through the jungle paralleling the Ho Chi Mihn trail and soon broke from the jungle into a great savannah covered with elephant grass. The ten foot tall green stuff was appropriately named because the area included villages of peasants who raised and trained Indian elephants.

The squad threaded its way through the tall thick grass. Breaking into the open, they came upon some locals bathing their elephants in a big pond which was fed by a little stream from the western slopes. The grass gave way to a low plain of pastures and rice paddies. A road at the edge led to a village. The squad followed the road toward the village.

Suddenly, the scout's whistle chirped. Coming towards them, from the jungle on the other side of the village, was a long column of uniformed troops, perhaps a full company. The squad dove into a nearby ditch. Lieutenant Baxter observed the troops closely with his binoculars.

"All right!" he shouted. "Republic of Korea troops."

Pete had heard there were other countries in the Southeast Asia Treaty Organization (SEATO) who sent troops to help in the war-torn southern part of Vietnam. This was one such group – a detachment of a hundred and twenty marines from the Republic of Korea.

Lieutenant Baxter sent out Harmon ahead of the squad with an American flag tied on his piece, held high above his head. Although the entire squad wore an American flag on the shoulder of their greens, the squad made this obvious gesture to ensure recognition.

Seeing Harmon, a South Korean soldier was sent out to meet him. They exchanged greetings and Harmon returned to the squad. "They're on a search and destroy mission," Harmon reported to Lieutenant Baxter. "They were about to inspect this village when they saw us."

The squad eagerly approached the open area about a hundred yards from the village where the ROK marines were taking "5." Lieutenant Baxter and the ROK Colonel conversed while the squad exchanged personal items such as candy, cigarettes, pocket knives and cigarette lighters.

An old man, an elder from the village, came out where the two units were gathered and talked to the squad's Vietnamese interpreter.

"This village is an open town," said Colonel Tsin. "All troops, VC and South Vietnamese are welcome as long as they leave their weapons outside. We can go in and have a beer at their town bar if we wish."

Lieutenant Baxter talked it over with the ROK commander. The ROK Colonel agreed to watch the American weapons while the squad took the first turn in town. Anticipating a beer to wash down some of the dust and grime, the squad stacked their weapons. Absentmindedly, all the marines forgot to take off their grenade belts. The lieutenant, the sergeant, and Pete kept their sidearm .45s. The squad was just interested in getting to the beer.

The bar reminded Pete of something out of a western movie, an old wooden frame building with a wood floor. It was apparent the building was leftover from the days of French occupation. Pete counted three frame buildings and about twenty thatch huts, or hooches, in the village as the squad entered. Perhaps the village had been a regional farming center at one time.

Entering the bar first, Lieutenant Baxter held the door for the others. "Just one beer, guys!" He held up the index finger of his left hand. "We've only got two hours to get to the LZ."

Leaving the bar, they headed toward the edge of the village. Everything appeared normal. People were going about their daily tasks, tending animals and their cooking fires. Children were running about shouting, or staring at the very tall strangers.

As they turned a corner, Willows grabbed Lieutenant Baxter by the arm. "Sir, I just saw people dressed like those two 'tiger hunters' on a corner a few buildings down from the bar."

"Stay alert and act as if you don't suspect anything," Baxter cautioned the squad. "We'll have to warn the ROK troops to keep a sharp eye." The squad nervously walked back to the outskirts where the ROK troops were waiting.

"Say, we saw a couple of men in town dressed similar to the VC we had a fire fight with yesterday," Lieutenant Baxter warned the ROK commander. "I wouldn't go in there without weapons if I were you."

Pete was relieved to hear the ROK Colonel being warned. Some of the villagers came out to greet the strangers. The American troops passed out candy to the children.

From behind the village elder, Pete noticed a woman approaching. It was hard to tell her age, because she was obviously worn out from hard toil and well past the age of fruition. Pete thought she looked rather peculiar because she had a strange leather thong around her neck, like a dog collar.

Pete's mind rambled as he watched the woman approach. *I've got to calm down. Yesterday had some weird events and this village could make anybody nervous. This woman has a dead stare in her eyes with no facial expression at all. C'mon boy, it's just your imagination.*

The woman approached a group of GI's talking with ROK soldiers. Pete eyed her strange neckwear. She said something and did a little bow. She put her right hand up under her blouse toward her neck.

Unexpectedly, Pete was knocked reeling by a football clip from Sergeant Perkins. His violent shove caused Pete to tumble sideways into the dirt.

"Grenade!"

Pete's ears were assaulted by three shots from Sergeant Perkins' .45.

The woman with the leather neck thong tumbled backwards and hit the ground; red stains appeared on the front of her blouse.

Pete popped up next to the sergeant's arm. "What's going on?" he hollered.

Sergeant Perkins tore the woman's blouse down. Pete was aghast to see the leather thong inserted through the pin of an American shrapnel grenade. The entire squad was dumbfounded to think this woman would so readily expend her life to kill a few marines.

On hearing the shots and seeing the woman fall, the other villagers scurried back to the safety of their town.

The squad picked up their weapons, thanked the ROK troops for their hospitality and started around the village.

Their pickup point was 5 klicks, a little over three miles away, on a hilltop on the other side of the village. The squad passed rapidly around the outskirts of the village with the scout ahead and the drag behind.

Suddenly, there was automatic weapons fire! The squad turned to find the drag man pinned down by fire coming from the bar and a hooch next to the bar. The squad ran back to cover him so he could get out of the hole. Harmon got close enough to lob a grenade into the hooch. The top blew off with a fierce bang, and the firing from the thatch building ceased. The rest of the squad opened up on the back of the bar and the firing from the bar quickly stopped.

An unarmed ROK Marine came running around the side of the bar. Stumbling, the ROK trooper was trying to escape pursuers.

He had already been hit. The squad watched from cover with weapons ready as he crawled to them and fell. Doc Davis got out his kit to tend him, but he was already dead from multiple bullet wounds in the head and back.

The squad heard more firing and grenades. They dug in and waited. The people doing most of the firing were the ROK Marines who emerged in the opening next to the bar. The ROK weapons went reflexively to the ready as they recognized the crumpled form at the feet of the Americans.

The Colonel approached and looked at his man lying in the deep grass. "Two of my men went ahead of the rest of the company without permission and without arms. They were unaware of possible enemy presence. While in the bar, VC came in and shot them down."

"We'll be glad to stay for a while if you need help cleaning up here," Lieutenant Baxter said.

"No, we'll take care of everything," the ROK Colonel said, smiling grimly, his eyes narrowing as he offered a handshake to Baxter.

The squad resumed their trek. No one said a word as they walked for about an hour into the hills. They had cleared the jungles and were nearly to the top of a plateau. The LZ lay just ahead.

The drag man's whistle cut into the quiet morning air. As Pete turned back, he saw the entire village burning.

The ROK Marines are cleaning it up all right! Pete thought.

The squad was too far away to hear anything but muffled sounds, but they could see the flames consuming everything. The squad could do nothing to intervene. They were too far away and it was getting near their extraction time.

Tired and weary from the two day adventure, the squad was glad to get to their pickup point. They rested and anxiously waited until half an hour before their pickup time and then transmitted their signal for pickup.

"Mother Hen, Mother Hen! This is chick one, come and get us. We're at point Bravo," called Willows over the radio. A single transmission was used with no reply necessary to confirm the message. The squad could not afford to transmit but the briefest signal.

The men spread out a yellow plastic 6 foot by 6 foot square for the pickup chopper to spot. The pickup chopper from an in-country base, along with a gunship, would arrive soon.

When the squad heard them approaching they stayed under cover while the gunship circled the area. The extraction chopper came in to land.

Panic hit Pete again as the gunship fired rounds into the trees above his head.

"What's he doing?" screeched Pete.

"Willows, tell that idiot to knock it off! We're down here getting hit with splinters and falling branches," Lieutenant Baxter commanded angrily.

"Oh, sorry, sir!" came a humble voice in the radio. "We were just checking out the area and the gunner got a little excited. This is his first extraction."

With the welcome smell of kerosene in their nostrils and the clatter of rotor blades in their ears, the squad clamored aboard, and the ship started to rise. Everyone hung on for dear life until it stabilized straight in cruise.

"Hey! You got a smoke?" Doc Davis asked Pete. Pete relaxed and handed Davis a cigarette.

Upon arrival at the base, the squad went immediately to debriefing. Everyone recounted the same story about the loss of Decker and the same description of the village burning.

"Well, this is still an undeclared war, and it's touchy for us to tell our allies how to fight it. They might take their troops and go home," shrugged the major in charge of intelligence.

A week later, Harmon came into the barracks with news. "Hey, you guys," he said, gesturing for everyone to come close. "There's a rumor at the EM Club. A village was burned by ROK Marines after two of their men were killed. They found five hooches full of weapons. All the inhabitants in the village were stood against a wall and shot."

What a rotten, mixed-up war this is, thought Pete.

Chapter 8

Revenge

Lieutenant Baxter poked his head into Pete's barracks and said, "Hey, you guys, we have a little Search and Destroy mission."

A few minutes later Sergeant Perkins opened the screen and stood in the doorway. "First Squad to Briefing!"

Eleven men from K company, First Squad, fell out with their gear. Pete, the Hospital Corpsman Davis, and the rest of the men from the tiger patrol were called out. In addition, Second Squad would be joining them.

Second Squad was twelve men strong and included a mortar team and a heavy weapons team. All together there would be twenty-three men in three choppers. The unit would be platoon strength when all hands were present.

At the briefing, Lieutenant Baxter explained, "The U.S. Navy is trying to reach the people in need with a project called 'Operation Handclasp.' All projects by the military have to be signified by some catchy phrase making it sound good."

Pete eyed his leader closely as he spoke. He could not decide if Baxter was a military school hard ball or a Princeton egghead. This officer was always kind, considerate and thoughtful of his men, but at the same time knowledgeable and tough as a Drill Sergeant.

"The ships off-loaded clothing, medical supplies, food and tons and tons of books. What these peasants will do with tons of English textbooks, I don't know, so don't ask. They surely can't eat 'em or trade 'em for sustenance.

"Our Navy medical teams have gone into villages distributing supplies and giving medical treatment the villagers desperately need but can't afford even if they can get to the proper facilities in a larger town. The children were given inoculations against various communicable diseases. Operation Handclasp was designed to be a public relations activity to help win the hearts and minds of the people. The Navy's good intentions, unfortunately, led to the death of some innocent children."

Lieutenant Baxter stopped momentarily and stared at the faces of the men before him.

"There's a rumor coming through refugees from this province that there's a village that's starving. The Viet Cong have recently visited them, stealing their food and harassing the people for allowing Operation Handclasp teams to come in. One child was brutally killed with a machete. They cut off his arm because he had an inoculation mark."

He put his finger on the wall map and continued. "Our job is to investigate, search out the VC, and destroy them before they can do any more harm to this village. Dismissed."

As the platoon filed out to the flight line, Doc Davis turned to Pete, "You know, they'll probably use those books for cooking."

"Okay, I give," said Pete, turning his head to see the expression on the corpsman's face. "I thought they were text books, not cook books."

Doc slapped Pete on the shoulder. "They're going to burn them in their cooking fires. Those pages will make great fire starter."

As the choppers sat down in a clearing in front of a village, the platoon heard the clatter of weapons fire, and radio chatter indicating a unit of the US Army 1st Cavalry was engaged and being pushed by a body of North Vietnamese Regular Army in a heavy engagement in the area.

"What's the NVR doing this far south and since when has the Army gotten into the act in this province?" asked Pete. "We sure are getting a lot of surprises."

As the troops hopped off the choppers, Willows turned to Sergeant Perkins. "Sarge, what's the possibility we could go help the army?"

"N.O.! That's a capital, no!" said Sergeant Perkins. "We're heading for the assigned village."

The flight crews dropped the unit off and the choppers, three Huey's and a gunship, departed. In the event of trouble, they would be a short radio call away.

The platoon gathered the villagers they could find for questioning. No one wanted to talk to the South Vietnamese interpreter. He kept walking among them, earnestly beseeching them to speak to him. The adults lowered their heads, and averted their eyes. The children cowered and clung to the legs of the adults.

After a few minutes, Colonel Tsin reported to Lieutenant Baxter. "They fear reprisal from the Viet Cong, but I'm not going to give up."

Finally, a woman told him there were enemy troops camped down the road, maybe 200 in number, all terrorist Viet Cong guerrillas.

Pete looked at the malnourished children and asked the interpreter. "Why are these people starving? Why hasn't the government distributed some of the food the Navy's making available through their aid program?"

"They're starving because the VC takes the food away from them. Our government doesn't give them food anymore because it will wind up in enemy hands," he explained with a shrug. "Besides, the government wants these people moved into resettlement areas and they don't wish to move."

The interpreter told Lieutenant Baxter the enemy was less than 2 klicks away. With anger in his voice, Lieutenant Baxter got on the radio and called for reinforcements before the platoon moved into position. Twenty marines, though angry and ready to take revenge for the village and for the loss of Decker, would still need reinforcements against possibly three-hundred enemy troops.

Within minutes, the platoon heard choppers, loaded with Army of the Republic of Viet Nam regulars, a full company of 120 men. The officers conferred; Lieutenant Baxter came back to where the platoon was standing.

"Wow!" Sergeant Perkins said. "That is what I call efficient support."

"OK, guys." Lieutenant Baxter said. "These troops are here to help." He gestured with his M-14 toward the column of Army of the Republic of Viet Nam. "To keep everything organized, we'll spread out among the ARVN troops, one marine for every four ARVN's, until we run out of marines. Then, the rest of the South Vietnamese troops will spread out behind us. They have twelve knee mortar teams and twelve automatic weapons teams. We have one knee mortar team and one automatic weapons team of our own. That's plenty of firepower for the size of enemy force we expect to engage."

As the platoon approached the enemy position, they walked a raised road on a dike running parallel to the VC camp, as the allied forces surrounded the camp.

Pete and Sergeant Perkins quietly peeked over the road. The VC appeared very nonchalant and extremely confident of their safety; there were no guards posted. Their weapons were stacked or lying against trees and most of them were standing in a chow line. The camp was in the bottom of a bowl-like ravine with the marines and ARVN troops on the road above them. It was a perfect ambush.

At the lieutenant's command, the entire company opened fire. A rocket propelled grenade from the heavy weapons team hit the hooch appearing to be the VC command post. The platoon concentrated their fire on the area near the stacks of weapons and on the men standing in the chow line. Anywhere the VC ran, they were caught in a crossfire. VC scattered everywhere. Grenades exploded, bullets kicked up dust, the fire was very heavy, cutting the VC down as they ran.

The platoon reloaded their weapons and heaved grenades as fast as they could get them off their clips. Pete did not have time to look around at his companions. He kept his attention riveted on the action in front of him. The combat lasted five minutes. Sporadic gun fire finally ceased.

When Pete took his eyes off the scene before him and looked to his right, he was surprised to see he was looking into the face of his radioman and on the other side of him, another marine.

"Where are the troops?" Pete asked as he stood and looked around. The ARVN troops were nowhere to be seen. As the platoon moved around the perimeter, only two dead South Vietnamese soldiers were found. Not one jarhead had been scratched.

"Evidently," said Willows. "once the dance started, they elected to bow out. For a moment there, I thought the Cong were going to rally."

The platoon walked into the compound, picked up the weapons and counted the bodies - 230 dead. The weapons would be turned over to the local militia for use in protecting their villages. Satisfied their mission was accomplished, the platoon started back up the embankment to the road.

Before the platoon could get to the top of the road, they were met by two patrols of 30 enemy troops each, coming down the road at a fast pace. A fire fight began.

The VC were on one side of the road and the platoon on the other. The VC had come looking for a fight, so the platoon threw everything they had at them. The platoon had a stand-off for 15 minutes, until they killed enough VC to force them back. The marines held the advantage. The Viet Cong had to withdraw.

In the middle of the shooting, a boy about eight years old started down the road from the village, between the platoon and the VC. He rode a water buffalo, kicking his heels into its front shoulders and hitting its sides with a bamboo stick. He was seemingly unaware of the danger. Only sporadic firing was going on now, but if the boy came between the two groups of fighters, he would be slaughtered. He either could not hear the firing or was oblivious to its danger. The platoon watched with open mouths as the boy came closer, never turning nor slowing in his efforts to get his buffalo up the road.

"Shoot that buffalo," shouted Sergeant Perkins to the automatic weapons team. Private Smith popped it in the head and as it fell over, the boy slid off and ran back toward the village.

The Viet Cong withdrew, firing ceased and the platoon went to check for dead and wounded. The platoon found no bodies. Pete knew he had shot someone because he had seen the enemy take a hit and fall behind the brush. The platoon knew they had beaten the VC, because they would not have backed off if the advantage had been theirs.

The platoon had two wounded; a marine from the mortar team had his ear clipped and Private Havers had sustained a crease wound in the fleshy part of his thigh. The corpsman had already bandaged and sedated them for pain. At least, they could walk back to the choppers.

The platoon gathered their gear and headed back up the road toward the village. Pete moved behind the sergeant who was conversing with the interpreter. "Thank you for shooting the buffalo in the head," Colonel Tsin bowed to Sergeant Perkins. "Why?" the sergeant grunted.

The interpreter pointed to a group of about fifteen people from the village already crouched over the buffalo. "That buffalo will make fine food until Handclasp personnel can get back with rations. The South Vietnamese government will now have to make the decision to offer this village protection from the Viet Cong or relocate it all together."

After their encounter with the VC patrol, the platoon prepared to board their waiting helicopters. The choppers of the South Vietnamese troops had landed and the ARVN troops were coming out of the jungle to board them. Colonel Tsin went over to speak to the ARVN Captain in charge of the troops.

Pete looked up to see a couple of Army patrols from 1st Cavalry coming out of the jungle. He was sickened to see trophies on a couple of helmets, human ears. His hand jerked to pull the bolt on his weapon, slamming it home in anger. Pete wanted to make the stupid ground pounders take the ears off their helmets. Sergeant Perkins caught his arm as Pete raised his weapon. "Don't bother, Peterson. People like that are sick."

Without speaking to the Army unit, the platoon gathered their gear and boarded their choppers. *Maybe the guy with the ear on his helmet felt justified after seeing the dead child by the road. If a man in the marine company had tried something like that, Sergeant Perkins would have...* Pete shuddered at the thought.

Colonel Tsin was the last man to get aboard. He spoke to Lieutenant Baxter as the chopper pitched and left the ground. "That company of ARVN troops did not desert us. They were not sent to help us. They were supposed to be relief for the 1st Cavalry unit that was having a hard go of it. As soon as they discovered they were in the wrong place, they left to join the 1st Cavalry."

As the helicopter gained altitude and streaked over the tree tops, Pete's thoughts rattled around. *Should the little children of this country have to pay the price for war? The VC use terror mercilessly. Wearing of enemy ears on the helmet may be the soldier's form of vengeance on this cruel enemy, the killer of his own kind.* Pete took a deep breath and closed his eyes. *Whatever the case, I have gained revenge against at least one group of Viet Cong for what they did to the innocent children of that village. Am I beginning to feel comfortable with this war? I hope not. Not ever!*

Chapter 9

MIA, Almost!

A week after their last patrol, the squad sat around their barracks playing cards, reading and writing letters. The wooden screen door to the barracks popped against its frame as the heavy spring pulled it closed. Pete looked up from the letter he was writing to see a small man in full combat gear, carrying a sea bag and an M-14. "Is this First Squad, Company K?" he asked. Everyone dropped what they were doing and approached the man.

"I'm Lance Corporal Gutierez," said the man, dropping his sea bag and weapon in a pile at his feet.

"Welcome to First Squad," said Doc Davis, extending his right hand in greeting.

"My friends call me Pancho," said Gutierez, taking Doc's hand.

"I'm Doc Davis and this is Pete, our com tech." He gestured to Pete who was now standing beside him.

Each man of the squad approached Gutierez, shaking his hand and introducing himself. After meeting the new man, the squad went back to what they had been doing.

Doc picked up Pancho's sea bag by the shoulder strap and started down the aisle between the bunks. "Let me show you to your rack and locker."

Pete returned to his bunk and picked up his letter. Pancho would be in Decker's bunk. The bunk right next to Pete.

After Pancho had stowed his gear, he laid his M14 out and began to take it apart and clean it. From his locker, he pulled a set of small aluminum rods that screwed together with a small brush on the end and began to clean the bore of his piece.

"What's with the cleaning kit?" Pete asked. "I've never seen anyone do that before."

"It's not regulation, just something I do," Pancho said. "My dad is a hunting guide in New Mexico and I've been shooting competition since I was six. I learned early on if you don't keep your firearm clean, it won't work right. I was talking to a ground pounder from 1st Cav at the EM Club the other day and he said his weapon had jammed in the field while he was under fire. Sounds pretty scary to me."

Pete looked over at his own weapon, leaning against the wall next to his bunk. He folded his letter, put it in his locker and picked up his piece, pulling the bolt back.

"I've fired over three hundred rounds through this, and it's never jammed," he said as he let the bolt slide forward. The bolt didn't slam forward as it normally did, so he looked closer at the breech. There was heavy carbon buildup and powder residue all along the slide and the breech felt gummy to the touch. "Holy cow!" Pete exclaimed. "This piece is filthy!"

Pete turned to his new acquaintance. "Pancho, how about the loan of your cleaning kit when you get done there?"

Pancho looked up as he finished pulling a small piece of cloth through the barrel of his piece. "You listen good, Pete. Where you from?"

"I'm from Utah, about a hundred miles north of the Four Corners area, a place called Moab. Ever hear of that?"

"Sure. I've heard of Moab. Uranium town, kinda hot, not much to do there."

"Wow! You hit the nail on the head," said Pete.

"Since we're neighbors, geographically speaking, you can use my kit any time you want; just be sure to put it back where you found it. The same goes for the rest of the guys in the squad. If they want to be eccentric, they can clean their pieces, too."

It wasn't long before all the men in the squad were cleaning their weapons. "One more thing the ground pounder from 1st Cav told me," said Pancho. "The spring in the clip on this rifle is weak and if you load it to full capacity, the spring wears out and the ammo won't feed. What he suggests is you keep out two or three rounds."

Pete went back to his ammo pack, pulled out four clips and pushed three cartridges out of each one. "I sure wouldn't want to run out of ammo when I still have bullets in the clip," said Pete. Pancho was a very sharp marine and he and Pete became fast friends. The fact they were neighbors, geographically speaking, didn't hurt either.

The next day, a replacement for Havers came into the squad. Private Anthony Certonio, a sharpshooter and demolitions man from New York.

A few days after the replacements reported to First Squad, Lieutenant Baxter came into the barracks. "Sergeant Perkins is busy rounding up a few maps. I want to see the entire squad at the briefing room as soon as you finish chow." He pointed a finger at Pancho. "Make sure everyone is ready. One day's rations."

Twenty minutes later the entire squad and Colonel Tsin were assembled in the briefing room.

"We're going to attack the Ho Chi Minh trail in another area," said Lieutenant Baxter as he pushed his pointer across an area on the wall map near the Mekong Delta. "The trail intersects the Mekong River right here. There are tributaries all through the Mekong Delta with a lot of good backwater in the jungle. The VC are using the waterways to move weapons down into the south off the Ho Chi Minh trail. The material is being picked up in the backwaters, taken down the tributaries and into the river. There, it is put back on land and sent 30 klicks overland, where it's put on more tributaries for distribution.

"Intelligence has good info on this distribution network. It has to be slowed. This squad has been assigned to blow up the docks where these supplies are off-loaded onto sampans and taken down river. A big shipment is expected soon. We have to get in there and blow up the sampans and docks."

The battalion commander was in on this briefing also. "Men," he said, clearing his throat for silence. "This is going to be a real ticklish mission, timing wise. Everything must go according to schedule in order for it to be a success. Your lives will depend on it. You cannot afford to be delayed or held up in getting to your pickup point when the objective is completed."

Lieutenant Baxter stepped back to the podium. "The squad will be dropped at a point some distance from the objective and slip into the area on foot. The pickup point will be right on the edge of the river on a high mound, the only place in the area the choppers can land. Once the squad loses the element of surprise, we won't have much time to get to the pickup point."

The squad always had a pickup point different from the drop zone. The enemy loved to booby trap areas troops had dropped into, so they could not go out the way they came in.

The choppers landed the combat team without incident. The squad faced three hours of moving through the brush before they reached their destination.

The going was slow, real slow. Booby traps were always a danger. Pete could feel the urgency of the squad to keep moving, but also, to watch for traps and trip wires.

As the squad was making their way down the trail through the thick jungle, the scout whistled a halt. Private Palmer pointed to a wire across the trail. He followed the wire into the brush and came up with a C-ration can with an American M70 hand grenade stuffed inside. The can would hold the fuse trip closed until the wire jerked the grenade out of the can, then - bang. "Be careful! All it takes is one careless step to set one of these babies off."

As Willows, who was behind Pete, stepped back off the trail to regain his balance after peering at the hand grenade over the shoulders of the two marines, Pete heard a strange whooshing sound from behind his head. He did not know whether to duck or stand still. A weighted punji stick, a large wooden mat with spines sticking out of it, the tips covered with water buffalo dung, came slinging into the group's midst.

The punji mat sailed past Pete's face and imbedded itself into the radio pack on Willows' back, lifting and spinning him through the air like a rag doll. Willows screamed with pain as it ripped through the flesh of his upper shoulder.

The squad had a chance to take a rest while Doc Davis tended to Willows' wounds. Though the spines of the punji sticks had penetrated the muscles of his upper shoulder, the radio pack had taken most of the blow. Doc Davis jabbed a needle of antibiotic and a needle of morphine into the wounded marine's thigh. Quickly and efficiently, he washed and wrapped the shoulder tightly.

"You'll be groggy on your feet for awhile and hurt a bit, but at least you can stay up with the unit and continue on the mission," Doc said.

Willows gritted his teeth, and grunted, "Yeah, I'm OK, Doc. Let's get going. Just a scratch!"

While Doc Davis worked on Willows, Pete worked on Willows' radio. There was no doubt his field pack and the thin-line field radio had saved his life. The punji sticks had penetrated through his field pack; they skewered a can of C-rations, hit the steel case of the radio and were deflected or broken off.

The squad was soon moving again, eyes wide open to traps. Edging along, it seemed like it took an eternity just to gain a kilometer.

The sergeant spotted the next booby trap. "Watch out," he cautioned, pointing to a soft area of dirt in the middle of the trail. It looked harmless enough, just an area covered with leaves. Perkins slowly moved the leaves aside and exposed a two foot deep hole dug in the middle of the trail. In the bottom were punji sticks, again dripping with foul-looking excrement. The unlucky person who stepped there would have sticks slashing into his foot and leg. For protection against such traps, all of the squad members wore the new neoprene rubber sole jungle boots with nylon net to the leather-covered steel toes. There were solid steel plates inserted in the bottoms to protect the foot from stabbing sticks.

The whole trail the squad was moving on was well-covered with more evil devices. Pete glanced up the trail, watching the squad leader move cautiously to the edge of the trail as he gave a hand signal, a closed fist followed by two extended fingers. He had found two "Bouncing Betty" mines. The trip mechanism on these looked like little pieces of bent metal sticking out of the ground and could easily be mistaken for a sprouting plant, like the fresh sprout of a bean with dirt mounded up toward it.

Stepping on the release or catching something on it would eject the bomb into the air 18-20 inches. It would explode, throwing whatever it contained, nails, rocks, pieces of metal or glass. These vile little devices would maim and disable the lower half of the body.

The squad stepped carefully and did not disturb them. All the men were tired. They could have been buffaloed by pieces of bent metal stuck in the ground with no bomb attached; however, they did not want to stop and investigate each detected booby trap, real threat or not.

After three hours of slithering through the jungle and circumventing more booby traps, Pete could see the water. It was a slow-moving, greenish, dirty tributary. He wondered how many snakes were in it. Ugh!

It was definitely their objective. Nestled down in the brush with the rest of the squad, Pete could see a dozen or more sampans tied up to the wooden dock extending out into the river from the front of several medium-sized wooden frame buildings used as warehouses. Men in loose black pajamas and large woven straw hats were unloading the supplies into the warehouses. There were no guards nor sentries posted.

Observing while Sparemont and Certonio sneaked up and disappeared underneath the warehouses, Pete hoped this time Sparebrains would use the right amount of explosives and not blow the marines up with the buildings. Maybe Certonio was a little more discerning in these matters. In a few minutes, their faces reappeared from underneath the buildings and they cautiously moved back to join the company.

As the squad waited for the attack to commence, Sergeant Perkins whispered, "Concentrate all your fire on the sampans and sink 'em."

Lance Corporal Sparemont triggered the explosives. Fire, smoke and debris shot into the air in all directions. Pete aimed his weapon at the sampans and raked the sides as fast as he could. The squad poured round, upon round into the sampans. Those still loaded with ammunition blew up, rolled over and sank, or caught fire. The smoke cast a dark blue haze over the water and the air smelled like sulphur and burning charcoal.

Figures were falling and being blown into the water or disintegrating in the explosions from the warehouses. The squad had completely surprised them, and there was no return fire. When there was no more movement around the sampans or the burning warehouses, Pete sighed in relief. The squad lowered their weapons and looked around for enemy troops.

"OK, men, let's move out as quickly as possible to the rendezvous point," Sergeant Perkins commanded. "We have just minutes to get there."

The squad had four hundred yards to move up the river to the pickup point. They were making good progress, and Pete could see the knoll where the chopper would land to get them out of this death trap. Pete knew the squad would make it if they could just keep moving.

Suddenly, small arms fire poured down on them from their front, commencing an intense fire fight. An enemy patrol had slipped up to cut off the marines from their rescue.

It took only a few minutes to clear out the dozen or so enemy troops blocking the way. The squad began moving toward their pickup point.

Again there was small-arms fire on the squad's position. An enemy patrol came from behind, and the squad took heavy fire. This larger group of well-armed VC pinned the squad down. They returned fire as hard and fast as they could, but the VC would not withdraw enough to permit the squad to move on.

Here we are, thought Pete, *within rock throwing distance of our pickup point, but it might as well be 10 klicks. The choppers will be coming in soon. This pickup has an assigned time. If the squad is not there, we will not get out. If the squad is not there in ten more minutes, we are out of luck. Maybe at the assigned time in twenty-four hours, they will come back to the pickup point just in case the squad is still around. Twenty-four hours to fight and hide in the jungle from VC patrols in the area.*

Pete thought about his family, *How will Marie Peterson take the news of the disappearance of her little boy in this foreign jungle?*

All the while, his ears strained to detect the whomp-whomp--whomp of approaching chopper rotors. "Come on, you guys!" he said aloud. He tried to shift his gaze from firing his weapon to sweep the sky for signs of the Hueys. Out of the corner of his eye, he could see Davis bending over a wounded marine. There was an increasing number of enemy. If the squad did not get out soon, they would be overrun.

Time was as much the enemy, as the aggressive forces trying to surround and overrun their command. Their backs were to the river, and their right flank near the high mound of the pickup point. Their front and left flank were raked by heavy gunfire.

Pete knew if the choppers did not arrive soon, the squad would be buying some of the river when their ammunition ran out. The term MIA again swept Pete's mind.

If the squad has to surrender to this hornet's nest, it would be missing in action. It could even become KIA, killed in action.

A welcome sound met Pete's ears, the unforgettable sweet sound of a chopper at 1200 feet, just a speck on the far horizon towards the east. Soon, Pete could make out two ships, a gunship and a Huey. The pickup commander would be in the rear bird, the gunship. It was his decision on when and how to execute the extraction.

The closer the choppers came, the more intense the enemy's fire became. They were determined to prevent the squad's escape. The VC started concentrating some of their fire on the choppers as the first chopper started to descend, getting ready to set down.

Lt. Baxter spoke to Willows, "Tell the pickup commander we're receiving heavy fire and are so engaged we cannot move the last few yards to the pickup spot. Tell him to bring his gunship in first and sweep our position to clear the area enough for us to be able to move and be picked up."

Incredulously, Pete saw the pickup chopper back off and hover into position beside the gunship just outside of small arms range. "What's going on?" Lieutenant Baxter roared.

The marine lieutenant on the gunship, the pickup commander, spoke to Willows over the radio. "It's too hot for me to order the pickup. We're not coming in for you. We'll call the Navy for some close support. They should be here in about twenty minutes."

Lieutenant Baxter's face grew red with fury as he jerked the phone from the hand of the radioman. Pete could distinctly hear him as he growled into the phone. "Cullen? You yellow coward! You bring that chopper in here right now and pick us up. If you don't, we'll bring you down and we have the weapons to do it. Now, get down here and get us out, right now." Baxter's face grew grimmer as he heard the negative reply from Cullen. Lieutenant Cullen ordered the aircraft to pull back even further.

Pete quickly glanced at the sky to confirm the action before slamming the next clip into his weapon to fire at the enemy. The gunship began a slow circling turn, bringing it down toward the warehouse area the squad had destroyed. The two helicopters got up to maneuvering speed to climb out of the valley.

Pete saw tracers coming from that direction, something really heavy, a .50 caliber machine gun. Willows was talking to the gunship again, beseeching him to return for the unit. Lieutenant Baxter grabbed the phone again and yelled, "You better not head out that way. You'll pick up heavy enemy fire."

The voice of Lieutenant Cullen crackled back, "Oh yeah? We'll see you guys tomorrow." Before he quit transmitting, Pete could hear the distinct sound of the chopper taking hits from the machine gun at the warehouse.

Suddenly, defying Lt. Cullen's orders to hold his aircraft clear of enemy fire, the young pilot of the pickup copter came swooping in and hovered. High RPM's of the rotors blew the brush flat. The skids were about three feet off the ground.

The squad ran toward the chopper, firing as they ran, hunched over and dragging their wounded with them. Pete could hear the ching-ching-ching of bullets hitting the metal skin of the rescue craft. Pete jumped up, sitting in the open door, his feet on one of the skids; he turned around, jerking up the wounded man behind him by his shirt collar.

"Thank God for strong material in these fatigues," screeched Pete as he rolled the wounded man into the chopper next to him. It was Certonio, the new guy.

A couple of able-bodied riflemen swung themselves up and helped Pete load the second wounded man, Sparemont. The men still on the ground threw their gear aboard and joined their comrades aboard the rescue copter.

Though it seemed like an eternity, the squad had their wounded aboard. The chopper heaved over abruptly and swung around, scooting out of the heavy fire zone as fast as it could lift and turn. The young pilot had just saved the lives of the entire unit.

As the rescue chopper cleared the area, the gunship came in, sweeping the area with its door gun, wracking the VC forces on the ground. Only then, did the heavy gunfire being directed at the helicopters cease.

Pete's knees felt weak. His mouth was dry and his hands began to shake. His mind tried to make sense of what had just happened. Pancho said the words Pete was thinking. "What kind of deal is this, where a pickup commander, supposedly on our side, refuses to complete his mission? He'd leave us in the jungle to be captured or killed? What a yellow-bellied chicken shit!"

Pete felt like he could use his last clip on the pickup commander when the squad landed. Slowly, he regained control as his breathing slowed and rationale returned. Pete was still in one piece without a scratch on him, just glad to be alive. He was exhausted and looked forward to his bunk.

When the squad landed, Lt. Baxter jumped out of the Huey first, dropping his gear and piece on the ground. The gunship landed just behind the rescue chopper, and Lt. Cullen took his time getting out. Baxter ran up to him with anger and rage masking his normal pleasant features. He smashed Cullen to the ground with his fist before Cullen could even say a word of explanation or apology.

"Cullen," Lt. Baxter growled down at him. "Don't you ever refuse to come and get me and my men. If I'm listed as MIA, someone is going to shoot or frag you. This is the way MIA's happen. Men are left in the jungle, pinned down and unable to be extracted, either from lack of support or lack of courage on the pickup commander's part. The lucky ones get out. The unlucky ones run into the brush or cry for help on a radio as their ammunition runs out, and the enemy closes in."

Lieutenant Cullen pulled himself up on his right elbow and placed his left hand on his face. Blood was gushing from his nose. "You broke my nose! You're not getting away with this, mister. You're going to the brig for this!" he said as he turned and attempted to gain his feet.

"Stay down, you yellow dog," said Baxter. "Snakes belong on the ground." He turned and rejoined the squad.

Pete's stomach was cramping and churning. He needed a good sleep, but first, the debriefing.

He watched as Davis supervised the off-loading of the wounded marines onto stretchers. Private Certonio and Lance Corporal Sparemont who had been hit during the fire fight would be taken to the camp hospital. The squad dragged their gear to the debriefing room and slumped in chairs, too tired and upset to care much about anything.

The Intelligence Officer came in, and each man gave his report on the mission and its objective. The results of this debriefing indicated the mission was successful. It had been designed in the Pentagon. The goal had been to look for and destroy supplies and support of enemy troops.

After the debriefing was finished, the Company Commander, Major Hatch, came in and offered each member of the squad a smoke. He shifted his weight on his feet as he leaned back on a desk top. "You guys did an excellent thing out there today. You completed the mission and destroyed a lot of enemy supplies. You showed great courage and the fighting ability of the Marine Corps operating as a rifle squad, deep in enemy territory. I am really proud of you guys, and I want you all to know you have been put in for a Presidential Unit Citation. The pickup chopper pilot, Lt. Spencer, has been put in for the Bronze Star.

"However," he continued as his face turned to a sterner set, "I have something unpleasant to tell you, too. I've had a report from Lt. Baxter about the incident at the pickup point, and I agree he did what he had to. Lt. Cullen has filed a formal complaint against your whole squad charging you with threatening an officer with bodily harm and loss of life. There is also a charge of insubordination, for disobeying his orders as pickup commander. The write-up report goes up to the battalion commander's desk tonight. I'll let you know what comes of it. You're all restricted to your barracks until this is resolved. Dismissed!"

Pete could not believe it. One minute the squad was being lauded as heroes and an example to the Corps and the next minute, some coward was hitting the entire squad with charges to bring them all up for court-martial if the battalion commander agreed with Cullen.

"What are they going to do," asked Pete of no one in particular as he left the briefing room, "kick us out of the war?" He decided the best spot for him would be in his bunk and let God take care of whatever was going to be his lot.

He could not forget the feeling of hopelessness he felt when the squad had been pinned down. There would have been no hope of rescue if Lt. Cullen's orders had been followed. He was grateful to be alive, no matter what the outcome of the charges.

He was happy that he would not be listed -- MIA.

Chapter 10

Rotation

Pete sat on the edge of his bunk and stared down at the page of orders Sergeant Perkins handed him. The *USS Kingston* had completed its tour of duty and was sailing for Long Beach. It was Pete's rotation. He could go stateside and forget about all the confusion he had been putting up with for the past several months. He had been authorized two weeks leave to go home and then he was assigned to the Electronics Technician Class A School at Treasure Island Naval Station in San Francisco. *Hot dog, what a set of orders!*

Pete looked up at the sergeant. "What about the court-martial for our patrol? Am I going to get out of that?"

Sergeant Perkins smiled like a kid with Disneyland tickets. He tipped his head and came back with a wide grin. "You know, Pete." There was an air in his voice, a secret he wanted to keep for just another moment. "You can't present a man with a Presidential Unit Citation one day and court-martial him the next!" He broke into laughter as he sat down on the bunk across from Pete. "How about that? You're scheduled to get your medal from the Commander of Marine Forces, South East Asia, on Wednesday and your court was to be Friday. Well, Lieutenant Cullen is out of luck. The General tore up the report chit. As a matter of fact, Lieutenant Cullen has been transferred to a noncombatant staff job in Saigon."

"All right!" Pete hollered, jumping to his feet. "I hope Lieutenant Baxter will get off too. I really don't think the pickup chopper would've landed for us if he hadn't threatened to blow the command chopper out of the sky."

When Davis, Harmon and Guiterez entered the barracks, Davis slugged Pete's arm and spoke in a jovial voice. "We just came from the Major's office. Bax was called on the carpet this morning to atone for his act of insubordination."

"Oh no!" Pete said, as he came crashing down from his high. "What did he get?"

"He got restricted to the post for three days!" spouted Harmon. The tent was filled with laughter as all the men roared at the punishment dealt their company commander.

"Come on you guys," laughed Sergeant Perkins, grabbing Pete's arm as he straightened to his full height. "Let's go over to the enlisted club and have a few brews. I'm buying!"

The balance of the afternoon was spent with good friends, swapping stories and toasting their company commander who was truly an example of leadership, honor and courage. They were all proud to serve with Bax. He was the kind of man nobody minds going to war with.

After the presentation of the unit citation, Pete was rotated to the *USS Kingston* which was pulling out for the continental United States. The trip would take seventeen days. On the eighteenth day the Kingston would be tied up in her home port of Long Beach, California.

During the trip back to the states, Pete was again assigned to his old division, Operations Electronics. His third day aboard he took the test for Seaman. On the morning of the forth day, he was standing with his division at Quarters For Muster on the hangar deck. There was a long veer of the Boatswain's Pipe, "Now, Peterson, Seaman Apprentice, OE Division, lay before the mast."

Pete's eyes grew wide. He looked at Sergeant Hana for an explanation as all the men of the division stared at him. "Fall out, sailor," said Sergeant Hana. "The Captain is waiting for you. 'Lay before the mast,' means stand before the Captain."

Pete broke formation and marched to the center of the hangar deck were he made a right turn and marched to the far end of the hangar bay. The Officer's Call detachment in front of the Captain split to either side and Pete could see the Captain standing behind the ship's microphone, waiting. Pete came to a halt, rendered his best salute and reported. "Peterson, Seaman Apprentice, OE Division reporting sir."

"I know this is a little unusual," said the Captain over the PA system. "Peterson took the test for Seaman yesterday and I want to personally award him his new stripes. Sure, lots of men make Seaman, but this is the first time I've seen anyone score 100 per-cent on the test in my career."

Commander Agies from Personnel stood next to the Captain holding up Pete's test with a big red 100% marked across the front. The Captain handed Pete his new stripes and shook his hand. "With your permission, Seaman Peterson, I'd like this test to be mounted under glass outside the Personnel Office for the whole crew to see."

"Yes, Sir," Pete said, his voice straining. He rendered a salute, did an about face and marched back to his waiting division. He could not contain the 'Cheshire cat' grin that plastered itself on his face. He was now a Seaman and he was already looking forward to the day when he would be able to sew on his Third Class Petty Officer insignia.

He spent the rest of his time on board with the communications gang, working on radios, the crew's entertainment television and keeping equipment operational.

When the Kingston tied up at pier Echo, the dock was filled with families and friends of the crew. The base band played martial music and there was a great celebration.

Pete began to have an unfamiliar feeling. It was pride in himself -- as he said goodbye to all his old friends and walked down the afterbrow of the *USS Kingston* for the last time. He was on his way; two weeks leave and then ETA School at TI.

* * *

"That'll be thirty-eight fifty, Mac," said the taxi driver as he closed the trunk and dropped Pete's seabag onto the sidewalk beside him. "This is the main gate for Treasure Island."

Pete handed the driver the exact change and hoisted his seabag to his shoulder. "Thanks."

The past two weeks had gone by quickly. The hour was late, nearly twenty-three-thirty hours, as Pete approached the main gate guard shack. His orders specified he must be aboard the base by midnight.

Four sets of glaring lights illuminated the small guard shack set high on a three foot, oval-shaped slab of concrete in the middle of the double driveway, which was the main gate to the station. As Pete walked up to the guard shack, a marine came out to meet him. The young man was a Lance Corporal. He was easily over six-foot--six and as he leaned over, his name tag, Lopez, winked under the harsh light.

"Just reporting, huh?" Pete handed over his orders. "You get used to these lights after awhile," he said, observing Pete's squint. He tore the report slip off of Pete's order packet, logged him in and signed the time. He pointed across the street to a large palm tree next to a beautiful marble fountain. "A bus comes through here every twenty minutes. It'll be here in less than five. It'll take you right to the incoming X Division barracks area."

Pete looked across at the well lighted marble fountain, a beautiful configuration of a group of sea birds with water gently flowing from the top and spraying out at the edges. "This sure isn't like any Navy base I've ever seen!" Pete said, hoisting his heavy sea bag to his shoulder.

Lopez spoke as Pete crossed the pavement to the park bench situated by the fountain. "I think you'll like it here. This was the site of the 1938 World Fair and most of the art and grounds work is still intact."

Within moments, the stubby Navy-gray bus arrived and carried Pete to "X Division" barracks where he would be assigned until his ET School class was formed. The Master-At-Arms personnel of the barracks were polite and very accommodating. Within half an hour, Pete was in his bunk fast asleep.

Reveille the next morning came at 0600, an hour Pete was not used to. As he turned over and sat up in his bunk, he found himself looking square across the aisle at a young fellow about his own age, but half-again as big, with dark hair. The young man's face was covered with a wide grin, and his huge right hand was already extended to Pete.

"Hi! My name's Michael Francis Duffy. I'm from Akron, Ohio. I've been here for two days. I don't have any duty assignments, so if you'd like, I'll be your guide for the day. It'll take you most of the day to get your records out to where they have to go if you don't have a guide."

Duffy took off his white hat and rolled the edges down. "As soon as you get dressed, I'll be back to pick you up, and we'll head out for some breakfast."

Pete shook the young man's hand, noticing the firm grip. "I'm Beuford Peterson. My friends call me Pete."

The sailor turned on his heel and left the berthing space.

Pete was amazed anyone could be so cheerful, and even more amazed anyone could be up and dressed so early in the morning. Pete tossed his sea bag on his bunk and took out his shaving kit, a towel and his shower shoes. The wearing of flip-flop thongs in the shower was a normal practice to ensure against disease in the shower, not to mention it gave better traction on tile or painted floors.

Pete had finished his shower and shave and was stowing the last of his gear in his locker when Duffy showed up again.

"Say, I didn't know you fleet sailors could shower that fast," he joked. "Grab your packet and let's head over to the administration building."

"How about the breakfast you mentioned?" Pete asked as they left the berthing compartment and started down the stairs to the street.

"That's the last thing you want to do just now, Pete. If we were to go over to the chow hall, the first thing they'd do is make you pay for your meal because you don't have your meal pass yet, and around here, your meal pass is as important as your ID or liberty card. On top of all that, the food around here is certainly not worth paying for. We can go to late breakfast at the visitor's section of the chow hall as soon as you pick up your meal pass at the administration office. We also won't have to put up with as many people over at administration, because the normal thing to do in the morning is go to breakfast and that's where the crowds will be. We'll be first in line to get all your paperwork done at admin."

Spending the day with this self-assured young man was quite an experience. He had been on the base for only two days, yet he knew where everything was and what was going on in each office. They went from administration to breakfast, to personnel, then medical, dental and finally, Pete's favorite, payroll.

Under normal conditions, it would have taken all day, but with Duffy's help it took only until noon.

At noon, they walked to the mess hall and enjoyed a delicious lunch. The pork chops were just a little tough, but other than that, it was great.

"I thought you said the food around here wasn't very good," Pete chided Duffy.

"Okay!" Duffy pushed his empty tray away and let his eyes wander across the clean white walls and spacious skylight covered ceiling. "You must admit, Navy cooks are the only people you know who can take triple grade A food and reduce the quality to A by the time it crosses the serving line onto the crew member's tray. Yes, I will admit someone in the kitchen probably screwed up today, because this was a good meal."

Pete broke out laughing. He had never thought of it before, but it really was the perfect analogy of Navy cooking. Duffy was pleasant and easy to be with, a good friend already. Pete knew his time here would go a lot faster and be a lot easier because of him.

Pete had met some really fantastic people in the past six months and some real turkeys too. As Pete readied for bed he realized what a true learning and maturing experience it had been for him. He remembered wondering if he would live through the combat. But, thanks to some great sergeants and courageous marines, he was on this incredible base looking forward to the next part of his Naval training. He could finally be trained for what he had enlisted to be, a nuclear power electronics technician. His rotation was complete.

Chapter 11

School Days

"Gentlemen!" Pete stood on his new billet number next to this new ET School barracks listening to the grating voice of Boatswain's Mate Third Class Stanley Benion. Benion acted like he had just received his stripes and was demanding the right to prove he was a born leader. He strutted up and down in the traditional style of a mud marine, his attitude reflecting a career of being the little guy always pushed around by the big guys. He seemed to have to prove he was in charge. He acted on people instead of interacting with them.

"I was a Marine Corporal and cross-rated to the Navy to become an ET. The pay is better here, and the chances for advancement are far better."

He had his rate crossed from Corporal, an E4 grade in the Marines, to Third Class Petty Officer, E4 in the Navy. He was a Boatswain's Mate because that was the oldest enlisted rate in the

Navy, and it was most equivalent to his infantry training as far as the Navy was concerned.

"As you all know, by my rate, I am the senior member of this newly formed class. Because of my military background, I have been selected by the Barracks Chief to be the company commander of ETA School Company 521. I will be responsible for your military bearing from 0700 when we form up here after chow until 1600 when we march back after class. If any of you want to act like girls, chit chat or be clowns, you'd better get out right now, because I won't stand for it." Benion was carrying his Basic Electronics textbook on a clipboard at his left side. He pulled it up briskly and slapped his hand down on the book to stress his point. "I won't stand for any skylarking while I'm in charge."

This cocky little rooster was about all Pete could handle. He treated the entire class like they were boots straight out of basic. As Pete looked around, he could count at least a half dozen sets of Seaman stripes, not to mention his own. Pete could feel heat boiling under his collar.

"Are there any questions?" asked the Petty Officer as he finished his spiel. He slapped his feet down in a perfect "parade rest" stance, his clipboard at his side, his right hand at waist level squarely against his spine.

He had opened the door. Pete couldn't resist just a little shot at him. Pete popped to attention. "With all due respect, Sarge," Pete could hear the sarcasm in his voice but was committed, "don't you think we could pretend we're a class of halfway intelligent people who are here to study and learn electronics together instead of a bunch of grunts you just dug out of a mud bog to assault a hill?"

The Petty Officer came to attention and spun on his heel, in a few quick steps he stood leering at Pete, just inches from his face. Pete had really jacked this boy up. He was hot!

A clamor of 'Hee Haw' came from the entire rank. There was even applause from the last row. Pete wanted to get a piece of this guy's goat, but he hadn't bargained for an entire herd.

The Petty Officer's eyes were wide, his face pale with rage. "You'd better not call me sarge again or I'll put you on report for insubordination. When you speak to me you'll say 'Sir!' Do you understand me, boot?"

This ding dong is really asking for it. Pete wasn't backing down. "Listen, Sarge." Pete felt the urge to mess up this guy's uniform in the dirt. "When you get gold bars on your collar, I'll call you sir. In the meantime you'll have to settle for the promotion to Sergeant."

The entire class roared with laughter. A few small snickers of "Sarge, Sarge," could be heard. Pete could see Benion was not only mad, he was getting frustrated.

"What's your name?" He demanded tracing his fingers up and down the class role. "What's your name?"

"My name's Peterson, I'm a Seaman, like many of these people here. We're not boots. We came here from sea duty, not from basic training. Most of us have probably got more salt in our sea bag than you've ever sailed on, so lay off the 'Saltier than thou' routine." Pete suddenly was feeling very mellow. *This guy's not too smart. A real marine would never have given me the opportunity to speak my piece without filling my mouth with a handful of knuckles.*

Benion's full attention was now on the clipboard in his hand. "Seaman, huh!" he exclaimed. "This roster shows you as being a Seaman Apprentice." He pointed to Pete's left sleeve. "You're wearing one too many stripes, Mister!"

Now Pete was taken by surprise. Pete had been awarded his seaman stripes aboard the *USS Kingston* just a week before he returned from WESTPAC.

"Wait just a minute!" Pete began feeling cornered. "Why don't you call Personnel and get this straightened out?"

Benion took the attack. "This list is from Personnel, dummy. It seems there's a mistake here. It's yours. You're wearing the insignia of a higher grade than you should be. That's a court-martial offense, Mister. You could go to the brig for this one."

"I think you'll find the proof is in the record, Sarge," Pete came back. "I don't think I'd waste my time writing up a report chit if I were you. You think payroll would give Seaman pay to a Seaman Duce?"

Benion flinched and walked away. Pete would not be a good example for him to display his leadership ability on.

The first day of class was fun and interesting, kind of a get the feet on the ground program. The school was a collection of old wooden barracks, converted to classrooms for training electronics technicians for the Navy in World War II. Not much had changed so far as the physical training facility was concerned. However, the material being taught was quite different than that taught to the first class.

Class was over at 1600 in the afternoon so there was plenty of time for doing homework, writing letters, getting the laundry done, shining shoes, or going to the Enlisted Men's Club for a coke or perhaps a small game of pool. The class was divided into three duty sections which obviously meant, on the night his section had duty, he could not leave the base.

The barracks Chief Petty Officer assigned each man to whatever military duties had to be done. Pete thought it strange to immediately draw a midwatch. *A lousy midnight to four in the morning sentry outside the barracks as a fire watch.*

The first night was not bad, but it wasn't long before he realized he was getting all of the midwatches for his duty section. The third midwatch Pete stood was very cold. The temperature was in the high thirties and the fog blowing off of San Francisco Bay was so thick he couldn't see his hand in front of his face. During this watch

Pete decided to find out how he had achieved such overwhelming popularity with the Barracks Chief.

Right after breakfast the next morning Pete went straight to the Barracks Chief's Office. He thought the root of the problem had to be some simple clerical error someone had overlooked. He sat down in a chair across the desk from a lovely young woman, a Third Class Yeoman, the Navy's rating group for sharp clerical and secretarial skills. The shining black name badge with white letters read, "Randall, YN3."

"Hey, Randy," he said, getting her attention. "I probably should come down here to talk to you instead of the Chief. You probably have the answer to my question."

A soft smile crossed the narrow mouth and the large blue eyes opened wide as she raised her eyebrows and noticed Pete for the first time. The YN3 looked hard at Pete as if trying to recognize him. "Do I know you?" Her voice was soft but demanding.

Pete tipped his head to one side dragging up his most sheepish grin. "I wish you did, Randy. If you knew me you'd probably help me get in to see the Chief so I won't be late for my next class."

"What's your question?" Her smile broadened as she turned fully toward him. "Maybe I can help you."

Randy was right, she could help him, and Pete definitely wasn't interested in seeing the Chief when she finished telling him about the line BM3 Benion had laid on the Chief. As a matter of fact, the next watch schedule was on her desk to be typed, Randy explained. "Once the schedules are hand-written by the Chief, he never sees them again. One copy is posted in the barracks, and the other goes into my file," she said.

"If the schedule gets typed wrong, Benion won't see it since he lives off the base with his wife and never stands military watches. He's just our nonresident company sergeant," Pete assured Randy.

As Pete left the office, Petty Officer Randall stood up. "Don't forget! You owe me a coke. I have every intention of collecting."

"Yes." Pete smiled back at the lovely young woman. "When next we meet, you shall be my guest."

From then on, Pete caught the midwatch on a regular rotation, after everyone else in his duty section.

* * *

Class was never easy, but the days began to pass quickly. There were new things to learn on a daily basis. There was a test every Thursday and if you did not pass, you were sent back one week on Friday. On Monday, you would retake the week with the class starting the week you failed. If you failed the test the following Thursday you were sent to 'X' Division to await assignment to sea duty.

By the fifth week, the class of thirty-eight men was down to twenty-three and some of them were set backs from other classes. One of the sweet faces missing was BM3 Benion. He had flunked and been set back during week three.

One day when Pete was on his way to return a textbook to the library, he passed the Barracks Chief's Office and glanced inside. He had planned to look in and just keep going, but what he saw brought him to a dead stop. There was a YNSN sitting where he expected to see Yeoman Third Class Randall, and the worst part was, this Yeoman Seaman was a male.

"Hey! What happened to Randy?" Pete asked from the hall not yet in the office.

The Seaman looked up with a smile. "Oh, she got promoted to Second Class. She's over cutting orders in Administration now. Why do you ask?"

Pete felt a little stupid. He had only talked to the girl once. "Why do I ask? I owe her a coke," Pete snapped off the top of his head. "Thanks." He spun around and left the office.

The same afternoon, Pete and Duffy were sitting in the EM club having a coke. They were in the billiards portion of the building because Pete had begun to fancy himself a pool player. They could get things going in the afternoon when a bunch of Petty Officers came in. They would win cokes or beer or even money once in a while, but there were often as many losses as there were wins.

They sat at their table eating hamburgers and drinking Pepsi Cola when a fight broke out two tables away. Like a shot, they were up and in the crowd to watch.

When a fight breaks out, it is good judgment to be close enough to enjoy all of the action but not so close as to be mistaken for one of the participants. Pete was standing next to his table when one of the participants came reeling back against him. The man's face was bleeding and his eyes were glazed with anger. He jerked a pool stick from a nearby observer's hand and turned back to his opponent.

"Something's a little unfair here," Pete grunted, grabbing the large end of the pool stick as the man drew it back like a baseball bat. *This could be considered aiding the man's foe*. Pete heard the hollow 'thwak' of the opponent's fist against the cheater's skull. The big sailor's body went slack, and he crumpled in front of Pete. Pete stood face-to-face with the opponent, holding the pool stick.

Large dark brown eyes peered up in recognition as a big smile flashed across the broad face before him. Pete knew this guy. It was Isidro Onisimo Gomez. At five-foot-five he was the fastest, strongest, toughest, meanest, nicest, swellest guy Pete had met at the hand-to-hand combat school. He had been there to train as a 'beach master' for a SEAL Team. A very special group of Navy ranger types.

Isidro extended his right hand and Pete could tell from the small "skull and crossed bones" patch four inches up his right sleeve, he had indeed completed his training successfully. He was one of the elite fighting men. For him, the use of a pool stick by the other sailor would not have been a disadvantage.

Pete dropped the pool cue to the table and grasped the little guy's huge hand. "Hey! It's great to see you, Isidro. What in the world are you doing here?"

A broad smile crossed Isidro's face. He spoke as they sat at Pete's table. "I'm just laying over here for a week. I've got orders for Saigon. I'm going in-country to take some names and kick some commie tails." He broke into laughter as he leaned back. "Naw! Really, I've been assigned to a Navy photography team as their escort so to speak, and at that, there are five of us."

"Say, why don't we go on the beach and have a little fun and see what San Francisco looks like at night?" said Isidro reaching his right hand out to Duffy. "My name is Gomez. If this wild man didn't tell you, he and I were tight buds down in Coronado when we were at hand to hand school. I always had to pull him out of scrapes. He seems to have a knack for attracting trouble."

Duffy laughed and leaned back in his chair. "We've all seen a little bit of that since he's been here at ETA School. He has a real bad habit of telling people what's on his mind."

"Come on, you guys," Pete said. "I'm not all that bad. To hear you tell it, I'm always trying to stir up something."

Within the hour the group had changed into their dress blue uniforms and were on the streets of San Francisco at North Beach. North Beach was the showplace of the city. The streets were lined with night clubs, theaters, bars and restaurants. There were neon signs, bright lights and strange people selling anything young military personnel might want to buy.

As the sailors walked down the street, the barkers in their tuxedo suits and ties stepped close to them as they passed each establishment.

"Come on in fellows. We've got topless and bottomless. We've got good booze at a good price. Come on in. We have a floor show about to start. We have some of the best looking girls in the city."

"Let's go in here, guys," Duffy said. "I'll buy the first round. The sailors were not twenty-one, but the establishments did not care as

long as they were wearing a uniform.

The darkness of the bar made Pete feel blind as they entered from the brightly lighted street. As his eyes began to adjust he felt very comfortable. They found a nice table under a large crystal chandelier.

A bar maid saw them sit down and was right there to take their order. She wore a deep blue satin outfit, the style made popular by the Playboy Bunnies. Looking around, the club was very nice with a small stage in the lowered center. There weren't too many people in the club, and the floor show had not yet started.

When the cocktail waitress returned with their drinks they were ready to party. This was just the right atmosphere for it. The tab for the drinks was eight dollars and Duffy had exact change. He was not a tipper so when he laid the money on the woman's tray, she just stood there looking at him. Pete was busy talking to Isidro so he wasn't watching the transaction too closely. He noticed the lady was kind of miffed.

It was almost twenty minutes before she returned to their table. When she finally returned, she stood directly across from Pete and said "Do you guys want another round?"

"Sure! It's my turn to buy," Pete said. "We'll all have the same, please."

When the waitress returned, Pete placed a twenty dollar bill on her serving tray. She set a smaller change tray down on the table containing a five dollar bill and three ones.

"Whoa," Pete said softly taking hold of the lady's wrist across the table. "I could've sworn you said the drinks were eight dollars when you delivered our last round. If that's the case, you owe me four more dollars."

"Oh, I'm sorry," she said, getting testy. "Your friend didn't give me a tip last time so I thought you wanted to cover both his tip and yours."

"You put the money on the change tray and I'll decide how much I'll give you as a tip. I've never heard of 'covering' a tip or 'paying' a tip. I was always taught it was a gift or reward for good service. It's been twenty minutes since you were here last. What kind of service is that?" Pete released her hand.

She reached into an ashtray on her service tray and withdrew four silver dollars and laid them atop the bills. She wheeled and left in a huff.

Pete quickly picked up the bills and two coins and stuffed them into his blouse pocket. As far as he was concerned, the service was far from superior.

As the conversation at their table was about to return to normal, a huge man with black hair and moustache, wearing a blue suit, appeared at their table.

"Looks like the bouncer is about to ask us to leave," Pete said.

"Why you guys want to make trouble for my girls?" asked the big man as he looked down with a sneer. "You guys expect service, you can expect to pay for it. It isn't right for you to come in here and expect to get everything for nothing. Now, why don't you be good sports and cough up the two bucks?"

Duffy, normally mild mannered, always got a little aggressive after one shot of booze, stood, towering over the man. He fingered the heavy bottomed highball glass in front of the man's face. "Listen, sea weed for brains," he began. The man backed up two feet from the harsh tone. "You have the nerve to try to jerk us around for two bucks when you have an establishment like this at stake. You're going to screw with us for two bucks and I'm going to throw this glass through your stinking chandelier. These guys here are going to throw chairs through your mirrors and bust up your glassware on the bar. For two lousy dollars this hole will be posted 'off limits' to all military personnel and all we'll get will be restriction to the base for a week. Now, if it's your intention to collect two bucks you'd better stand up and get into motion."

The man took another step back. "No. No. Fellas." His whole tone and bearing changed. "I, I'm the manager. I just didn't want a misunderstanding. Maybe I could buy you fellows a drink."

"Maybe you could learn a little respect," Isidro came to Duffy's aid, "and stop treating Naval personnel like dirt."

The man quickly faded into the background and out of sight, issuing apologies all the way. The three sailors finished their drinks and left the bar.

As the men walked down the sidewalk, Isidro pointed out a previous observation to Duffy. "I told you this wild guy has a bad habit of attracting trouble. I have to step in and bail him out."

The next day a messenger came to Pete's third period class and delivered a note to the instructor. Pete was to report to the Administration Building within the hour. He had an appointment with the base Legal Officer.

Pete double timed all the way to the Admin building. He couldn't figure why anyone in the legal department would want him. "I'm pretty sure the club manager last night didn't know my name or what command I'm from," he grumbled as he approached the Legal Office.

Entering the Legal Office, Pete found a seat with four other sailors waiting in an outer office across from a lovely Wave, a Yeoman Third Class. Pete looked at her a second time as he tucked his white hat into his waistband at the small of his back and took a chair. Yes. He knew this girl. It was Patty Lingester. Pete had met her in the Barracks Chief's office while she was visiting her friend YN2 Randall. Randy had been transferred to this building. She was down in the 'Orders' section.

"How are you Pete?" she said as he sat down. "I wasn't sure you would make it. Your appointment with Commander Hallis is next. You were just about late."

She lifted the receiver of her telephone and pressed a button. "Sir, Seaman Peterson is here for his appointment."

She smiled returning the receiver to its rest. "Go right in." She gestured to a door behind her and to her left. "It's that door."

Pete opened the green wooden door and entered the commander's office. What a difference. When the door was closed, Pete was standing in a large spacious office with a rich carpet on the floor. All of the walls were hardwood paneled and on the other side of the green door was a bright rich walnut finish. *So this is a legal office. This guy really has it made. A big desk, plush chairs and couches and to top it all off, a large window looking out on San Francisco Bay.*

"Come in, Peterson." A large man, a little on the chubby side, rose from the overstuffed chair behind the large desk and extended his right hand to Pete. "I'm Commander Hallis. I've asked you to come and see me because we have a problem we have to resolve very early on in your career." He held up a form in his right hand. "This is your last medical evaluation. You have a vision problem. I'm afraid the vision standards for nuclear power ETs is so strict, you cannot qualify. Someone should have found this and brought it to your attention long ago, but since it's here now, it's my job. The reason you've come to Legal instead of going over to Medical to get this news is because, as I said, it plays on your whole career."

Pete winced a little as he sat in the large armchair in front of the officer's desk. Commander Hallis seemed very well versed on Pete's case.

Squinting his eyes down and leaning forward, elbows on his desk as if to give out a secret, the Commander said, "I'm here to tear up your contract with the U.S. Navy and either write you a new one or let you walk out that door as a civilian. It's your option. The only option you don't get is nuclear power school because of your eyes. The Navy doesn't want anyone on a submarine, working in a life and death situation, and risk a whole crew on a guy who loses his glasses. I'm sorry you had to serve more than a year of a six year enlistment before you were told this. The rule clearly specifies, no one with less than twenty-twenty vision will be allowed into nuclear power. Sorry!"

Pete sat there, his mind reeling with questions. He had received new glasses at his last physical. He knew he didn't have perfect vision. He also didn't have all of his teeth.

The commander pressed a button on his telephone and spoke into the receiver. "Pat. Would you please bring a couple of cups of coffee? We have a guest who could use one."

He had no sooner set the phone down than the door opened. Pat walked in with two large mugs of coffee. Pete watched the lovely young woman cross the room and set the cups on the Commander's desk. He recalled a comment an ET friend had made once. 'The Army may run on its stomach but the Navy runs on coffee.' Pat turned and was gone as quickly and silently as she had appeared.

As the two men drank their coffee, Commander Hallis explained all of Pete's choices. "It says here in your record, you're a decorated Field Electronics Technician. A Presidential Unit Citation, that's hot stuff.

"You have several options to choose from: You can go on and finish Electronics Technician 'A' School here at TI and be assigned back to the fleet. You can select any other class 'A' school in the Navy. You can just go back to sea duty, or you can sign your DD 214 and walk out the door as an honorably discharged veteran of the armed forces of the United States."

Pete set his empty cup on Commander Hallis' desk. His decision had come to him. *I have a goal to be a Second Class Petty Officer at the end of my tour and I'm still a Seaman.* "Commander," Pete said, feeling good about his decision already. "I'd like to convert to a standard four-year contract and go back to sea duty."

"Which A School would you like?" Commander Hallis asked.

"None, thank you, I'll just return to sea duty."

"I think you're doing an awful foolish thing," said the officer leaning forward on his desk again. "The Navy is offering you the brass ring here. You can go to any school you want, get a another grade of rate. You can't just turn it all down and say send me back to sea. You have to be crazy to say that. You're an undesignated Seaman. You could wind up as a Boatswain's Mate striker, chipping and painting for the rest of your tour."

Pete rose to his feet, extending his right hand, which the Commander took by reflex. Pete pointed to the form on Commander Hallis' desk with his left hand. "Put on there, I'm blind and crazy. It seems that since I came into this man's Navy, I've been prodded, pushed and directed by someone else. I'm disappointed and a little fed up. I think I'll make my own decisions for a while. Thanks for all your help. I'll pull my gear from the school barracks and report to "X" Division to await my orders." Pete turned and left the office.

On his way out, he stopped at Pat's desk, leaned down and gave her a rub on the shoulder. "Thanks. I want you to know you make the best coffee in the fleet. Tell Randy I said Hi. I'll see you around."

Pete left Admin and literally skipped the four blocks to his barracks. His mates were still at class so he left a note on Duffy's bunk, packed his seabag and headed over to "X" Division. His school days were over.

Chapter 12

An "X" Rated Division

Pete walked to the Master At Arms shack in the new Transit Division Barracks, next to the main chow hall. The office was new and well-lighted with a cheery atmosphere. Pete dropped his sea bag on the floor and leaned over the half door. A Third Class Aerographer looked up from a desk.

"I'm not the MAA," he said. "I'm in transit barracks here and I just watch the place while he's on his rounds or when he goes for coffee. He's gone for a cup of java right now. Is there anything I can do for you?"

This Navy weather man seems all right, Pete thought. "I just left the A school," Pete replied. "I'll be a guest here until I get my orders."

The AG3 came to the door and spoke in a hushed tone. "Don't let Boats find out you were kicked out of school or you'll be in hot water with him."

"I didn't get kicked out," Pete protested. "I quit, so to speak."

"Oh, man. Don't say that," The Airedale's voice softened. "Boats hates people who get kicked out but he's sudden death on quitters."

Pete placed his hand on the Petty Officer's shoulder. "I elected not to continue my education. That's all there is to it. I don't think what I do should be the concern of any 'X' Division Master At Arms."

The young Petty Officer extended his right hand with his introduction, "My name is Paul Newstead. Just don't talk about where you came from too much, okay?"

"Okay," Pete took his hand. "My name's Pete. I'm here to await orders for sea duty. Do you have your orders yet?" Pete asked the lanky young man.

"No I don't, but I hear they're picking up a few guys to send to the *USS Blue Island Sound* (AV-77), out of San Diego. I'd sure like to get that duty," Paul said. Talking about a subject the Petty Officer obviously enjoyed put him at ease. "The Blue Island Sound is a sea plane tender of the *Currituck* class, the flag ship for the Commander Patrol Forces, Pacific Fleet when it's in WESTPAC. Don't you know, flag ships always get to make more port calls than any other ship?"

The weather guesser seemed to really know his stuff. "Say," Pete chided him a little, "if you're in such a hurry to get aboard a specific ship, why don't you go over to Admin and see a Second Class Yeoman named Randall? Tell her you're a friend of mine, and she'll get you out on the next plane."

Newstead laughed as he handed Pete an issue of bedding and a pillow over the half door. "You'll be in bunk number twenty-eight, upstairs. Enjoy your stay."

The next morning at Quarters For Muster outside the X Division barracks, Pete met Boats. He was Boatswain's Mate First Class Henry Gofsmucker, better known as Boats. He was a tall heavy man with a stout body and a sharp tongue, with no patience and no respect for anyone below the rate of Third Class. But, Pete didn't mind one bit; he had seen this type in the fleet and sooner or later they always got what was coming to them. Pete had resolved to mind his own business until his orders came.

For the day's work Pete was assigned to sweep out the MAA's office and dump the trash. After this chore, he was given the rest of the day off. He went to the library to find a quiet place to write a letter or two home. He figured his mom would be upset when she got the news her little boy was no longer in school, but there were some things in life one must do for oneself and getting out of Schools Command was one of those things as far as Pete was concerned.

About seven that night Pete returned to the X Division barracks. He glanced into the MAA shack as he passed and noted it was untended. From the MAA lounge next door, he heard a commotion. Boats' voice came to Pete's ears along with some pounding. "This piece of junk! You'd think, right here among all these ETs you could have a TV that'd work. We just got this piece of junk three months ago, and it hasn't ever worked!"

Curious, Pete opened the door. The faces of five Petty Officers turned toward him. "If you wouldn't mind letting a Seaman take a look at your set, I might be able to get it working."

"Say," said Boats motioning Pete into the lounge. "You're the new guy!" He snapped the fingers of his right hand as if to make his memory work. "Newstead logged you in as being from Administration. How would you know about televisions? Is Newstead trying to hide another ET failure in our midst?"

"No!" Pete laughed quickly, since the guy seemed totally psychotic about ETs. "I used to help my dad repair appliances in his little shop back home. I don't know everything there is to know, but I'll help if I can. Have you got a screwdriver?"

One of the Petty Officers handed him a screwdriver. Pete pulled the plug from the wall and pushed the set around so he could get light into the back.

In just a few minutes Pete had checked every tube in the set by feel and found three to be loose, including the power amplifier tube, a very important part of the picture.

Thank goodness for my training with the ship's entertainment system aboard the old Kingston, thought Pete as he plugged the set back into the wall and turned it on. The picture was perfect and the sound was great.

"Hey! All right!" Boats exclaimed. "Why don't you join us for a cup of coffee and watch a movie?"

Since televisions were at a premium on the base and restricted to a select group of people, Pete was flattered. He had not seen a TV show in almost a month. "I'll be happy to," he said.

One of the other Petty Officers was already handing Pete a steaming cup of fresh coffee. "Here ya go, buddy. My name's Smithy. I'm the MAA next door at the chow hall." He looked over at Boats who was taking his chair. "Boats, you're gonna hafta give this guy his first week's rent free."

Boats turned his head up with a little smirk. "I think I can take care of it with the Chief for this week."

Pete sat down to watch TV and the meaning of the short conversation passed over his head.

The next few days at X Division were great. Pete laid around and enjoyed his holiday. He had plenty of time to write letters, visit the library and even go over to the school barracks and jaw with the old gang.

When pay day came, Newstead delivered Pete's check to him. "That'll be five bucks," he said, handing Pete his check. "You have to pay your rent in advance."

Pete leaned back on his bunk, laughing. "Paul you've got to be kidding. This is the US Navy. We don't pay rent. That's a pretty good joke."

Newstead grabbed Pete's arm as he sat down beside him and began to speak in a very serious voice. "You've got to listen up and listen up good." The Petty Officer's voice was barely a whisper as his eyes darted here and there checking for other people. "This is really serious, Pete. Have you noticed you haven't had any watches since you've been here? Well, that's because your rent was paid. There's some kind of giant control over this X Division. I've been here almost nine weeks. I've been playing along, trying to find out what's going on so I can turn someone in to Naval Intelligence and get this ring of crooks thrown in jail. But, I haven't been able to find out what the story is. If you want to get along, you've got to pay your rent. If you don't, you'll find yourself with all the watches on the pier. If you object to that, you'll find yourself on mess cooking at the chow hall. All the mess cooks bunk in the other wing of this same barracks and you're still under Boats' control through Smithy, who is one of his henchmen."

Pete was a little irritated to think anyone would try to charge rent for a bunk on a Navy base. "I'm not going to pay," Pete stated flatly. "I've seen some real strange things in this man's Navy, but this takes the cake. You can go back and tell that ugly old Boatswain's Mate, I said he can turn gray before I'll pay him anything"

"Shhh!" Newstead pleaded. "There's more to it than just Boats. There's someone in Administration that's involved, someone who controls orders. Nobody gets out of here quickly or easily. Everyone seems to go from here to mess cooking or some other crappy detail on the base, and then they get their orders within a month or so. But, if they pay their rent, they're gone within three weeks. I've been hanging around in hopes I could find the answer and give the entire package to NI-7. There's a Naval Intelligence Internal Group Seven office on this base, and they could clean up Boats and *all* his friends in a hurry if they could get the poop on them. There's a rumor NI-7 sent one of their guys over here, but he wound up in the bay."

Pete was getting shook up. "You know so much and you're still here? It sounds to me like you're from NI-7. You know you could get killed doing what you're doing?"

"Okay, Pete. I'll tell you why I'm trying to catch Boats and his friends," Paul said, his voice sinking in his throat. "The NI-7 man they found in the bay was my brother."

"Oh, no!" Pete said. He stood, taking his check from Paul's clinched fist. "Let's go to the chow hall and get some food. We'll eat in the Open Mess with the officers and guests so we can talk more freely. There will be fewer mess cooks and MAAs around."

As they sat down to their meal, Pete related what he had overheard in the MAA lounge the night he had worked on their television.

"So there must be a Chief Petty Officer in Admin or Personnel who's in on this with Boats and his bunch," said Paul. "I've got to find out. I'm going to do a little checking around over there. Do you want to pay your rent to Boats this week or say no and see what happens?"

"I don't think I want to pay the fat old sea rat anything," Pete said, shoving the last fork of food into his mouth. "Have you been over to NI-7 with the information you have?"

"Not yet," said Newstead, setting his coffee cup down. "I may just go see them while I'm out poking around in the morning."

After lunch, Pete was lying on his bunk when a Seaman Apprentice came up from Boats' office. "Pete, 'the man' wants to see you," he said. Pete was expecting this, so he took his time slipping into his shoes and going down the two flights of stairs.

"Hey, Boats! What's up?" Pete tried to act as innocent as he could. "The messenger told me you were looking for me. What can I do for you?"

"Don't you give me any of your hayseed -- I don't know what's going on -- business!" His face was reddening. Pete was getting

Boats' goat. "You ain't so smart! I can pick up this phone and find out all about you."

He snatched up the receiver and began to dial. There was a brief pause and then he spoke. "Pat, this is Boats at X Division. Is Chief Acres there?" His eyes moved up to meet Pete's as the conversation paused. "Yeah. What it is, I need a run down on a Seaman Peterson. Maybe you could leave the chief a note to call me when he gets back." There was another pause. "Oh, you can? Well, shoot." The First Class PO's eyes rolled as he listened for a few moments. "You mean this is just a dumb black shoe Seaman off the *USS Kingston* awaiting orders? That's hard to believe. He acts as smart as one of those dumb ET strikers. Well, thanks, Pat."

He set the receiver down on the phone. "Well, no matter. You have the twenty to twenty-four hundred watch on the pier. Be down here at eight PM in full dress blues."

Pete stared into the big man's eyes. He had more than a few things he wanted to say to this pig. He took a deep breath, turned on his heel and marched away.

At twenty hundred hours Pete reported to the Master At Arms shack and picked up an old M-1 carbine, a white duty belt, helmet and leggings. A typical school's command sentry watch lay ahead of him.

The watch on the pier was cold, foggy and very dark. It was, however, the first watch Pete had stood since leaving School's Command. His post was on the seawall across from the Petty Officer's Club. He found himself enjoying the beauty of the old fountains along the seawall. Great statues posed in the darkness with water dripping off of them. The view, like much of Treasure Island, was beautiful, with the brightly lit city of San Francisco across the bay. Other than a couple of drunks, he saw and heard nothing the entire watch.

When Pete got back to the MAA shack at midnight, Boats was waiting. "You've been assigned to mess cooking, Peterson. You're to report at O'five hundred to the mess deck MAA." Boats took great delight in delivering the message. "You have to move your gear down to the main wing with the mess cooks, tonight. You wouldn't want to be written up for being late the first day on the job, would you?"

Pete was not in a good mood as he pulled uniforms from his locker. He was even a little noisy, kicking the door closed, waking men sleeping in the area.

At zero four-thirty hours Pete was rudely awakened by Smithy, "You decided to come on over and join us did you? That's just great." He smirked. "We'll do our best to make sure you remember your time with us."

After showering and dressing in whites, Pete joined the rest of the first shift mess cooks on the main mess deck of the galley for Quarters For Muster.

While they were standing in the table area getting their morning pep talk from Smithy, a very large black man came out of the kitchen area. "Smithy!" he growled. He wore a Commissaryman First Class insignia on his tall chef's hat. "You gots ta fine me a country boy. I need somebody who knows the difference 'tween a spud and an egg. 'Dese city boys you keep givin' me don't know nothin' 'bout food."

It was Pete's chance to avoid wiping table tops and picking up trays all day. "Cookie! I might be able to give you a hand. I'm told I make the best hash-browned potatoes in the state of Utah."

A broad smile crossed the CS1's face. He pointed a large finger at Pete. "You come wid' me, boy! We gots ta get hot on some breakfast for the crew. They'll be here in 'bout two hours."

Pete broke from ranks to join the big Commissaryman as Smithy turned to the CS1 and started to speak. "Cookie, this guy is a special case. I have to take care of him. Boats told me to watch..." His voice trailed as the cook interrupted.

"Smithy, I don't give a crumb what your personal problems are. This is my galley, and in *my* galley, everybody works for me!" The CS1 gestured with his right thumb to the middle of his huge chest.

"Come on, boy," he motioned to Pete. "Let's turn to."

Within fifteen minutes, Pete had pressure cooked over two hundred pounds of red potatoes and was helping three other men peel and shred them for hashed browns.

After breakfast, Cookie called Pete into his small office just off the main kitchen. "You know food pretty good. I can get you a permanent assignment here at the galley if you'd like to have it. I can get you a Commissaryman Third Class crow in less than six months"

Pete was amazed to run into a real person on the base after all the stuff he had been through. Pete looked across the desk at the big man. He couldn't help noticing the wall behind his desk, covered with certificates and awards. Pete raised his right hand as if he were in a class. "Can I ask a question, Cookie?"

"Shoot." said the CS1. "What's on your mind?"

"I don't mean to be insubordinate," Pete felt he was touching thin ice with his toe. "But, what happened to the accent? The 'down-home-country' or ghetto or whatever it was?"

The Petty Officer leaned back in his chair, pounded his desk with a huge open hand and laughed loud and long.

"I tell you, Pete," said Cookie. "You are very sharp! You're one of the few people who has caught me." He muffled his laughter down to a chuckle. "I jus talk like dat for dem's dat thinks they's smarter'n me." He chuckled once more. "I have a good time with it. Now, back to you, how about being my striker?"

"If you don't mind, Cookie, I'd rather just work for you until I get my orders. I do like working for you here, but I'd rather be at sea, if you know what I mean."

The big Commissaryman looked across the desk with a broad smile, a look of understanding in his eyes. "Yeah. I know what you mean. I spent sixteen years at sea, and loved every minute of it. You can go out and help the boys with lunch. I'm assigning you to be in charge of the Spud Locker and the salad bar while you're here. I want you to move your gear into the cooks berthing compartment. You'll be my 'Spud King' until your orders come through."

The large man reached into his desk and brought out a cloth chef's hat. "Get rid of the paper hat. I don't want anyone to mistake you for a mess cook," he said, handing Pete the hat.

What a treat. The spud locker was a large room equipped with a lot of stainless steel tables and four automatic potato-peeling machines resembling large upright washers with course sandpaper inside. Pete could make any kind of salad he wanted to try; he just had to meet the menu requirements on a daily basis. *What a fun job!*

At noon Pete was working the serving line in the Open Mess, serving visitors, officers and some base personnel. There had been several Waves, female sailors, come through from Admin so Pete was on the lookout for Pat or Randy. At twelve fifteen, they showed up together and were quite surprised to see Pete standing behind the serving line.

"Can you get out of there, and come to our table?" asked Randy. "We sure would like to talk to you. We'll be over by the front windows in our favorite spot. We like to look out at the rose garden."

In a few minutes, Pete joined the girls at their table. Their beaming smiles welcomed him as he sat down. "How have you girls been?" Pete straightened the napkin holder on the table. "What's in the good news department? Have either of you girls seen an AG3 named Newstead?"

Randy's face beamed. "You won't be seeing him again, Pete. He came over the other day and said he wanted to go aboard the sea plane tender, *Blue Island Sound*. He said he was a friend of yours, so I cut a set of orders and sent him out. There was something funny though." She tilted her head and Pete could not help looking into her big blue eyes. "When I pulled his record of transfer I discovered I had sent him to the *USS Coral Sea* almost five weeks before, and to the *USS Lexington* three weeks before that. I was surprised to see his orders had never been delivered to him"

Pete was interested. "What do you think happened to Newstead's orders, Randy? Is there a Chief in your section by the name of Acres? Do you think he could've had anything to do with the lost orders?"

"Gee, Pete. You seem to know as much as we do," said Randy. "As a matter of fact, Chief Acres heads up the order review and transmittal section. Basically, he gets all the orders for anyone who is assigned to X Division. He reviews them and then notifies the sailor involved through the Transit Division MAA. He only handles one section. I knew that, so I called Pat and asked her to look around. She found your friend's original set of orders. Isn't that a kick? You know, sometimes I think Chief Acres is smoking something. He's always misplacing or losing orders"

Pete turned to Pat. "Pat, when you found Newstead's orders did you happen to see any others?"

Pat smiled. "To be honest Pete, I just opened the file up to the letter 'N' and pulled out Newstead. Randy asked me to look for a specific name, so I didn't think to look for anyone else. If you want me to, I'll go back this afternoon and see if I can find the orders Randy cut for you the day after you were in to see Commander Hallis"

"Oh no!" Pete put his hand up to indicate silence, one finger in front of his pursed lips. "At this point in time, I don't want you girls to do anything. You can go back and cut me a set of orders to join Newstead if you want, and throw in a couple of weeks of leave while you're at it. I have to go back to work now."

Pete started to get up. Randy took his hand and held it as tight as she could. She had a pleading look in her eyes. Pete leaned over and kissed her on the cheek and smiled. "I get off at two, so I'll see you at two-thirty."

Pete left the table and returned to his work station. The rest of the lunch hour went quickly, and the second shift was there to take over, so Cookie allowed Pete to leave a half an hour early.

Pete arrived at the Admin building and went straight to the NI-7 office. The office was at the far end of a dark corridor.

The hallway leading to the office was unkept and in need of paint. When he opened the door, a different world met his eyes. There was a clean modern office with computer terminals here and there. A Third Class Yeoman came to the desk where Pete was standing. "What can we do for you?" He seemed awfully warm for a person Pete didn't know.

Pete suddenly felt cold and uncomfortable. Am I here to do good or am I here to make trouble for some good, yet misunderstood, people? Pete had a lump in his throat and at first it was hard to get the words to come. "I need to talk to an officer about internal intelligence," he stammered.

"I see," said the Third Class slumping into his chair and leaning back. "Since internal intelligence is the only function of NI-7, could you be more specific?"

"I'd like to talk about X Division," Pete said. He was starting to get angry.

The Petty Officer jumped from his chair holding up his right hand. "Whoa, hold it right there. You're the second person in a week, and I know Commander Maxwell has been waiting to see you. Sit down right here for just a second." He gestured to a chair by his desk and left the room.

Returning momentarily, the Petty Officer guided Pete to a back office with lush hardwood-paneled walls and a large desk. Behind the desk sat a very small man with gray hair. The man was dressed in working khakis. The silver oak leaves on his collar indicated he was a full Commander. He stood up extending his right hand to

Pete. "Hi there. I'm Commander Maxwell. I understand you have information about X Division."

Pete became cautious. "Before we get started," he said. "I want to know if AG3 Newstead has been here to see you."

The officer dismissed the Third Class showing Pete in. "Newstead. A sharp young man. Yes, he's been here. He gave us some very valuable information. I think we're very close to breaking up a ring of extortionists here on the base."

He pressed a button on his intercom. "Before we start. I have some people in another room who would like to listen to this interview if you don't mind." He spoke in the direction of a little black box on the desk near Pete. "Mr. Peterson and Mr. Walls, have you got all of your group there?"

A man's voice came back on the box. "Yes, we're ready. You can begin any time"

"Well sir..." Pete related everything he knew and everything he could think of, right up to the minute he entered the Commander's office. The whole story took an hour and a half. When it was over, Commander Maxwell said, "We got most of the story from Newstead but the scoop on where the orders actually are and the top man being Chief Acres is all news. Good news."

Pete left the office of NI-7 and went down to the Orders and Transfers Office where both Randy and Pat were waiting for him. They had a surprise.

Pat got up from the chair beside Randy's desk. "I guess you're here to see about a set of orders. Right?" She was beaming from ear to ear. "We might have the set you've been looking for."

"I'll say, I'd like a set of orders," Pete replied as he took Pat's outstretched hand and clasp it in both of his. "I want to thank you two wonderful ladies for being my friends while I've been here. You've both been very good to me."

Randy reached across her desk and shook Pete's hand. "Here." She smiled as she handed Pete a pay envelope. "I have something for you. It's your final pay from this station, your travel pay and a two-week pay advance for leave." Her smile got bigger as she picked up the next sheet of paper. "You are to report on December 24th to the same ship we sent your weatherman buddy, Newstead. It's the *USS Blue Island Sound* (AV77)."

"Wow!" Pete exclaimed. He went around the desk to give Randy a hug. "This is terrific!" The little hug he expected to give her turned into a long passionate kiss and embrace combination.

Randy gave Pete one more little squeeze for good measure before letting him go. "I've been trying to figure out how to get ahold of you since the first time we met." Her smile dropped into a frown. "Now, it's too late."

"Hey!" Pete realized what she was getting at. "I still have to pick up my gear. We can go out tonight! What do you say?" He brushed her shoulder and looked into her face.

Her frown broke. She buried her face in the front of Pete's shirt and burst into tears. She turned away from him and left the room. It was during the break period for the office staff, so everyone else was out. Pete felt really stupid. *What have I done?* "What's wrong?" Pete pleaded, turning to Pat. "What can I do?"

"Life is wrong and there's nothing you can do. You won't have time to take her to dinner." Pat picked an envelope up from Randy's desk. "Here's your plane ticket. Your seabag is under Randy's desk. We had a couple of guys from Admin go over and get it for you. Your plane leaves from the San Francisco International Airport in three hours. You'd best catch a bus and get going."

Her face took on a very serious look as she put an arm around him. "Don't worry about Randy. She knows where you'll be. She can write if she's hung up on you." Pat pointed to the seabag Pete had not noticed. "Now, get your gear and get going, sailor!"

Pete sat in the airport terminal waiting for his flight to be called reflecting on his last days at Treasure Island. He had come from one temporary assignment after another and hoped beautiful Treasure

Island would lead to something permanent in his life and his Navy service. Instead, he found disappointment and frustration. Pete had been in the Navy a year and five months and the rest of his four-year enlistment seemed blurred with uncertainty. He had met a lot of genuine people and some crooks. He supposed the Navy was no better or worse than the general population. It had all kinds of people serving. One thing was for sure, there would be changes made. In the future, temporary personnel would not have to face the harassment of Boats, his friends and *their* X Division.

Chapter 13

Back to Sea

A soft rain swirled down from the black sky as the taxi rolled through the gate at the 32nd Street Naval Station in San Diego. The night was quiet, the weather lousy, cold, with a soft drizzle that spun and churned in the air like the wind didn't know which way to blow. Pete was looking for a ship he had not seen before on an unfamiliar base. The Marine at the gate told the driver the ship was on pier 6. The driver nodded as if knew the base and headed toward the waterfront.

"Here you are, son," the cabbie said pointing a finger toward the passenger side of the car. "Your ship is the big one, second one down." He turned halfway around in his seat and gave a big smile. "That'll be sixteen thirty-five. For you, sixteen. Remember, call for Yellow the next time you need a cab."

Pete handed the driver the money and stepped into the dark inhospitable night. "What a Christmas present!" Pete muttered, closing the door and dragging his seabag behind him as the taxi pulled away.

It was Christmas Eve. As a matter of fact, it would be Christmas Day in about twenty-four minutes – just enough time to report to his new duty station.

As Pete approached from the head of the pier, there was a street lamp shining down on the bow of a destroyer escort. The ship was at 'dress ship' so there were lights strung all around it and up to the masthead. It was like a giant Christmas tree except all the lights were white. A sentry, posted about twenty feet out from the ship, walked the familiar 'last watch.' But, this sentry was not a fire watch; Pete could see he was armed with an automatic weapon. Pete walked far out of the perimeter of the sentry post to avoid being challenged and slowed from his path by a bunch of questions.

The next ship on the pier was definitely what Pete was looking for. The bow alone stood forty feet higher than the fantail deck of the tin can in front of it. The huge dark gray shadow now towering above him was his destination. As Pete drew closer the twelve-foot high white letters painted on the bow plates let him know he was almost home. 'AV77' was the designation on the seaplane tender.

A feeling of warmth flushed through Pete as he approached the forward gangway of the ship. He could hear the purring of the big pier-side generators pumping life into the metal hulk making it even more inviting. A single long gangway stretched from the pier to the forward quarterdeck of the ship. Along its length, in large black letters on a white field was the ship's name, *USS Blue Island Sound* (AV77) .

Pete's seabag felt like a hundred pounds as he shifted it to his left shoulder and reached out for the handrail of the gangway with his right hand.

"Hey, sailor!" A voice cut the icy drizzle. "This is the officers' brow. The enlisted brow is down the pier another four-hundred feet." The enlisted brow was a welcome sight. A double staircase system similar to the *Kingston,* with a flat gangway at the top, was much easier on the legs than the direct pier to ship gangway the officers had.

Pete stopped at the edge of the ship just before the end of the gangway and turned to salute the ensign flying from the fantail. Turning forward, a figure appeared from a nearby doorway at the back of the ship's hangar. "Request permission to come aboard, sir."

A right hand raised to the plastic-covered Chief Petty Officer's hat, and a husky voice reached Pete. "Permission granted! Now, get your back side in here out of the rain."

Pete gave the Chief his travel orders and his packet of files. "This is great!" said the Chief. "I'm glad to see they're finally sending us some ETs."

"Are you the ET Chief?" asked Pete.

"Oh, hell no! I'm a Machinists Mate. Name's McDonald. I've got plenty of men in my division. I just get tired of the ET Chief complaining all the time that he doesn't have enough help for all the equipment aboard."

Within the hour, Pete was in a bunk in the X Division berthing compartment. As soon as his head touched the pillow he was out. Reveille was not a welcome experience. At first Pete thought there was a drunk loose in the compartment so he didn't pay much attention. As the man drew closer to his bunk, Pete realized he was trying to wake all of the people in the berthing space, and was being neither gentle nor polite. He banged on lockers with his fist, slammed doors and jerked blankets.

Pete watched for a moment through barely opened eyes, wondering who this intruder was. The stripes on his shoulder indicated he was one rate junior to Pete as far as military grade – a Fireman Apprentice.

He was obviously another ignorant arrogant bully in the same mold as BM3 Benion. Benion had tried to run roughshod over

Pete's class at ET school and had then unceremoniously flunked out. The puke, a good two inches taller than Pete, was at the foot of his bunk, pulling at his covers. One hard jerk, and Pete lay uncovered, in his skivvies.

Pete's anger exploded like the time he had tried to pig-stick Sergeant Walters in combat school. All of Pete's bad experiences in the Navy were now focused on this man.

Springing from his bed with a long guttural screech, Pete caught the man's throat between his first finger and thumb of his left hand and slammed the man's head back against a tier of aluminum lockers. There was a loud pop as Pete's right fist smashed into the man's sternum just below the 'V' of his undress blue jumper.

The man reeled back into the lockers a second time with a loud crash and slid down to the deck, legs folding under and knees turning inward. A blank stare filled his wide eyes, as he gasped for breath.

The other men in the compartment quietly retrieved their towels from their lockers and went to the shower, stepping over Pete's victim as if they didn't see him. Pete shook his head. He was awake now. "Oh shit! Shame on me!" Pete exclaimed. He pulled his douche kit and towel from his seabag. He glanced back over his shoulder at the crumpled figure on the deck as he followed the last man out to the head for a nice warm shower.

The person Pete followed turned out to be Ted Winston, who had been aboard the *Blue Island Sound* for two weeks. He was an undesignated striker, a Seaman Apprentice without a definite job classification or assignment. In as much as Pete was not a designated striker, they were in the same situation. He would stay in X Division until the ship's Personnel Department decided which division could best use his talents. Ted was a reservist, which was a dirty word to the regular Navy sailors aboard the ship. Without a job training classification he could easily become a Boatswain's Mate – a deck hand with First Division.

The men talked while they shaved. Ted was from Portland, Oregon. Most of the experience he had in the reserves and in civilian life led him to believe he could be assigned to the ship's real X Division as a Yeoman or Personnelman, Lithographer or Postal Clerk. *At least Ted can get himself out of this ratty 'X' transit division,* Pete thought.

Like so many other instances in the Navy, where a person became your fast friend or your lifelong enemy at the first meeting, Ted became Pete's friend.

"The MAA force on this boat has two lackeys you have to keep an eye on," Ted said, smearing shave cream over his long face. "One is Bales, the guy you met in the berthing space. The other is Greek – a lackluster Seaman who came aboard a couple of years ago and was adopted by the Master At Arms force as their own. He has a real hard-to-say last name, so everybody just calls him Greek." Ted finished his shave.

When they got back to the berthing space, the big bad fireman deuce was gone. He had apparently slunk back to the MAA shack to report Pete's brutality to the MAAs.

"We'd best be getting down to the MAA shack for muster," Ted said, putting on his white hat.

Pete snatched his hat from his bunk, where he had laid it with the rest of his uniform, slipped it on and followed Ted out the door. They made their way down the stairwell to the forward mess deck and through the large double doors to a great mezzanine deck into the crew's main lounge.

The crew's lounge was flanked on the port side by the ship's library and on the starboard side by the Master At Arms' Office. Pete and his new friend quickly formed ranks with the other men from the berthing compartment. In the first line of the formation, was the Fireman Apprentice Pete had bounced off the lockers and beside him, a butterball about five-foot-five. The butterball was more than fat. He bordered on obese. He wore a tee-shirt with his dungaree trousers instead of the chambray or dungaree shirt the rest of the formation wore. Pete recalled tee-shirts could only be worn while the ship was underway. Since this guy was in front of Pete, he could read the name, which was nicely embroidered over the right back pocket of his dungaree trousers; it read simply "Greek."

Regulations require MAA personnel wear their badges at all times aboard ship. They have developed a nickname over the years. In the alligator navy, they were called 'badgers.' To Pete's mind, the perfect example of a badger was now stepping out of the MAA office. He was a short man with well-muscled arms and an air that told everyone to beware of this bantam fighting cock.

He carried a clipboard in his left hand as he approached the formation. "Attention!" he trumpeted. "Greek, take the roll." He handed the clipboard to the butterball in front of Pete. "Bales. Come stand by me." He pointed to a spot near him on the shiny green tile floor. The fireman deuce stepped from the formation and stood beside him.

After Greek had finished the roll, on which Pete was surprised to already find his name, the badger stepped up to speak to the formation. "For those of you who don't know it, Greek and Bales are assistant MAAs. If they give you an order, you *will* react as though that order," he paused for effect, "were given by a member of the MAA force." He pointed his right hand at Pete. "You're very lucky regs allow a man sixty seconds to wake up or you'd be in the brig, right now!" the rooster crowed.

Pete stared at the little man with the badge of authority and worse yet, Petty Officer Second Class stripes on his sleeve. He was arrogant and ignorant like his wormy-eyed little messenger. The name on the badger's shirt read 'MOLINI.' Pete was getting very frazzled! *This is ridiculous!* he thought.

"Listen, Molini," Pete found himself talking out of turn. "You can send a Seaman or a Fireman or an Airman to tell me what to do and I'll do it, but if this little fireman deuce tries to approach me with anything other than a direct message..." Pete's voice trailed as he realized he was about to make a bodily threat in front of the cops of the ship. *Not a red hot idea!*

"Greek, give out liberty cards to everyone here except this guy." Molini pointed to Pete again. "Mister, you're restricted to the ship for the day. X Division dismissed!" Molini turned away with a hard look on his face.

Pete left Quarters For Muster and walked around the ship with Ted, getting a complete tour. It seemed Ted had plenty of time to become well acquainted with most of it.

Pete was not too concerned about going anywhere on Christmas day. He had just had two weeks of leave and certainly didn't have enough money to go party in San Diego.

The next day at noon muster of X Division, Molini gave Pete his divisional transfer. Molini had arranged for Pete to go to S2 Division. It sounded neat at first. The assignment was mess cooking again.

Molini took Pete aside for a one-on-one face chewing as he gave him his transfer chit. "I'm going to watch you like a hawk. You step out of line and I'll personally see you get busted so fast you won't know what hit you. You're mine, you smart ass!"

Pete leaned down into the Petty Officer's face so he knew Pete was listening to him. Pete's lip curled, his face reddened. "Someday Molini," Pete drew up his most threatening tone. "Someday, I'm going to sew on a Second Class crow and when that day comes, I'm going to look you up and tell you to eat my shorts." Pete snatched the chit from Molini's hand and walked away. Pete was back on sea duty.

Chapter 14

Looking for a Home

Pete had gained a knowledge of what made cooks tick while he was on Treasure Island. He was glad he had escaped the holding division in favor of an active part of the ship's company. Although mess cooking meant berthing in a transient kind of compartment with people being rotated in and out every week from all the various departments of the ship. At least they were permanent crew members and by getting to know them, Pete could find out what was going on throughout the ship.

His first morning in the galley, he went to the Chief Commissaryman's office for a little chat. "My name is Peterson. I'm a Seaman, recently assigned here from Treasure Island Naval Training Station." Pete was looking at the back of a set of khakis.

The chief's desk was turned, facing the bulkhead. "Are you a Commissaryman striker?" the Chief asked, not turning around. He was involved in drawing up a menu. "What experience do you have in a galley?" he asked. The Chief's tone was anything but friendly.

"I was in charge of the spud locker at TI, Chief. I'm told I make a fantastic salad and my prep work for vegetable soup, stews and hash browned potatoes makes it so the cook has nothing to do but heat it up and serve it."

The chair spun around. Pete could see this guy did not like to be bothered when he was doing his paperwork. "Benson!" the Chief bawled.

A chubby Commissaryman Second Class, almost as wide as he was tall, came scooting from the galley kitchen, at the Chief's beckoning. "Yeah, Chief. Is there somethin' I kin gitcha?" he drawled as he stuck his head through the doorway.

The Chief acted as if he was short on temper. He motioned toward Pete. "This is your new man in the spud locker. Give him whatever he needs and send him on his way. If the salad bar doesn't improve remarkably by the middle of the week, I want him in the soup." The Chief made a sharp motion with his right hand. "Now, get out of here and leave me alone." He jerked his hand up, as if struck by a last minute thought. "Tell that Storekeeper to get in here. I need him."

"Aye, aye, Chief," said Benson, motioning Pete to follow him from the office. They crossed the main mess deck. A First Class Storekeeper sat alone at a table reading a newspaper and drinking a cup of coffee. Benson spoke to him as if he knew him well. "Muggs, you best get your face outa that paper and go see Chief Black."

The SK1 quickly folded back the paper to stare at the front page. "Oh, rats!" Muggs exclaimed. "It's the third Friday of the month again! He wants his blasted menu typed, and he doesn't allow any errors. Can't you go back and tell him you didn't find me?"

The chubby CS2 turned to Pete with his hands on his wide hips. "The third Friday of every month, Chief Black has to hunt Muggs down and force him to type the menu. I don't know exactly what the story is, but Muggs sure hates to type anything." He poked Pete in the ribs. "Come on kid, we'll show you your new office."

The spud locker was a large, spacious room, walls covered halfway down with stainless steel, plenty of counter space and two new potato peeling machines. They looked very much like the ones he had used on Treasure Island, except they had their sand paper interior surface recently replaced. As far as working conditions went, the spud locker was the greatest. Pete had two helpers to aid in the preparation of produce and set up of the salad bar.

As CS2 Benson conducted the introductions with Mats and Booker, Pete's two helpers, Pete stuck his hand out to Petty Officer Benson, also. "My name's Peterson. But, please call me Pete. I like it much better than kid."

Benson lifted his round face and laughed as he shook Pete's hand. "Well Pete, old man, since this is your first day on the job, what're you going to prepare to win the Chief's favor? I guess I should tell you, the last spud king was fired this morning. He's scraping trays in the scullery now. Captain Hamblin eats with the crew every Thursday night. Last night the Captain said the salad dressing was soured. That's all it took." Benson put his hands into the pockets of his white trousers under his apron and turned toward the door. The rotund Petty Officer spoke over his shoulder. "I'd have a look at the salad dressing if I were you, Pete."

Pete immediately had Mats, a bright Fireman Apprentice from M Division, take him to the storeroom where the salad dressing was kept so he could have a firsthand look. As the men descended the ladder into the storeroom, Pete detected a slight odor. Upon further investigation, he discovered a plastic jug of salad dressing leaking. He looked carefully at the contents of the four other cases. All the lids were swollen, and the contents spoiled.

"These are all ruined, Mats!" Pete explained. "It looks like they've been exposed to heat, and it's spoiled the whole lot."

The FA interrupted him. "That can't be, Pete. We just took these stores on from the Naval Supply Station at 32nd Street. I was in the working party. They just came aboard a week before Christmas."

"If that's the case," Pete said, closing the flap on the box, "we'd better go see if we can get the Chief to bring the S2 Division Officer or the Supply Officer down here to verify this. It seems to me, the Naval Supply Center folks owe us sixteen gallons of fresh dressing."

For the evening meal, Pete had fresh dressing for the salads. He spent a lot of time preparing the saladbar. He made a green salad, a carrot and raisin salad, a bean salad and the traditional coleslaw. He also whipped up four kinds of dressings and as an extra touch, he added a bowl of black olives, a cheese plate and a relish tray. The cheese plate had never been served before and was a real success. Pete's assistants had to fill it up three times.

The evening meal was being served and the preparation areas were being cleaned. Pete was in the spud locker, his back to the door. He was wiping down the large stainless steel preparation table when he heard a voice from the main passageway. "Spud king. You had an excellent salad bar, tonight." Pete turned to see the speaker. In the doorway stood a very large man in officer's seagoing khaki.

Pete instantly recognized the silver eagle on his collar and the gold star set in a gold circle above his left shirt pocket. It was the Captain. Pete popped tall, a little startled to see the Captain at his work station. The large man smiled as he spoke again. "Next Thursday, I've invited Admiral Moore of the North Island Naval Air Station to have dinner here on the 'Blue Goose.' I hope we'll be able to have some of that excellent carrot salad."

"Yes, sir!" Pete said, trying to regain his composure. "I'll see it's on the salad bar. Thank you, Sir."

The Captain turned and was gone. Pete was still in a state of shock. *Pretty good, having the old man himself speak to me, and better yet, to have the Captain look me up to give a compliment. What a guy! The only bad thing is, I don't even know the Captain's name. Did CS2 Benson say, Captain Hamblin?*

When Pete finished cleaning up the spud locker, he hurried to find Benson to tell him of his experience. Pete was very pleased with himself as he bounced into the galley kitchen. "Hey, Benson!" He was talking to the back of a sailor he didn't know. "Have I got a surprise for you?"

Pete hesitated. He didn't recognize the giant man turning around. He was black, at least six-foot-four and well over two-hundred and fifty pounds. He was not fat like most cooks, this guy looked like Mr. America.

The large man extended his right hand to Pete. "I'm CS1 Moon. You must be the new spud king. I'm the head cook and leading Petty Officer of S2 Division. I work the afternoon shift and Benson works the mornings. It works out real good for us that way."

As Pete shook the giant's hand, he was amazed. Pete could have put both his hands in one of Moon's with room to spare. "My name's Pete," he said, feeling it was necessary to spill his whole life story in ten seconds. "I'm an undesignated Seaman, here courtesy of a frustrated badger by the name of Molini in the MAA force. I guess it's just as well though. I'm a little confused about what rating group I'd like to work in. I worked as an ET aboard the *USS Kingston,* but I'm not sure what I want to do with the rest of my career."

The Commissaryman walked to his preparation table and pulled up a large ball of dough he had rising in a bowl. He pinched off small pieces and put them onto a baking tray for breakfast rolls. "You know, you already have a real good reputation here on the mess deck. You sure don't have to worry about a cook giving you up to the badgers for any reason. Why, today alone, you made us a lot of points with the old man and the whole crew. If you want to strike for Commissaryman, you've got the job, and I can promise you in May when the exams come up, you'll earn your crow."

The attitude of this man was overwhelming Pete. He was open, warm and, most importantly, sincere, like walking in the door at home to the aroma of fresh baked bread.

"I thank you for your offer, and I might take you up on it," Pete said with a smile. "There are a lot of really nice people on this ship, so all I have to do is decide, but for the moment, I'm not in any hurry."

Moon tossed Pete a ball of dough, and Pete began to pinch off rolls and place them in the greased pan next to the ones Moon had made. "You do that pretty good, Pete. You sure you're not a cook in disguise?"

"I'm not a cook!" Pete said. "I just used to help my mother in the restaurant where she worked. Now, that lady is a real cook."

"Well." Moon smiled. "Do you have any really good, down home recipes for great soups? You know, the Admiral is coming over for supper next Thursday, and the Captain always likes to treat him to a new or special item. I'm long out of new and just about out of special. You got anything in the bean line?"

Pete thought for a second. "Why do you ask for beans?" he asked.

"That's easy," said Moon. "This is the one branch of the service where you never see beans except as a cold item on the salad bar or as pork and beans on a Sunday cold food tray. Besides, the Admiral is from the south. I hear he's a real nut about every kind of bean. I'm just like any other Navy cook though; I hate to cook or serve beans of any kind."

Dropping his last roll in the tray, he patted the big friendly man on the shoulder as he began to leave the kitchen. "I'm going out on the pier to call my mom right now. By tomorrow, I'll have a recipe for beans that'll knock the Admiral's socks off. See ya later."

Returning to the S2 berthing compartment, Pete finished unpacking his sea bag into a clean locker. He took a shower, changed into his undress blues and headed for the pier.

He found a pay phone next to a geedunk vending machine at the end of the pier and made a phone call home. Pete's mother was very happy to give him one of her old family recipes and delighted to hear her son had an interest in cooking.

The next day, after Pete had finished the salad bar preparations for the noon meal and turned over potatoes, onions and carrots to CS2 Benson, he sat at a table on the forward mess deck reading a book. Mess cooks were busy setting up condiments on every table. When the task was completed, Benson would inspect the setup and call all galley personnel for their meal.

Pete looked up from his book to see BM2 Molini strut through the double doors at the far end of the mess deck, walk to the giant coffee urn and begin to fill his mug. The mug was white, decorated on one side with a Second Class Boatswains Mate rating insignia. Molini's name was under it. The other side, in large black letters, read MAA. As soon as his cup was filled, Molini walked over to where Pete was sitting. "You tryin' to get written up, Mess Cook?" he crowed, pressing uncomfortably close to Pete.

Pete fixed his gaze on Molini's weathered face. "Is there something going on here?"

"You need to get off your can and help these people get this mess deck set up. What gives you the right to sit around while all these people are working?" He gestured toward the other side of the mess deck.

The five mess cooks setting up the tables saw Molini enter the area and had moved to the farthest end of the mess deck. They didn't want to chance getting into the MAA's line of sight.

"He's doing what the Spud King's supposed to do," came a husky voice from behind Molini. It was Moon, coming back from liberty. Molini spun around to find a giant in dress blues standing right behind him. "And, if you want to keep your privileges of early meals and coffee any time, you'd be wise to leave him alone. If you have anything to say to him in the future, you say it through me," said the big CS1. His right eyebrow was raised and his eyes were half closed in a serious expression.

"Fine!" Molini grunted. He turned and left the mess deck toward the MAA shack.

"I can't leave you alone for a minute, can I?" Moon joked as he sat down across from Pete.

"I didn't think I'd need to be rescued, but I'm sure glad you came along," Pete said.

"I was just coming back from the base gym," said Moon. "We're going to change moorings to our home berth at North Island Naval Air Station tomorrow. I'm glad 'cause I like the gym at the air station much better. So tell me, did you get the recipe?"

"I did, indeed," Pete said as he laid a three by five index card on the table. "Here's a recipe straight from my mom's mouth. It used to warm my family up on cold winter nights in Utah."

The recipe:

Mom's Bean Soup

2 cups dried pinto beans

2 cups chopped onions

2 cups bacon, cut into 1" strips

1/4 cup brown sugar

1/2 teaspoon salt

1 tablespoon vinegar

1 teaspoon black pepper

1 teaspoon of dry mustard

Wash dry beans thoroughly. Allow beans to sit over night in a pan of hot salted water. This will enhance their tenderness. Be sure to cover the beans. Wash the beans in the morning and cook with salt added. When beans are about half done, add all other ingredients and cook over medium flame, stirring occasionally until beans are done enough to be smashed with a fork. Serve hot with corn bread.

Moon picked up the card and studied it with professional scrutiny. "This looks like a good recipe, Pete." The CS1 raised both eyebrows. "Let's put some beans to soak this afternoon and when the soup's ready, send it to the Officer's Wardroom so the Captain can sample it." He turned his head and squinted one eye down at Pete. "If the Skipper likes this recipe, we'll lay it on the entire crew next Thursday when Admiral Moore comes aboard. If Captain Hamblin likes the soup, you can bet we've got a winner."

At Sixteen Hundred the next afternoon, Moon called Pete to sample the bean soup. As far as Pete was concerned, it was great. Moon gave Pete a two-gallon pot and instructed him to take it to the Chief Steward in the officers wardroom kitchen.

The head man in the officer's mess was a black Steward Chief Petty Officer. He had a kitchen full of Filipino Steward strikers and Petty Officers. This man was a light-weight compared to Moon. Pete hoisted the heavy pot of beans onto the stainless steel counter by the stove. The Chief kept his head down as he rolled out dough for some pies.

"Here's the bean soup from the crew's galley," Pete said. He beamed as he released the bail on the large pot. "Petty Officer Moon said you'd be serving it tonight."

The Chief spun around from his work, his face casting a look of rage. "Where the hell does that uppity nigger get off, sending one of his white lackeys to tell me what to serve in *my* Wardroom?"

Pete stepped back. "Hey! I'm just the messenger."

"I'm serving fried chicken tonight, and I don't see how bean soup can be served, too," the Chief growled, wringing his hands in his apron.

"I guess Moon was wrong." Pete picked up the pot and started for the door.

The Chief snatched a large knife from the counter top and jumped in front of Pete. "What did Moon say?"

Pete was ready. He shrugged and looked down as if he didn't want to tell. "Just that you are the best baker in the fleet, and this would be a chance for you to make your world class corn bread for the Captain. He said it would be a challenge, but you'd meet it. I guess he doesn't know you *that* well."

The Chief burst out laughing. "You like Moon, don't you?"

"Yes, I do." Pete glared at the Chief, ready to give him a piece of his mind.

The Chief was laughing hard now. "Well, give me those beans."

He took the pot and set it on the stove. "I guess I'll tell you. The corn bread's in the oven. Moon and I go back a long way. We're good friends, and I think Moon has another good friend in you."

Pete laughed out loud all the way back to the galley. He had just had one of those good tricks played on him by a couple of old friends.

Pete reported to Moon in the crew's galley. "What are you doing to me?" He demanded nervously, as though he hadn't caught on to the joke. "That Chief Steward is a real tough nut. I don't think he's going to serve your beans tonight! He thinks you're trying to tell him what to do, and you're only a First Class. You need a rocker over your chevrons if you plan to talk to him." It was Pete's turn to pull a trick. He left the galley with a smile on his face.

Pete heard Moon's comment as he picked up the telephone from the wall and started to dial. "I'll set that nigger straight!" he mumbled.

After the evening meal, Pete cleaned the spud locker and walked next door to the galley to see Moon. The Chief steward was leaning against the preparation table. He jumped the minute Pete came in. "Hey! Here's the spud king!" He seemed happy to see Pete.

"What're you doin' here, Chief?" Pete wasn't sure if he should trust him or not.

"I'm here to give you and your buddy, Moon, a message from the Skipper." The Chief was standing at his full height, strutting his stuff. Moon was just walking in from the other end of the kitchen. "He said to tell you guys..." he paused for a second to look at Moon's face, who was listening hard. "...that you have a winner for tomorrow night's supper. I guess the Admiral will be here at five sharp and that's why I'm here. I'm going to whip up some corn bread you can bake tomorrow. You guys better put a few beans on to soak." He folded his arms and leaned against the prep table grinning.

Raising a giant fist in jubilation, Moon motioned to Pete with a wide grin. "Pete. Head down to the storeroom and bring up fifty pounds of dry pintos. I'll start cutting up the bacon. When you get back, see what you can do about getting us forty pounds of onions chopped."

"Aye, aye!" Pete replied and headed for the dry stores stockroom.

The next day an electricity buzzed about the mess deck. Every member of the crew was aware of the special preparations going on in the galley. The Commissary Chief had five requests from officers for permission to join the crew for supper. Without the Commissary Chief's permission, only the Captain, his guests, the S2 Division Officer and the Supply Officer were allowed to eat in the crew's mess.

At fourteen-thirty in the afternoon, Pete sat at a table with Mats and Booker on the main mess deck. "I want you guys to be sure to chill down the carrot and raisin salad, per Captain Hamblin's request; and put it on the salad bar at sixteen-thirty hours. Captain Hamblin and Admiral Moore will be coming through at seventeen hundred."

Just then Muggs came strolling through. "This has got to stop!" he muttered. "I'm tired of being that Commissaryman's Yeoman. Who does he think he is, anyway?"

Pete decided he would take a shot at smoothing out the SK1's ruffled feathers.

"How about a cup of coffee, Muggs?" he asked as the big Storekeeper started to pass. Until Pete spoke, Muggs had not noticed the group sitting at the table.

"Sure, I'll take a cup, if you can type," he said, wrestling his overweight frame into the chair beside Pete. "I'll give you five bucks if you can type this stupid menu without any errors." He held up a legal size sheet of paper with splotches of correction fluid all over it. "This is the second time I've typed it. I just can't get it good enough to satisfy the Chief."

"What kind of typewriter do you have?" Pete asked. "There's a chance I could help you out. I had a couple years of typing in high school."

Muggs sprang from the chair. "What're we waiting for? Let's go!" In less than a minute, the two men were in Muggs' office.

Muggs had a brand new, full size, electric Olympia typewriter.

"Wow!" Pete exclaimed. "This is a beaut. Either you don't do much typing, or you haven't had this machine very long."

"Okay!" Muggs said sharply. "I got it last week. I thought if I got a new machine, I'd get this stinking menu done without a hitch. Problem is, they just don't make a machine for a man with hands like outfielder's mitts." he said, holding up his hands.

Pete had not noticed Muggs' hands before. He studied them. For such a big man, he did have peculiarly shaped hands. The palms were large and the fingers were thick but very short in comparison to the rest of his hand.

I've heard of fat people before, thought Pete. *I guess, when you can't get any fatter elsewhere, your fingers get fat. He had to be able to type 40 words a minute to get his First Class crow, but that was propaably fifteen years and two-hundred pound ago.*

"Don't worry, Muggs, old buddy." Pete said, rolling a fresh mimeograph mat into the platen and adjusting it evenly across the carrier. "As long as I'm here, you'll be able to get this menu out on time. I can do this and take care of the spud locker, too. No sweat." Pete's hands flew over the keyboard like a concert pianist.

Twenty minutes later, the menu was finished. Pete threw the carriage one last time to eject the stencil. Muggs grabbed it as if it were gold and bolted for the Chief's office. Pete reached for the typewriter cover, looking up just in time to catch Muggs' back going out the door. "Guess my work here is done," he sighed and walked back to the mess deck to finish his coffee.

Ten minutes later Fireman Apprentice Booker looked up from the book he was reading, past Pete who was sitting across from him. "Pete. It looks like you have company."

A long, tall Third Class Electronics Technician sat down beside Pete. "Hi, Pete. Remember me? I came down to see you on your first day on the mess decks." He leaned forward on the table. "I'm Robert W. Washington, III. My Chief sent me to see you about joining OE Division. It's an excellent division with little or no duty and lots of benefits."

Pete knew it was a good division, he had been in OE on the *Kingston.*

"The Operations Electronics Division is starving for help, and you're the first person to come aboard ship in four months who even knows what an ET is."

Pete had not had a lot of wonderful experiences as an Electronics Technician striker, and for *that* reason, he was not in a hurry to join them.

"Pete." Washington had a crooked grin on his face. "You've been down here on this mess deck for a whole week. You should be getting tired of scrubbing and cleaning up after people. I've got a chit in my back pocket. All you have to do is sign it and you'll be an ET this afternoon."

"I'm sorry, Bob," Pete said, sympathetically. "But, mess cooking isn't bad. I work four days and get three days off. Now that's good duty. The work is hard, but someone has to do it, and besides I like the work."

In frustration, Washington got up. "Pete," he pleaded, "we've got a work load that would choke a horse. Half of the division is on leave. The other half is away at school, and there are only five of us to take care of the entire ship's problems. Most of the problems are communications issues. Radios and like that. I'm a radar tech not a com tech." The young man was practally in tears. "Personnel said you were a communications technician. Can't you see we need your help?" He started to walk away.

"Bob!" Pete spoke to his back. "I'll be up when I finish my shift."

Washington spun around, joyful surprise crossing his face as his hand reached for his back pocket.

"I'm not joining your division." Pete waved his hand. "I'll just be up to help out."

Pete had just started back on his newspaper when Booker again raised his eyebrows indicating someone was behind him. Pete turned to find a tall, thin, sharp looking black man. The stripes on the left sleeve of his undress blue jumper indicated he was a First Class Storekeeper. The fact that he had blues on, meant he was either an office worker or he was coming off in-port watch duty.
"I'm SK1 Lee." The Petty Officer extended his hand to Pete. "The Supply Officer, Commander Webster, would like to see you right away."

"Oh boy, Pete." Mats piped up. "You're in trouble now. Webster's a real hellcat. He gets his jollies by eating enlisted men for breakfast."

"Thanks a lot!" Pete smirked, throwing the open newspaper at Matts as he rose to follow the Petty Officer.

When the two men entered the well-staffed Supply Office, all work seemed to stop. It was dead quiet. All eyes were on the newcomers. Pete's eyes ranged around the room as he followed Petty Officer Lee toward the back of the large office.

So this is Supply. I remember Mom telling me that Bill is a Second Class StoreKeeper. If he likes it so much after all these years, this is the place for me, thought Pete.

Along the wall next to the door, there were three sets of huge loose-leaf books like one might see at an auto parts store. But, each of these books was twelve feet long, each on a separate shelf, one above the other. There was a table with a five-inch deep insert running the entire length of the left wall. This table was filled with cards. One sailor was posting information to these from small chits. There were six gray metal desks, set strategically around the large office. Against the back wall under an open porthole was the only wooden desk in the office. A shiny brass nameplate stood on the desk, "Lieutenant Commander Webster, Supply Officer." Lee and Pete popped tall as they got to the front of the desk. "Sir, this is Seaman Peterson," reported SK1 Lee as he slid into a chair behind a gray metal desk near the wall.

"Very well, Lee. Thank you," the officer said, laying down his pencil and picking up the menu Pete had typed. "Did you type this?"

"Yes, sir. I did," Pete replied. This line of questioning was puzzling to Pete. Perhaps it was against regulations to help the Commissary Storekeeper.

"Peterson, I'd like you to accept an assignment to the S1 Division. We need Storekeepers with good typing skills. If you accept my offer, you can count on having your third class crow within two months provided you study." He placed a chit in front of Pete for his signature. "We'll have you off the mess decks within the hour. What do you say?"

"I'd like to finish out the day if you don't mind, sir. I feel like there are people counting on me." Pete leaned over and began to sign the chit. This seemed as good a place as any on the friendly ship, even though he enjoyed the mess decks, too.

"Are you the spud king the whole crew is talking about?" asked Lt. Commander Webster.

"I guess I am," Pete said as he stood. "I don't know what the big deal is though."

"I'll tell you what the deal is," said the officer. "Captain Hamblin is bucking for the rarely awarded rank of Commodore. I figure if he makes a good impression on the Admiral at dinner tonight, he'll be promoted within six months. There are a lot of politics in this Navy, you know."

Ha, that's for sure! Pete thought as he smiled to himself, remembering some of the back-stabbing politics he had seen.

As Pete walked back to the mess decks, he felt confident he had made the right decision. Now, he really did have a home.

Approaching the main mess deck double doors, Pete could not help noticing the door was flanked on either side by two Shore Patrolmen in full dress blues, white helmet, duty belt and leggings. They carried eighteen inch night-sticks on their left side and holstered .45 pistols on their right side.

You can bet there's an Admiral within twenty paces of these two guys, thought Pete as he stepped over the sill of the watertight door and headed down the passageway to the spud locker.

The meal was winding down as Pete finished his clean up.

A familiar voice came to him from the passageway. "Spud King, you in there?" It was Captain Hamblin.

"Yes, sir!" Pete said, dropping his dishrag on the counter and turning around at attention. The large man in the door was not Captain Hamblin, he wore two silver stars on his khaki collar.

"Commissaryman Moon, sure can cook beans, but I hear you had a little something to do with the great meal this evening." The large, gray haired man smiled and reached out his right hand. "Congratulations on a job well done."

By reflex, Pete took the officer's hand. For a moment he was reminded of the time he met John Wayne in Moab. Wayne's comment was, "You shake hands like an Indian pumping a well." The comment later appeared as a line in the movie *Commancheros*. Pete held a firm grip as he shook the Admiral's hand – *two shakes -- that's all.* "Thank you, sir."

The Admiral and his entourage was gone, but Pete just stood there, gripped by wonder, excitement, amazement-- *this was just too cool!*

"I'd say your last day in the galley was a successful one," Moon said, as he stepped through the spud locker door. "So, what you gonna do? Go get drunk and try to figure out if it really was the Admiral."

Pete shook his head and came down off of his cloud. "No, but thanks for reminding me. I do have to be somewhere as soon as I can get a shower and change into dungarees. I promised the ETs I'd come and help them this evening."

After working on equipment until twenty-one hundred, Pete and the two other young men took a break. Washington and an ETNSN named Albright had worked with Pete all evening to get several of the ship's entertainment televisions working.

"This is great, Pete!" exclaimed Washington, slapping Pete on the back. "We sure appreciate all your help!"

The door to the shop opened and ET Chief Burns stepped in. He eyed the four TV sets ready to go out. A broad smile crossed his face. "Looks like you boys've been working hard."

"We couldn't have done it without Pete's help," said Washington. "He's a great TV repairman."

The Chief slid into a chair at the table to join the other three men having coffee. "Why don't you come join us, Pete?" Chief Burns asked. "You'd sure have a good home here."

"Thanks Chief, but I signed the chit this afternoon," Pete said. "I have a home. I joined the S1 Division. I'm going to strike for Storekeeper."

The Chief looked a little disappointed. "You know, the average time in grade for Second Class in the Storekeeper rate is fourteen years. But, if you were an ET, you'd have Second Class stripes in two years."

"S-1 has a First Class named Lee who wears only two four year service stripes on his left sleeve," argued Pete.

"You're right, but Lee is unusually smart," said the Chief, standing. "Just remember, if you decide you don't like your new home, you're always welcome in the ET Shop,"

Chief Burns gave a quick wink and walked from the compartment. Pete knew he was surrounded by friends here in the OE Division and looked forward to his new home in the S-1 Division.

Chapter 15

On Being a Petty Officer

The next day, the *USS Blue Island Sound* changed its anchorage from the 32nd Street Pier to Naval Air Station, North Island. NAS North Island was a fitting place for a seaplane tender to tie up. The ship had an excellent berth. It was only a few yards from a small ferry the crew called the 'nickel snatcher' as well as close to the Enlisted Men's Club.

On this facility, Pete discovered all the base services were handy. The nickel snatcher was the civilian operated, high speed motor launch which ran from the NAS North Island landing to the foot of Harbor Boulevard in San Diego. North Island was not really an island, but a long jetty of land called the Coronado Peninsula. The crew members could easily catch a bus into town but the trip was almost an hour longer than if they jumped aboard the nickel snatcher.

"It's funny, how they call the ferry a 'nickel snatcher,'" Pete said, looking up from his typewriter. "It costs fifty cents."

"I'll bet, at some time in the past, it had cost only a nickel and that's where the name came from," SK1 Lee said.

Pete was welcomed into the S1 Division with open arms by all hands. SK1 Lee was a particularly good boss. He set right to work grooming Pete for the SK3 exam he would have to take within three months. Robert E. Lee was a very conscientious leading Petty Officer and personally undertook Pete's tutelage. He was going to make good on his statement about Pete being a Third Class Storekeeper within ninety days.

During his third week in the division, Pete went to Lee and got permission to go back to the X Division and sign up his friend, Ted Winston. Ted was quite happy to get into S1; "Yahoo!" he yelled out, slapping Pete on the back. Ted was assigned to GSK, the ship's main storeroom and control center of all stores aboard the ship. GSK was under the control of a recently promoted Storekeeper Chief by the name of Wilks. Although Wilks was in charge by name and military rank, he was only a figurehead for a Third Class by the name of Bagzendel.

This little man who could easily pass as Red Skelton's twin brother, with his balding head and round shiny nose, was comical and fun to be around. And yet, there seemed to be a darker side -- a side not readily visible. Pete quickly discovered Bags used GSK for his personal as well as Navy business. From GSK, this happy little man ran the ship's largest slush fund and other racketeering functions such as crap games and card games.

Generally, one would think an underworld figure would be disliked. Bags, as the crew called him, was well liked by all hands. He didn't participate in the military or work functions of the division; he was just there. No one seemed to mind or perhaps they didn't notice him. Since Ted liked the little man and liked working in GSK, Pete didn't worry.

Pete was assigned to the stock control cardex in the Supply Office. There were six SKs in the office all together. SK1 R. E. Lee was at the first desk and handled all of the administrative duties. Pete was at the cardex and handled the locating of stock. SKSN Dave Vickers ran the massive parts catalog section.

SK3 John Maynard handled the ship's budget or OPTAR, as the chief accountant. Seaman Charlie Whipple was the Supply Officer's Yeoman and took care of all of the Supply Officer's secretarial requirements as well as typing requisitions for merchandise. Storekeeper Master Chief T. A. Paul, the first E9 rate Pete had ever seen, had his desk in the back of the office near the Supply Officer.

Master Chief Paul was also the senior enlisted man aboard ship. He was responsible for the administration of S1 Division. There were also two officers in the office, Lieutenant Commander Webster, Supply Officer, and Ensign George, the S1 Division Officer.

Since Pete didn't have any particular reason for going on the beach with the guys, he spent many evening hours working in the Supply Office or helping out in the ET Shack. Pete really did enjoy his work, and there was always something to do. If Pete got bored with work, he could always read something, and Lee always made sure he had more than enough to read. Pete had completed the two extension courses for advancement in less than two weeks. Military Requirements for Petty Officer 3&2 was easy, but the Storekeeper 3&2 course was not. When Pete finished, he turned it in to Personnel, but he did not totally understand it. He just tried to memorize as fast as he could, because Lee would spend hours drilling him.

One evening, during a memorization drill, Lee and Pete heard the Supply Office door open. It was Storekeeper Seaman Ditka. Pete rolled his eyes at Lee. Ditka was an antagonist and made it clear that he should work in the office and Pete should be in GSK. After all, he was the Storekeeper 'A' School graduate, a designated Seaman and Pete was the know-nothing Seaman off the mess decks.

"Hi, guys," Ditka said, lifting his square chin. He closed the door and plopped down in Chief Paul's chair. Ditka was a large man with dark hair and hazel eyes. His 'better than thou' attitude caused everyone to be cautious of him. "You'd better get hot, Pete, if you're going to be rated in the first increment. You know, if you get rated in the second increment, you'll be in line for a job back on the mess decks again." He leaned back and the leather chair groaned. "Muggs is going to retire, and S1 has to send a Third Class or higher down there to replace him.

"The way I see it, it'll be you or me. Probably you. I'm an 'A' School graduate, so I'm assured of being rated on the first increment," he said. As he stood and started for the door, the chair creaked in relief. "I think I'll go down to the forward mess deck and watch the evening movie." He paused, with an over-the-shoulder snear, the door half open. "We'll see you at the test tomorrow, Pete!"

Lee looked hard at Pete, a twinkle in his large round eyes, a subtle smirk across his shiny black face. "Don't you worry, Pete. You will be fine. The test is nowhere near as hard as those guys in GSK would lead you to believe. The only reason most of them haven't passed it is because they're too lazy to apply themselves or they lack a skill called reading."

The next day, a third of the enlisted men aboard ship were assembled on the main mess deck to take tests for advancement in rate. Pete could feel nervous perspiration on his face as his eyes darted around the large spacious room to see if he recognized anyone. There was Alphie L. Johnston, the 'Pooh Bear,' an Aviation Storekeeper striker who had graduated from 'A' school, and there was Chip Dale who had graduated from ET A school. Yep, then there was Pete, an unschooled, undesignated Seaman, trying to grow up to be a Storekeeper Third Class.

Master Chief Paul was one of the proctors, handing out the tests. He set the white-covered leaflet in front of Pete, the bold letters SK3 stared up from the clean surface. Pete's stomach churned as the next proctor handed him a pencil. Chief Paul moved to the front of the mess deck getting everyone's attention. "You have your tests. Begin."

Pete's heart jumped as he picked up the shaking pencil, took a deep breath and opened the booklet. He read the first question with resolve. *It's too late to give up now.*

Pete completed his test in a couple of hours, with surprising ease. He only had to reason out a couple of questions he could not answer with confidence.

Pete was back at his desk in the Supply Office, catching up requisitions from the morning when Ditka and Lee came in. "Pete," said Lee, "you don't have to work today. The Captain has declared the rest of the day to be Rope Yarn Sunday. You can go on the beach or do whatever you'd like, but you don't have to work."

"He probably feels he needs the work," Ditka said. "I turned in my test and went to the Geedunk for a Coke before Pete here put his pencil down." Ditka dropped into the chair next to Pete. "You know, Pete, there were some questions on the test I didn't even know." He fidgeted with a pencil. "I think all the crap about electronics supply should be left off the third class test. I can see it for second or the first class test, but it just isn't right to have it on the third class test. What do you think?"

Pete felt the urge to stab Ditka's intellect. His heart began to pound, like the pre-seismic rumblings of an earthquake, a Richter eight to be sure. *Might not be smart in the long run. Maybe I should cool down until the test results are in.* "I used to be an ET striker, so a lot of those questions were very easy; it's the rest that worry me." Pete turned back to his typewriter and resumed his work.

A month later, Ditka and Pete stood across the passageway from the Personnel Department bulletin board as a First Class Yeoman posted the results. Pete stood back against the far bulkhead, giving everyone else their chance to see how they had done. Pete felt weak and wasn't sure he wanted to look. *I guessed at too many of the answers. I tried to answer with common sense rather than knowledge.*

Ditka was now at the board, his finger making two passes up and down the rows of names. The crowd had dwindled down so there were only eight sailors present. Pete stood stiffly listening to the groans of failure and the shouts of success.

"Crap!" Ditka roared as he smashed a large fist onto the list of names.

Pete turned and started to walk away. *If the glorious 'A' School graduate didn't make it, why should I bother to look?*

Pete stopped for a drink at the scuttle butt across from the Personnel Office. The Pooh Bear, his little roly-poly AK buddy, came up jubilantly slapping Pete on the back. "Congratulations, Pete," he shouted, his round face covered from ear to ear with a smile. Pete turned his head to see Alphie's face and got squirted in the eye.

"What do you mean?" Pete sputtered. "I haven't seen the list. Am I on it?"

"Are you on it?" Alphie laughed. "You are the first name on the list, buddy!" He grabbed Pete's sleeve and pulled him to the bulletin board. He held a chubby finger under the first name on the list, and read it aloud to Pete.

"B. Peterson, SK3. How do you like that, my friend?" Then he ran his finger down the list and stopped at his name, A. Johnston, AK3.

"Hot dog!" Pete screeched. "I made it! Now, I can say I know something about being a Storekeeper." Pete could not contain himself and did a little jig around Pooh Bear. "Now, I won't feel like an outsider anymore!"

As the two men walked down the passageway toward the Supply Office, Alphie turned to Pete. "I guess you can put that smart aleck, Ditka, in his place. Even if he gets rated on the second increment, you'll still be senior to him. He'll have to shut up and listen when you talk."

"Thanks, Pooh, but you don't have to make such a big deal out of it. All it really means, is you and I will get out of mess cooking and laundry detail assignments. But, we'll also get an increase in pay!"

As the two new Petty Officers entered the Supply Office, applause filled the room. There was a cake in the middle of Pete's desk, and Moon was lighting three candles on it. There was a handshake from the Master Chief. Lee stood next to Moon holding up a brand new blue chambray shirt with a third class crow sewn on the left sleeve. Pete swallowed hard and blinked back tears.

SK1 Lee handed Pete the shirt and put his arm around his shoulders and whispered into his ear. "On being a Petty Officer. You must lead and teach your men. Never push or abuse them."

Chapter 16

Underway for WESTPAC

Chief Paul stood rigid as he looked down the ranks of the S1 Division at Quarters For Muster. Twenty-six Storekeepers and Aviation Storekeepers, all present. "Gentlemen, we'll be getting underway for WESTPAC tomorrow. We'll be in the Western Pacific Theater for six months.

"I'll expect every man jack of you to be ready to 'turn to' as soon as the ship hits the breakwater." The grey haired Chief Petty Officer walked down the line, meeting each set of eyes as he spoke. "I'll have the underway billet board posted. This division has the responsibility of standing all the bridge plotter watches. You know your underway jobs, and I'm confident we won't have any screw-ups." He gave a right hand salute, which was quickly returned by all. "Division, dismissed."

At 0900 the next morning, the brows and gangways would be pulled away for the last time stateside. Pete faced a tour that would not culminate in constant danger of hostile enemy action as had his tour on the *Kingston*. He might even get to see something other than the jungles of South Vietnam, though the war zone, he was certain, was their ultimate destination. At least, he would not have to sleep in elephant grass filled with enemy infiltrators or fear stalking tigers in the dead of night.

Right after reveille, all hands changed into dress uniforms for leaving port and went topside to the seaplane deck to visit friends and loved ones who were coming aboard at the afterbrow to bid them a fond farewell.

Pete marveled as he drifted through the crowds of people. *There are almost more civilians aboard than sailors. I didn't realize sailors had such large families!*

At 0830, a short veer of the boatswain's pipe, and the word was passed. "All visitors are requested to leave the ship." This was followed by a long veer. "Now, set the Special Sea and Anchor Detail for getting underway." Designated personnel manned the lines and prepared to cast the ship free from the pier.

Some of the sailors walked down the brow with their families for a last 'good-bye' kiss. One Pete noticed, in particular, was Bill Mackey, an SK3 from GSK. This was the third cruise for Mac, and his wife cried just as hard every time. Mac's three-year-old daughter was more interested in walking to the edge of the pier, throwing small stones into the water and worrying her parents.

Another short veer echoed from the boatswain's pipe. "All hands lay aboard and man the rails." It only took one call to get the crew to do this. The rail is the best place to get a 'last look.' The crew lined the perimeter of the ship, standing against the lifelines waving their last good-bye as all lines were cast free from the pier. A long blast on the ship's fog horn signalled the ship was 'Underway.' Three small tugboats quickly filled the gap between the ship and the pier pushing the ship further out into Mission Bay.

"Now, shift colors. The ship is underway," the Boatswain's Mate called over the ship's 1MC PA system. The American flag was lowered at the fantail pole and another was raised to the highest point on the main mast.

As the distance between the ship and the pier grew, all hands, especially those who were superstitious, took part in one of the oldest traditions of the Navy. Each sailor's white hat, with the brim rolled down, was cast, like a frisbee, toward the pier with a flick of the wrist. Old maritime lore says, if the white hat lands on the pier, the sailor will be back. If the white hat goes into the water, that is a bad omen. Pete knew this crew would be back -- Not one hat missed its mark.

The people on the pier were picking up the hats like kids on an Easter egg hunt. Pete's hat and the hat of his division mate, AK3 Cagney, was picked up by a lovely lady about eighty-five years old. For just a moment Pete imagined his mother on the pier bidding him farewell and picking up his hat. *I'll have to make a point of writing mom tonight and let her know her little boy is okay,* Pete thought.

As the ship passed the breakwater and headed for open sea off Point Loma, the ship's 1MC came alive with a long whistle of the Boatswain's pipe, "Now. All Hands Turn To. Commence ship's work!" Pete cast a last look at the lovely San Diego harbor and turned to go below.

The second day at sea, the mercury fell to a damp 48 degrees, and there was a brisk wind of 14 knots blowing from port to starboard all day. Low clouds cut the visibility from fourteen miles to five.

Pete stood the 0400 to 0800 'plotter watch.' Spray and gray seas splashed against the windows of the bridge, 60 feet from the water line. Pete watched a port window, and thought, *It's like watching a washer at a laundromat.*

On the third day at sea, Pete was amazed at the contrast in the weather. The sea was like a giant inkwell, solid purple and very still.

Pete had the midwatch on the bridge again from midnight to 0400. At 0130, the Combat Information Center hailed Pete over the sound powered phone system, "Pete, this is CIC. We have a 'skunk,' dead in the water, range - fifteen miles." Pete recognized the term 'skunk' for floating object and reported to the OOD.

It was not long before the lookouts reported visual contact. As the *Blue Island Sound* drew closer, the Officer Of the Deck focused the telescope on the wing of the bridge and could clearly see it was a Russian trawler with its nets out. The area covered by the nets was marked with lighted buoys.

That's quite a place to fish, Pete thought. *Eight-hundred miles from nowhere? In the middle of the night? And by sheer coincidence, right on the exact course the Blue Island Sound has been following for two days.*

Rules of the road required *Blue Island Sound* to take evasive action, so the OOD gave the order. The 'Blue Goose' passed the trawler at three hundred yards to port.

What a joke! Thought Pete sarcastically. *A combat vessel going around a trawler is like a bear edging around a porcupine.*

The next day, Pete was called to the desk of Ensign George. The S1 Division Officer was an Annapolis graduate who did not fit the traditional military mold. He had chosen to become a Supply Corps Officer instead of a Line Officer which made him all right in Pete's book. Although Pete had been in the division for only three months, he felt like a charter member.

Pointing at the chit in front of him, "I'm going to reassign you and SK3 Ditka," he said. Pete's eyebrows raised. Mr. George gave a soft chuckle. "Since Muggs retired and our Electronics Store-keeper Stephens left the ship before we sailed, the empty billets have to be filled." He laid a pen on the chit and slid it toward Pete. "I'm going to send Ditka to the S2 Division as Commissary Storekeeper. I'm assigning you to the Electronics Supply Office.

Pete, with your electronics background, you'll be a great help, to both the ETs and to our stock control problem in ESO."

Pete was thrilled, and although he didn't think he had the experience or the time in grade to get such a terrific job – here it was. He would have his own office! He would be his own boss! Ditka, on the other hand, would be working for a very temperamental Commissary Chief.

Pete signed the chit and Ensign George handed him the keys to the office on the 02 level. "I'm sure you'll do us a good job. But, there's quite a bit of stock to be put away before we reach the Philippines, our first port of call. You should get right to it."

"Thank you, sir!" Pete smiled as he took the keys and shook his Division Officer's hand. "I'll keep ESO in tip-top shape, sir."

As Pete left the office, he looked at the keys. Excitement rushed through him, like the first time he got the keys to the family car. Pete had made good friends with the ETs while the ship was in port, and now he would be working with them every day. Perfect as far as he was concerned. He tossed the keys into the air and snatched them back with exhilaration. ESO was just down the passageway, twenty feet from the ET Shop, across the hall from the Chief ET's office.

He skipped up the stairs two at a time, to the 02 level and burst into the ET shop. "Hey!" Pete exclaimed, shoving the door back against its stop. He threw open his arms like a performer on a stage. "Guess who's your new ESO Storekeeper?" He was answered with a round of applause, pats on the back and a fresh hot cup of coffee. Pete had never been in the ESO Office before, so the whole gang accompanied him as he turned the key and pushed the door open. Across from the doorway, twelve feet in, stood a metal desk against the far bulkhead. On both sides of the small stockroom were rows and rows of aluminum parts drawers, from the deck to within two feet of the overhead. The desk was covered with mail bags and small envelopes full of parts. The entire floor of the compartment was covered with boxes and bags of parts, leaving no space to walk. "What a mess!" Pete said, his mouth agape.

"A little more than you bargained for, Pete?" ET2 Washington chided, nudging him from behind.

"Mr. George said he wanted this stockroom shipshape by the time we get to the PI. I'm not sure I can get the job done in a month of twenty-four hour days." Pete said.

Washington, who had been promoted to ET2 at the same time Pete was promoted to SK3, stepped past Pete and picked up a handful of padded manila envelopes from the desk. "It seems to me, when we were way behind in our work a few months ago, a Storekeeper came along and helped us out, and now my friend, the tables are turned. I've got plenty of extra time on my hands, and I can help you."

A chorus of "Me too!" echoed from the unseen group of men behind Pete. He could not believe the support rallying around him. Over the next few days, Pete developed a habit of working until midnight, showering in the Fox, G and W head before turning in and getting up in time for late breakfast at 0730. Several days passed as Pete got the last of the stock into its proper location and the Electronics Supply Office cleaned up.

It was after 2330, almost midnight when a knock came on the door of his office. Ted Winston pushed the door open. "Hey, Pete. I was just going up to relieve the bridge plotter watch, by way of the weather decks and guess what's dead ahead of us?" He waved a left hand in a 'come on' motion and disappeared toward the weather deck. Pete jumped to his feet and followed, literally being dragged by his curiosity. Pete stood against the life-line of the 02 level and strained his eyes into the darkness to make out what all the excitement was about. About three miles ahead lay a trawler, dead in the water with nets out, and marker lights on.

It was obvious this Russian ship was with the other trawler they had passed a week earlier. The crew had heard of harassment by Russian destroyers and nuclear-powered submarines. The word was, the Russians would cut the path of a ship in an effort to get them to change course.

They probably feel they are helping the war effort of their allies in communist North Vietnam by holding up or delaying anything American, Pete thought.

Ted turned to Pete. "You know, this can't be accidental. It's got to be orchestrated by the Kremlin. I guess those communist buggers just don't like us."

The *Blue Island Sound* changed course once again to avoid hitting the nets of the fishing vessel. The US Navy ship was closed up tight for the night, with no lights showing except for the running lights on the mast, red on the port and green on the starboard side. The trawler had people on deck taking pictures, even in the dark. It was obvious this trawler was not fishing.

Rumors concerning shipping harassment by both the Russian Navy and their commercial fleet caused tension to rise like heat in a pressure cooker for the next few days throughout the ship's company. It was reported that a Russian submarine had actually been hit by a merchantman flying the US colors near Singapore.

Several days passed, and the crew calmed down. As Pete stood his favorite watch, the midwatch as plotter on the bridge, he was behind the large plexiglass board, plotting the contacts sent up to him by CIC or by the lookouts.

The ship had just crossed the International Date Line and was now in the eastern hemisphere. As part of the traditional International Date Line initiation, Pete and Dave Vickers had their heads shaved on top, leaving a full growth of hair around the ears, making them both look like Bagsendell or little old men. The Captain was quick to react to this new look. "Before I allow you to go on liberty, your hair will be the same length all over you head."

Naturally this resulted in the 'Q' ball look. Their heads were shaved bald.

Pete looked at the backside of the clear plastic board on which he wrote the information given to him by CIC and the lookouts. The board started with a dot in the middle representing the ship and had circles around the center, every few inches in a widening pattern indicating distance from the ship in hundreds of yards. Each circle indicated distance to a target in the water, which was called a "skunk," or in the air, which was called a "bogie." Pete marked the contacts on the lighted plastic surface with a yellow grease pencil and wrote the actual yardage information backwards so the officer of the deck could quickly read the information being fed to the bridge.

Pete talked to CIC and the lookouts through the sound-powered telephones he wore. The phones were fashioned in such a manner as to leave his hands free except when he spoke, then he would depress the button on the mouthpiece, which stood up from a breastplate fastened around his neck by a strap. He listened through the two padded ear muffs of his headset.

"Port lookout, bridge. How is it going up there?" Pete released the talk button.

"Bridge, port lookout. Pete, it's Kinghorn from 2nd Division," a strong voice came back. "Looks like another quiet night at sea. Aren't we supposed to meet up with the Australian and Canadian Navies out here somewhere for a SEATO exercise?"

"Yes, we are." It was the voice of the Radarman watching the scopes in CIC. "We'll be joining up with the British, too. We'll complete a month of exercises, and then we'll make a port call, but we won't know what port until the Admiral decides, and the Admiral is aboard the *USS Pine Island Sound*. "Whatever port the Admiral chooses will be where we'll change the flag to the *Blue*

Island Sound. You can bet it'll be a fun port, because it'll be the Piney Maru's last port before heading back stateside."

"What do you mean, change the flag?" Pete asked, releasing the button on his mouth piece.

"Changing the flag means taking the admiral aboard our ship," came the voice from the Combat Information Center. "He'll be aboard the *Blue Island Sound* and we'll fly his two star flag from our starboard yardarm."

"Bridge, port lookout." Kinghorn's voice sounded agitated. Chit-chat was cut short. "I have a large reddish light dead in the water thirty degrees to the port bow. Range, 14 miles."

Pete touched his yellow crayon to the lighted plotting board and marked the spot close to the horizon the lookout had reported. At the same time, he made his report to the OOD. "Sir, port lookout reports we have a skunk bearing three zero degrees on the port bow. Range, fourteen miles."

The Officer Of the Deck, Lieutenant Junior Grade Hunsaker, was an easy-going guy with a lot of smarts about running a ship. He was the Fox Division Officer (fire control) and could be trusted with any command decision. "What the ...?" he said, looking at the plotting board. He rushed out to the port wing of the bridge and turned to Pete. "I can't see a thing out there, Pete. Ask your starboard lookout if he sees anything, and what about CIC?"

"Starboard lookout, bridge. Do you see the red light? CIC, can you confirm?" Pete repeated into the rubber cup of his mouthpiece. "Bridge, starboard lookout. You won't believe it, Pete. I see it, too. It's right where Kinghorn said it was. It looks like a ..." There was hesitation. "It looks like the top of a flying saucer!"

Pressing his talk button, Pete spoke. "Starboard lookout, bridge. Do you want me to tell the Officer Of the Deck, it's a UFO?"

The Boatswain's Mate's voice from starboard lookout post rang in Pete's ears. "Tell him whatever you want, Pete. I can only tell you, I see what I see."

"Bridge, CIC. I don't have anything on the scope. I think someone up there is full of it."

Pete turned to the OOD. "Sir, both lookouts report sighting a large red light dead ahead off the port bow, but CIC cannot confirm."

For a good twenty minutes, Lieutenant Junior Grade Hunsaker paced back and forth from one wing of the bridge to the other, stopping on the port wing each time to study the horizon through his binoculars.

Pete could see the large red light looming like a red fire ball on the horizon. It sat motionless on the water as the ship grew ever closer. The rest of the sky was an eerie pitch black. Pete's heart skipped and the palms of his hands became cold and clammy.

"CIC, bridge. Can you confirm a skunk dead ahead? You must be picking up something," Pete pleaded.

"Listen, Pete. I went out on the weather deck on the port side for a second, and I see what you're all seeing, but I can't give you a fix on the darned thing. I just don't have it on the radar," said the CIC Radarman.

Lieutenant Junior Grade Hunsaker now stopped in the middle of his pacing and looked at the Quartermaster Of The Watch. "Call the Captain from his sea cabin." He pointed to the Boatswain's Mate Of the Watch. "Sound General Quarters."

The veer of the boatswain's pipe cut through the warm night air as the alarm klaxon brought the ship to life with a loud chilling *bong... bong... bong*. "Now, General Quarters!! General Quarters! This is not a drill! All hands, man your battle stations!" commanded the Boatswain's Mate of the Watch into the ship's 1MC system.

The Quartermaster reappeared on the bridge saying, "The Captain's on the bridge. Attention on deck!"

"As you were," said the Captain as he stepped through the open doorway from his sea cabin. "What have we got here, Mr.

Hunsaker?" he asked, placing his binoculars to his eyes and peering at the red half-ball shape growing ever closer.

"We don't know what we have, sir," reported the young officer. "Our lookouts have a visual, but we can't seem to get it on the radar."

"That's quite the phenomenon," said the Captain. "Visible to the naked eye but invisible to radar. Just to be prepared, tell gunnery to train on that thing."

"Request permission to come on the bridge, sir," came a voice from the port door of the bridge. It was Pete's old friend AG2 Newstead from Treasure Island. He too, had been promoted another grade since coming aboard ship. "Sir," he said, rendering the Captain a salute. "I think if you'll check with the Chief Meteorologist down in Areography, he'll tell you the red ball is the planet Mars, rising."

The Quartermaster Of The Watch was just hanging up his telephone. "It's true, sir. I just spoke to the Weather Officer, and he confirms what Newstead just said."

The Captain burst into laughter and slapped the younger officer on the back. "Secure from General Quarters and take the Deck and the Con, Mr. Hunsaker. I'm going to bed."

"I have the Deck and the Con, sir," said the younger officer sheepishly as the Captain stepped from the bridge.

Pete thought of Mars, not as a planet but as the Roman god of war. It had suddenly called the ship's company to prepare to join battle. *Now that's ironic!* Pete thought.

Two days later, as all hands stood along the rail at quarters for entering port, the *Blue Island Sound* was making its first WESTPAC stop of the cruise. The ship was pulling into Subic Bay in the Philippines. Beyond the gate of the base lay the famous port city of Olongapo.

AK3 Cagney elbowed Pete to get his attention. The division was at 'parade rest' in formation, so Pete turned his head slightly to see

Cagney's long thin face. A smile erupted as Cagney whispered, "Look aft. There's your old boat."

Looking back toward the starboard quarter, like a giant post card picture, the *USS Kingston* was crossing the breakwater and entering the channel to Subic Bay. She too, had just begun her WESTPAC cruise.

Chapter 17

In Port, Subic Bay

The jungle seemed to glide by as the *USS Blue Island Sound* cleared the narrows and moved into Subic Bay proper. Pete remembered the jungle in South Vietnam, but this was different. Sprays of huge tall palm trees lined the rocky shore, while other great trees hung heavy with leafy vines. Bright, colorful flowers and birds seemed to be everywhere like an orchestra warming up its instruments. *This is breathtaking!* Pete thought.

The early morning sun spread its warmth across Pete's face as the crew stood Quarters For Entering Port. He looked out in awe because this was his first time in the Philippines and he wanted to see as much as he could. He pressed against the wire rope handrail and gazed down at the still, clear, blue green water. He could easily make out coral on the bottom.

Jim Cagney nudged Pete. "Hey!" Cagney's face brightened, the smile he always wore was even bigger today. "Want to go on the beach? I've heard of a place called the White Hat Club that's supposed to be great fun."

"I don't care about the entertainment." Pete grinned and nudged Cagney back. "As long as they have cold beer, I'll be happy."

Jim was an Aviation Storekeeper Third Class. An 'A' School graduate who had received his Third Class crow the month after Pete and the Pooh Bear. The wiry Oklahoma college graduate was a lot of fun to be around.

Pete met Jim at the afterbrow as soon as the *Blue Island Sound* was tied to the pier. The Boatswain's Mate Of the Watch was just piping down 'Liberty Call.' It would be "Cinderella Liberty," meaning all hands had to be back aboard ship by midnight.

Jim and Pete caught the first base transport they saw, which took them to the front gate of the base. The gate stood next to a small creek and as they walked from the base they had to cross a bridge to get to the city of Olongapo.

Pete flipped open his wallet, showing his ID card to the Marine gate guard as they passed.

"Wow!" Pete flinched, his head drawing back as if to avoid the odor reaching his nostrils. "What's that stink?"

The Marine Lance Corporal at the gate roared with laughter. "This must be your first trip to Olongapo! That's the Olongapo River you smell." He pointed to the small stream. "This is how all the sewage in the city is transported to the sea." He slapped Pete on the shoulder. "You stay around here long enough, and you'll get used to it."

Jim and Pete hurried over the bridge, relieved that the air was better on the windward side. As they crossed, Pete looked down on the banks of the river where children were diving for coins tossed by passing sailors.

Pete watched one small boy, not more than six, dive from an old truck tire stuck in the mud, into the slow flowing, murky brown water for a silver coin. The boy came up with the coin held high in one hand as he jubilantly waved the other hand. It was fun for the sailors to watch the children dive and swim, but Pete doubted that anyone gave a thought to the health or safety of the children. For the moment, it was just a bright warm day with laughing children chasing coins.

A jeepnee driver grabbed Pete's arm as they reached the other side. "You fellows would like to go down town to a very nice club? Many beautiful girls. Two dollar."

"Okay!" Jim said, pulling Pete up the back step of the jeepnee to the bench seat across from him as he handed the driver two dollars in military pay certificates. There was no US currency allowed here, just MPC or the Filipino peso.

The driver sprang to his seat and cranked up the vintage jeep engine, and away they went.

"This is a pretty neat rig," said Pete, to no one in particular.
A senior Petty Officer sitting next to Jim answered Pete's comment. "The jeepnee is the most common form of transportation in the Philippine Islands. After the Second World War, there were thousands of jeeps left on the islands. The chassis were just extended, the back bench seats enlarged, turned to face each other, and a canopy put across the top for shade."

As they drove up the street to the main part of town, it was evident that the owners of these jeepnees were very proud of them. The little vehicles seen speeding all over had the most lavish paint jobs Pete had ever seen. *A custom car fan would go absolutely nuts looking at some of the detail work on these outfits.*

"We're here, Pete," said Jim as he stepped off the chrome bottom step and into the dirt street. "This is it, or so it seems."

Pete looked around as he stepped down, noticing the front of a building looking as though it were straight out of an old western movie. The sign above the swinging cafe door read 'Golden Girl Saloon.'

Pete had a momentary flashback of another dirt street and western-type setting in the village the ROK troops had burned, until his gaze focused on the other end of the street. Pete could easily make out the main gate of the Naval base. They had barely traveled six blocks.

Quite an expensive taxi ride, Pete thought as he ascended the wooden steps onto the boardwalk in front of the saloon.

Jim did not bother with the stairs. Instead, he sprang to Pete's side from the street. "We have just one purpose in being here, my friend!" Jim slapped Pete on the back. "We have to get rolling in the gutter, puking straight-up drunk! That's our mission for this day." The air-conditioned comfort of the building was welcoming as they entered the saloon. Although it was a bright early morning outside, inside, it was a cool quiet evening. A long bar ran along the far wall, as the cafe doors closed behind them. The main floor, except for the area in front of the bandstand, was crowded with tables and chairs. Along two walls, there were rows of heavily padded booths done in some kind of purple artificial leather.

The wall behind them was lined with a row of high bar stools and on each bar stool sat a young woman. The women were of all shapes and sizes, each with her own beckoning smile. They each wore a green brocade dress with a deep slit up the left side, reminiscent of the movie, "Suzie Wong." The diving necklines revealed more than Pete wanted to see.

Pete felt a small hand on his arm. "You like nice girl? Yes? Joe?" A very pretty, dark eyed girl smiled up at him.

He was certain this girl had not seen the Navy VD film the ship's crew had been shown on the way over. Pete had too many things to do and too much to see to be getting himself on medical restriction. Pete's face turned beet red as he gently pulled away, "No, thank you, honey," he said sincerely. "My friend and I have been at sea for a long time and we have some very serious drinking to take care of."

Jim and Pete found their way to a corner booth and ordered up two beers. Before long, a band was on the stage and the whole place was jumping. Soon, the place was packed. The fleet was in.

After the two young sailors had finished their eighth beer (or was it the twenty-eighth?), they stumbled into the street and realized this was definitely no place to be. It was dark and the only light came from the building fronts along the board walk. There was no traffic on the dirt street.

They discovered there was a bar almost every forty paces down the street as they headed for the base, and naturally, they had to stop and check the quality of each establishment's libations.

As they reached the corner of the last block, they came to a street vendor who was selling a nifty looking shishkebob on an eighteen-inch sliver of bamboo. The tiny man prepared the stuff over hot coals in a small hibachi barbecue. The smell was delicious! Pete's stomach growled with delight!

"What do you have there?" Pete demanded, bumping into the small table. "What's the price?" Pete didn't give him a chance to answer the first question.

"One dollar MPC," the man answered, handing Pete the large end of one of the sticks. Pete clumsily drew out a one dollar military pay certificate and gave it to the street vendor as he eyed this obvious gourmet's delight. The shishkebob was layered, meat and pineapple all the way up the stick.

Jim followed suit and the two men chewed, chatted, joked and carried on all the way back to the ship. It had been a fun liberty, one Pete would remember for a long time.

As they approached the afterbrow of their ship, they could see their own Chief Wilks from GSK had Officer Of the Deck duty for the enlisted brow. Jim had finished his barbecue and had both hands free so he was ahead of Pete. Pete was trying very hard to get his eaten before he boarded.

"Request permission to come aboard, sir!" Jim said, trying not to slur, saluting the Ensign on the fantail and turning back to the Chief with another salute.

"Permission granted," said Chief Wilks, returning Jim's salute. The Chief broke into laughter. "Pete! What are you doing with monkey meat?"

Pete's mouth hung open in mid chew -- he felt the stick slide from his hand as he leaned over the gangway lifeline to watch the stick plunge into the water. Suddenly, the pit of his stomach was trying to bounce off the roof of his mouth. The first piece of monkey meat was trying to follow the last into the bay.

"Oh! I'm gonna be..." Vomit sprayed from Pete's mouth and nose. The meat, followed by a rush of warm beer, reminded Pete of an out-of-control one and a half inch fire hose.

Pete didn't remember getting into his bunk, but at 0500 when Quarters For Leaving Port was sounded, he was still in his uniform. He stood Quarters For Leaving Port in a stupor. He seemed to be getting drunker and drunker with every passing minute. When the crew was excused from quarters, Pete went straight to his bunk. His fun liberty had backfired on him. Pete made a note not to drink quite so much in the future.

As Pete dropped into his bunk, he heard a moaning voice from across the berthing compartment. "Pete," called Cagney in a pitiful voice. "Did we ever find the White Hat Club? Did we have fun?"
"I'm not sure, Jim," Pete replied as he pulled his sheet up over his pounding head. The ship was in WESTPAC.

Chapter 18

War Games

It took Pete three days to start feeling like his old self as the ship steamed into the South China Sea. Bright rays of sunshine danced on the calm ocean. It was terrific weather for getting a tan or just lounging about on the weather decks as the crew relaxed and enjoyed the cruise.

Bong...Bong...Bong! The General Quarters klaxon throbbed its loud angry sound. Pete left the 02 level handrail where he had been watching a Light Guided Missile Cruiser take up a position about a half-mile away on the port quarter of the *Blue Island Sound*. It was obviously in 'escort' formation.

Pete reached his sound powered headset and had just put it on when the ship suddenly lurched hard to starboard. It was such a sharp turn that it tossed Pete across the office and into the port bulkhead. At that moment the collision alarm sounded, with its eerie hoot, hoot, hoot, like a screaming train out of control.

"Bridge, ESO, what's going on?" Pete demanded.

"ESO, Bridge. Relax, Pete," said the voice from the bridge. "We just took a torpedo to the port quarter, and the ship is being abandoned from the starboard side." The voice hesitated for a moment and began again. "Oh, by the way, Pete. You're dead! You and everyone on the port side up to the 02 level. Sorry!"

At that moment, Chip Dale pushed the door to Pete's office open. A large yellow sticker on the left pocket of his dungaree shirt read "CASUALTY." He carried another in his right hand.

"This is for you. You're out of action," he said plastering the adhesive sticker on the front of Pete's shirt. "Come on! Let's go watch the war."

Pete took off his headset and let it fall to the deck. He felt as though he was deserting his post. "Well, I guess if I'm dead, I can come."

The two friends stepped out onto the starboard 02 level weather deck and looked down toward the main deck. Life jacket clad men were rushing from all parts of the ship while men carrying stokes stretchers came up through the lower deck hatches. The wire baskets were occupied by men wearing the ominous yellow, "injured" tags.

"Look at that!" Chip said, pointing to a young Boatswains Mate standing next to a life raft rack, the discharge lanyard of a life raft wrapped around his left hand.

"He's not going to really..." Pete's comment was interrupted by the explosion that pushed the huge life raft off of its rack and plunged it into the ocean.

Pete and Chip watched, their mouths agape as the huge, twenty feet long, ten feet wide, four feet thick package splashed on the surface and went out of sight in the clear blue water.

"Aren't those things supposed to open up and pop back to the surface?" Pete gasped.

"They are indeed!" Chip said, pressing closer to the lifeline for a better look. "Those things have a shell in them that explodes like a depth charge after they get twelve feet deep. That thing is supposed to unfold and make a life raft forty feet long."

The Deck Officer, Lieutenant Gerber, was now on the scene. Pete could see by his gestures, he was chewing out the Seaman for releasing the raft. As soon as he realized that the raft was not coming up, he turned his ire on the Boatswain Mate Chief, with whom responsibility for the maintenance of the life raft lay.

Pete surmised that he and Chip were not the only observers to the fiasco. The ultimate responsibility lay with Lieutenant Gerber, the Deck Division Officer.

A short chirp of the Boatswain's pipe brought the 1MC to life. "Now, the Deck Officer to the Bridge!"

The *USS Blue Island Sound* and the surface vessels accompanying her were the blue navy and the submarine force was the green navy. Ships from many South East Asia Treaty Organization nations participated in the war game maneuvers. The *Blue Island Sound* assumed the stature of an aircraft carrier and was escorted by two British Destroyers and an Australian Light Guided Missile Cruiser.

Five days after the "Blue" pulled out of Subic Bay, she was joined by the Australian frigate, *HMAS Piedmont*. Two hours later, she was engaged in mock battle by a US nuclear-powered submarine and sunk! The Captain of the sub said he just bird-dogged the frigate on the chance she might be going to perform escort duty. After thirty-two days of war games, the *USS Blue Island Sound* had killed the sub twenty-one times and the submarine had destroyed the entire patrol squadron sixteen times.

Pete sat in ESO writing a letter to his mother, *I'm not sure I'd want to be in the fleet in the event of a shooting war involving submarines. I'm soo glad these are just war games.*

Chapter 19

Changing the Flag

War games were over and orders were received from the Commander Patrol Forces Pacific Fleet. Admiral Anderson was aboard the *USS Pine Island Sound,* but in a few days the *USS Blue Island Sound* would become the "flag ship" of the Commander Patrol Forces Pacific Fleet.

"Gentlemen," Captain Hamblin announced over the 1MC. "We've received orders to sail for Bangkok, Thailand."

The ship steamed up the Bangkok River for several hours before 'Quarters For Entering Port' was called. The river was wide and deep, with dark swirls of greenish brown. There was the usual array of sampans and junks moored along the bank. But, Pete was most fascinated by the World War Two surplus US and Japanese destroyers tied up here and there along the shore. The ships were nothing more than old rust buckets, and the people on them appeared to be dressed in civilian clothing. There were women aboard and laundry seemed to be hanging everywhere even though they flew the Thai national colors from the fantail.

"What's the story on those old tin cans?" Pete asked SK1 Lee.

"Don't laugh," Lee said. "That's the Royal Thia Navy. They have quite a problem with pirates along their coast and every once in a while those old ships go on patrol and blow up a few junks."

Pete squinted at his leader.

"Oh, I see! You mean the women on board," said Lee. "This is one of the few navies in the world where they allow the families of the officers and senior men to live aboard."

Pete shook his head and went back to watching the scenery flow by.

When the *USS Blue Island Sound* tied up, it was at an excellent mooring, a long narrow pier with the *USS Pine Island Sound* right along side. The *Blue Island* was actually moored against the *Pine Island*, on her outboard side. To go on the beach, the crew of the *Blue Island Sound* had to cross the seaplane deck of the *Pine Island*. The crew members of the *Pine Island* were yelling and jeering at the crew of the "Blue Goose" as they tied up. "Where have you been?" was the most common question. They had been in WESTPAC for seven months and their relief was thirty days late according to *their* schedule.

A working party was called away, and within six hours the transfer was complete. The Admiral (the Flag) and his personal staff, along with all the records of his command were transferred aboard the *USS Blue Island Sound*.

Captain Hamblin's voice sounded over the 1MC with an announcement about liberty. "Gentlemen, we will be in port for five days with minimum duty status. We will have three section liberty, so let's go out there and enjoy ourselves, but please remember, you are the ambassadors of your country. Conduct yourselves accordingly."

Pete would have the duty only one of the five days the ship would be in port, so, naturally he called AK3 Cagney at the Air

GSK Office. "Would you like to go on the beach with me, ol' bud?" He asked with a laugh. "We can make a point of not getting as drunk as we did in the Philippines."

"Okay." Cagney replied. "I've got a couple more merchandise orders to type up and get off on the wire for Yokosuka, then I'll meet you in the compartment. We can change and leave from there."

Pete had purchase orders for merchandise to take to the radio shack for transmission to the Naval Supply Center, Yokosuka, Japan. In less than a month the "Blue" would be making port there, and there would be a tremendous amount of stores to take aboard to replenish the stock used up.

Jim and Pete stopped by the Disbursing Office and changed their US currency for the Thai national currency called the 'baht' (pronounced bought). The exchange rate was twenty to one, making each baht worth a nickel.

The moment they hit the pier from the *Pine Island's* gang plank, they were assailed by a dozen taxi drivers. The cabbies apparently knew exactly what every American sailor wanted. They rattled off, in excellent English, the names of several bars, night clubs, and red light houses, the latter of which Doctor Vesper had told every crew member to avoid like the plague.

Pete stuck his right hand up in the air to silence the crowd. As the group quieted, Jim asked, "Who's familiar with the temples and the diamond market?"

Everyone stayed quiet, except one driver. "I'll show you around the city," he announced with great confidence.

The sailors followed their driver to his small car. As they started through the city, Pete noticed the meter, running as fast as the second hand on a clock. The figure on the meter was at nine point eight five when Pete finally spoke. "Those aren't dollars on the meter, are they?" Pete asked, remembering he paid two US dollars in Olongapo for a quarter of a mile ride.

"Oh, no," replied the driver in a cheerful tone. "I can see you two are very unusual men, so I will give you a very good tour of the whole city at a very good price." He turned and smiled at Pete, sitting in the front seat beside him. The inflection of the driver's speech sounded as if he were singing a tune, going up and down the scales. "I will show you the whole city, except for the race tracks and have you back to your ship or to the bar of your choice by eight PM for only 200 baht."

Jim leaned over the seat, putting his hand on Pete's shoulder and gave him a pat. "Sounds like a great deal to me, Pete."

"Okay. We'll take it," Pete said. "What is this about race tracks?"

"We have two major horse tracks here in Bangkok," he answered, his eyes dancing in his olive face. He was a fan all right. "Horse racing is so big here, we have a track for the week days and another track across the street for Sunday."

They spent the whole day eating, drinking and looking. By eight o'clock they were back at the after brow of the *Pine Island*. It had been a most enjoyable day. Pete remembered his lesson from the Philippines.

The next day, Jim and Pete both had the duty and stayed aboard, getting all of the supply department details cleared up for having the Flag (Admiral) aboard ship. Pete had just left the Supply Office and was crossing the passageway in front of the Captain's office when a deep voice stopped him in his tracks.

"Hey, Spud King!" Pete knew it was the Skipper who had called Pete that since his days on the mess decks. Pete turned and went into the office. "Spud, do you remember Admiral Moore from North Island? He relieved Admiral Anderson this morning."

Pete stood at attention, leaned over and shook the hand of the large man sitting in an armchair across from the Captain's desk. "I am honored, sir." Pete was quite surprised at the introduction. *This guy is a legend. An Air Rescue flying boat pilot during the second world war. Decorated several times as I recall.*

"No. I think the honor is mine. If I could make bean soup like you, I'd be in the restaurant business. I'm sure we'll see your recipe in the Officer's Wardroom galley soon." The Admiral glanced at Captain Hamblin, then winked at Pete.

"As a matter of fact, Sir..." the Captain spoke as he seated himself behind the desk. "Bean soup is on the menu for this evening's meal."

The Admiral's face came back to a serious feature. "Spud. You don't mind if I call you Spud, do you?"

Pete shook his head 'no.' *You're the Admiral and you can call me whatever you want.*

"While I'm aboard the 'Blue Goose,' I want you to work for me as my liaison with the Supply Department. You'll continue with your normal duties and responsibilities. I understand you've been promoted to Petty Officer Third Class and are the ESO Storekeeper now. But, you'll be on call if I need your expertise." The Admiral rose to his full height and placed a large left hand on Pete's right shoulder. "Well, Spud. What do you say?"

Pete could feel the smile crossing his face. "I'd be happy to, sir."

"Okay, Spud," said Admiral Moore, patting Pete's shoulder. "On your way. I'll call you later. Be sure to go past the Personnel Office and pick up your special ID card."

Pete turned and floated out of the office. He had just been handed quite a shock. *Not everyone in the fleet gets a chance to be the Admiral's gopher. It might sound like menial chasing-around tasks, but why not, I'm doing it for one of the most powerful men in the Western Pacific.*

Pete couldn't wait to tell Cagney.

At supper on the after mess deck, Pete shared the news of his good fortune with Jim.

"Tomorrow, we'll have to go on the beach and celebrate in a big way," Jim said as he crumbled crackers into his bean soup. "With the Admiral aboard, I think the food will improve a little, too."

"Oh yes! One more thing," Pete said. "SK1 Lee told me he got a special request chit from the Deck Division today. An order for eleven life raft charges."

A good laugh was had at the expense of the Boatswains Mates. Changing of the Flag was complete and Pete had an additional assignment!

Chapter 20

Some People Never Learn

The next day liberty call went down at eleven-hundred hours. Jim and Pete were in the city by eleven fifteen. They walked down the sunny sidewalks of the narrow paved streets and watched the traffic dodging in and out in the morning hustle and bustle of the city's downtown area. They stopped along the way to look into shop windows. It did not take them long to discover English was the second language of these people.

Many times they were approached by young children asking for money or offering their older sister for a price. Of course, their older sister was eighteen and a virgin. Pete found it hard to believe there were so many virgins in the whole world.

Needless to say, Doctor Vesper had scared him into believing he didn't want to be caught with any woman in Bangkok. Doc Vesper had a way of turning a simple VD lecture into the most frightening horror story ever told. As for Pete, the stories always seemed to work. Hearing the average rate of VD was two hundred and ten percent higher than any other seventh fleet port had a way of curtailing any wild animal drive he might have.

About noon the boys found their first bar. A modern bar with small tables and large booths covered with imitation leather. The lights were low, and the juke box played an old Elvis love song as they entered and found a booth near the back.

They settled in, stacked their white hats against the wall on the table top and ordered two beers from the pretty little waitress. The charge for the beer was eighteen baht each, eighty cents, but they were hurricane bottles, just over a quart, and the labels read 18% alcohol. The taste was excellent, very much like a good German malt liquor.

Three hours passed, and they were very near the end of their second beer when the front door opened and three Royal Navy sailors walked in. At first, Pete thought they were British, like the four sailors near the door, and they had come in to join their mates who had arrived an hour before. The British sailors, at the table, whose band on their flat hats read HMS or Her Majesty's Ship had been drinking, dancing and flirting with women. The bands on the hats of the three big fellows walking in said HMAS or Her Majesty's *Australian* Ship.

The Brits had their flat hats stacked one atop the other in the middle of the table. The Aussies walked in and stood around the table. Pete stared as one of the Aussies swept the hats off the table onto the floor, not a word being spoken. The war was on! There were flying chairs, fists and bottles. As quickly as it started, the fight was over. The Aussies had thrown the Limey's out into the street and their flat hats after them.

The Aussies now settled down and began to drink and flirt with the women just as the British before them had done. Pete thought it was kind of comical and snickered his point of view to Jim. The biggest sailor of the bunch got up and approached their table.

"Quick! Jim, sit on your hat." Pete tossed Jim's hat across the table to him and slid his under his right leg. "I'm not having a giant throw me out in the street."

"How's things in the colonies, mates?" the Aussie asked as he stood, towering over the table. He slid into the booth next to Jim, across from Pete. "I was just joking!" He laughed. "You don't have to answer that for us, we're colonials, too!" He stuck a large right hand in Pete's face. It was obvious he had been drinking. "I'm Jesse James. What are your names, mates?"

This guy saying his name was the same as an American legend from Pete's birth state of Missouri caused a strangled snicker to catch in his throat, so Jim answered.

"This is Pete Peterson and my name is Jim Cagney. We're off the *USS Blue Island Sound*." Jim did not wait for Pete to ask. "Is Jesse James your real name?"

"It sure is," the sailor cocked his head to one side and smiled a toothy grin. "I always get asked that by you Yanks. How about if I buy you lads a drink?"

Pete found his voice. "Great, and maybe you'd let us buy the second round."

Jesse called the waitress over, and the young men settled down to some serious drinking and story telling.

Pete counted himself lucky not to have burst out laughing in front of Jesse James. The fellow seemed to have a tremendous sense of humor, but Pete still wasn't sure he would understand.

They finished their beer as the sun was setting. Jesse invited the Americans to join him and his two cronies at the Royal Navy Enlisted Men's Club. Pete thought it was a great idea and Jim agreed.

A short taxi ride later they entered a building that looked like a giant gymnasium from the outside. Once inside, past the armed guards, they stood on a giant hardwood floor. On the other side of the room a large band played live music. On their right was a raised floor, four feet higher than the main floor, on their left another raised floor ten feet higher than the main floor. Under the floor of the higher section Pete could see the main bar, kitchen and rest rooms.

Jesse noticed the look of wonderment on Pete's face. "Pete, when you come into a Royal Navy club, it is very important to know who everyone is, so the Seamen sit on the main floor, the Petty Officers sit on the lower raised level and the Noncommissioned Officers sit in the highest area. Come on. We'll all be up in the Petty Officer's section."

The two Yanks followed Jesse and were soon seated at a large round table with the two other sailors from the *HMAS Piedmont.* The table was covered with a white linen cloth and seated seven people and the furnishings were a little nicer than the main floor. "You fellows drink rum, don't you?" asked one of the men already at the table.

"I've never tasted it before," Pete answered without thinking. He was not going to appear as an 'old salt' to these guys. "I usually drink Kentucky bourbon whiskey," Pete followed up quickly.

"Well, sit yourself down, mate," the Petty Officer offered, pointing to a chair next to himself. The other chairs at the table filled quickly. "My name is John. I've already ordered the first round," said the Aussie Petty Officer.

The drinks arrived shortly, carried by a pretty young Thai woman with flashing dark eyes. John paid her and slapped Pete on the shoulder. "It's your turn, Pete," he said.

Pete had watched the exchange of drinks for currency very carefully. Each drink was two baht or ten cents US. He laid a twenty baht bill on the girl's tray with the change the Aussie had left and spoke up in his most mature bravado. "Another round, please."

Pete looked at the drink in front of him, a glass smaller than a little juice glass from the average restaurant, filled with coke and one small round ice cube. Pete tasted his drink. The liquid was rich, sweet and smooth. He could barely taste the alcohol, sort of an after-taste as he swallowed the coke.

One good Yankee swig, and the drink was gone. Pete noticed his hosts were drinking theirs a little slower, but the girl was back already and she had brought double rounds, knowing the next person at the table would want to order another round. It was Jesse's turn, and he did just that.

Eight rounds had passed, and Pete had not noticed the effect of the rum, yet something warned him that he should be as conservative as possible if he was going to last the night. He thought back to what an old cowboy had told him when he was in high school. 'If you drink too much, just put your finger down your throat and get rid of it. Then get some butter and eat it. The butter will coat your stomach and the alcohol won't get you as drunk.' Pete knew he would be getting drunk soon, and he would be hard pressed to keep the fact from his comrades who sat laughing and having a good time.

Pete pushed his chair from the table and stood feeling the fire of the rum warming his cheeks. "If you fellows will excuse me," he pointed toward the other end of the building. "I need to go to the head. I'll be right back." He turned and walked down the short stairwell onto the main floor. He had his eyes set on the large oak door marked "men." Suddenly, a large hand grabbed his arm, and he was pulled down into a chair. His eyes met the face of a young British sailor. "Hey, Yank. What do you say? How about joining us for a drink?" A drink was slapped into Pete's hand, and he was pronounced the guest of honor.

"Here's to the Queen!" Pete heard himself say in a loud slurred voice.

He did not realize what he was doing. About half of the people within earshot jumped to their feet and chanted, "The Queen!" and downed their drinks. Pete did the same and hurried away so as not to be noticed. He would not say that again.

He was half way to the men's room when he was again arrested by strange hands all over his arms. Pete grabbed the drink from in front of his face and said, "To England." *Oh rats, it happened again!* Everyone around him jumped to their feet and sounded off, "To England!" and downed their drinks. There were obviously a few Canadians and Australians around this time because Pete could hear "Screw England!" in the distance.

A young Canadian sailor put his hand on Pete's arm as he passed. Knowing what he wanted, Pete answered before he asked. "I've got to pee so bad I can't see good, so how 'bout when I get back?" The hand released him, and he staggered through the door into the head.

Pete found a quiet stall, closed the door and began the ritual as he thought it should be done. His eyes bulged and his throat convulsed.

Coke and the warm beer from the earlier part of the day filled his mouth to the shape of a balloon as his belly button tried to shake hands with his spine. The warm liquid tasted awful, and perspiration poured from his over heated face. When it was over, Pete was supremely grateful. He found his way to a sink and splashed cold water over his face. His confidence had returned by the time he threw the brown paper towel into the trash.

Pete turned outside and found the kitchen. A cook stared up at him. "What can I do for you, Yank?"

Pete felt a little sheepish. Maybe the cook knew what he had in mind. "Could I trouble you for a pat of butter?" Pete asked.

"Sure, mate. No trouble at all." The man in dress whites and a chef's hat handed Pete a finely sculptured butter rosette which he downed quickly and left to rejoin his group.

Pete was starting across the main floor when a hand took his sleeve. It was the Canadian again. "You said you'd have a drink with us on your way back. We have it. Come and join us!"

Pete dropped into the chair beside the sailor. He looked at the face that had called to him. The sailor could not have been fifteen years old. It was understandable, since the British allowed their men to join at the age of fourteen, but their enlistments are fourteen year stints.

Pete had a drink and started on his way, but he was yanked down at three more tables before he finally rejoined his group. *It must be unusual to have a drink with a Yank.* Every member of the Royal Navy seemed to want to hear the Yanks speak because they talked so funny.

When Pete reached his table, he was well on his way to being drunk. He wanted to find the old cowboy and tell him he was wrong – beyond a shadow of a doubt! As Pete slid into his chair, the sight in front of him was amazing. There were at least sixteen glasses of rum and coke at his place.

How am I ever going to drink all of these drinks and get back to my ship alive? He picked up the glass nearest him and raised his hand in salute. "To the Queen!" He shouted. As he raised his glass, his elbow ***accidentally*** knocked over all of the drinks but two. He tossed his drink down and dropped into his chair. Things were getting fuzzy.

* * *

Pete was coming out of a deep sleep. He fought the thick haze and opened his eyes as wide as the narrow slits in his face would allow. Someone was tapping heavily on the sole of his right shoe with an oak night stick. He could barely make out the face. It was Molini! The Master At Arms! *What have I done?* Pete looked at his watch. It was nine in the morning! *I missed reveille! No. We're in port, it's a holiday routine day.*

Molini leaned toward Pete's head, a bright smirk covered his face. "The Captain wants to see you on the forward mess deck, right now!" He gave one more hard tap on the bottom of Pete's foot. "You're in a world of trouble this time, and there's no way out. You're going to lose your stripes and get three days in the brig on piss and punk."

Pete was shocked. His mind raced. *What have I done so awful as to get called before the mast? Why would I get three days in the brig on bread and water, let alone lose my rate?*

As Pete peeled out of his bunk, he saw he was still dressed. He straightened down the front of his uniform and picked up the flat hat from beside his pillow. *Flat hat!* He looked down hard. He was wearing a Royal Navy uniform. The inscription on the blue band of white flat hat read *HMAS Piedmont.*

Now, Pete knew why the Captain wanted to see him. He had gotten so drunk that he traded uniforms with one of the Aussie sailors. Guessing by the loose fit, it had been Jesse James.

When Pete got to the forward mess deck, he found he was not the only one on board who had traded uniforms. There were four other men dressed for Halloween. The Captain sat at a large oak desk reading the charges and counts against each man to himself. When he was done, he looked up and gave a stern lecture on being representatives of the United States and the importance of staying in uniform when on liberty.

After his lecture, he began to administer what the Navy calls 'Captain's Mast.' He had Molini read the charges, asked the defendant for an explanation and then rendered a sentence like a judge.

Molini was right. The first guy lost his rate and got sent to the brig for three days on bread and water. He had, of course, been quite unruly during his arrest. He had broken the jaw of the British Shore Patrol Officer who arrested him for disorderly conduct. The rest of the punishments were not so bad, but they were administered in such a manner as to get everyone's attention in a hurry.

Now, it was Pete's turn. "Pete," the Captain began. "The report simply says you came aboard wearing a Royal Navy uniform, and when you were questioned about it by the Officer Of the Deck, you fell asleep in the arms of the Messenger Of The Watch."

Pete was relieved to hear the charges were not more serious. *Maybe I'll only get restriction to the ship for the next two or three port calls.*

"What do you have to say for yourself, Pete?" asked the Captain.

"I ran into some Aussie sailors, sir, they were drinking rum and I . . . ." Pete felt his voice trying to hide so none of the other sailors in the room would hear he wasn't an old salt, "...never drank rum before."

The Captain leaned back in his chair, laughing. "I'll never forget the first time I got drunk on rum." But, his face lost its laughter and became stern again. "I don't care whether you get your uniform back or not, but by sixteen hundred today, you will return *that* uniform to its rightful owner. Is that clear?"

Pete popped tall. "Yes sir!" His head throbbed like a toe that had been stepped on by a horse.

The Captain made a sign with his right hand as if to show Pete the door. "Now, get out of my sight!"

Within the hour, Pete had showered, shaved and changed into his own undress whites uniform and was standing on the pier looking toward the fantail of the ship moored right in front of the 'Blue Goose.' Pete didn't have far to go to return the uniform. The name on the stern of the ship read *HMAS PIEDMONT*. .

Pete approached the quarterdeck of the guided missile frigate, saluted the British Ensign flying from a pole on the fantail and turned to the Officer Of the Deck. "Request permission to come aboard, sir?"

The officer acknowledged his salute.

"What is your business here, mate?" asked the officer.

"I'm here to see one of your quartermasters named James," Pete replied.

The officer went to the ship's 1MC and picked up the microphone. His announcement boomed in Pete's head as it came loud and clear over the ship's PA system. "Hey, James! You got company down 'ere."

James appeared on the 01 level weather deck above the quarter deck. His working uniform was not exactly what Pete had expected. James had on a pair of white shorts, a white tee shirt with blue piping around the collar, low-cut white tennis shoes and his flat hat. "Come on up, Pete," he said, motioning to the stairwell of the port weather deck ladder.

After Pete explained what had happened, Jesse smiled. "I'll not be giving you back your uniform, mate. Yank uniforms are too hard to come by."

"That's just fine with me," said Pete, handing Jesse a brown paper bag containing the Aussie uniform. "My orders are to return your uniform, not to get mine back. I have to be back aboard my ship by sixteen hundred."

The big man looked down at his watch. "It's nearly noon and the galley is open. You have plenty of time. Why don't you join me for rations?" Jesse asked.

Pete touched his stomach with his left hand, realizing he had not eaten since breakfast the day before. "I'd be delighted," he said. When the two friends reached the galley, they fell in line behind other sailors waiting at a half-wall, the top of which was a heavy wire screen with a small arch shaped window and a protruding stainless steel shelf.

As they reached the window, Jesse spoke. "One for me and one for my mate, here." he said. He stuck both of his large hands through the cage window and withdrew two large flagons of dark ale.

"Oh no!" Pete exclaimed. "I thought rations were food, not more booze! Booze got me into trouble in the first place!"

"Don't get excited, mate," Jesse reassured him. "You don't think we'd be allowed to drink hard liquor and return to work, do you? This is just a very good, light drink. You'll enjoy it. Now, sit down and let's chat."

At fifteen forty-five, Pete was back aboard his own ship.

I made it! Pete thought. *It's a quarter till four and I'm back. Just a little drunk, but I am back. I thought I learned my lesson about booze in the Philippines. I guess it's like Mother always says,* **"Some people never learn."**

Chapter 21

On with Work

The remaining days in Bangkok passed quickly. It was time to return to sea and assume the stature of a flagship of the Seventh Fleet.

Pete had just changed into his dress whites for leaving port when the 1MC blared out, "Now SK3 Peterson, lay to the after brow." Pete hurried to the after gangway to find he had a last minute visitor.

Jesse James was happy to see Pete and smiled as he clasped his hand in greeting. "I just couldn't let you leave without saying good-bye. My ship will be putting to sea in a short time, too, so I thought I'd stop by and say God-be-with-yee." He reached into his jumper pocket and drew out a large silver cigarette lighter. "I had this engraved with both our names so you wouldn't be forgetting this port of call," he said, handing Pete the lighter.

Pete smiled. "Wow! Thank you very much. I doubt I'll forget this port, and the next time I go into a bar, I promise I'll be ordering rum and coke. How about that?"

The Boatswain's pipe peeled a final call for all ashore. Jesse saluted Pete, turned and saluted the Ensign on the fantail, then walked smartly down the after gangway. Pete swallowed the lump in his throat as he watched his good friend leave. He gripped the lighter firmly and waved a final farewell.

Pete walked to his station for getting underway on the 02 level. His division was already assembled. He watched the *Pine Island* drift back as lines were cast off bollards. The *Blue Island* moved into the Bangkok River. Two tugboats quickly filled the gap between the *Blue Island Sound* and the *Pine Island.*

Unexpectedly, several members of the *Pine Island* crew appeared on their seaplane deck with buckets of eggs. The crew of the 'Blue Goose' was totally unprepared. Before the *Blue Island Sound* was able to get underway, the entire port side of the ship was colored with dripping yellow and white. *What a rotten prank!*
The crew was dismissed from quarters quickly, but by the time they had returned to the weather decks with their ammunition from the galley, the 'Blue' was out of range and the best throws fell short of the laughing faces on the *Pine Island.*

Egging wasn't the only humiliation the *Blue Island Sound* had to suffer at the hands of the 'Piney Maru.' Somehow, members of her crew had sneaked on board and painted the *Pine Island's* hull number on the *Blue Island Sound's* crash boat. Captain Hamblin was so upset he complained to the Admiral. The Admiral laughed and said, "Doesn't that give you some ideas for when you're relieved?"

The weather was clear as the ship broke into the open sea. This crew was on its way to perform their wartime function. The Captain was relieved of the 'Deck and The Con' on the bridge by a junior officer and retired to his cabin for supper.

On being relieved of his bridge plotter position by Cagney, Pete went below for dinner and contemplated the ship's schedule. ***Maybe** the ship wouldn't be held in WESTPAC for the whole six months.*

***Maybe** it would be in San Diego home port for Christmas.* In the meantime, there was a lot of work to be done and a lot of missions to be accomplished by the ship's squadron of seaplanes.

The days at sea now turned into months, and the port calls were highly anticipated. Liberty was a good way to forget the military life aboard the *Blue Island Sound*.

Pete took advantage of the time at sea to complete his correspondence courses to qualify for the SK2 examination. The only requirement left was the commanding officer's recommendation. Pete was not sure the Captain would be willing to recommend him after the Bangkok incident.

Pete was sitting at his desk typing orders for parts the ship would be picking up in Yokosuka when SK1 Lee came in. His face was beaming with happiness as he thrust a sheet of paper in front of Pete. It was the recommendation list from the Captain's office. There were three Storekeepers on the list. Cagney for AK2, Alphie "the Pooh Bear" Johnston for AK2 and Pete for SK2. As Pete picked up the list, a bolt of excitement shot through him. He had been recommended for advancement in rate. All he had to do now was pass the test.

The ship would be in Yokosuka in a few days, and the written tests would be given before the ship reached port. Pete could easily be a Second Class Storekeeper by the time this WESTPAC cruise was half over.

"Well, my friend," said Lee, opening the office door to leave, "you know, you can't work here all night. You have the twenty to twenty-four-hundred watch, so you better get dressed for it and report to the bridge."

Pete winged the tall black man a quick salute as he disappeared through the closing door. Pete opened the bottom drawer of his desk and pulled out his trusty can of Kiwi black polish and buffing brush. After a couple of minutes of polishing his shoes, he was ready to stand his watch.

Pete reported to Lt. Taylor, the Officer Of The Deck on the bridge. He was the ship's "Air Boss." Lt. Taylor had a reputation among the crew as a real squared away officer. He never played hard ass or the "I'm an officer, you're enlisted," game a number of the younger officers enjoyed so much.

Pete looked at the plotter board. It was completely void of any marks. AKAN Evans handed over the yellow grease pencil and the sound-powered head set.

"It's been real quiet tonight, Pete. I don't think there's another ship in the entire ocean," he said straightening his seagoing ball cap. He turned to the OOD and requested permission to leave the bridge. He gave a salute and was gone onto the darkened weather decks.

Lt. Taylor paced, back and forth, raised his field glasses to his eyes and peered into the black night. Because of the heavy overcast, Pete was not sure where the sky ended and the sea began.

The ship had been running in a westerly monsoonal flow for days. The dense humidity and lack of a horizon was just about to get to the crew. Pete stood next to an open starboard port hole feeling a little breeze. He listened to the rush of the ocean against the forward hull. It sounded like a fast running waterfall in the mountains back home. He pushed back a sudden tinge of homesickness.

"Pete!" A voice vibrated in his headset. "Pete, it's me, Henderson in CIC."

Henderson was the Third Class Radarman watching the scopes and listening to the radios down in the Combat Information Center. He was a good kid who had reported aboard the same time as Pete. They had worked on the mess decks together.

"Pete, tell Mr. Taylor to turn on the commercial shipping channel on the bridge radio."

"Sir," Pete called, hailing the attention of the OOD. "CIC requests you turn on the radio to channel three and listen."

"Go ahead, Pete," he responded. "See what's on. You might come up with the latest weather report. Maybe this muck will go away before breakfast."

Pete flipped the knob of the radio console clockwise until it came to rest on the number three. A low, strained voice came through the heavy weather static.

". . . emergency transmission. I repeat. This is an emergency transmission. This is the merchant vessel *Audrey J. Luckenbach.* Any ship picking up this transmission, please respond."

Lt. Taylor picked up the hand set and spoke into the mouth piece as he depressed the transmit button. "*Audrey J. Luckenbach,* this is the *USS Blue Island Sound.* Please state your problem? Can we be of assistance? What is your current position?"

There was a momentary silence as the radio spat and crackled, then the bridge was filled with the excited voice of the radio operator transmitting the distress signal. "Hey, there is somebody else on this pond besides us! I sure appreciate you guys answering me. We've been at sea for three weeks. We are on our way to Vietnam with supplies for the army." He took a deep breath. "Can I get back to you with our position? Our problem is, one of our shipmates has been taken seriously ill with pneumonia and we have no medical staff nor medicines aboard this ship. We're strictly a merchant vessel. I guess no one's supposed to get sick while we're at sea."

The radio on the darkened bridge went silent. Everyone on the bridge stared at the radio as if to will it back to life. The merchant-man started up again. "Are you guys a 'man-of-war,' a tin can, or what? We really need a doctor."

The *USS Blue Island Sound* was indeed a man-of-war and this was near the war zone. Lt. Taylor was very careful not to give away his position to the distressed ship. He simply scribbled down the longitude and latitude provided by the radio operator and told the merchantman to heave to and stand by. "We'll come along side at 0800 and pick up your seaman in a motorized whale boat. We have two very fine surgeons aboard and your mate will get the best of care."

Lt. Taylor turned to Pete after he had completed his communications. His voice was serious. "We'll approach this situation with caution. This is just the kind of trick a German U boat might have tried."

His words smacked of paranoia, but all precautions had to be taken to protect the ship.

As hazy daylight began to break, Pete stood on the weather deck with RD3 Henderson outside of CIC watching the horizon. The little dot was now easily identified as a merchant vessel flying the Ensign of the United States.

I wonder what brought this ship here? Pete scratched his head as the light came on in his mind. *Oh, yeah! Most of the ships sailing the world's oceans are civilian owned and operated.*

Boatswain's Mate Third Class Smith launched a motor whaleboat with a crew of four in a gray choppy sea heading for the *SS Audrey J. Luckenbach.* Within the hour, the boat was back alongside, and Boatswain's Mates hoisted the ill seaman in a stokes stretcher, to the seaplane deck. Winches quickly recovered the whale boat, and the 'Blue Goose' was underway as if nothing had happened. The seaman would be cared for until *USS Blue Island Sound* reached Yokosuka, where he would be transferred to a civilian hospital for final recovery.

Pete spent the rest of the day at his typewriter in the Supply Office getting the last of his orders for ESO out. He was just finishing when Pooh Bear came into the office. "Hey, Pete," he said, his round face glowing, "tomorrow is test day, old buddy. What do you say we grab a couple of Pepsi Colas from the geedunk and go up to ESO for some last minute studying?"

Pete threw the cover on the typewriter he was using and pushed his chair back. "I would love to spend the evening studying with you, Pooh, but you have to spring for the sodas."

All the ship's store had left was Shasta®, which wasn't Pete's favorite, but, they had a good assortment of flavors, and they were so cold little ice chunks floated around in them.

For the past two weeks the ship's refrigeration had been on the fritz and Pete wasn't sure whether he would get a cold drink or a hot one. The bad part was a lot of the guys would take the hot canned drinks, put them into the plastic exhaust cone of a CO2 fire extinguisher and blast away until the freezing chemical had cooled their drink. This made the Captain angry because the crew's desire for a cold drink had created a dangerous situation in many areas of the ship. In the event of a fire, there would be trouble if a crew member attacked the fire with an empty extinguisher.

The end result was the ship's machinists and air-conditioning specialists were sent to repair the geedunk refrigeration before they were allowed to repair the air-conditioning in officer's country. The refrigeration was back on line and the crew was happy to have cold drinks again.

Pooh and Pete retired to ESO for the evening to study their Military Requirements for Petty Officer and their other manuals for the big test in the morning.

At 0900 hours, all of the recommended men assembled on the forward mess decks, ready to take their tests for advancement in rate. By noon, almost everyone had finished. In six days, the ship would pull into Yokosuka, and the promotions would be posted. Pete felt good about the test. He left the forward mess deck and went aft to get into the chow line. He had been a Third Class Petty Officer for over six months, the minimum requirement for advancement to Second Class. If he passed the test, there would be several people actually working for him who had been in the service longer. The way he saw it, if they wanted to be his boss, they had better study hard and earn their stripes like he had.

There was one more thing he wanted to do as soon as he made rate. He had made a promise to Molini and had every intention of keeping it.

A firm slap hit Pete's back as he mused. He turned quickly to find Chip Dale with his toothy smile standing right behind him. "You know we made third class at the same time, do you think we'll do the same with second?"

"Sure we will," Pete replied. "We're prepared, and that's all it takes."

"Are you ready for this?" Chip laughed. He was obviously holding out a bigger than average secret as he ducked his head slightly and cupped his hand over his mouth so only Pete could hear.

"I just came from the Com shack and the word is we're not being relieved when we get into Yoko. The *USS Salisbury Sound* hasn't even left San Diego. Instead of our tour being over at the end of six months like normal, we'll have a change of command. Captain Hamblin is being promoted to Commodore. His relief is a real heavyweight named O'Hara. We'll stand for change of command ceremony as soon as we get to Yokosuka."

Pete didn't eat much supper. The news from Chip was still classified, and it would not do for him to start talking about it before the Captain made his normal address to the crew. Pete could barely hide his disappointment. This would ruin Christmas plans for the whole crew.

The only thing I can do is get some rest and go on with work. So much for going home!

Chapter 22

Changing of the Guard

The high pitched whistle of the Boatswain's pipe yanked Pete's mind from a long night of rest. He had retired early to be fresh for entering Yokosuka. Today would be a big day, and he wanted to be ready. He had no intention of going on the beach; there would be enough excitement aboard.

Pete jumped from his rack, opened his locker and took out his douche kit along with a large white towel. He juggled the shaving kit in his hand as he stepped over the threshold into the S-2 Division head.

Pete smiled to himself as he tossed his shaving kit into the air and caught it. *Some sailor probably christened it a douche kit years ago because all he could get from the shower spigots was a healthy splash of water, a douche if you will, while the ship was underway. Undoubtedly in Napoleon's navy.*

Many times in the past few months the ship had opened whole boilers to sea water. The crew was forced to take salty showers because the desalinization plant was on the fritz. Pete hesitated before stepping into the warm spray, remembering to keep his mouth closed.

In a few hours, the ship would be in Yokosuka, and fresh water lines would be hooked between the base and the ship. Sewer, telephone and electrical lines would be run, and the ship would, in effect, become another building on the base. All hands would stand clear of the weather decks while the ship underwent her 'fresh water wash down' to cleanse her of salt deposits she had picked up since the last port call. This procedure reduced the amount of chipping and painting by the deck force. After the *Blue Island Sound* got her bath, all hands would be crowding the showers for their own fresh water wash down.

I can't wait to feel fresh water on my face, Pete thought. The warm salt water splashed over his head and down his back. There were fourteen showers in the S-2 Division head, and they were all in use from 0600 until 0730. For a short period of time, the head was very popular.

Taking another deep breath, Pete smelled diesel oil. "What the hell?" he screeched. He quickly shut off the shower. Not only was it salt water, but, now it smelled of diesel fuel. *I don't mind smelling like an old salt, but I sure don't want to smell like a bilge rat!* He stepped out of the shower, jerking his towel from the overhead loop.

As he wrapped his towel around his lower half, the main door at the other end of the compartment burst open. Through the steam, Pete could see AK3 Cagney squirreling his head around in search of someone. He was in full dress whites and wore the duty belt and arm band of the Petty Officer Of The Watch. "Any of you guys seen Pete?" Cagney hollered.

"Down here, Jim," Pete shouted over the running water of the showers.

Cagney crossed the compartment in three steps and a hop. "They're posting the results of the tests outside Personnel right now." His face was dripping from the steam, making his usually pale complexion turn rosy from the heat. "Guess what?" He slapped Pete's wet shoulder almost knocking him back into the shower. "You're on the first increment again! You get to sew on your Second Class crow at midnight!"

Pete jumped with the excitement of this news. He slapped Cagney on the back as he turned toward the door. "Yahoo! Let's go see!" Pete said, tightening his towel around him.

He quickly followed Jim up two flights of stairs and down the long passageway to the bulletin board by the X Division Office where the list was posted. Sure enough, there was Pete's name, right at the top of the list, and there was the Pooh Bear, A. L. Johnston AK2, right under Pete.

Pete looked hard at the board. Cagney's name was conspicuously absent. Pete turned from the board, his excitement draining as he looked into Cagney's eyes. Cagney's voice cracked as he spoke quickly. "Maybe next time."

Later, Pete was alone in the S-1 berthing compartment putting on his dress white uniform for entering port. He looked at the Third Class Petty Officer rating badge on his short-sleeved dress shirt as he pulled it from the hanger. The American eagle perched proudly over a single chevron with the crossed Storekeeper keys in the middle.

At midnight, Pete would change rate. He would have two chevrons, more responsibilities, more pay and a stronger leadership roll in the division.

Slipping into his shirt, he grinned from ear to ear. ***I've got my Second Class crow!*** He had worked long and hard to attain the Second Class rate. There were three men in the division who had been in the Navy for thirteen or fourteen years that had taken the test a number of times, and had still not been rated. Pete would now be their superior. Pete realized he had worked and fought to gain this rate, not only because it had been his career goal for this four-year hitch, but also, he was now the same rate as BM2 Molini. Under naval regulation, Pete was now his peer. Pete would no longer have to fear charges of insubordination or disrespect to a superior and could speak his mind to the little wormy-eyed mutt from the Master At Arms force.

An hour later, Pete stood at parade rest, elbow to elbow with Pooh Bear. The entire ship's company, except for those actually on watch, was assembled in the huge hangar overflowing onto the open seaplane deck. The men were gathered to hear a special announcement from Captain Hamblin before the ship entered port.

"Gentlemen," Captain Hamblin spoke through a microphone located on a podium just outside the hangar bay doors. "I know many of you were looking forward to being relieved by the *USS Salisbury Sound.*" The large man shifted his weight. "The only way to tell you this, is to just tell you. The *Blue Island Sound* will not be relieved. Tomorrow morning, there will be a change of command ceremony and you will have a new Commanding Officer.

"I've been promoted to the rank of Commodore and am being assigned as U.S. Military Advisor in London. I don't know why the boys in Washington have decided to have you do a double tour, but I'll tell you this. The SP5B seaplane is on its way out as a war machine. Therefore, the seaplane tender, the 'Blue Goose' will soon be gone." The Captain lowered his head and took a deep breath.

"I would like to congratulate those of you who passed your rating examinations, and I encourage you to work hard toward your next promotion. You have all served faithfully while you've been under my command. I hope you serve your new Captain as well. Thank you and the best of luck to each and every one of you."

As Captain Hamblin turned and stepped from the speaker's stand, the crowd went completely silent. As his foot touched the seaplane deck, the entire ship's company broke into a thunderous roar of applause. Captain Hamblin was well liked by his crew and would undoubtedly be missed. As Pete applauded, he looked around at the faces of his shipmates. He was part of this great crew.

Later, quarters for entering port was piped down. The ship's company laid to the weather decks to man the rails, and stood at parade rest for an hour. The ship rolled over the breakwater and came alongside the pier at the U.S. Naval Supply Center, Yokosuka.

Yokosuka had not changed much since the last time *Blue Island Sound* was in port. The blue waters of the Pacific turned into gray clabber from the dumping of diesel by ships for the past thirty years. The stench assaulted Pete's nose. Still, it smelled better than many of the ports of the Orient Pete had visited. The base was clean, neat and always ship shape.

Pete wasn't surprised when they tied up just one pier away from the *USS Provincetown*, a heavy guided missile cruiser. This ship spent so much time in port the crew of the 'Blue Goose' had started calling her "building 66," sixty-six being her hull number. Immediately after the ship's fresh water wash down, "Liberty Call" was passed over the 1MC. Pete was glad he had not planned to go on the beach because he drew the onboard duty section for the first night in port.

The exciting day Pete expected had not come to pass. On the contrary, it was very quiet. The Captain declared Holiday Routine for all hands not actually on watch and Pete spent the evening in the ET shack watching reruns of Lassie.

The channel came in with Japanese voices, so the ET's turned down the sound and turned on an armed forces radio simulcast in English. Never once did the radio get out of sequence with the television. Well, except for commercials when the two different stations did their own thing, but when the show came on, everything was synchronized.

In the early evening, a "roach coach," a food and drink vending truck, pulled up on the pier. Crew members swarmed around it. Any food, not from the ship's mess, was a treat.

As midnight approached, Pete and Chip Dale got out the OE Division ironing board and began getting clean dungaree shirts ready to receive their new iron-on rating badges.

At five minutes to twelve, both men buttoned their shirts. They faced toward each other and made similar motions as if looking into a mirror. Pete looked up at the large clock on the bulkhead while Chip sat down and resumed watching the late movie. The time had finally come. Pete turned toward the door. He had something to take care of, something he had waited two years to do.

Pete walked through the dark outside passageway and headed for the main deck. He entered the skin of the ship and crept down the ladder to the forward mess deck. He crossed the shiny green tile floor glowing red from night lights here and there, to the metal half-door which was the entrance to the Master At Arms office. The lights were off. Pete listened to the sound of heavy breathing, a person in deep sleep. The duty MAA bunk was behind the open top half of the door to Pete's right. A snore echoed to his ears. His heart pounded hard. It was time. "Molini!" Pete growled in his deepest, harshest tone.

A sucking stumbling voice snorted back to Pete. "Uh. Yeah. Who is it?"

"Molini! **Eat my shorts!**" Pete yelled at the top of his lungs. Pete relished the scene for a moment and then quickly faded into the shadows making his way back to the ET shack.

Chip handed Pete a cup of coffee as he sat down to enjoy the rest of the movie. Pete could feel the warmth of laughter boiling up as a big grin of satisfaction tore at the edges of his mouth. He took a sip of coffee.

Just then, the door burst open. Molini stood in the doorway, hands on his hips, wearing nothing but trousers and flip flops. His face was white as though he had been frightened awake. He pointed with his report chit book held out in his chunky fist. "You!

You sea scum! You're on report! I've finally got you, and you're gonna pay!"

Chip leaned back in his chair with a conspiratorial smirk on his face. "Listen, shorty," he grunted in a matter-of-fact tone, gaining Molini's undivided attention. "If I were you, I wouldn't bust into a classified space in the middle of the night, without clearance, cursing at people and making threats. The Captain might not like that." Chip took a sip of his coffee and went on. "Besides, Pete has been sitting right there all evening. Now, why don't you go muscle a couple of drunk Seamen."

Pete sensed Molini knew he couldn't win this one. He jerked the door and put both feet into the passageway. He pointed the middle finger of his right hand at Pete. "You! Slime-boy! Some day I'll get you." He slammed the door and was gone.

Pete exploded like a volcano, laughing so hard he dropped his coffee cup and slipped off his chair into the puddle on the floor.

"Sweet revenge!" Pete said. "That crazy Boatswain's Mate has been hassling me since the day I stepped aboard this tub. Now, we're even."

Chip handed his laughing friend a roll of paper towels as his voice took on a serious tone. "You'd better hope that crazy Boatswain's Mate doesn't hold grudges or this could be a long cruise."

The next morning Pete enjoyed a fresh water shower. There was plenty of chatter about all the fun on liberty from the night before. Word had been passed right after reveille, today would be Holiday Routine with 'change of command ceremonies' at eleven hundred hours.

As soon as the new skipper was installed, the crew would have Liberty Call. Chip, Cagney and Pete could go on the beach. They were looking forward to it, like kids watching the clock on the last day of school.

Breakfast was special, not only the usual bacon floating in grease and green scrambled eggs, but also, a beautiful fresh fruit buffet. The spud locker had done a terrific job, and Pete couldn't resist making three trips before he had his fill of the delicious treat. The entire ship's company was present for the change of command ceremony. They stood at parade rest on the seaplane deck and listened to the two Captains read their orders and the Admiral pay each one a personal tribute. The new skipper, Captain O'Hara, was last on the podium, concluding his remarks.

Pete studied him as he spoke. He was a big man, well over six-foot-four, with a square face written with lines which spoke of naval history and command decisions. His hair was gray at the temples but otherwise jet black. He wore the large signet ring of the Naval Academy on his right hand, and gestured with it as he spoke. "I want you men to be aware that the days of this ship being a floating hotel are over. You will learn what it is to be sailors again. I expect nothing less than the finest military bearing from each and every one of you. Thank you."

I wonder what Captain Hamblin thinks about Captain O'Hara calling our ship a floating hotel? Pete was not impressed. *And why are we being sent a 'Battleship Navy' Captain, when all of the previous Captains have been flying officers or some kind of Airedale?*

The entire ship's company came to attention as Captain O'Hara stepped down from the speaker's stand. There was absolute silence as he and the procession of officers with him wound their way through the formation on the seaplane deck, into the hangar bay and the ship.

The realization that the ship would not be relieved hit Pete like a hammer smashing a goblet. *By changing Captains, the Department of the Navy has accomplished a complete changing of the guard. Now it's a new command. They have effectively replaced the ship and its crew.*

Chapter 23

The Boys

Howell and Racozad reported aboard the *USS Blue Island Sound* in Yokosuka, as Seaman Recruits with two-year hitches to serve as Naval Reservists. Howell was from Oklahoma and Racozad from Oregon, but the way they were always together, you would have thought they were from the same home town.

They worked hard at their jobs and studied on their training courses for advancement in rate. They stood their bridge plotter watches in a military manner and always conducted themselves with the best military bearing aboard ship.

They weren't bad kids. But, when they were on the beach, their behavior was another story. They were not the contemporary Mutt and Jeff duo, but they were opposites in a lot of ways. Howell was a half an inch taller than the minimum Navy requirement of height to get into the service. A wiry little guy who tipped the scale at ninety pounds on a wet day, with sandy hair and a square face, he had a temper like a firecracker he kept under control for the most part. He was absolutely woman crazy, a man on a mission. He wanted to get into the pants of anyone who wore a skirt. Most of the division thought, if there was one single woman in any given port, Howell could find her.

Racozad was a few inches taller than Howell, with dark hair, deep brown eyes, a pale pockmarked complexion on a round face, all set on a slightly rotund, larger than average, stocky frame. He had a mellow temperament, but could drink anyone under the table.

One night, several men from the S-1 Division were out drinking in Yokosuka. It was the boys' first cruise, so old Uncle Pete was showing them around to all the bars in Thieves Alley.

The group went into a bar frequented primarily by the silent service, the submarine fleet. Most of the bars on the alley catered to just one type of ship, thereby making it unsafe for anyone from a destroyer or carrier to go into a submarine bar. In smaller ports, like White Beach in Okinawa, the bars were territorialized by division rather than by ship because it was a small port city with a lot of bars. Pete was sure all the submarines of the Seventh Fleet were at sea, and when the Storekeepers and Aviation Storekeepers went into the bar, it was so dimly lit Pete could not make out any distinguishing marks on the uniforms of the few sailors.

Pete and his friends were on their second beer at a quiet, table in a corner when, from out of nowhere, a submariner towered over them. He straightened his neckerchief, drawing up his composure. "Don't you Airedale Navy people drink wine?" he slurred as he slammed a bottle of Akadama wine down on the table.

Howell looked up. He stretched his right arm and placed his forefinger on the sailor's silver dolphins and said, "How do they get a giant aboard a submarine?"

Not being in the mood for combat, Pete brushed Howell's hand down and responded to the question. "Sure, we drink wine. We just don't make as much money as some people, so we'll have to stick to drinking beer. That's all we can afford."

The submariner grabbed a chair and slammed it back-first into the table and dropped down with both hands on the wine bottle. "You know what?" His wine was talking. "You Airedales are all lower than whale shit, and that's on the bottom of the ocean. One of you couldn't drink this bottle. I doubt if all three of you together could down this bottle."

Racozad fingered his glass. "Sounds like quite a challenge from a man who spends six months of the year in a stinking pig boat." The hair on the back of Pete's neck stood up. Comparing the two men was like pitting a pint jar against a five-gallon jug. The big man thrust two fingers into his jumper pocket and slapped a bill on the table. "Here's twenty bucks that says you can't drink all this bottle of wine, big mouth!"

Racozad nudged Pete. "You got any money, Pete?" A thin smile crossed his face, and his eyes narrowed. "If you do, this bubble head is offering to treat us all to dinner."

"Hey!" Pete turned to face Racozad who was wearing the grin of the devil, himself. The single candle flame on the table danced in his eyes. "All I have is the money I've been saving for leave when we get to the States." Pete said, drawing a small wallet from his inside jumper pocket. "I guess I can cover twenty bucks."

Pete locked eyes with the submariner, who smiled and jerked around on his chair toward the bar where another ten submariners were drinking. "You guys!" he yelled, motioning for them to join him in his bold attack of the carrier group. "You want some easy money? We got an Airedale over here who thinks he can drink my bottle of wine, and he's got a banker who's backin' up his big mouth."

"Wait just a minute!" Pete protested, putting a bill on the table and pushing it toward the sub-sailor. "I'm covering your bet, not the whole fleet's."

A lanky Third Class Torpedoman put his hand on Pete's left shoulder and snatched the wallet away and began to count the contents. Another TM3 was at Pete's right shoulder, and a Machinist Mate stood behind him breathing down his neck. Pete made the quick decision to avoid a scene at this point.

The lanky Third Class Torpedoman who was whispering something to the others threw Pete's wallet onto the table. "Your bet is covered Naval Air *Farce,*" he snarled, as he began to peel bills from a wad he took from his jumper pocket. The Torpedoman threw the money on the table with smug confidence.

Two of the other sailors followed suit until the Torpedoman put up his hand and said. "The pot is right, boys. Now, on with the really big shoe!" His shipmates laughed at his Ed Sullivan impression, but Pete was far from impressed.

"Wait just a minute here!" Pete argued. "Who do you people think you are? You can't go around pulling this stunt on anybody that comes along. The bet was for twenty, and we covered that..."

Pete was interrupted by the huge TM3 on his right. "Your bet is covered Airedale, and if you don't like it, you can take a walk, and leave the wallet."

"I'll referee this drinking match!" A raspy voice intervened from behind the group gathered at Pete's table. "And if this youngster only wants to cover twenty bucks, that's the way it'll be." It was the bartender, a giant of a man with a white apron and bald head which made him appear threatening. He was carrying a major league baseball bat in his huge right hand. "Now, I've always catered to you submarine sailors, but there is something you ought to know. I was aboard the *USS Hornet* during the last war. Now, this little drinking match is going to be fair, or it ain't going to be at all!"

Racozad stood up, pushing Pete's wallet and the money toward the bartender. "Forget these bubble heads, Pete! We don't have to take their guff!" Anger was beginning to show in his face. "Bartender, if you would please, make sure the pot is right."

He went on as he broke the seal on the large wine bottle. "There's just one more little point of satisfaction I'd like to see in this bet. Just one thing to make it worth my while." He pointed to the sailor who had started the discussion. "You! Jolly blue giant. You've got the mouth. Drop your dolphins in this bottle!" Racozad uncorked the bottle and held it across the table into the giant's face.

The crowd broke into laughter and began to chide the big sailor on. "Go ahead, Rudy. If this guy can drink that much wine and live, he deserves to be one of us," said the Third Class who had taken Pete's wallet. Begrudgingly, the big man took off his silver dolphins and dropped them into the wine bottle.

Racozad tipped the large bottle up with both hands. He didn't take a breath after the bottle touched his lips. With each chug, the dolphins dropped closer to his lips, but when he swallowed, the dolphins shot back up the neck of the bottle.

Pete watched silently for what seemed like forever as his friend sucked and chugged at the contents. Racozad's pale complexion began to change from pink to a deep rose and then his teeth plucked the evasive dolphins from the bottle as he jerked it down hard onto the table. It was empty!

Moans of disbelief and cheers of admiration filled the bar as Pete grabbed the money, Howell and Cagney grabbed Racozad, and the group made a quick exit from the bar.

Every time Racozad went on liberty after that, he wore his dolphins, symbol of the silent service. He called the dolphin pin his 'intraservice victory medal.'

Chapter 24

Ko Samui

Two months had passed since the ship last visited Yokosuka. The crew had been at work, carrying out the orders of their new Captain, ensuring their days as a hotel were over. All hands worked long hard hours both underway and on seadrome operations. The months the *USS Blue Island Sound* had spent with Captain Hamblin now seemed like a vacation compared to serving with Captain O'Hara.

The crew had spent most of the two months in the war zone. The General Quarters klaxon was sounded two or three times a day, and all hands were standing 'battle ready' watches. So much time was spent at battle stations that GQ began to be treated as casual and routine by the crew. The serious, sharp, anxious, alert attitude was becoming complacency.

Pete's ESO battle station was right next to the ammo handling room under gun mount 51. Many times he heard the men complain that the job wasn't hard, but the air quality had a lot to be desired. When condition 'Zebra' was set throughout the ship, all ventilation was closed off and the temperature in the ammo handling room shot up to one hundred and thirty degrees in minutes.

There seemed to be a tendency to use the General Quarters klaxon in place of the Boatswain's pipe for reveille call.

Pete sat at his desk, his office door open. He had come to his battle station early today. He watched as Gunner's Mates scurried through the passageway and ascended the vertical ladder right next to his office door. Five men clambered up the ladder, the heavy steel hatch banged shut and Pete heard the whir of large electric motors as the gun mount came to life, turned and trained on an imaginary enemy vessel.

Pete trained his ears above him and to the right. He could barely make out the sound as a low clicking noise told him that the breech of the big gun was being opened.

All was quite for a moment, then **BANG**, a loud popping sound. Pete's mind raced. *I know that sound. Not a pistol shot, too loud. Not the big gun, too small for that. A hand grenade? Oh my gosh! A grenade in a gun turret.*

Pete jumped to his feet and headed for the door. As he reached the door, the round handle on the hatch above the hallway spun and the hatch opened. Feet appeared. "I've got to get to sickbay!" the man said as he descended the ladder. Pete could now see it was GM3 Allen.

He had his blue chambray shirt wrapped around his right hand. The shirt was red, soaked with blood.

"What happened, Greg?" Pete asked. "02 level Corpsman to ESO!" Pete screamed as he ushered the injured man into his office. Pete snatched two blankets from a shelf, threw one on the floor for Allen to lie on, slid a box under his feet and covered him with the other blanket.

The 02 level Hospital Corpsman appeared in the doorway with his medical kit. "What's up Pete?" he asked.

"Allen is hurt pretty bad. He could probably use a shot of morphine," Pete said.

The Corpsman had seen the blood and had already set to work, giving the Third Class Gunner's Mate a shot in the leg. He was unwrapping Allen's hand as he spoke to him. "Okay, Gunner, didn't your mama tell you not to play with firecrackers?"

Pete could now see the injury. The last two fingers on Allen's right hand were missing.

"So, what happened?" asked the Corpsman as he deftly applied a pressure dressing.

"Ensign Palmer had a couple of his Signalmen set three cases of hand grenade fuses inside the turret yesterday to get them out of the weather. He had been training his division on assembling grenades and maybe they were too lazy to carry them back to the armory with the grenades. I guess the lid on the top box was open a little. I sat down on it during loading exercises and when I stood up, my keys must have caught a fuse pin. I felt extra weight on my belt. I reached back and pulled the extra weight off of my keys and there I stood looking at a hand grenade fuse. The pin had been pulled by my key chain. Then, POW! No fuse, no fingers."

Stretcher bearers from sickbay appeared with their Stokes stretcher. Allen was placed in the wire basket and the group was gone.

After the early morning drill the crew was called to Quarters For Muster. Commander Hatchfield called the Supply Department together in their assembly area afterward. To Pete's way of thinking, he was an excellent officer when it came to the treatment of his men. Commander Hatchfield was nothing like Commander Webster, the Supply Officer he had relieved in Yokosuka. He was a bit of a nonconformist. He wore cowboy boots with his working khaki uniform.

"Fellas," Commander Hatchfield said, shifting his lanky frame, checking to see all eyes were on him. "How about some good news?" A smile came over his face as he pushed back his sea going ball cap. "How about a break from this war business?" The response was applause and shouts. When the noise quieted, he continued. "We're going into the Gulf of Siam for a peace mission. An island called Ko Samui. We'll still be at sea, but we won't be at GQ."

In the early afternoon, the *USS Reclaimer*, a submarine retrieval and salvage vessel, came along side with a medical problem. One of her seaman had appendicitis. Doctor Vespers operated, and the young man was listed in good condition by evening.

The next morning reveille was at zero six hundred as usual. The entire day followed normal routine, but everyone was uneasy, waiting for the GQ gong to go off at any moment. Instead, the special sea and anchor detail was set at zero nine hundred. Pete rushed out onto the weather deck to see the sights. The port bow anchor was just going into the water.

The Airedales running the huge crane on the fantail set a crash boat into the crystalline blue water. Pete could easily see to the bottom. It looked like the ship's thirty-foot draft might touch the coral at any moment.

Doctor Vespers was leaning over the life rail looking at the water as Pete came up. "Hi, Pete!" The doctor smiled. "Get a load of this place, would you? Did you ever, in your entire life, see anything as beautiful as this?" He pointed at a small island with shining white beaches and lush greenery in the middle.

At first glance, Pete had the impression of a green yoked egg sitting in a great blue fry pan. "This is kind of pretty, isn't it?" Pete managed as the breath-taking beauty filled his eyes. "I got the impression there was only one island. It seems we're anchored between two." Pete pointed to the island behind on the port quarter as the ship swung around the anchor and came to rest.

"Oh yes, Pete," the doctor said, as he put his pipe back to his mouth and then withdrew it. "There are two islands. The one we're interested in is that one, there." He gestured with his pipe. "The other one is a leper colony, and the Thai government has forbidden us to visit it."

As the two men watched, several small boats came out from the island and began to circle the ship. They yelled up, but there wasn't much the crew could understand. It reminded Pete of the bum boats in the Philippines. They would circle the ship and ask you to throw down money or anything else useful. Pete noticed one boat in particular, loaded with school-age children. It looked very much like a class outing had come to see an American man-of-war.

Pete reached into his trouser pocket where he had several coins. He tossed a quarter and it was caught by a young man who showed it off like an American kid might show off a freshly caught fly ball at a major league game. Excitedly, all the occupants of the boat watched as Pete tossed the next coin. Pete could tell it was going to fall short of the boat by inches. Pete expected what he had seen in the Philippines. The coin would hit the water and one of the children would dive and catch it before it sank a foot. This didn't happen. To Pete's amazement, the coin fell short by no more than eight inches and no one even extended a hand over the water to catch it.

With raised eyebrows, Pete turned to Doctor Vespers. "What?"

"It's because of the sharks, Pete." He pointed toward the open lagoon.

"That's where they bury their dead. Human flesh is part of the diet of the sharks in this area. The people here regard the shark as a god, but they don't take any chances by entering the water."

After 'knock-off-ship's-work' was sounded at sixteen-thirty, many of the crew went to the Geedunk and bought boxes of candy bars to toss over the side to the people in the small boats. Pete had the midwatch. He would be supervising the armed sentries walking posts along the perimeter of the ship on the main deck from the bow to the fantail. When he went on watch at 2345, the air was still and muggy. He got a kick out of watching the flying fish play in the water alongside the ship. The water was illuminated by several twenty-four-inch spotlights which shone from fore and aft on both sides of the seaplane deck. He saw a lot of different kinds of fish, rays, sharks and very large sea snakes. The sight of the sharks bothered him, but the giant snakes, with six inch diameters and twelve feet or more long, really got to him.

After the first hour on watch, the still, greenish blue water became restless and rose with whitecaps. There was lightning and thunder as dark clouds, driven by the soft breeze, blotted out the moon and stars. There was a smell in the air denoting the coming of warm tropical rain.

At zero two-fifteen Pete put on his foul-weather gear, just in time. The sky broke open and large drops of warm rain came down as if poured from an enormous pitcher. He thought of the announcement the XO had made earlier, about the ship needing more fresh water. Each crew member was allotted twenty-four gallons per day and were currently using seventy-two. *By golly, you're getting it!* Pete thought as he sloshed through the downpour that made the seaplane deck awash with two inches of fresh water.

At zero eight hundred Pete's division assembled on the open seaplane deck for muster. There was no sign of the tropical rain that gave him a good soaking the night before. A torrential downpour passes quickly and goes unnoticed in the tropics.

At eleven hundred hours, plane service boats and crash boats began shuttle runs between the ship and the island. On their way in, they carried food, medicine, books and clothing. On the return trip, they brought school children from the island.

The children wore school uniforms, the boys in tan shorts and short-sleeved shirts, the girls in blue skirts with white blouses and blue ties, topped by small white straw hats. They ranged in age from seven to ten. Three or four adults who spoke English came aboard with the children for their tour of the ship. Two were very pretty young women. One was a school teacher, the other a twenty-two year old coed from the University of Bangkok, named Loni. Pete had occasion to talk to Loni while he was conducting a tour of the ship. The tour was stopped on the main mess deck for a special treat.

"It's wonderful of your Captain to give the children ice cream and cookies," Loni said, licking her spoon. "This is one thing most of these children have never seen before."

"Only the best for our guests," Pete said. "You speak better English than I do. Did you study in the US?"

"No." Loni smiled, stirring the ice cream in her bowl. "I have a brother who is studying medicine at the University of Virginia in the United States, but I received all of my education at the University of Bangkok."

By late afternoon, all the guests had left the ship and Pete was back pacing the deck as Petty Officer of the Watch.

The people of the island had decided to repay the ship's hospitality with a version of their own graciousness. Small boats came alongside again, but this time the people in the boats were a little older, and they were not just catching the things crew members were throwing down. They threw fresh fruit and coconuts up to the main deck.

Pete walked his post in a military manner, munching a large chunk of sweet delicious pineapple. Juice dripped from his chin, collecting on the front of his dungaree shirt.

Too soon, the ship's week at Ko Samui Island was over, and it was time to resume its duties as a warrior. The *USS Blue Island Sound* left the island and steamed back into the war zone.

Dr. Vesper told Pete that GM3 Allen would be flown to the Naval Hospital in Tokyo and then transferred home. "It's not the million dollar wound you hear about, but it is a ticket home," he said.

Pete thought of the beautiful island and its tranquil surroundings. *I hope war never comes to Ko Samui!*

Chapter 25

Home for Christmas

Days turned into weeks and weeks to months as the ship moved silently from one seadrome operation to another, replenishing stores, fuel and aviation gasoline at sea. Port calls seemed a thing of the past.

Captain O'Hara's words from the Change of Command ceremony in Yokosuka echoed in Pete's mind. *"Your days as a floating hotel are over."*

The Captain was right and the morale of the crew was beginning to drop right off the scale. There were more and more fist fights between old friends and a higher frequency of illegal crap games. The master at arms force was having a field day raiding them. The culprits were sent to Captain's Mast and ended up with their heads shaved and three days in the brig on bread and water.

The discipline in Pete's own division was starting to deteriorate. Almost every day the Master Chief threatened someone with two hours of 'extra duty,' which meant military drill on the seaplane deck. Pete had not seen military drill 'extra duty' since he left the

Kingston. "You keep this up and you'll get two hours!" This seemed to be the watchword around S-1 division, and it was one of the more mellow divisions aboard ship.

Captain O'Hara was not like Captain Hamblin in a lot of ways. He never called the crew to quarters on the seaplane deck to speak to them. He simply used the ship's PA system every time he had something to say. He would pass whatever word he had at morning muster through 'officer's call,' and the crew would accept his words as part of the 'plan of the day.'

It was now late December. The crew had spent Thanksgiving in the war zone acting as a fire support station. *Blue Island Sound* had fired sixty-nine salvos on the beach to destroy an enemy staging area and supply depot. From eight miles at sea, the ship took firing instructions from an army light observation aircraft.

Pete wondered as the five-inch guns fired each round controlled by the aircraft, if the ship wasn't just blowing up a bunch of sticks in the middle of the jungle. He remembered the "suspension bridge" his squad had launched when he was with the Third Marine Division.

"*Staging area. Supply depot.*" Pete knew exactly what this meant to the us, but what did it translate to in the terms of Viet Cong? He thought about the supply depot he helped raid in the Mekong Delta. It was two shacks and a three-foot wide, twenty-foot long pier. A place with such simple construction that all the enemy had to do was bend down a palm tree and cover the edges with palm fronds, and they were back in business.

* * *

Pete sat in the crew's library paging through *Moby Dick* when Howell opened the door. "Say, Pete. You'd best come out to the mess deck. The Skipper is about to make an announcement. Lt.

Taylor told us at movie call that the Captain would speak at twenty-one hundred." Howell looked down at his watch and motioned for Pete to follow. "Three minutes. We had best hustle up."

A long veer of the Boatswain's pipe, followed by three sharp chirps told the crew the Captain was about to address them. "Gentlemen..."

There was a pause as if he were searching for words. "Many of you have saved up quite a bundle, with all the time we've been in the war zone. I talked it over with Admiral Moore, and we've decided to give you a chance to spend some money. We're going to spend Christmas at home – at our home port that is." There was a pause.

The entire ship rocked with applause, cheers and laughter. For a moment there was absolute bedlam. "We'll pull into White Beach, Okinawa at zero eight-thirty on the twenty-third, and liberty will commence at ten hundred hours. Thank you and good evening." Again the ship came alive with a cacophony of joy, like seniors on their last day of high school.

The ship pulled into the harbor at White Beach and dropped anchor at zero eight-thirty on the twenty-third and 'Cinderella liberty' was sounded for sections one and three. Pete was in section three so he put on his dress blues and went on the beach with the Pooh Bear. The two men spent the whole day eating, drinking and traveling around the island. It was wonderful to taste fresh vegetables and fruits again after such a long period at sea. The libations were not bad either. The rest of the time was spent shopping. Pete had a list a mile long the Admiral had given him for his family back home. The Admiral absolutely hated shopping, but loved gifting.

On the twenty-fourth, Pete's section of the ship's crew had duty, so he expected to stay aboard and watch TV and write a few letters home. There was no work to be done because the Captain had declared 'holiday routine' for the entire period in port. Pete was not so fortunate this time. As luck would have it, Pete drew Shore Patrol duty for Christmas Eve!

It was late afternoon when Pete reported to the Shore Patrol Officer at the afterbrow. He was pleased to see which officer had drawn the duty with him, Commander Hatchfield. He had relieved Commander Webster in Yokosuka at the same time Captain O'Hara had relieved Captain Hamblin.

The ride to the pier took only five minutes in the landing craft borrowed from the Marine Corps. The LCVP could easily carry a hundred men without crowding. It was certainly faster than twenty-two men in a Plane Service Boat or thirty men in a forty foot Crew's Launch.

The patrol area was divided up, beginning at the pier where two men would be stationed for the balance of the day. The next two went to Village One, and Pete drew Village Two with a Second Class Radioman named Mitchell off of the *USS Provincetown* (CG-66).

The little villages that sprang up around military facilities were rarely called by their local names. It was much easier to just specify them by number. Two other men were assigned to Village Three, and the balance of the force was assigned to the night club section of Koza, the major city of the island.

Sailors were not the only service men on the beach. There were also Marines and Air Force Personnel from Kadena Air Force Base, but they generally stayed in Koza. If they did venture out, they came all the way to the Enlisted Men's Club at White Beach.

Commander Hatchfield would stay with the 'hard hat shore patrol' in Koza next to the phone and take hourly reports from each patrol as they called in. The hard hats were the permanent military police of the area and were men rated in military police activities. Jeeps from the hard hats picked the group up and dropped them off at their assigned area. There were two in the jeep which carried

Mitchell and Pete. These men were giants compared to the two shipboard sailors. The fearsome looking duo were two feet wider and a foot and a half taller. Their dress blues were immaculate with white duty belts, leggings and yellow lettered SP bands on their right arm. Since they were the military police specialists of the Navy, they were allowed to carry firearms. Pete had never personally met one of these men before, but their reputation in the Philippines preceded them. It was said that they would bust your head first, throw you in jail and then ask if you were involved in the problem.

As Pete and Mitchell stepped from the jeep, the Petty Officer driving turned and spoke in a gravely voice. "If you boys run into anything you can't handle, just give us a call. We can be here in two minutes flat."

"Okay. Thanks." Pete said into the exhaust of the jeep as they drove away. Pete turned to Mitchell and shrugged his shoulders in disbelief.

Mitchell was a small man of five-foot-six, with a very cocky self-assured attitude. He had enough confidence for both men. "We won't need those chrome-domed jerks," he said, spitting into the dirt.

The next five hours crawled by as the men walked in one door and out another of the sixteen bars on their beat. The Bar Happy was the hardest bar for Pete to check because it was the one frequented by the men of his own division, and every time they went in they were greeted with invitations to join their mates for a drink, stories of how much fun they were having and other nuisance chatter from his friends.

Mitchell had received his Second Class crow two weeks before Pete, so that made him the senior Shore Patrolman. It was his responsibility to make reports, calls, arrests and other military decisions.

Each bar was territorialized by rating type, and unless you were wearing a Shore Patrol uniform, you were not welcome in a bar which was the territory of another rating type or at least of a different classification: Airedale, Black Shoe, or Snipe. The Airedales worked with the aircraft of the VP squadron. The Snipes tended the internal workings of the ship below the water line, and then there were the Black Shoes, like himself, who took care of clerical, supply, communications and everything above the water line and on the exterior of the ship.

As a Shore Patrolman, it paid to know the troublesome characteristics of each class. If a Black Shoe got into a disagreement, they tended to work it out or walk off. If an Airedale got upset, they tended to break things. If a Snipe got riled up, they tended to break people. The two patrolmen knew they had to pay the closest attention to the Bar New York, which was frequented by Snipes. The Bar New York was right on Highway One between three other bars that were entertaining Black Shoes.

Pete pulled the collar of his peacoat up against the damp night breeze coming off the ocean. The men had just turned the corner of the block onto Highway One.

"Shore Patrol! Shore Patrol!" A woman's voice came screeching through the damp darkness.

Pete squinted through the shadows of the window-lit street and saw the mamasan of the Bar New York jumping up and down on her toes waving her hands over her head. "He's killing him! He's killing him!" she shouted.

Mitchell leaned forward to quicken his pace. Pete took hold of his elbow. "You don't have to stop a fight. We'll arrest the winner when we get there," Pete stated philosophically.

"Come on!" Mitchell growled. " I get a chance to bust some heads and you want to hold me up!" Mitchell took off. Fearing he might cause some grief, Pete increased his stride and stayed right with him.

The Shore Patrolmen burst into the bar, their night sticks at the ready, expecting the place to be alive with flying chairs and bottles. Music was playing, the lights were low, people were dancing and sitting quietly in the booths. Every sailor seemed to be snuggled up to a pretty young woman.

The mamasan was now bouncing up and down at the edge of the dance floor next to the street front windows at the end of the bar. "He's killing him!" she screamed again.

When Pete reached the spot, he was relieved to see he knew at least one of the combatants. The larger black man doing "the killing" was Steam Pipe Smith, Machinist Mate Fireman. Pete had served on the mess deck with Steam Pipe two years earlier, and although they were not best buds, they were well acquainted.

Steam Pipe sat astraddle a young black Fireman's chest and his left hand held the man's head by the hair. The man on the floor was taking a real beating as Steam Pipe's huge right fist bore down on him striking him in the head.

Mitchell drew back his night stick about to strike Steam Pipe. Pete grabbed his arm. "How about letting me handle this, Mitch?" he pleaded. "I know this guy. He's not really a maniac." Mitchell lowered his stick, and Pete holstered his.

Pete leaned over face to face with the huge man on top. Steam Pipe's eight inch knuckles grazed Pete's face as he tapped him on the shoulder to get his attention. "Steam Pipe! What're you doing?" Pete demanded.

Steam Pipe's head turned up slightly and his eyes met Pete's. A smile of recognition broke over his big face and a soft deep voice came from his grinning mouth. "Hi, Pete. I saw you. You got Shore Patrol duty."

"That's right, Steamer." Pete smiled. "And I can't let you beat this man to a pulp. It's against the law. Why are you doing this?"

"He won't let me buy him a drink, Pete," Steam Pipe said, looking down only long enough to bounce another fist off of the man's forehead.

The man was bleeding from the nose, but his eyes were clear, and he was alert. He didn't appear to be in as much pain as Pete had expected.

Pete spoke to him. "How about if you let my friend here buy you a drink and I can be on my way and we don't have to call in the hard hats. What do you say?"

The man on the bottom jerked sideways, his eyes meeting Pete's. The man sneered his answer as Pete read his shoulder patch with his ship's name, *USS Ogden* (LPD-5). "Screw you, honky! Take yer nigger lovin' ass out'a here. I don't need yoe help. I can ..." He didn't finish the statement. Steam Pipe's gigantic fist slammed into the man's mouth.

"Don't talk like that Leroy, Pete's ma friend!" Steam Pipe screeched.

Mitchell was getting more frustrated and angry by the second. His patience wore out. He shoved his night stick into the side of Steam Pipe's huge neck. "I don't care if you blacks want to beat each other to death, but don't do it on my beat. Now, get off of him!"

Steam Pipe looked out of the corner of his eye at Mitchell and smashed another fist into the man on the floor.

"I warned you!" Mitchell screamed and his heavy oak stick cracked alongside Steam Pipe's ear.

Steam Pipe barely flinched. He took his left hand from the man on the floor and grabbed Mitchell's white duty belt. He raised Mitchell above his head like a rag doll and tossed him over a booth full of revelers, through the paper and bamboo wall into the street.
"Hey!" Pete said, after the amazement wore off. "You can't do..."
Steam Pipe's right hand took hold of Pete's duty belt and the next thing Pete knew, he was lying on the sidewalk next to Mitchell.

Mitchell had already pulled one leg up under himself getting ready to rush back into the bar. "We can take care of this big lug," he growled, giving Pete a hand up. "Let's go back in there and bust his coconut!"

Pete put a hand on the smaller man's shoulder. "I don't think that's the answer, Mitch. How 'bout letting me have one more crack at this guy?"

Mitchell said nothing. He just gave Pete a hard sideways glance, shook his head and followed him into the bar.

This time, instead of standing over Steam Pipe, Pete took out two one dollar bills, held them away from himself and lay down on the floor beside the two men. "Hey! You guys! How 'bout letting me buy you ***both*** a drink? Hey! How about it?" Pete prodded Steam Pipe under the chin with the bills. "What do you say? It's Christmas Eve, you know. Goodwill toward men! How 'bout it?"

Steam Pipe smiled down at the man on the floor. "I will if you will, Leroy."

The man on the floor seemed to think for a second or two before answering. "Only 'cause it's Christmas. I don't drink with white folks, and this honky is a Black Shoe and that's worse than bein' a honky!"

Steam Pipe let the man up as the blood from his nose was wiped away. "Leroy, this is ma friend, Pete. Pete, this is Leroy Hastings." Pete didn't ask about the dispute for fear of fueling the fire. He just slid onto a stool at the bar and ordered a round of drinks while Mitchell stewed quietly in a corner booth.

"Whatever these gents are drinking, fill 'em up. I'll have a Coke." Pete held the two dollar bills across the bar.

The bartender quickly filled the request, setting liquor across the bar to the combatants and handing a Coke up to Pete.

"Hold it, honky," Leroy spat, as he sucked the dry blood from his lower lip. "If yer gonna drink wid' me, *drink* wid' me. Don't gimme none a that, I'll have a Coke, shit!"

Pete fidgeted for a second, rubbing his thumb with the first finger of his right hand.

Steam Pipe leaned forward on the bar, his massive body in front of Pete as he spoke to Leroy. "Pete's from Utah, an' he don't drink much. Besides, he gots the duty!"

"I don't care!" Leroy spat. "If this honky wants to drink wid' me, he hasta *drink* and not be pretending he's no Shirley Temple!"

"It's Okay!" Pete said, pushing his glass across the bar. "Bartender, add a little rum to this Coke, please."

After the first drink was gone, Pete pointed to Leroy, "Okay, Pal. It's your turn to buy." The bartender set up another round of drinks, and Leroy instinctively shoveled out two dollars. After Leroy, Steam Pipe bought, and Pete felt satisfied that the men had drank together.

"Leroy, it's your turn to buy, but I have to be on my way. We have a lot of rounds to make before Santa comes."

Pete picked his white hat off the bar and motioned to Mitchell. The Shore Patrolmen started for the door, but Steam Pipe's huge right hand grabbed Pete's arm. Standing, he pulled Pete up close so he could whisper.

"Thanks for showing me that this guy is Okay, Pete. I just haven't liked him since he married my sister." Steam Pipe released his grip and the Shore Patrolmen left the bar shaking their heads. Pete and Mitchell had not traveled thirty steps down the pavement when the mama-san was behind them screaming. "Shore Patrol! Shore Patrol!"

"Oh, boy!" Mitchell grumped. "Your way didn't work." He turned and asked the woman as she approached, "Are they at it again?"

"No. I'm here to collect," she said emphatically, her left hand extended palm up.

"Collect for what?" Pete demanded.

"A hundred bucks, Joe!" Her eyes pierced into Pete's and she spoke with rigid determination as she pointed to the front of her establishment.

"You knock out wall! You pay to fix wall!"

Mitchell extended both his hands and patted his backside as if feeling for a wallet. "Hey man, I'm tapped out until payday."

Pete fished his wallet from an inside jumper pocket and looked at the contents. There were three one hundred dollar bills, a twenty, a five and three ones. He thumbed the contents.

Pete's first thought was to argue. *Steam Pipe broke the wall! Or it's Mitchell's wall, he went through it first. Arguing, who knows what that will lead to? I can see her calling the hard hats on us.* "Here!" Pete slapped a hundred dollar bill into her hand. *I was going to buy Mom a new set of china when the ship reached Yokosuka,* Pete thought. *Looks like that Christmas present can wait.*

"Thanks, Joe. You a very good Shore Patrol. I hope you have this beat often. Merry Christmas!" She winked and danced back into the bar.

It was half an hour before midnight and Cinderella liberty was about to expire. The bars were closing and the Shore Patrol was making sure all the men got back to their ships.

When they got to the Bar New York, Steam Pipe and Leroy were walking down the sidewalk arm in arm singing Christmas carols. With all the sailors gone from the street, the hard hat jeep picked them up, taking Mitchell to headquarters to fill out a final report and dropping Pete at the pier.

Arriving at the pier, over two-hundred sailors waited on the covered landing for the boat to make its round trip from their ship. Three crews mingled on the pier, the *Provincetown,* the *Ogden* and the *Blue Island Sound.*

Pete reported to Commander Hatchfield and stood around with everyone else to await the arrival of the next launch. One of the two

Shore Patrolmen assigned to the pier came up to the Commander and spoke in a low whisper. "Sir, we need to do something. There's a lot of tension in the air." His eyes darted around at the large group of men. " I'm afraid we might have a riot on our hands if we don't do something."

Commander Hatchfield turned to Pete. "What do you think Pete?"

"I've seen two fist fights already, sir. For most of these men, this is their first cruise. They're away from home, away from all they hold dear at Christmas." Pete shook his head. "They've been drinking, they're lonely and feeling remorseful."

The Commander folded his arms across his chest and smiled. "You're from Utah. What do they do in Utah when a tense herd of cows starts milling around."

Pete's brow furrowed at the thought. "We sing to 'em, sir," Pete answered.

"So go sing to 'em, Pete," said the Commander, pointing toward the crowd.

Pete walked to the edge of the herd and started tapping his night stick on the concrete to get attention and clear a path. When he reached the center of the milling melancholy men, he raised his nightstick like a giant baton, made motions like an orchestra leader and began to serenade them with the first bars of "Rudolph The Red Nose Reindeer."

Surprised by the sudden joining of voices, Pete sang louder. He had his own giant choir. They sang songs of Christmas until the last launch was on its way to it's ship. The caroling continued in the launches as they disappeared in the darkness. There was not a single incident on the pier.

The next day, Holiday Routine was declared throughout the ship as the ship got underway for Yokosuka, Japan, a beautiful port city with lots of friendly people, plenty of shopping and other things to do. Only the duty section had to respond to their work stations. That meant the cooks in the galley and the 'underway duty section' had to work. Pete spent part of the day in his bunk, catching up on his rest.

About two in the afternoon Pete was sitting at his desk in the Electronics Supply Office when an announcement came over the public address system. "Now Storekeeper Second Class Peterson. Lay before the mast. The Captain is on the bridge."

In Navy jargon, 'lay before the mast' means appear before the Captain of the ship. You would do this only to meet with a military court. To be summoned in this manner, without notice meant that Pete must be in serious trouble. Pete called down to the Supply Office to see if anyone knew what he was wanted for, but the phone just rang and rang. Pete looked at his uniform. He was wearing dungarees, clean but not pressed. *There is no time to change, I'm wanted NOW!*

Pete hurried up the two flights of stairs to the bridge. He saluted the Officer of the Deck and requested permission to enter the bridge. He entered and stood at attention several feet back, but directly behind the Captain, who was sitting in a large elevated chair looking out at the open sea.

Pete was sure he was in deep *kimshi* as the Captain's chair spun around and he noticed for the first time that the Chief Master At Arms, Commander Hatchfield, Admiral Moore and several Storekeepers were also there.

There are men from my division present. I guess everybody needs a witness.

The Chief Master At Arms was carrying a clipboard, presumably a good place to carry a list of charges to be read to the accused. He raised the board and began. "Petty Officer Second Class Peterson. We have a memo from the Captain of the *USS Provincetown* (CG-66)." He hesitated for a second looking at the Captain who raised one eyebrow. "The communication reads: Due to your instigation, on the night of 24 December, the shore party returning from liberty arrived at the ship singing Christmas carols and sang them all the way through the ship and into the bunking spaces where they woke their shipmates. Because of the attitude that my crew returned to the ship with, all incidents were resolved without confrontation. A first for this command. Thank you Petty Officer Peterson." The Master At Arms came to attention and retired to a position behind the officers.

"I have a more serious matter here," said the Captain, opening a folder in front of him. "I have a report of one of my Shore Patrolmen drinking on duty."

A wry smile came to the Admiral's face as he interjected. "Or did that Shore Patrolman simulate drinking in an effort to resolve a potentially dangerous incident and bring all of his shipmates home safely?"

"Pete," Captain O'Hara said. "We're here as the officers and men of this command to say a heartfelt thank you for caring about your fellow man under these conditions in these times. Thank you!"

"I have a little something personal for you, Pete," said the Admiral, handing him a white envelope and shaking his hand.

Pete took the envelope and came to attention.

"You are all dismissed," said the Captain as he rose and shook Pete's hand. The men from Pete's division broke into cheers and applause.

When Pete got back to the privacy of the Electronics Supply Office, he opened the envelope from Admiral Moore. There was a crisp $100 dollar bill and a note. "I'm sure this will serve a special purpose. Merry Christmas and God Bless."

It's great, being home for Christmas. In your home port, that is. Pete thought as he stuffed his Christmas present into his shirt pocket.

Chapter 26

On Report

On the third of January, the *USS Blue Island Sound* was taking on aviation gasoline at the Yokosuka pier prior to getting underway. The Boatswain's Mate of the Watch, working from the after brow, had passed the word, "The smoking lamp is out throughout the ship with the exception of the Fox, G and W head, where the lamp will remain lighted." For the rest of the ship, the smoking lamp was out as long as the orange gas truck sat on the pier. The *Blue Island Sound* was due to take on three loads, and the one on the dock would be the last.

Pete peered out a porthole in the Supply Office where he had been typing purchase orders all morning. He had just arrived in the office from lunch and the rest of the office staff was not back yet. He fidgeted with his shirt pocket, hunting for his pack of cigarettes. The big orange gas truck was now rolling up its final length of hose and pulling away.

Pete was excitedly waiting to hear the Boatswain relight the smoking lamp throughout the ship. The announcement did not come. He put an unlit cigarette into his mouth, then tossed his lighter into the air and caught it. He laid the lighter on his desk, anticipating the lighting of the smoking lamp. He had not had a cigarette all day, and they always seemed to taste best right after a meal. *Well, what the heck*, thought Pete as he picked up the phone on his desk and dialed.

"After brow. Petty Officer Of The Watch speaking. Can I help you?" came the voice at the other end.

"May I speak to the Junior Officer Of The Deck?" Pete asked impatiently.

Momentarily a familiar voice came on. "Storekeeper First Class Lee speaking. May I help you?"

"Lee, it's Pete. How come you haven't announced the smoking lamp yet?"

"Oh, the smoking lamp is lit all right. I just can't announce it because the 1MC is on the blink and hasn't worked at all for the last half hour. I just hung up from registering a formal complaint with those Communication Electricians down in Engineering. I had to send my Boatswain's Mate of the Watch up to the bridge to make the announcement from there," continued Lee in an agitated voice.

Pete didn't wait for him to finish. He flicked his lighter and lit his smoke. "You say it is lit though, right?"

"Yes, Pete!" First Class Lee snarled. "I know you have better ears than that."

"Thanks!" Pete said and hung up the phone. It sounded like Lee had enough trouble without Pete adding to it.

Pete took a deep drag on his cigarette and leaned back in his chair with his eyes closed. He savored the smoke as the golden flavor drifted out of his mouth and past his nostrils. Suddenly, he sensed a presence. Someone else was in the office with him – someone unfamiliar. He opened his eyes and let the front legs of his chair drop to the deck. Pete was startled by the presence of ***Molini***, master at arms.

Molini was half crouching as he walked. He screamed and pointed a stubby finger at Pete. "I gotcha! I gotcha! I've gotcha now, you bag of spit! Your ass is mine now! What time is it?" He screeched, almost in laughter.

In his shock, Pete could not answer. Molini took the time from a large clock on the wall. "What's your name?" he heckled, trying not to break into laughter. His face making angry contortions. "What's your name?"

"Molini, you dipstick!" Pete exclaimed. "You know very well what my name is. Now, what's this about?" Pete thought he had better take the offensive until he was sure of what was going on. "Listen, mister. If you don't have business with Supply, I suggest you leave this office."

Molini was writing on his report chit pad as fast as he could write. He tore out the chit with a sudden jerk and handed it to Pete. He turned and started for the door, laughing and muttering to himself. "I can't believe it. I can't believe it. I got him, I finally got him!"

Pete looked down at the white chit in his hand. At fourteen-thirty hours – two thirty in the afternoon of January third, Pete had been placed on report for 'Smoking while the smoking lamp was out.'

As the office door closed behind Molini, the word was passed over the 1MC from the bridge. "Now, the smoking lamp is lighted throughout the ship."

There was little sense in trying to explain the situation to Molini, and besides the ship was getting underway in an hour.

The next morning, a Messenger Of The Watch came to Pete's table on the main mess deck. "Your Captain's Mast is set for eleven hundred hours on the forward mess deck. You are to appear with any witnesses you think can be beneficial to your case."

Pete looked around the ship for SK1 Lee and was told he had flown to Kobi in the HU16 Charlie mail plane at the last moment to pick up a part for the ship's radar system.

Since Pete didn't have the Petty Officer that had issued the order, maybe he could get a copy of the engineering log showing the time Lee had reported the 1MC as being in a disabled condition. He rushed down to the engineering log room and asked the Petty Officer on duty if he could see yesterday's log. He scanned the page for an entry in the afternoon. There was none!

"I know for a fact, the 1MC on the after Quarterdeck was reported down about fourteen hundred yesterday. What happened to the record?" Pete demanded.

"Don't get so hot, buddy." said the Second Class IC Electrician. "We got called away to do a rush job for the master at arms Office." He turned the time report page and put his finger under an entry. "See. Right there is your precious call. The log read *fifteen hundred*. "See there." His finger slid down one space. "We had the entire ship's PA system back on line by fifteen-thirty. The afterbrow section was only down for a half an hour."

Pete left Engineering feeling very frustrated. Lee was gone, and he didn't know of any way to prove his innocence. It seemed Molini had seen to that. There had been no witnesses to Pete's end of this conversation. The office had been empty.

It was time for his mast. Pete returned to his compartment and put on his best dress blues and reported to the Chief Master At Arms on the forward mess deck.

This time, Pete was the only man before the mast. The legal orderly started the proceedings. "SK2 Peterson, lay before the mast!"

Pete wheeled and marched to within three feet of the Captain's desk.

The orderly went on. "Storekeeper Second Class Peterson, you are called here to answer the charge of smoking while the smoking lamp was out throughout the ship. To whit, while taking on aviation gasoline at the Yokosuka pier at fourteen-thirty hours on the third day of January this year."

Pete could feel his pulse rate rising. His hands were beginning to sweat as they hung lifeless at his side.

"Storekeeper Second Class, Peterson. How do you plead to the charges as read here?" asked the orderly.

Pete's mouth was dry. The words stuck in his throat as he struggled to answer. "Not guilty."

"Be seated," commanded the orderly. "Boatswain's Mate Second Class Molini, before the mast."

Pete sat at the accused table a little behind and to his left and watched Molini romp jubilantly from his station beside the Chief Master At Arms, before the Captain.

The orderly went on. "Master At Arms Molini, state the case as you see it."

Molini glanced sideways at Pete, then turned back full face to the Captain to boast his story in his raspy little voice like a tattling child.

When Molini finished, the Captain spoke as he closed a file folder in front of him. "Petty Officer Peterson, this is a very serious offense for a person with a service record that reads like the history of Mr. Clean. What have you got to say for yourself?"

Pete rose to attention and related his story as best he could recall it, pointing out, "If Lee were here he could verify my statement."

Pete told the Captain he had tried to track down anyone who had been on watch with Lee but could not find anyone. He told the Captain of trying to check the Engineering log that Lee had told him about, but all he could say in the end was that he was not lying and the smoking lamp was lighted, it just wasn't announced yet.

As Pete took his seat, Molini became enraged and blurted out. "You can't believe this man, sir. He and Lee are both Storekeepers and they'll lie for each other. This man is guilty and should be busted to Seaman and given thirty days in the brig."

Captain O'Hara raised his left hand to quell Molini's outburst.

"Petty Officer Peterson, there is one place you forgot to check when you were trying to clear yourself."

The Messenger Of The Watch entered the mess deck and laid the Ship's Log from the bridge on the desk by the Captain's left hand. The Captain opened the book and ran his finger down the page.

"Entry by the Quartermaster of the Watch for the Junior Officer of the Deck, January three at fourteen-o-six hours." The Captain read from the page. 'The 1MC is not working from the After Quarterdeck brow station, it has been reported to Engineering as of fourteen-o-five. The Boatswain's Mate of the Watch has been sent to the bridge to pass the word, 'The smoking lamp is lighted throughout the ship. Refueling of aviation gasoline is completed.'"

The Captain closed the log with a thundering fist. "Petty Officer Peterson, it seems you have been dealt an injustice."

He glared sideways at Molini. "I hope you will forgive the system, and my Chief Master At Arms will personally see that such a thing never happens again." He waved his large right hand. "Dismissed!"

"Thank you, sir!" Pete said, scooping up his white hat and leaving the mess deck.

Pete knew two things right there and then. Number one, he would give up smoking and number two, he would make it a point to never get put on report again.

Chapter 27

On the Beach in Tokyo

Pete sat in the Electronics Supply Office studying his World History 101 extension course from the University of Michigan when a knock came at the door. It was his long-time friend, Chip Dale. Where his parents ever got the name would always be a mystery to Pete.

"Hey, Pete." His smile was broad and bright as he pushed his glasses back on his broad Ceasar-like nose. "Why don't you go on the beach with me in Yokosuka? We'll tie up in the morning, and you and I can make a day of shopping for cameras and stereo equipment. I hear the base exchange here is the biggest store the U.S. Navy has in the world and they have everything. They can even ship sets of china to the folks back home. You have to pay the handling and duty, but it would still be worth it."

Chip was one of the brightest people Pete knew. Very young for being a Second Class Electronics Technician. His specialty was radar, and he was the best on the ship. He was always saving money and concerned about the family back home. He was the example of the clean-cut American boy.

"I don't know, Chip," Pete sighed, closing his text book. "I got a C on my last exam in this subject, and if I don't get hot, I'll fail the course."

"Come on!" He put his hand pleadingly on Pete's shoulder. "We've been at sea for a long time. You can do this when we get back. Besides, I know you promised the Admiral you'd pick up a new camera for his granddaughter. It beats me how you can make a promise to the Admiral and leave it until the last minute, and then, half the time you have his staff car take you to wherever it is you have to go." Chip tipped his head slightly. "You can take care of your promise early, and after, we can go into Tokyo and see a stage show at the Nichigeki Theater."

Pete started to laugh. "You dummy! The Nichigeki Theater is in Tokyo! You can't expect to go shopping in Yokosuka in the morning, see a stage show in Tokyo and be back aboard by the time Cinderella liberty expires at midnight."

Chip's smile got bigger. "All you do is tell the Admiral you'd like a three-day pass when you get his money for the camera this afternoon."

In the afternoon Pete went to the Admiral's stateroom, a luxurious place by naval standards. There were couches and chairs, overstuffed, of course, and even a queen-size bed.

So this was what Captain O'Hara was talking about when he said our days as a floating hotel were over.

Pete spent several minutes with the Admiral shooting the breeze. Of all the people in the supply department, Pete was his favorite. Admiral Moore said Pete reminded him of his grandson. The nice thing was the Admiral was very likable, and Pete enjoyed being his gopher.

The next morning, about a half an hour after 'liberty call' went down, Chip and Pete left the ship and started for the pier compound gates. The pier gates were a security area manned by the finest fleet marines. Their job was to keep the piers safe and not allow unauthorized people near the ships.

As the two men left the after brow of the ship for the gates, a half mile away, they started seeing sailors they recognized, walking back toward the ship. Two of them were Howell and Racozad, Pete's good buddies. Pete stopped them as they approached. "What's with you guys? I've never seen a port you returned from early. Did you already burn all the bars down or did you just forget your money?"

"Rats!" Howell said, kicking up gravel at his feet. "There's a jarhead Sergeant at the gate. I think he's the head MP. He won't let us go onto the base." Howell put his closed fists on his hips. "You guys might make it because you're Petty Officers of the same rank." He stomped an errant bug beneath the glassy spit-shined shoe of his right foot and continued to look down. "He's pulling dress inspections on everybody. He's even checking dog tags! If you ain't got 'em, you go back to the boat."

Pete pointed his friends back to the gate with his 'sailor's rights' speech. "That's a bunch of bilge water! We don't have to take this kind of treatment from any Mud Marine!"

When they got to the gate, Howell was right. The Sergeant was inspecting a sailor's dog tags.

Seeing a sailor humiliated by a Marine Corps door monitor disgusted Pete. "What's going on here, Sarge?" Pete growled as he approached the sentry. "We've been at sea! Our uniforms are sharp! We have good military bearing, and you're not going to play bully boy with this ship's company any more! I'm talking to you bellhop, so listen up!" Boy, did Pete know how to pick a fight.

The jarhead did a perfect military about face and stepped up nose-to-nose with Pete. Two more MPs were suddenly on either side of him. A dozen sailors were crowding around with angry faces. The Sergeant placed his finger on the eagle of Pete's Second Class insignia.

"Bellhop, huh?" He spoke like the traditional Marine Corps Sergeant: open mouth, snaggle-toothed expression. "You're under arrest, wise-ass!" He ground the sole of his boot over the spit-shine on the toe of Pete's left shoe. The two MPs beside Pete grabbed his arms. Pete stared stiffly into the man's eyes as he heard handcuffs coming out of a belt on his left.

"You're not dressed for liberty, squid! Your shoes need shining! You're under arrest for interfering with the military police in the course of their duty, and attempting to start a riot." He gestured to the guard station building. "Take him inside and call his CO." The Sergeant put his finger on Pete's chest. "You're going to our brig here on the station, Mr. Alligator Mouth."

Whoa! The memory of the Brig Chaser incident aboard the *Kingston* raced through Pete's mind. *What have I gotten myself into? These guys can get real nasty if they want to.* The difference was, Pete was being nasty right back, and he knew it. Pete was determined to raise the biggest stink he could.

Pete's two body guards were putting the handcuffs on him just as the Admiral's car rolled up right beside the group. Everybody popped tall. The Sergeant saw the flag on the fender with two stars waving in the breeze and immediately fired off a sharp military salute. "You may pass, sir!" The car idled on the tarmac, not moving.

The rear window of the car came down, and the smiling face of the Admiral appeared. "Pete, did you. . . ?" His voice trailed off for a moment as he looked at Pete's hands. His eyes narrowed, his brow furrowed and his right eyebrow raised. "What's going on here?" Admiral Moore demanded with a heavy growling voice. "Sergeant! You get on the phone and get the Officer Of the Guard down here on the double!" The window went back up.

Within two minutes, a jeep came roaring up. A young marine Lieutenant jumped out and stood at attention on the other side of the Admiral's car. There must have been some chewing going on, because the young officer's face grew quite rosy.

"Thank you, sir!" The Officer Of the Guard said, popping tall with a salute.

The Lieutenant walked into the guard station as the car pulled away. He made a hand motion as he entered. "Wilson!" he said in a harsh voice.

The Sergeant dashed into the station. Muffled yelling and profanity could be heard from where Pete stood, his heart still pumping double-time.

The MP on Pete's left unlocked the handcuffs and said, "I think you guys had best leave now." He took out his handkerchief and wiped the toe of Pete's shoe. "Sorry, guys, but I just work here. We tried to tell this dope when the first *Blue Island* sailor showed up, our job is to keep people off the pier, not to keep sailors off the base." Without further interference, all the sailors were passed onto the base.

In a couple of hours, Chip and Pete had completed their shopping at the Navy Exchange and were on their way back to the ship in a taxi. Taxi cabs were not allowed onto the pier, so the two friends started to get out of the cab at the gate guard station. Pete was just clearing the taxi door when a familiar voice got his attention.

"Hey, Storekeeper!" It was the Marine Lance Corporal who had dusted his shoe off. "We have a special pass for you if you should want to bring a taxi onto the pier. You tell the guard on duty the code words, 'Admiral 13 red.'" He held out a plastic card with the seal of the Commander, Naval Patrol Force, Pacific Fleet on it.

"For an enlisted man, you sure carry a lot of clout. I've never seen this base so turned upside down," he whispered, handing Pete the pass.

Pete smiled and handed the pass to the driver, and the two men hopped back into the taxi. Pete noticed the marine was no longer wearing his comfortable khaki uniform, instead he wore full dress blues with red jacket and white hat. "Kind of hot for full dress canvas, isn't it?" Pete asked as he closed the car door.

A small wry smile accompanied the young marine's answer. "We'll be wearing this uniform until your ship pulls out of port."

Chip was leaning across the seat with his question. "Where's the Sergeant who was here when we came out?"

The young jarhead shifted his weight uneasily from his left side to his right, leaning inside the window to speak in a clear whisper. "Do we really have a base on the South Pole?"

His question was answered with laughter from the car. Chip patted the driver on the shoulder, and the small compact lurched forward and sped off down the pier to the afterbrow of the *Blue Island Sound.*

Within the hour, the two friends had stowed their gear aboard ship and were back on the highway leading from Yokosuka around Tokyo Bay to the beautiful capitol city and its exotic, exciting Ginza Strip, second only to the Las Vegas strip. Their objective was at the other end of the Ginza, the Nichigeki Theater.

In Pete's opinion, it was one of the world's foremost entertainment centers. The theater featured plays, stage productions, operas and reviews from all parts of the world. The most popular show was naturally the Paris Review with all the beautiful, scantily-clad ladies, prancing, dancing and showing off their feathers.

In the area between Yokosuka and Tokyo, there is a vast plain covered with rice fields, an agricultural belt much like Kansas – extremely boring to drive across as a passenger in a taxi going forty kilometers per hour, a twenty-four mile an hour snail's pace by western standards.

"How do we get this driver to go faster?" Chip queried. "Do you suppose we could offer him a couple of bucks like they do in the movies? Maybe he'd step on it a little bit."

Mustering up his best Japanese, Pete spoke. "Hioko, dozo!" This, Pete recalled, meant 'at one hundred, please.' The car sped up just a little. Pete took out a five hundred yen bill and handed it over the seat. "Hioko, dozo?"

The driver took the bill. The automobile had right side steering so Pete had a good view of the odometer, which now was registering 70 kilometers per hour. Chip took out a bill and did the same thing. Up went the speedometer to eighty. The speed limit was fifty.

The taxi was speeding along to the outskirts of Tokyo when a motorcycle cop on a shining white Honda pulled the taxi over and gave the driver a ticket. After the policeman left, the driver studied the ticket for a minute, then turned to the back seat and said. "Forty thousand yen, please!"

The impatient passengers placed a hundred and twelve dollars American, at the exchange rate, in the driver's outstretched hand and the conversation ended.

The driver let the men off at a fine French hotel right on the Ginza Strip. "I know there are American hotels around, but this one's only two blocks from the theater." Chip said. "Just look at it, Pete! It's so worth it!"

Chip took a deep breath as he stepped from the taxi and handed his overnight bag to one of the bellmen who met them graciously on the front sidewalk. "What a fantastic city Tokyo is. It's really remarkable to think every piece of wood, nearly every stone and piece of steel in this city had to be shipped in."

He must have done some reading.

The men checked the theater schedule while they registered. A Paris Review was playing! Exactly what they had hoped for, a musical.

They followed a bellman to the eighth floor and watched as he opened the drapes to show a beautiful view of the city and Tokyo Bay.

It didn't take them long to settle into their luxurious suite. A bathroom adjoined two large areas with king size beds. A privacy wall ran from inside the front door to the bathroom, creating two spacious compartments.

The walls were painted with picturesque dragons, tigers and the ever-present oriental scene. A bridge from nowhere crossed a great gorge and a path that wound up to a hill into the clouds -- on top of the hill there is always only one bonsai tree in this breathtaking scene.

Chip threw his overnight bag on the floor, stomped off his shoes and jumped onto a bed. "Hot dawg! A real bed! This one's mine!" The bed sagged, rocked and rolled into the wall with a whack as Chip lunged forward and bunched the polyester pillow under his head. "Man, this feels good! Why didn't you ask the Admiral for a week? I could easily stand this for a few days!"

Pete called room service and had two rum and Cokes sent up, wondering if there was anywhere in the world that you could not get a rum and Coke.

The two friends kicked back on their beds and sipped their drinks and soaked up the soft jazz playing on the radio. One of the things Pete liked most about Japan, was that he never felt like he was in a foreign country. They were deep into a discussion of Japanese surface culture versus subculture when a soft knock came at the door.

Chip sprang from his bed and opened the door. Pete could not make out the conversation being conducted at the half-closed entry until Chip threw the door open. "Hey! Let's ask my partner here."

A small man in a white coat, the floor boy, advanced into the room and spoke to Pete. "Would you like some very high quality girls?" he asked, a smile spreading across his round face. "We have some very nice girls who work this hotel. We take care of all kinds of big shots here. We serve both the military and civilian world." He winked and continued. "We do not get many enlisted men."

Chip paced around Pete, grabbing his shoulder. "Pete, we got two months pay to burn! We're fixin' to go to sea again and we've sent presents home to everybody we know. Now, it's our turn to grab some fun." His face was plaintive as he eyed Pete's conservative frown. Chip was usually the one who was concerned about saving money. "Come on, Pete! Let's at least talk to these ladies."

A short 30 seconds later, the door opened and in walked two lovely young Japanese women. "To talk is five dollar. A short time is ten dollar and an overnight is thirty dollar. Please." The floor boy extended an open hand. "We are talking American, U.S. dollars. Please pay now."

"I'm sorry," Pete said, half turning away. "All we have is MPC, Military Pay Certificates, or yen. If you're looking for a little American green to peddle on the black market, you've come to the wrong place."

"No. No. No!" exclaimed the floor boy, reaching out to arrest Pete's departure. "You misunderstand! We just want the price to be clear! So everyone can agree."

Chip grabbed the shorter of the two girls and waltzed her off to his side of the room. "Put us down for two overnights!" He guided his girl onto a leather-backed bar stool. "This little honey reminds me of my 'tight podner' in Okinawa." He whipped out his wallet and slapped the equivalent of thirty U.S. dollars on the bar.

Pete was still trying to retrieve his wallet from his inside jumper pocket. From the moment the young women entered the room, Pete had been captivated by this young woman's eyes; she was now awaiting his big decision. "Come on, Pete! Pay up!" Chip chided as he crossed the room and slipped his money into the floor boy's open hand.

"I am, I am." Pete stammered, as he wrestled the money from his wallet and laid it on top of Chip's.

The floor boy took the money in two cupped hands and leaned forward, bowing his grey head gracefully. "Please have a most enjoyable night, gentlemen," he said as the door closed.

The girl next to Pete now spoke for the first time. "Hi," she beamed. "My name is Rose. This is my first night, so you'll have to pardon me if I'm a little backward at first."

Pete took her hand, and they sat down on a nearby sofa. Pete couldn't get over how lovely she was. She stood five foot six, extremely tall for a Japanese girl. Her skin was a golden bronze color, not the normal olive brown Pete was so used to seeing. Her face was a delicate oval, with a turned up pixie nose and her eyes were large and round. Her mouth was wide and her thick supple lips were a perfect pout which matched her narrow chin. This was quite a contrast to the round faces he was used to seeing in the Orient. This girl looked almost like an American. Whatever the case, Pete had never been close to such pure natural beauty before.

There was giggling through the partition, but for Pete, it went unheard. He was drinking in the beauty of this young woman before him. Long radiant, dark hair with a slight reddish sheen to it, an hour glass figure, and on top of all that, a stunning command of the English language.

"My name's Pete," he said. "We're on a pass for this evening and we're going to the theater. I'd like very much if you would come with me." Pete looked at his watch. It was nearly time for the show to start at the Nichigeki.

Pete started changing into his civilian clothes from his overnight bag. He spoke through the partition to Chip as he buttoned the last button on his shirt. "It's just about show time, old buddy! If you have any intention of going you'd better get some kind of hot, and in a hurry."

The voice of a happy man reached Pete's ears. "I'm hot, partner! Red hot! You, go ahead. You can tell me all about it tomorrow."

Rose and Pete left for the theater and saw one of the finest live stage productions Pete had ever seen. Of course, it was in French, as most French Reviews are. Rose told Pete what was going on. Another pleasant surprise, she spoke French.

After the show they went to several casinos along the Ginza Strip and then to a fine restaurant for dinner and drinks. Rose also proved to be a fine dancer.

It was well past one in the morning when they got back to the room. Pete fumbled in the darkness and turned on the small lamp by his bed. He undressed and showered first. While Rose was in the shower, Pete nuzzled down between the fresh sheets waiting with anticipation of the beautiful shadowy form approaching the bed with just a towel around her.

She clicked off the lamp just as she released the towel and let it fall to the floor. It was only for a second that Pete had the opportunity to look upon what he considered to be the world's most perfect woman.

Pete was totally awed and infatuated. He was completely under this beauty's spell. She slid between the sheets, her warm soft body next to his. Her hand was on Pete's chest. He could feel the fire welling up inside of him as his left hand found its way over her leg, her thigh, her tiny waist. Pete touched her firm, fully rounded breasts.

What an absolutely perfect woman for fate to treat me to!

"I want to thank you for the most enjoyable evening I've had for a long time." She spoke softly, as if not wishing to disturb Pete. She pressed her cheek close to his. Pete could feel a tear on his face. It wasn't his! Pete was in no mood for tears.

"Hey! What's with the tears?" Pete asked, sitting up. He could see the tears making angular streaks down her face in the soft moonlight shining through the window. Pete sighed deeply. He was no longer in the mood for romance. "Maybe we'd better talk. Why don't you tell me a little about yourself and what's bothering you."

A sad story unfolded. Rose was the daughter of a French army officer who was killed in Vietnam when she was only two years old. Her mother was Vietnamese, not Japanese. She had been raised in a French Catholic school near Tokyo. Rose's uncle had arranged for her and her mother, who was a nurse at the Catholic school, to join him in Los Angeles where he had obtained U.S. citizenship. Rose was to go to school at UCLA on a scholarship to study acting. Unfortunately, Rose's mother died suddenly, and the money her uncle sent was used for expenses.

Rose was only a hundred dollars shy of having enough money for her airfare to the States, and if she worked the hotel for only five nights, she'd have enough money for the flight. If it were not for her financial woes, she would not be in this situation. She told Pete she had never been with a man before, but she was willing to do whatever she must to get to the free shores of the U.S.A.

Pete was destroyed. *What if this were my sister trying to get to a safe sanctuary and had to go through this kind of ordeal?* Pete knew there was only one thing to do. He leaped from the bed. "Get your clothes on," he snapped, grabbing his undershirt off the dresser and sliding it over his head.

"Are you mad at me, Pete?" Rose asked plaintively. "I don't want you to be mad at me. You are the nicest person I have met in a long time. You are very kind and considerate."

Pete smiled and kissed her on the cheek. "No, I'm not mad at you. Do you have a passport? Where are your belongings?"

* * *

It was almost eight-thirty the next morning when Chip entered the third floor coffee shop where Pete was slowly finishing his fourth cup of coffee. "You lucky son of a gun, you!" Chip exclaimed as he pulled up his chair and motioned the waiter to bring him a cup of coffee.

"You spent the night with a Tokyo legend! The gal you were with is really a story. She blew into town six months ago and started working the best hotels. She hasn't actually slept with but two or three of her clients. She's got this terrific story she tells the john, and before you know it, he slips her a hundred dollars and throws her out of the room. The girl I was with has been her sidekick for four months."

Pete felt his face warming, turning red. A small surge of anger raced up from the knot in the pit of his stomach. "Oh," Pete said, "so tell me more. It seems to me the little honey you were with is a regular fountain of information."

The waiter delivered the coffee and menu as Chip went on. " I guess it's true. When she first started, she was on her way to some of her relatives in the States. She was going to attend UCLA, but she found the pickings so easy here she just stayed on and took the johns down the primrose lane as fast as they could line up."

The waiter interrupted Chip long enough to take their orders for breakfast and left. "I'm proud of you! You old sea dog. I'll bet you had a night with her that neither of you will ever forget. Tell me. Was it a night you'll not soon forget?" He leaned across the table in anticipation of Pete's story of a night of love making with the goddess of prostitutes of the Orient.

Pete felt a smile of irony trickle across his confused face. It was funny! Pete began to laugh aloud.

"Pete!" Chip pulled at his friend's elbow. "I've heard of it being good, but never funny. What's the joke?"

Pete looked him in the eye, watching his reaction as he spoke. "I put Rose on a plane for LA this morning at zero four thirty-two. It cost me one hundred and twenty bucks. I guess this john ***really*** kicked her out of his room."

Chip roared with laughter. The irony of Pete's story was more than he could take, and he could not conceal his feelings.

* * *

By sundown the two friends were back in the bars along saloon row in Yokosuka, having a few drinks, and a few more drinks. There were plenty of girls who were interested in drinking and dancing, and that is what these guys wanted to do on their last night in town. It was nearly twenty-three hundred hours, and liberty for the crew expired on board ship at midnight. *Good old Cinderella Liberty!*

Chip gave Pete a little shove, knocking his drink over. "Hey, old stick! It's time to go back to the boat. We have to get underway for the good old South China Sea in the morning, and we'd better be there or your Admiral will never give us another pass."

The men pulled themselves together as best they could and caught a cab outside the bar. When they got to the main gate the driver spoke. "You must get out now. No taxi is allowed on the base after twenty-two hundred hours. It's only a twenty-minute walk from here to your ship."

Pete leaned out the window as the marine gate guard began to approach.

"Admiral 13 red!" he slurred.

The guard did an about face and went into the guard shack. He came out carrying the pier pass. He handed it to the driver with a reminder,

"This is a pier pass. Return it to me as you leave the base." He popped tall, rendered his best military salute and sounded off. "You may pass!" The taxi was also passed on immediately by the marine in full dress blues at the pier gate.

During all of this, the driver did not speak, but as the men got out at the ship's after brow he declared his amazement. "You must be officers playing a game!"

"Not us!" Chip slurred as he paid the driver. "We're the game, playing officers!" Chip leaned back and roared a heavy guttural laugh that only people from Minnesota can produce.

By now, all the rum Pete had drunk was settling in on him. He was truly plowed, the drunkest he had been since the Royal Navy Club in Bangkok.

The enlisted men's gangway, the after brow, closed at twenty-three hundred so the men were obliged to board the ship via the officer's gangway, the forward brow and the ship's most sacred Quarterdeck. Pete could see the Officer Of the Deck clearly now.

"What's that piss ant doing on the Quarterdeck?" Pete asked, trying unsuccessfully to straighten himself up. It was Ensign Palmer, a fresh Annapolis graduate. "He thinks he's the cream of the military crop. He believes he's always better, sharper, and smarter than any other officer aboard ship. He's as big a dope as Molini in my book."

"Be cool, Pete," Chip cautioned. "He'll have you sleeping this one off in the brig. All officers have to stand a watch now and then. It's probably just his turn." Chip leaned against the ropes at the top of the gangway and turned toward the stern to salute the ship's Ensign and then back to the Officer Of the Deck. "Request permission to come aboard, sir," Chip tried to muster up his best military tone. The young officer kept his eyes directly on Pete as he returned Chip's salute. "This man looks very drunk. You men haven't been out giving our country a bad name in a foreign port, have you?"

It was Pete's turn to step onto the Quarterdeck. He released his death grip on the handrail, irritated to see this newcomer hassling everybody for things that were no big deal.

The heat of anger flushed through Pete, and he came upright with a salute. "Request permission to cross your patio, Daddio!" Pete shot off a smile and his best salute for the little twerp.

The Boatswain's Mate Of the Watch was Edwards, a well-muscled black man about twice Pete's size, also a friend. Edwards was at Pete's side like a shot, scooping him over his shoulder like a sack of potatoes.

"I'll take him to his bunk, sir," he said as he began to pass the officer.

"I want this man on report!" The young Ensign scowled. "No one gets to insult me on my Quarterdeck."

The Boatswain's Mate turned back to the officer. "I don't think you want this guy, sir."

"Why not?" Ensign Palmer barked. "You heard him insult me. He's deliberately being a smart ass. He can pay with his stripes!"

The Boatswain's Mate shifted Pete's weight on his shoulder and leaned down into the officer's face speaking softly as if conveying a secret. "The first reason you don't want this guy is because our Captain doesn't like anyone bothering the crew when they're returning from liberty. The second reason is, this guy is the Admiral's gopher. No disrespect, but this boy packs more weight in his pencil than you do in your whole seabag, Sir."

"Gopher? What do you mean gopher?" puzzled the Ensign.

"Come on, sir. Errand boy. You know, go for this, go for that. Gopher." With that, Edwards slipped through the open doorway and down a ladder onto the mess deck.

Edwards sat Pete at a table and drew him a cup of coffee from the large urn. "You'd better drink this, Pete, and square away or you're gonna be in trouble," he said. "You remember this sometime when you have Shore Patrol, and it's your turn." He turned and left the mess deck.

Chip sat and wiped his brow as Pete took a long drink from his cup. "Boy! I thought you were going to get us both thrown in the brig!"

After two cups of coffee, the men were in fair shape for a couple of drunks, so they staggered off to the Fox, G and W head, which was located on the second deck above Chip's berthing compartment and two frames forward of Pete's. It was a favorite head for many of the men who berthed near it because it was always so clean. The three divisions which were responsible for it, did a great job of keeping it spotless at all times. It was a full service head with urinals, commodes, and showers -- lots of showers.

"I'm going to pump the bilges and hit the rack," Pete grumbled. "I've had it."

Chip walked toward a shower and turned the water on. "I think I'll take a nice hot shower before I hit the rack," he said.

"Okay. I'll see you in the morning for breakfast before we leave port," Pete mumbled, and entered the passageway leading to his compartment and his warm bunk.

The long piercing veer of the Boatswain's pipe over the loudspeaker in his berthing space woke Pete. The other guys in his division were already peeling out of their bunks and heading around the corner to the S-2 Division head for their shower. "Now reveille, reveille! All hands heave out and trice up!" came the Boatswain's command.

Another day aboard the old *Blue Island Sound* was about to begin. Pete pulled himself from his bunk, folded his blanket neatly at the foot and pulled the anti-flotation strap tightly across it.

Opening his locker, he put his shaving kit under his arm, a towel over his shoulder and went to the Fox, G and W head. When he got there, he noticed someone showering in the corner stall where Chip had been the night before. "How's the water?" Pete asked, raising his voice to ensure the man could hear him over the water.

There was no answer from the shower stall. Pete had finished shaving and was about to step into his own shower, when he realized the water was still running in the corner stall. "Hey, fella," Pete said in a critical tone, sure he was talking to a young Gunner's Mate. "You're lucky we're in port or you'd get put on report for wasting water." No response. Pete's curiosity piqued. He pulled the curtain back and looked inside the shower. Some idiot had gone off and left the shower running. He reached for the valve.

There sat Chip on the floor of the shower, fully clothed. He was still wearing his best dress blue uniform. He had passed out, his feet against the shower wall, his face turned down to one side. He was fast asleep with the warm water running over his head.

"Hey, Chip!" Pete shook a soggy shoulder. "You better wake up and dry off! I'll loan you my towel and go back for another. You're going to have to hurry to be in time for Quarters For Muster."

Chip looked up sleepy and confused. "Let's not party so hearty anymore," he said as he picked himself up off the shower floor and sloshed to an upright position.

"Don't worry," Pete said. "It'll be awhile before we're on the beach in Tokyo again."

It appeared Chip had been soaked as bad as Pete.

Chapter 28

Playing Navy

Pete had just completed his bridge plotter watch and was about to join some of the guys on the forward mess deck for the four o'clock meal. It had been hot on the bridge, but the air conditioning was working great on the mess deck, and today's fare looked excellent! There were pork chops or hamburgers, french fries, vegetables, soup or salad and assorted breads. The galley was still putting out a first class meal, even though the ship had been at sea for seventy-eight days. Pete realized one of the reasons for tomorrow's underway replenishment when he went to the milk dispenser.

Yuk! The milk is reconstituted. The ship's out of fresh! I can't stand reconstituted or evaporated milk! I'll drink iced tea.

"Hey, Pete!" It was Cagney. Even though they were in the same supply support division, they never actually worked together. Sure, they shared the same berthing compartment and the same military responsibilities, but their only common ground so far as work went was the Supply Office. Cagney was in the aviation branch and Pete was from the surface ship branch. Cagney's branch kept the aircraft up, and Pete's took care of the ship's needs. Pete was an electronics specialist, so he concentrated on the ship's communication and surveillance needs.

Every time a radar repeater broke down or even a television set, it was supply's fault. If an aircraft couldn't fly, it was supply's fault, so it was right that they were in the same division.

"Come over and join us," Cagney hollered, motioning with both arms. "How are things up on the bridge? I was just telling the guys here that it looks more like we're on our way to Hong Kong than to an UNREP rendezvous."

Pete finished filling his glass with tea and walked to the six-man table. "Cagney, what's up these days? I know it's not the air squadron's gooney birds." Pete drew a laugh from the other blackshoe men at the table.

"Listen, Pete." Cagney lowered his voice. "Our seaplanes have been flying twenty-four hours a day for seventy-two days, and you know it. You also know very well, we haven't had one minute of downtime on a single aircraft in the squadron."

Racozad sat next to Cagney, a wide grin on his face. It was obviously 'pick on the air force' day. "Yeh!" Racozad chided. "You know, Pete, we're on the high sea replenishing food and aviation gasoline while our squadron has flown back to the Philippines for repairs. They could've stayed at the seadrome, but we didn't have the parts aboard the *Blue*."

Cagney was getting agitated. "Now that's not right, you guys. You know very well we could've gone to the P.I. or Hong Kong to get our stores, but our illustrious Executive Officer wants to get on Captain O'Hara's good side. He deliberately scheduled four days of underway replenishment so we could play at being ***Real Navy***. I think the Captain is wishing he were back aboard a heavy cruiser." His tone softened.

"You guys, mark my words. The Captain will have us playing 'beat to quarters' in the middle of the night to prove to the Exec that we can't button this ship up in less than four minutes." Cagney took a quick drink. "Then we'll have 'General Quarters' drills whenever the Exec wants them until we can make the ship airtight in less than three. The XO can't afford to be easy on us with this new Captain."

"Come on, Cagney!" Howell said, lighting a cigarette. "The XO isn't a bad guy, and if he puts us through a few drills, it'll be for our benefit. He just wants to prove to Captain O'Hara that we're a fighting force and not just a floating hotel."

Chip was sitting with Pooh Bear at the end of the table and added his two cents worth. "You guys know when Captain O'Hara was with the battleship navy, they called him the Jolly Green Giant. No wonder. Did you ever notice how tall the Captain is? If he's got a temper to match his size, you can bet he's a mean mutha." Chip finished his coffee and stood with his tray. He added one more thought before heading for the scullery. "If I were you guys, I'd probably sleep at my battle station tonight. I can feel a GQ coming on."

It was zero two hundred hours when the General Quarters alarm and the screeching voice of the young Boatswain's Mate Of the Watch shook Pete out of his bunk. "Bong! Bong! Bong!" went the alarm. "This is a drill! This is a drill! Now, General Quarters! General Quarters! All hands, man your battle stations!" boomed the Boatswain's voice.

Pete shoveled on his dungarees, slipped into his shoes, then grabbed his coat and ball cap. The lights flashed on in the berthing compartment as everyone rushed out.

Pete raced for his battle station, the Electronics Supply Office on the 02 level. His bunk was on the first deck below the main deck, and he had less than two minutes to plug in his sound-powered telephone and announce his battle station ready for action. Running forward up the starboard ladders three decks seemed like a simple task but it was complex to accomplish. Many of the passageways were dark for night running as the crew scurried through the narrow corridors and up the ladders to the decks above. There was only the red night lights to guide them.

Just as Pete crossed the threshold of the main deck hatch, the 'on scene officer' yelled, "Clear the hatch! Give way!" The hatch hold-back bolts were about to be knocked out and the eight-inch thick steel hatch would come crashing down. Pete ducked and rolled through the upward opening. The twelve-hundred-pound hatch slammed into place at his feet. Pete jumped and climbed the next ladder onto the 01 deck and then to the 02 level and the Electronics Supply Office. He stumbled through the door of his office and picked up the sound-powered phone set. "ESO at battle stations!" He panted.

Pete looked down at his trembling hands as he sat down at his desk. He was shaking as he remembered the voice that ordered the final closure of the watertight hatch on the main deck. *It was Ensign Palmer. The bird-brained little bugger didn't even look to see if the hatch was clear. He just ordered it shut. Thank God he used military procedure in giving his order to close it. Maybe I'll get a chance to do something for him some day*. Pete shook his head in disgust.

Five minutes after the crew had reached their battle stations, GQ was secured. Pete returned to his bunk and spent the rest of the night dreaming of being beheaded by flying hatches commanded by a skinny little Napoleon. Maybe it was an accident that every time anything happened that didn't make sense, Ensign Palmer was involved.

The next day, Ensign Palmer was promoted from the deck force group to the Signal Division Officer. He would be in charge of all visual communication. He would be in charge of the boys that blink lights, wave skivvies at each other and raise flags on the mast for passing various types of information between ships.

At fifteen-hundred hours, lookouts picked up the supply ship on the horizon. Within the hour, *Blue Island Sound* was alongside, and the supply ship was ready to start passing stores across the heavy cables to the 'Blue.'

As in most military situations, before the transfer could start, there was a little ceremony called 'colors to the mast' that the Captain of each ship conducted for the benefit of the other Captain. It was the only time the personal flag of the ship's Captain was flown under the American colors. The Captain's pride was on display.

Chip and Pete stood on the catwalk of the 02 level watching to see whose colors would hit the yardarm first. The Captain of the supply ship was first. His rolled colors hit the supply ship's yardarm and a giant pork chop unfurled on a beautiful field of green lettuce leaves, dotted with apples and oranges. Captain O'Hara's colors were now unfurling as they struck the yardarm. A great white field with a silhouette of the *Blue Island Sound* surrounded by seaplanes in a seadrome, and over all stood the massive figure of the 'Jolly Green Giant.'

Chip poked Pete in the ribs. "Now, that's not a fitting flag for the 'Jolly Green Giant.' I'll have to talk it over with the boys and see what can be done about getting Captain O'Hara a new one when we get to Hong Kong."

Pete looked hard into Chip's face as he spoke with one eyebrow raised. "You know, we might be able to give Ensign Palmer the credit," he said.

The ship had barely finished the food replenishment operation, when the voice of the Boatswain's Mate Of the Watch came over the PA system. "Now stand by for the Captain." The 1MC went dead. "Gentlemen," announced the Captain, "I have just received word, one of our seaplanes has sunk in the bay at Olongapo in the

Philippines. For this reason, the squadron will be delayed in returning to our seadrome sight for six days. We will pull into Hong Kong the day after tomorrow for some well-earned R and R. In the meantime, however, we will continue with our military drill procedures. Thank you. That is all."

Chip and Pete were sitting in the ET shack when the Captain had announced the well-deserved R and R. Chip turned to Pete with a rosy, tooth-filled smile. "Hey!" He raised his coffee cup. "Let's go over to your office. Maybe we can come up with a radioman on the way who can give us the scuttlebutt on how the gooney bird sank."

Pete's office was just down the hall. The men looked in as they passed the Communications Office. The young officer hunched over the desk puffing a cigar as he read a paperback was Lieutenant Junior Grade Bobby Doug Turnbull. The crew lovingly referred to him as 'Gabby' because he would always spill the beans about anything. He was from Mississippi and seemed to have some kind of disease. Doc Vesper said he had diarrhea of the mouth. This guy just had to be talking. He talked anytime, anywhere and about anything.

As the men stopped by the Com Office door, Chip reached out and caught Pete's sleeve. "Look no farther!" he whispered.

Both men made a quick right turn and entered the Communications Department Office. They slid into chairs directly across the desk and sipped their coffee awaiting acknowledgment from the young officer. His head was bent forward, the top of which was shining through the short blonde hair from beneath his crew cut. His thick glasses seemed to cut into his chubby round cheeks. His attention waned slightly as he reached to turn the next page.

Chip set his cup on the edge of the desk. "How's it going, sir?" he asked sincerely. "Do you think it's really true, what the Skipper said, I mean." He avoided being direct right away.

The officer tilted his round head back slightly and stuffed the cigar between his teeth. He worked his lips around the lush tobacco, puffing on it methodically and eyeing the two petty officers, first one and then the other. He jerked the cigar from his mouth, spouted a large flume of smoke and came to rest, both elbows on the desk. "You know I don't give out the contents of the Captain's personal communications. When the Captain gets a message, it's his message, and nobody sees it or hears about it unless they really have a need to know. We here in the radio shack are not in the habit of repeating what we see in other people's mail." He rested his chin on his right hand, elbow on the desk, the stogie sending up curling smoke trails from between his fingers.

"I didn't think you'd know anyway, sir," Chip said as the men rose to leave.

"Know what?" The young officer's curiosity was piqued. "You can't just come in here and sit down and have me tell you what you want to know. I'm no mind reader, you know," he whined.

"Is it true, sir?" Chip hesitated. "Did one of our seaplanes really sink or is the 'Old Man' just planning an unscheduled stop in Hong Kong?"

Gabby put his cigar into the ashtray and ran his knuckles over his little pot belly as if preparing to give a professional lecture. He turned around and pulled the picture of a Martin SP5B seaplane off the wall behind the com officer's desk. "I know why Commander Johnson has this picture here. It's to explain to you enlisted, exactly what happened to a fine piece of military hardware being improperly handled by a bunch of dummies. Drunk dummies at that." He laid the picture on the desk and pointed with a pudgy finger.

"You see, the entire squadron, all sixteen aircraft were under the strictest of orders when they left the ship. They were to fly into Olongapo and get their tune up parts and whatever else they needed and fly right back to the seadrome and meet us there tomorrow as soon as we finished our UNREP. Well, you know those Airedales, they can't do anything according to orders." Gabby puffed up with pride as he continued. "As soon as they flew into the PI, they went straight to the officer's club and started having a few. Needless to say, they had a few too many. When the boats took them back to their birds, they loaded through the front hatch here in the bow like always." He pointed to the front door of the aircraft, right at the waterline.

"I'm not exactly sure what happened, but the air crew of one of the SP5B's was apparently still drunk. They turned their aircraft into the wind and fired their 'jet assisted take off' boosters! Those dummies had left the forward hatch open, so they started taking on water almost the instant the JATO tanks were fired." Gabby took a puff. "You know a jet assisted take off can't be shut down once those tanks start their burn!"

Gabby paused, grinning at the men. "They came back to their aircraft drunk, forgot to close the hatch, filled her up with water and sunk her. The crew got out through a cockpit window." The officer dusted his cigar in a butt kit as he shook his head in disgust.

Chip and Pete were about to bust a gut. They started their exit with Chip speaking over his shoulder. "Thank you, sir. We sure appreciate the story."

The thought of a seaplane zipping across the water sucking up half the bay made for a very comical mental picture, and the final floundering when the JATO tanks burned out would have been riotous to watch. The two friends laughed all the way to the Electronics Supply Office.

"There really is some fun to be had, playing Navy!" Chip said.

Chapter 29

Hong Kong

Two days later, at zero nine hundred, the crew stood at full dress parade along the weather decks as the *Blue Island Sound* entered the port city of Hong Kong.

After forty-five minutes, the crew was secured from Quarters For Entering Port and the ship tied up at an anchorage. All hands crowded the seaplane deck waiting for the after brow to be lowered so they could hit the beach in the most beautiful city in the world.

"Now hear this! Now hear this!" It was the Boatswain's Mate Of the Watch. "Liberty will commence for sections one and three at thirteen hundred hours. Duty Petty Officers of M, A, G, and S-1 Division report to the Officer Of the Deck for Shore Patrol duty."

"Rats!" Pete grumbled, "I drew Shore Patrol! What a rotten deal! The entire crew will have to wait three more hours before they can go on liberty. *That* will boost moral!"

The Pooh Bear stood beside Pete as he leaned against the wire rope handrail. Bum boats were now circling the ship, throwing packets of small cards up on to the main weather deck. Pooh leaned over and picked up one of the packets tucking it into Pete's hand. "Just think about it this way, Pete. You can visit every one of the bars in this pack of cards, and you won't even have to buy a drink." He laughed as he picked up a second pack and stuffed it into his shirt pocket. "Of course, you won't be able to buy any drinks on this trip, but there is always next time." He patted Pete's shoulder with a chubby left hand, as if to console him. "I'll see you on the beach, ol' bud." He laughed again as he turned and walked away.

* * *

A slight breeze blew the moist tropical air into Pete's face. He leaned over the white rail on Fenwick Pier looking down into the water lapping the filth of carelessly tossed debris and human excrement on the rocks next to the Shore Patrol headquarters. His concentration centered on a small milk carton. The little box splashed up and down, its small yellow form caught in the grasp of the sludgy black sea water as it danced and chugged against the seawall stones.

It's been more than two months since the crew had seen a port, and now we're in my favorite and I draw a ten-hour stint on Shore Patrol. Oh well, the ship will be here for the better part of three days, so tomorrow will be my day to hit the beach, have a little fun and eat my favorite black pepper steak at the Hilton Hotel.

"Pete! Come on!" It was Snell, a First Class Boatswain's Mate off of the *USS Provincetown,* a heavy guided missile cruiser which was also in port. The British Shore Patrol commander had chosen to put one surface sailor and one Airedale together for reinforced harmony in the event they ran across a brawl between personnel of their two ships. It was well known, even among the British sailors, that Airedales and "black shoes" of the 7th Fleet did not get along very well. "Pete! Let's turn to! Let's get out there and protect all the beautiful people in the city from Uncle Sam's animals."

Pete joined Snell at the crosswalk in front of the patrol station and the Hong Kong police officer directing traffic waved them to cross the street.

"What district do we have?" Pete asked as they crossed the street in a nonchalant manner.

"We've got the basin. I love to work the basin when I've got the duty. You're only six blocks away from headquarters, your backup is the hard hats, plus, your beat covers ten percent of the nastiest clubs in the City of Hong Kong."

The basin was a square mile of the city nestled in a low spot near the harbor. It was full of towering buildings, laced up with narrow streets sporting a night club every one hundred paces. The area was apparently designed and built for the specific purpose of entertaining the merchant and war fleets of the world.

Pete had pulled Shore Patrol several times in Hong Kong, but never in the basin. He usually drew the garment district or one of the nice hotel areas with little to do but enjoy the scenery and talk to people from all over the world who were on vacation. The basin was a pit, with brothels of all kinds, a hot spot where a sailor could do or get anything his heart desired – *for a price.* The 'rooftops' were also in the basin.

The rooftops comprised an area where illegal Chinese squatters set up cardboard and tin shacks on top of the buildings that towered skyward from the narrow streets below. The rooftops were strictly out of bounds to all military personnel. On the rooftops, illicit sex acts of the most animalistic nature were available along with any drug from mainland China.

The orders were very clear regarding the rooftops. Any sailor caught there would be clamped in irons and do three days on bread and water even before his trial came to Captain's mast.

The Shore Patrol team walked the streets and entered every club, letting the troops see they were around. It also reassured tavern owners and bartenders, knowing a police force was in the area.

It was six o'clock, and the early April sun began to set. The few existing street lights would be blinking to life. The patrolmen rounded a corner and started up the stairs on the side of a warehouse. In less than a minute, they were on the rooftop.

The terrible sight seemed as if they were on the ground again. A landscape of tumbled down shacks and shanties all over the place. Sleeping mats were scattered around, some unrolled in contemplation of a night of rest. Small children played stick ball with a large wad of paper. The stomachs of the children were distended, an obvious sign of malnutrition. Most of the people were nearly naked, sitting in small groups working on what appeared to be handy crafts. There was a central cooking station located near the center of the building. In this type of transient society, all food brought to the rooftop became community property, and one man took responsibility for its preparation and distribution. He was called a 'Wo Chi,' and was the group elder and head man.

The patrol was nearly to the other side of the roof. They had seen no white uniforms, so their business was completed. Pete marveled at how they had crossed the entire rooftop apparently unnoticed. No one looked at them nor indicated in any way they were under observation.

Suddenly a small man, his skeleton shinning through his opaque olive skin, appeared in front of them from beside a small shack that looked like an outhouse with a curtain for a door.

"I am Wo Chi. Yankee sailors come to make trade? Yankee sailors want girls? We have many girls. All girls virgin. You want honker? We have best honker in Hong Kong here." He pulled back the curtain to reveal a very old woman crouched on a small stool.

She opened her mouth to show she had no teeth and made a half round smile while gesturing a come-here-motion with her decrepit hand. Pete was not quite ready for this experience. His stomach churned and he swallowed hard to keep from gagging.

The little man released the curtain and turned his face back to the patrolmen. "You know what they say in fleet? You not a man 'til have a good honker! We give you best honker in Hong Kong!" Pete was appalled; he cleared his throat and tried to smile. "No thank you, Wo Chi. We're here to look for our friends who want to trade today."

Wo Chi thrust a bony finger toward Pete. The impatient old man glared. "You got cigarettes? You got cigarette, we talk. No cigarette, you go!"

Snell pulled a cigarette from his belt pouch and held it up tantilizing the ragged man. He spoke softly, but firmly. "First we talk, then I give you the cigarette."

Wo Chi dropped into the traditional Oriental sit, both feet flat on the ground, arms locked around his knees. "Okay, Joe. We talk. We make one trade today. Good trade to *Provincetown*. He gestured to the ship's patch on Snell's right shoulder. "We got whole carton of Salem for just one spoon of rainbow dust. You like to ride the rainbow, too?"

Snell's face grew pale. "Tell me about your *Provincetown* trader, and I'll give you another cigarette."

The old man reached out and snatched the cigarette from between Snell's fingers. "Okay, Joe. For three cigarettes. Joe like you, big. Hair like me. Age like him," he pointed to Pete. "Two stripes on sleeve, red."

Snell jerked upright throwing the two cigarettes down. "Come on, Pete, let's hit it! We may just have some really big trouble cooking here."

The men scurried over the roof edge onto a winding fire escape and down into the street. Snell kept scrutinizing the face of every passing sailor.

Pete took his arm and stopped him. "I'm sorry pal, but I have no idea what you're so worked up about. How 'bout letting me in on the story?"

"Holy cow! Do they keep you Airedale sailors in a bottle? Don't you know what that man was telling us?" Snell pulled away and started the pace again.

Pete was dismayed at the retort. "Very frankly, I don't have any idea of what you're talking about!"

"Look, stupid!" Snell raised his right hand, as if he was going to hit something. Snell looked around, then spoke in low whispers.

"What we have here," he glanced around again. "is a teenager from my boat, less than six months away from his parents, running around Hong Kong with a full ounce of cocaine. If he sniffs that stuff, he could go off to never-never land and do something really stupid, or worse – wind up dead."

Pete turned his watch up to the neons the men were standing under. "It's check in time. Let's go into the Suzy Wong Bar and make our call to headquarters before they send the hard hats out to look for us."

Snell held the bar door open for Pete, as he explained a snippet of history of the place. "Jack, the bartender at the Suzy Wong, is a retired G.I. who took his pension and made a nice home for himself in Hong Kong." The musty smell of smoke and beer hit the patrolmen as they found their way through the dimly lit cabaret to a wall table with a phone outlet jack and sat down. They stacked their white hats, indicating they would be staying for a while. Jack appeared at the table, carrying a telephone and two cups of coffee.

"Hey, Snell. What's with the down look? The night's young. You can't have had a bad day already." Jack flashed a smile as he set the tray down.

Snell looked up, locking the fingers of his hands together. "We've got a kid off my boat, running around with an ounce of cocaine." Snell lowered his voice. "My ship has already had one bad scrape with drugs this year. A Gunner's Mate sniffed up and went over the side, right after he set off an M-70 hand grenade in the forward gun turret."

Jack, a youthful looking, grey-haired man, slid the phone from the tray and plugged it into an outlet. "Be cool. Make your call and think about the problem. I'll get you guys a nice steak for lunch." A wide grin crossed his tan face. "On the house!"

Jack slipped away to the kitchen. Snell reported to headquarters and Pete began to think out loud, trying to make sense of the conversation with the old man.

"The old man said he was about my age, a Joe like you. Maybe he meant the uniform. Maybe this cat was wearing a dress white jumper and a neckerchief like you are, instead of a short-sleeved tropical white shirt like I'm wearing. Big like you and straight black hair like the old man. Two red stripes. A Fireman Apprentice. Maybe we do have a complete description of this joker. A Fireman deuce wearing full dress whites, six-foot-two, one-hundred-eighty pounds, straight black hair."

Snell snapped up the phone again and called the description into headquarters while Pete walked to the bar to pick up their meal. Pete set the food down just as Snell was hanging up the phone. He drew in a deep breath of concern.

"How'd we do?" Pete asked in a cheery tone.

Snell looked up, puckering a half smile. "Great! We're doing just great! There are only sixty Firemen Apprentices on my ship. One third of them have the duty. That means there are only forty of them on the beach." He gave Pete a big fake smile as the sarcasm continued to drip from his lips. "We're doing just great!"

Snell took his last swallow of coffee. "What we've got here, Pete, is a snipe. A young red striper with absolutely no sense of self preservation, and pity the poor soul that gets in his way while he's trying to go over the rainbow. Let's hit the street! We'll check the British pubs on the water front!"

Leaving their half-eaten meal, the patrolmen quickly crossed the four blocks to the waterfront where the scene changed to match the old pubs of England. Rowdy and loud laughter echoed into the streets. They looked through every window they passed. They saw no Americans, just Royal Navy drinking lots of grog. Though the streets in this area of the basin were much dimmer to the eye, it struck Pete that this was a happy place. The pubs were a warm reminder of home for the Britts.

Two British Shore Patrolmen joined them as they pushed through an alley, walking to the far corner of their beat where they would break off and go back into the basin.

Suddenly, they heard a woman screaming, "Shore Patrol! Shore Patrol! Help! Help!"

The disturbance was in the middle of the next block, toward Fenwick Pier, away from the American beat. One of the Britts motioned. "Come on, Yanks. It might be one of your lads!"

The group rushed down the street where a crowd was gathering. A young American sailor bent a taxi driver backward over the hood of his car as he furiously beat his face. "Try to take me, you scum bag! I'll kick your ass from here to Texas! You'll learn not to hijack American sailors!" he screamed as he pulverized the driver's face.

Pete arrived first and threw his oak baton across the sailor's throat in a choke-hold from behind. Pete was raised off of the ground by the man's height. Pete was mad, he put both his feet against the car and pulled up and back against the man's chin and jaw bone, hoping this would make him pass out.

"This is the Shore Patrol!" Pete yelled in the man's ear, pulling up fiercely. "Let him go, or I'll break your neck!"

The raging man turned on Pete, arms flailing in the air, spinning around and around. Pete was spun away from his huge frame like a tether ball. His baton was still around the man's neck, but now Pete hung like a rag doll in front of him. His fists, at close range, pounded Pete's chest like hammers. Pete heard the air leaving his body. It seemed like an eternity before the other patrolmen arrived. They handcuffed the big man's hands like an "X" on his opposite ankles and were finally able to subdue him. He was still on top of Pete, wrenching, convulsing, and cursing. When the two men were finally separated, Pete felt as though he had been run over by a Mack truck.

The young man lay in the gutter face-to-face with Pete who could hear the bell of an ambulance. Pete shook his head, trying to get his faculties back. He studied the man's face. The man was crying, his face was swollen, his nose was huge. His eyes were bloodshot. His bloodshot eyes had pupils nearly twice their normal size.

Snell and a Brit pulled Pete upright to the curb; the other Briton handed Pete his night stick. "You alright, Pete?" Snell huffed. "You must be as crazy as that Fireman deuce! Whew! He sure was a wild man. You okay man?"

Pete held his weight up against a nearby car. The hard hat patrol car arrived, and the ambulance pulled out with both the sailor and the taxi driver. Pete straightened his white hat with shaking hands. "Snell, what happened?"

Snell put his hand on Pete's bruised shoulder sending a shooting pain through his body. Pete winced "Pete, my boy," he said, his face drawing a shallow smile behind cold, knowing eyes. "We got our man. His name is Simon Kalis. He's off my boat. I know he's our man because of this!" His hand opened to reveal a small cellophane package with white powder in it. "This is only twenty-percent of what he bought, if that old man was on the square. I got this out of Kalis' jumper pocket in the scuffle. The dummy is going to jail for sure!" He shook his head in disgust and spoke softly. "When will these kids ever learn?"

A jeep pulled up with two Shore Patrolmen in the back. "You chaps are relieved," pronounced the British officer behind the wheel as the reliefs stepped from the vehicle. "Hop in. You have a few reports to file at headquarters."

As Snell and Pete sat quietly working on their reports, a British officer came into the room accompanied by a man in a grey suit carrying a cane. "Chaps," he said. "This is Mr. Henning from your foreign office. He'd like a word with you."

The stately looking gentleman took a chair between the two Petty Officers. "Boys, I'm from the American embassy here. *Provincetown*," he said, pointing to Snell. "You're on a two-hour recall. *Blue Island*, you carry a flag, Commander of the Patrol Force Pacific Fleet, so you have to be out of the harbor by zero five hundred hours. An American seaman has been involved in a civil incident. The matter is out of the hands of the military." The regal gentleman pushed away from the table and stood up. "The taxi driver is dead. It's true he tried to charge the sailor seventeen dollars instead of the seven on the meter. The ten-dollar overcharge has a U.S. currency value of little more than two dollars. I think something must be wrong with our system when we will kill our fellow man for less than two dollars." The man looked down at Pete and Snell for a moment and then he was gone.

The British officer stood with a long face. He spoke just as he got to the door. "Zip it up, lads. You've got a lot of people to round up in a very short time." His sad eyes looked at Pete's partner. "Snell, I am sorry about your mate."

In frustration, Pete slapped the table top. "How did this all happen? I don't understand what's going on."

Snell's answer came quick and angry. "Are you a monk? He gestured to the front of Pete's uniform. "You're wearing Vietnam combat ribbons, and you ain't seen any of this?"

Snell's anger heightened and his tan complexion began to redden. "For cryin' out loud, Pete! Dope is worth money! It's a new experience for these kids! There are a hundred reasons for it. The crime is, it's easy access. You want some dope? All you have to do is take a carton of cigarettes to the rooftops. If you want a lot of dope – say a thousand dollars worth, all you have to do is steal a ten-pound canned ham from the galley. Drop the ham in a camera bag and pretend you're on a tour and head across to the peninsula city of Kowloon. And for that ham, if you trade it in the new territories, you can fill your camera bag with dope!

"Nobody's going to notice a swabby with a camera bag. You can even take it on the beach in the States, and nobody will notice you. As long as this world has poor people in need of food, you can get anything you want. Nobody in this Navy is going to notice the sailors holding it until some senior turkey in the Navy Department figures out this kind of thing is going on. We've got a whole new breed of young people coming into the service now, and a lot of people are going to die before somebody wakes up and writes new rules to this game."

Pete was shocked by this Snell's in-depth understanding of the situation. Pete had always classed any boatswain's mate he ran across with the likes of Second Class BM Mollini from his ship, almost as smart as a can of paint. This one was not dumb - not by a long shot!

Pete finished signing his report and stacked the papers neatly on the table. "You okay?" He asked, staring across at Snell with concern.

As the men were leaving the office, an officer from the *Provincetown* came in. "You fellows should probably be aware of this," he said. "Fireman Kalis died in the hospital a few minutes ago. The doctors said it was an overdose of cocaine."

Pete's stomach churned. He had seen more than enough of Hong Kong for this trip.

Chapter 30

Rounding Up the Boys

It was half past midnight when Pete stepped off the service boat from Fenwick Pier onto the after ladder of his ship. It had been a bad day by anyone's standards. He had been exposed to narcotics, beaten up by a dead man and now, forced to leave port before he had a chance to eat his favorite steak dinner. What a dirty deal!

Pete reached the top landing, gave a salute and reported. "I'm back from Shore Patrol duty, sir. May I come aboard?" A crazy thought crossed his mind. *What if, after all I've been through today, this guy says no?*

"Permission granted!" replied the young Ensign on the Quarterdeck as he passed Pete a snappy salute.

As Pete crossed the Quarterdeck, a familiar face approached from the shadows. It was the Pooh Bear, AK2 Johnston. Pete was glad to see his longtime sidekick and compatriot.

"I think you've got a problem, Peter. Two of your boys aren't back from Cinderella Liberty." His face had a half smile. "You may not be able to bail them out of this one. If they don't get back before we pull out, they'll be AWOL and go to the brig for sure."

Angry at the day's events, Pete lashed out. "I'm not standing brig watches over my own men! I've got better things to do than that. Go get your baton and duty belt, and don't forget your Shore Patrol armband. We're going on the beach to get them. Meet me at the Quarter-deck in ten minutes."

After convincing the Ensign on the Quarterdeck that the Admiral was sending the two men on an errand, they departed the ship. They told the Ensign they were wearing their Shore Patrol gear to avoid being detained by the Royal Navy as curfew violators, which, in fact, was true. But, they were on Pete's errand – not the Admiral's.

To their surprise, as they reached the pier, they found three men from their ship awaiting a boat. These men had been on leave in the city, and were just answering the recall order closing the port to American ships.

"Mandrake," Pete called as he approached the man from his division. "Did you happen to see Howell and Racozad on the beach?"

"As a matter of fact," Mandrake's face lit up as he spoke. "I saw them at the Hilton. They said they were registered under one of Racozad's aliases. His favorite is Williams. Seems like they said Room 1223." He scratched his head. "Oh rats, I'm not sure Pete. I just know they're over there." He waved a hand as the service boat pulled out into the darkness of the unlit harbor.

Within minutes, Pooh Bear and Pete were on an elevator in the Hilton Hotel. Pete watched the green floor numbers flash. "Here we are, Pooh. Let's kick 'em all the way back to the ship. Floor boy. Floor boy." Pete called as they started down the long carpeted corridor.

A young man, dressed in white, appeared with a ring of keys. Pete motioned, and the man followed along until the group reached

1223. "Open the door," Pete commanded. "This is official business!" Pete pointed to his arm band. The floor boy stared up at Pete as if in disbelief.

"Do I have to kick the thing in?"

"No sir! No sir!" the small man pleaded, turning the key and standing to one side as the sailors rushed in.

The bed was covered completely with a quilt, but the shape under it and the motion of the blanket told Pete who it was. "Okay, Racozad! You're under arrest! You're mine this time, you little bugger!" Pete jerked the covers back. "Where is...Oh, my Gosh!"

Before his eyes lay a British sailor and a beautiful Chinese girl in the most promising embrace he had ever seen. "Oh my! Excuse me!" Pete threw the covers back over them and the Shore Patrolmen fled the room.

Outside the room, Johnston's face was flushed with laughter about to break. "Now that, my friend, is what I call a major screw up!" The laughter broke. "Will you please call the desk and get the room number of an American registered as Williams? Hey, one more thing. When we get to the room, will you please knock?"

Pete called the desk. After being reassured room 1124 was positively an American registered as Williams, the men changed floors. Pete took out his night stick and rapped on the door. "Howell and Racozad of the *USS Blue Island*, you are under arrest." Pete spoke loud enough for the occupants to hear him.

The door opened just a crack and Pete was staring down, eye to eye with a grey-haired, round-eyed woman. "There's no one in here by that name, sonny," she spoke softly. "We're the Williams' from Detroit."

The door closed as Pete's jaw dropped. Pooh was practically on the floor with laughter. It was all he could do to walk away. Pete had to gather his composure before he could follow.

Pete grabbed Pooh's arm, and they headed for the elevator. The two men walked briskly across the lobby. Once they reached the front desk, there was no problem getting access to the register. It was a great heavy ledger with a hundred lines per page. As Pete paged slowly through it, he noticed the guests were from all over the world, but primarily England and the United States. Then he found it. Racozad's handwriting. Registered as Mr. Peterson, Salt Lake City, Utah. They were in room 1224. Pete's mind raced, *I should have realized they may use a friend's name and home state... Mine!*

Most of Pete's anger and frustration had been burned up by now, so this time he knocked softly with his hand. No answer. Pete had the floor boy open the door. It was definitely the right room. "Hey Pete," Pooh said. "They left their uniforms hanging in the closet. They must be dressed in civvies."

"Bag the uniforms while I check the room for anything else these twerps might be up to," Pete said.

On a table, Pete found a hurricane jug of rum, the finest Puerto Rican rum, worth about twenty-eight dollars U.S. Determined to foul any booze smuggling by his men, Pete opened a window and looked down at the empty parking lot below. No sign of life. He dropped the bottle. It made a lovely splash on the pavement below.

Unable to find Howell and Racozad in the Hilton, Pooh and Pete returned to the ship. Pete was exhausted. He threw his whites on the foot of his bunk and fell asleep as soon as the side of his face touched the pillow. It seemed he had been asleep for a long time when a whispering voice called him awake.

"Pete. Pete. We're getting underway. It's 0400." It was Howell. His small square face held in his hands, his elbows on his knees as he sat on the edge of the empty lower bunk across from Pete's. He was dressed in civilian clothes.

"You know what, Pete?" He was visibly down in the mouth. "Racozad and I got put on report for being four hours AWOL, but that's not the bad part. We bought a beautiful bottle of rum to bring back for you and some skunk stole it. We reported it to the management of the hotel, but they said the Shore Patrol had searched several rooms, and I guess they got it."

Pete turned over in his bunk. *What a day this has been! I chucked my own gift into the street on top of everything else that has happened.* "It's okay, Howell." Pete managed. "We'll be in Hong Kong, again. You can get another bottle of rum. Just promise me, you guys will never have anything to do with dope."

Howell stood in an obviously inebriated manner and began to leave the Petty Officer berthing section. "Don't worry about us and dope," he said. "We already do enough stupid things."

Pete flipped over on his back as Howell left. He could feel the ship begin to roll over the ground swells as it entered the open sea. The entire crew was aboard.

Chapter 31

Replenishment

The next afternoon Pete sat in front of his Olympia typewriter in the main Supply Office pounding out parts requisitions which had piled up over the past week. He prided himself on the fact that there was never a piece of equipment down for lack of parts. Pete transmitted his orders while the *Blue Island Sound* was at sea, and when the ship pulled into Yokosuka, all of his merchandise would be waiting at the Naval Supply Center. The other option was a cargo ship or heavy oiler might pick up his merchandise and transfer it aboard during underway replenishment at sea.

The Supply Officer came in and sat down at his desk. Commander Hatchfield was an outstanding officer and a heck of a nice guy. He was a graduate of the University of Texas, but the men of his department didn't hold it against him. He was a typical picture of a Texan, long and lanky with a big heart for his men.

"Hey, Pete!" He motioned Pete to come to his desk. Commander Hatchfield held up a paper marked "confidential," a shipping schedule from the radio room. He handed the form to Pete and smiled like a new bride at on her wedding day.

"We have underway replenishment tomorrow, and the Admiral said you might like to help select the oil tanker we rendezvous with to take on aviation gasoline."

Pete looked at the list. On top was the *USS Caliente* (AO-53).

"Wow!" Pete exclaimed, looking down at the smiling officer. "This is terrific! The *Caliente* is my brother's ship. I haven't seen nor talked to him in almost three years. Do you think I could get some sound-powered telephone time to visit with him while we UNREP?" Pete's hands were shaking, and a lump stuck in his throat.

"I think that might be arranged," said the Commander, leaning back in his chair and lacing his fingers behind his head. He kicked back from his desk and crossed his nonregulation cowboy boots at the ankle on his desk. "So that settles it. We'll come along side the '*Flying Red Horse*' at zero seven hundred hours."

The next morning, Pete scurried to his favorite observation spot on the 02 weather deck. The men of the "special sea detail" had been at their stations since a half hour after reveille. The Gunner's Mate Of the Watch stood on the forward main deck ready to fire the 'shot-line' from his sawed-off shotgun across to the deck of the *Caliente.*

The two ships drew closer and closer and Pete's heart thumped as the gap of sea grew narrow between them. Pete could hear the PA system from the *Caliente* as her Boatswain's Mate barked orders to her deck crew. "Now stand by to receive shot-line. Clear the main deck and weather decks, port side."

Now it was the *Blue Island's* turn. "Fire!" commanded the Boatswain's Mate. There was a loud crack from the shotgun and a puff of smoke as the small rubber projectile carried a tiny nylon line between the two ships. The projectile struck the *Caliente* just below the wing of the bridge and fell to the main deck. The *Caliente's* deck crew snatched up the line and began pulling it across. As they pulled, it grew in size. A lanyard was fast becoming a hawser. The oiler crew attached a steel passing cable to the three-inch line and the *Blue Island's* deck crew began pulling it back. Within ten minutes, there were five cables strung and three aviation gasoline hoses hooked up and ready to pump.

Chip stepped through the 02 level doorway onto the catwalk where Pete was standing. He pointed to the *Blue Island's* masthead. "You want to see what some of the boys were doing yesterday while you were on Shore Patrol?" A gigantic grin covered his round face to the point of squinting his eyes half shut.

Pete was looking toward the *Caliente,* listening to their Boatswain's Mate. "Colors to the mast!" his voice echoed, and his Captain's colors hit the yardarm and broke open. A giant white field with nothing on it but a beautiful "flying red horse."

Pete quickly turned his head to watch for his ship's colors, ignoring Chip. Captain O'Hara's flag hit the yard and didn't pop open right away. Pete knew some young Signalman would have to answer for this embarrassment to the Captain. Skivvy wavers were supposed to roll all their flags so they opened the instant they hit the yardarm. The *Blue Island's* colors stuttered for a moment and then unfurled. A great white field, a silhouette of the *Blue Island* with seaplanes around it, and above it all, the Jolly Green Giant. "Oh, my gosh!" Pete exclaimed. "That's not the CO's flag!"

The Jolly Green Giant on this flag was not standing over the *Blue Island* with scarf flying, arms folded. Instead, this Green Giant had screws in one hand and giant screwdriver in his other. It was clear the silhouette of the hunching Green Giant was putting the screws to the *Blue Island.*

A familiar voice on the PA system sounded irate. It was the Captain!

"Strike those colors! Ensign Palmer, to the bridge!"

The flag was hauled from the mast as fast as three Signalmen could get it down.

"My aching ass!" Pete groaned, turning toward Chip. "I'll never get to talk to my brother now!" Chip burst into laughter as Pete shoved past him.

There were several minutes of silence about the ship, and then the Boatswain's voice was heard again. "Commence underway replenishment."

The heavy rubber hoses jiggled and gurgled as *Blue Island* began to take on liquid fuel. "The smoking lamp is out throughout the ship while taking on aviation gasoline!" barked the Boatswain's Mate of the Watch.

The next call rocked Pete out of his fixation with the deck of the *Caliente*. Pete was trying to catch a glimpse of his brother. "Now, Storekeeper Second Class Peterson, lay to the bridge."

Pete hurried up the 02 level staircase to the bridge.

Oh Boy! Now I've had it. Pete worried. *Somehow, I've been connected to that crazy flag. Palmer probably named me as someone trying to get at him.*

Pete reported to the Officer Of the Deck on the bridge, and was directed to the wing of the bridge where the Captain sat in his high backed swivel chair. Pete popped tall and passed his sharpest military salute as he stopped next to the Captain's chair. "Peterson, Storekeeper Second Class, reporting sir."

The Captain handed Pete the telephone handset he was talking on. "It's for you," he said with a grin and eased Pete's obvious case of nerves. "Go ahead and say hello, Pete. It won't bite." The Captain spun his chair back so it faced the *Caliente*. From where Pete stood, it was easy to make out the faces of the men standing on the other bridge.

"Bill?" Pete queried in anticipation of his brother's voice. Pete looked across the open space to see who had a phone to his ear.

"This is the Captain of the *Caliente,*" a deep voice responded. "Your brother was hurt in a scuffle aboard, yesterday. He fell off a catwalk.

He's in sick bay now, and we're transferring him to the *USS Bon Home Richard* tomorrow."

Pete's heart sank. He knew there was no chance to talk to Bill now. The voice on the other end of the sound-powered telephone continued.

"Look down on the bow of your ship." Pete complied. "You see, we've rigged a high line between the two ships. We've been carrying mail for you as well as personnel. The underway replenishment will last at least another hour. I think I can make arrangements with your Skipper for you to ride the boatswain's chair across so you can visit your brother."

"Hot dog! Sounds terrific, sir!" Pete exclaimed, and handed the phone back to his Captain.

"Go on down there, Pete," said Captain O'Hara. "No, first go in on the bridge and see the Admiral."

Pete reported to the Admiral on the bridge. He was sitting at the Quartermaster's table putting his seal on the closure flap of a large manila envelope. He turned as Pete approached. "Pete. You're going to hand deliver these orders to the Captain of the *Caliente.*"

The Admiral looked past Pete, his eyes focusing on the crystal blue South China Sea. He went on, "We're starting a new project. It's called Operation Market Time. The supply line will become very important during this operation. If you go in the drink," he smiled handing Pete the envelope, "make sure this package is torn into small pieces before you hit the water."

Pete returned the Admiral's salute and hurried from the bridge toward the forecastle where the high line crew was bringing the last of the new personnel aboard from the *Caliente*.

Boatswain Williams was in charge of the deck crew working the high line. He was a large man with graying temples, twenty-four years as enlisted, recently promoted to Warrant Officer. He was truly a Chief Boatswain who knew his business. Pete was not worried one bit as the Seaman pushed him back into the small metal frame and snapped the buckle of the safety belt.

"Don't worry, Pete," said the Chief, checking the rigging. "I've only lost one man over the side in my whole career. We'll get you over and back safely." He leaned forward, close to Pete's head and spoke softly in a threatening tone. "Don't tell those guys on the 'Flyin' Red Horse' you're Bill Peterson's brother. They might take a notion to put you in the drink."

He stood again, removing his hard hat. "Hoist away!" he sounded off as he waved his hat. Pete felt the cable chair rise. In an instant he was away, over the handrail and lost in the great void between the two behemoths of the sea. Fear clutched him as he looked down the forty feet to the churning surface. The ships were cutting deep swaths in the water, and the spray from the racing bows came up close to where he sat. The entire one-hundred and fifty-foot space between the ships was filled with boiling, churning foam as the water turned.

The next thing Pete knew, he was being pulled down onto the deck of the *Caliente*. As he stepped out of the chair, a messenger from the bridge met him. "This way," was all he said.

Pete followed the messenger through catwalks and up deck ladders to the bridge where he reported to the Captain. Pete gave the Captain the envelope he had been entrusted with and followed the messenger to where his brother, Bill, was waiting. He was on the mess deck instead of in the sick bay as Pete had expected.

Bill was sitting at a table drinking coffee as Pete approached. He extended his hand. As Pete took it, he spoke. "I'd get up," he said with a wry smile, "But I took a little fall yesterday, and I'm not feeling that good. I was breaking up a fight out on the weather deck and got knocked off a catwalk, two levels to the main deck."

Pete looked hard at him. "What were you doing in a fight? Don't you people have a master at arms force aboard this boat? It seems to me, fights are the business of the ship's police force."

Bill laughed, but quelled the laughter in favor of an expression of pain. "I am the Master At Arms. It was not a big thing. Just a little argument about some money. Enough of that. How are you doing? The last time I saw you, you were a Seaman Apprentice going to Vietnam with a marine unit. Hey, what are you doing wearing those stripes on your shirt? You can get into trouble impersonating a Petty Officer, particularly a Second Class." He gestured to Pete's sleeve.

"Oh, don't worry about that," Pete said, sitting down. "These are my stripes. I changed my rate after my experience in Vietnam. I became a Storekeeper, just like you. I studied hard for each exam and was recommended by my Captain for promotion."

Pete squirmed in his chair. "I know it's taken me less time to make rate than it did you, but you have to remember I don't spend all my spare time playing cards. I put in a lot of time with the books."

It was as though Pete had lit a fuse. Bill was instantly on the attack. He was in no mood for any good-natured truth. "If you're going to come aboard and insult me, you can just take yourself off this boat!" He scowled. "You and Rick were always Mamma's boys. You always got everything."

"Hey! Be cool." Pete countered. "You asked me, and I told you. You're the one who ran away to join the Navy. I was only five years old when you left. I don't remember getting any special favors from you." It seemed Pete's happy reunion was getting out of hand.

"That's right!" Bill's face was reddening. "You were only five. I was sixteen and had to lie to get into the Navy, and now here you are, trying to show the world you're better than me. Why don't you get out of here?"

"Aw, come on, Bill! I didn't mean it like that," Pete broke in. Their eyes locked. The moment of happiness Pete had experienced when he stepped through the mess deck doorway had flown from him. He got up and left feeling confused and crushed. As he left the messdeck he saw a shadowy figure rise from a corner table and quickly slip out a side door.

Three years! I can't believe this! Pete's heart sank. He was coming off an uncomfortable roller coaster ride.

Since their father died, Pete had always tried to model himself after the person he imagined Bill to be. He had never come home on leave and had not written to mother much at all, so for Pete, he was just an imaginary character. Pete had seen him only a couple of times, and both times were since he had come on active duty. It seemed every time Pete tried to get close to him, he would detect Pete's feelings and push him away. He seemed to want to follow the code of the strong silent type. Pete would go back to his ship and write his mother that he had seen "her boy" Bill and he was fine.

After underway replenishment with the *Caliente* was completed, Pete looked up Chief Warrant Officer Williams for a short visit.

"Chief," Pete began, "what did you mean when you told me not to tell the guys on the *Cal* I'm Bill's brother?"

The officer turned half away from Pete and put his forearms on the life rail and looked down into the water. "You know Pete, there are a lot of rumors. After a while, you hear so many that facts seem to start popping up here and there. I only know what I know, and I'm not sure what I know is the truth. When I first came into the Navy, I went aboard the *USS Fox* with your brother. We boarded her on the same day as a matter of fact. Your brother was a heck of a nice guy. He was the apple of the Captain's eye. Bill was selected for officer training command and was sent off to school to learn to be an officer. He and I were pretty close, and he wrote one letter when he first got to school, something about trying for Naval Intelligence. He never wrote again. When he rejoined the ship three years later, he was still a Seaman. He said he had washed out of Naval Intelligence. He fell in with a bad bunch of guys almost immediately. He was gambling, drinking, and was even caught in a smuggling deal, but they couldn't seem to pin anything on him." The officer looked at Pete. "They did, however, prosecute all the bad guys Bill was associated with."

The big man shifted his weight and spat into the sea. "I don't know exactly how it worked out, but Bill was transferred out almost at the same time an entire smuggling ring was arrested and taken off the *Fox*. That was when Bill and I were separated. He began to make rate, and it looked as though he'd be okay, but then he got hooked up with some of those guys who run slush funds. You know, a slush fund can make you a lot of money in a hurry."

The Chief paused to light a cigarette and looked studiously at the skies of the northern horizon. The monsoons had begun, and the skies were dark and foreboding. For the most part, they were just clouds laden with tropical moisture, but once in a while a typhoon kicked up out of nowhere and an unprepared deck force would be in serious trouble. "Those clouds don't seem to have any wind in them," he said taking a long drag from his cigarette. "A slush fund is where a sailor wants to borrow five bucks to go on the beach. You loan it to him with the understanding that on payday, he'll pay you back seven dollars. It seems, every ship has a slush fund. Here aboard our ship, the major slusher is one of your Storekeepers, a Third Class named Bagzendel. That little bald-headed rat probably makes enough money every cruise to buy a new Cadillac.

"The thing is, if no one makes a complaint against these people, there's not a thing that can be done. They're kinda like prostitutes, they've always existed. Your brother Bill is just a little more into it than the average guy, that's all. He doesn't just slush his division or his department or even his own ship, he's one of the biggest slush operators in the Pacific Fleet."

The Warrant Officer turned his attention back to Pete, trying to read the clouds in his face. "Usually, eight to twelve guys aboard a ship have slushes. On the *Cal* there's only your brother, and he's very much feared. It doesn't matter what ship or station he gets assigned to, he brings large sums of money and buys up the existing slush men. Then he uses them as his front, and he's never involved in a transaction, so nobody can touch him. He uses his position as a Master at Arms to ensure that everyone pays up. How do you report the chief of police to? If you squeal, you could get seriously hurt."

The Chief took a final draw on his cigarette and flicked it from between his fingers into the fourteen-knot breeze. Pete watched it as it somersaulted down to the quiet surface, broken only by the backwash of the bow. "You know, Pete," he went on. "The word is pretty much out. Bill is not a small time operator. I've heard he controls slushes on as many as twelve ships, and one of them is a carrier. I'd guess you can really pick up a piece of change aboard a 'bird farm'."

Pete left the conversation feeling his older brother was now a military gangland chieftain. The man Pete had worshipped as a boy was rotten to the core.

There must be something Pete could do to put a stop to this. He walked slowly to his office to be alone and ponder the possibilities. As he sat in his office with the door open, he heard a familiar voice coming from down the passageway. It was Commander Larkin, the Operations Officer. Pete left his desk and went to the open door.

"Commander, could I have a word with you, sir?" Pete asked as he motioned for the officer to come into his office.

As Commander Larkin entered the office, Pete closed the door and took his seat. "I'd like to talk to you about breaking up a slush fund operation, sir."

"Pete, you look a little troubled. Are you into these guys for a bundle?" he asked as he lit his pipe and leaned back in the chair across from Pete.

"No, sir," Pete said. "I was thinking of a bigger operation than the one Bagzendel is running aboard our ship. I was thinking of the one my brother runs."

"Whoa!" said the Commander, pulling his pipe from his mouth. He leaned across Pete's desk to speak in confidence. "I have a friend in Naval Intelligence, and NI-7 is working on the slush problem real hard right now. They're working all kinds of scams on these guys to bust up these rings. Tell me what you know, and I'll pass it along. Who knows, maybe you and I can get something done."

Pete told the Commander everything he knew and everything he suspected with regard to his brother's operation. Bagzendel's name came up, too. Another fourteen-year veteran of fleet service, and a known slush operator, but no one would appear against him.

Commander Larkin agreed to talk to Chief Warrant Officer Williams and gather as much information as he could, then he would pass it along to his friend at NI-7 Fleet Headquarters in the Philippines. Pete felt confused and relieved as the officer left his office. He seemed to know what was going on without Pete giving him the whole story.

Pete turned to a history text book and opened the pages. A tear fell on the book. He was grief-stricken to think his brother, the man he once adored, was a lowlife gangster.

He wanted to return to his world, his happy little world of ignorance. He had had enough of underway replenishment.

Chapter 32

On Station

The next day the seaplane tender was back on station at its seadrome near Con Son Island, off the coast of Vietnam. The runway marker lights were set into large buoys, looking like giant inner tubes. Heavy bottom-dragging anchors kept them in place. They sat two-hundred feet apart in two parallel lines a half mile long. At night, on the calm sea, the seadrome looked like any other long concrete runway, stuck out in the big flat open space, a quarter mile from the ship.

When the plane service boats and the crash boats were ready, the big lumbering seaplanes began to land in the seadrome. The crash boats, painted red like fire engines, would wait at the outer marker of the seadrome for the seaplanes to come in. Just as the Martin SP5B touched the water, the coxswain driving the crash boat would kick on the twin Chevy 409 V-8 engines and the "escorting" would begin.

The crash boat raced along beside the landing aircraft at the same rate of speed, about two-hundred feet away until the aircraft came to a safe stop. In the event of a problem, the crash boat would be right there to fight a fire, rescue the flight crew or whatever else might be required.

When the aircraft came to a halt and turned off its engines, the plane service boats or PSBs took over and towed the aircraft to its individual tie-up buoy or to the refueling station next to the ship. One of the several PSBs in the area then picked up the crew of the aircraft and brought them back to the *Blue Island* for debriefing with the Air Operations Officer.

By sundown, eighteen aircraft nestled in the seadrome, including Lieutenant Patric's – the one that had sunk and given the crew an opportunity to go to Hong Kong. The entire VP49 Squadron was aboard and resting easy, except for Lt. Patric and his crew. They were on the hot seat in the squad room with the Senior Air Officer!

Pete made a point of picking up his duty belt, .45 pistol and armband from the ship's armory early. The OOD for his watch had not reported yet, so Pete saluted the officer on duty. "Petty Officer Peterson assuming Petty Officer of the Watch, sir," and left the bridge to begin his rounds.

As the sun dropped behind the island and darkness fell, Pete began his assignment. It was his job, for the four hours he was on watch, to check on all of the sentry posts and ensure the security of the ship from any seaborne assault. Pete would make his rounds, speaking to each sentry, and report the status of the watch to the Officer Of the Deck by telephone from the after seaplane deck. It was the first watch of the evening, 8 PM to midnight, generally an easy one to stand.

Numerous spotlights had been hung over the side, so the sentries could see practically to the bottom of the bay, forty feet below. There were five sentry posts. One on the forecastle to watch the bow, one on each side, port and starboard, and two on the fantail to watch the hangar deck area and the stern, both port and starboard.

As Pete approached the starboard fantail sentry, he was greeted with a salute. "Starboard fantail all secure, sir!" It was Racozad. He had a transistor radio on a strap over his left shoulder and his M-1 carbine slung on his right shoulder.

"What are you doing with a radio?" Pete snapped as he returned the hand salute.

"Come on, Pete. I can still hear anything from the waterline and I'm being extra watchful. I'm just listening to Hanoi Hanna. She's a real kick!" Racozad kicked up a foot. "Did you know she has our position here, and she's talking about us? She's saying they're going to blow our ship up, tonight. It's just propaganda I know, and I shouldn't be listening to it, but she is playing the Beatles every other record."

Pete peered over the handrail into the brightly lit crystal clear water and stared at the beautiful orange, blue and green coral bottom.

"Okay!" he growled. "If there's the slightest disturbance in the water, I want you to start blowing that policeman's whistle around your neck, and start throwing depth grenades over the side. There's always the possibility that someone isn't just passing propaganda to us this time."

Leaving Racozad, Pete made a complete tour of the sentry posts, telling each sentry the same thing he had told Racozad.

After Pete had spoken to his last sentry, he called the OOD on the bridge to tell him of the instructions he had given. The voice on the other end of the line was squeaky little Ensign Palmer who had relieved the OOD on the bridge. *He was late for his watch, of course!* Pete thought.

Ensign Palmer's response was sharp. "Now you listen to me, Peterson. I remember you from Yokosuka. You're not pulling any of your tricks on me. Being the Admiral's gopher is not going to do you any good tonight. ***I'm*** giving the orders and if you disobey them, you're in deep *kimshi*. Throwing depth grenades in the water is a command decision! No one, I repeat, no one will give orders to throw depth grenades over the side but me! If I hear one rifle shot while I'm on watch, you'll be placed on report. Is that understood?"

Pete managed to muster up a weak "Yes, sir." and slammed down the telephone receiver onto the hook. For the next two hours, he walked the weather decks taking sentry reports and reporting to the Quartermaster Of the Watch on the bridge. The OOD was too busy to take his reports. *Probably having coffee!*

The night air was thick and clammy. There was so much moisture Pete could almost hold the air in his hand. The monsoons were on their way in, and had there been a moon, it would have been blotted out by the heavy stale overcast.

There's nothing like the darkness of night at sea, thought Pete. *I think it's the only place I've ever been where there's absolute blackness. Of course, the jungles of Vietnam are a close second.*

It began to rain; the water dripping from the sky was as warm as the air. There was no chance to go below for rain gear. Pete knew it was raining by the puddles beginning to pool on the weather decks. As he walked near the life rails he could see the downpour in the large spotlights on the still water. The rain fell without noise, seeming to leave the sky and join the sea in one motion like a silent orchestra. *And all my life, I thought only snow could do this.* The only noise came from the rain dripping off the men's clothing onto the deck.

Pete was passing from the port side of the ship onto the fantail hangar deck when he heard the whistle. It was Racozad's station. Pete rushed aft as fast as he could, and just as he reached him, Racozad released a depth grenade. It hit the water and sank, swirling bubbles to the rain splattered surface. There was a hollow bonking sound and the sea's surface erupted with a geyser of water and a loud boom. The salt spray shot fifty feet into the air splashing both men.

There was a slight splashing of water at the edge of a spotlight. Pete saw a form in motion, a wide dark body coming into the light. Without realizing it, his .45 caliber automatic was in his hand. He was firing the second shot when the form he fired at came into the light, a stingray, which was attacking the schools of squid at the center of the light. Pete had hit it twice. It floated for a second like a plate in a dishpan, and sank, sliding lifelessly back and forth as it descended. Pete recovered his faculties.

"What did you see?" Pete demanded. "I hope you saw more than a fish." Pete pointed to the water.

"I saw a frogman, Pete! I know it was a frogman!" Racozad hollered frantically.

There were dead fish and squid popping to the surface, victims of the depth charge. A frogman's foot flipper drifted near the surface and slid away under the water at the edge of the spot light.

"More grenades! More grenades!" Pete yelled. Both fantail sentries were now lobbing the large twelve-pound depth grenades over the side as fast as they could. "Give it to 'em, boys," Pete encouraged. "I'll call in the alarm to the OOD. Damn!! It looks like Hanoi Hanna wasn't kidding this time. She actually helped us without knowing it."

Pete rushed across the open seaplane deck to the hangar and the after Quarterdeck. There, an electronic command post similar to the one on the bridge exists for in-port use of the 1MC. Pete grabbed the phone and called the bridge. Ensign Palmer answered.

"We're under attack, sir!" Pete yelled.

"Now, just a minute, Peterson! I told you not to discharge any grenades until I gave the order! I'm going to have your stripes for this!" His voice droned on as Pete let the phone slip through his fingers and drop to the deck.

This idiot's crazy! He's busting my chops while enemy divers are planting charges along the hull of this ship. Pete could still hear Mr. Palmer's squalling reprimand as he turned to the ship's in-port alarm panel.

The ship's alarm levers were all in the open position above his head. Pete wasn't sure which was which. These switches were usually operated by the Boatswain's Mate Of the Watch.

"What the..." Pete muttered as he started pulling all of the levers into the locked closed position. He grabbed the 1MC hand-held mike and threw switches until all the lights were on. "The ship is under attack! The ship is under attack! General Quarters! General Quarters everybody!" Pete screamed into the PA mike. There were gongs and sirens and all kinds of noises going off from the alarm system. Pete wanted everyone to their battle station, but he was afraid to turn any of the switches off, for fear he'd turn off the GQ alarm.

Pete jumped as the PA barked an order directly at him. It was the Boatswains Mate Of the Watch. "Get off the 1MC, Peterson! The Captain is on the bridge!"

Pete dropped the microphone like a hot potato and quickly snapped off all the switches he had thrown. The General Quarters alarm continued its methodical *bong, bong, bong.*

The Boatswain's Mate Of the Watch was now heard throughout the ship. "General Quarters! General Quarters! This is NOT a drill! All hands, man your battle stations! Surface attack light weapons team to your boats! UDT Team to your stations! All frogmen be advised, your armband color is yellow!"

Flares were now being fired into the air by the five-inch guns. The area around the ship for a half a mile was lit up like daylight.

The light weapons team appeared in full combat gear and began loading into PSBs and crash boats. The boats were quickly away, and the ship's Underwater Demolition Team, with scuba tanks, was on deck in wet suits. They wore yellow bands around their left arm for identification. The UDT Officer ordered them down the ladder into the water. They were gone with a splash.

The ship suddenly seemed as though it were dead. It was totally buttoned up for battle. It felt eerie to Pete, standing on the fantail in the rain with two sentries and two officers, not knowing exactly what was going on. The ship was quiet. All alarms were silent and there was only the occasional crack of the five inch guns firing off another flare.

One of the ship's frogmen silently appeared under a starboard searchlight. He was holding a fifteen-inch diameter, four-inch thick magnetic discharge mine. A simple radio transmitter could set it off. "There are three like this, sir. It looks like they were about one fourth of the way finished when they were detected."

The mines were carefully placed into a Plane Service Boat and taken out about two miles from the ship where they were exploded. They created a nice yellow and orange fireworks display in the night sky.

An hour later, the light weapons team came back aboard. As they disembarked their boats, Pete counted three litter cases and one obvious prisoner. Two of the litters had wounded sailors on them. The third was a dead North Vietnamese diver. He had shrapnel in his chest and shoulder from a depth grenade.

The balance of the night was restless for the entire ship's company. Some of the Storekeepers stayed up listening to the radio.

At breakfast, Racozad came to Pete's table with a broad smile on his face. "Have you heard what Hanoi Hanna has to say this morning, Pete?" he offered as he sat down with a cup of coffee. "She's expressing her sympathy to the families of the crew of the *USS Blue Island Sound* which was sunk in Con Son Bay last night."

Pete looked up at Racozad. "Well, if Hanoi Hanna wants us, she's going to have ample opportunity. We are scheduled to be on station for at least another sixty days."

Pete set his coffee cup down. "Then again, we may move just to confuse the enemy. Wherever we are, we'll be on station, flying seadrome operations."

"Oh, yeah," said Racozad, handing Pete a folded sheet of paper. "Here is a note from Commander Larkin.

Pete unfolded the quickly scrawled note and read it with interest.

Pete, Admiral Moore thought you would appreciate knowing that one of your favorite officer, Ensign Palmer has been transferred. He left this morning on the HU16C mail plane for Saigon. It seems the Admiral feels he would be more valuable to the war effort if he were assigned to an ice breaker off Alaska. CMDR Larkin.

Pete quickly folded the note and stuffed it into his shirt pocket. He knew it was wrong but he could not help feeling joy.

Racozad burst into laughter. "Pete, I read your note." He turned slightly in his chair. "I must confess. I had a chat with the Admiral last night after GQ. He wanted to know why you sounded the alarm instead of the Boatswain's Mate of the Watch."

Pete looked up in amazement at his young friend.

"I just told him that the little pipsqueak has been gunning for you since he came aboard in Yokosuka. I didn't lie or exaggerate. Of course, Chip Dale went in to see the Admiral when I left. I don't know what he said."

Chapter 33

Air Force vs Navy

Two days after the attack by the North Vietnamese frogmen, the *USS Blue Island Sound* pulled in its buoys and moved to a protected harbor. The ship set up seadrome operations at Cam Ranh Bay, South Vietnam.

"Gentlemen." Captain O'Hara's deep voice rang out over the 1MC speaker outside Pete's office. "A new Air Force base has recently been completed here and a new Naval Air Facility is under construction. The Officer's Club and the Enlisted Men's Club on this new base belong exclusively to the Air Force." The Captain's voice trailed for a moment and Pete turned his head to listen hard.

"As you know men, one of the requirements of a ship in port at an air base is that the ship provide additional security personnel. This means whatever number the base commander deems necessary to handle the two services on his base.

"For this reason, selected NCO's have been assigned as Shore Patrol at the Officer's Club on their duty days, others have been assigned to the EM Club. Men – let's mind our manners when we're on the beach. A list of Petty Officers has been posted outside the X Division Office."

Pete's office door sprung open and there stood Chip. "Hey man! You've been selected to watch over the Cam Ranh Bay Officer's Club on your duty days! I was at the EM Club yesterday and you'd think the Navy was the enemy. Fist fights between the Air Force and the Navy were everywhere."

Pete drew in a deep breath and leaned back, realizing that this could be a "long" port call.

* * *

Pete's third duty day at the 'O' Club was well underway as the sun went down. A thick blackness came with evening and the base was frequently attacked at night. For this reason, the club was closed just before sundown and the crew had to be back aboard ship in time for 'eight o'clock reports.'

Pete was just inside the door of the 'O' club checking IDs on all incoming personnel. He had reported to the Duty Officer at 1400, and the Navy pilots started to show up shortly thereafter. By the time the Air Force pilots started to arrive two hours later, the Navy pilots already had a buzz on and some were very inebriated.

Pete noticed Lt. Patric and a couple of his crew members at a table near the front of the club next to the bandstand. They were two sheets to the wind. They had been joined by some Navy "air-sea-rescue" boys, and were getting so rowdy they could be heard laughing over the band. Lt. James, an HU16 Charlie rescue seaplane pilot, was the loudest of the bunch and Pete was a little embarrassed.

To think 'these' are 'my' officers and worse yet, they're guests in an Air Force Officer's Club. It wouldn't be so bad if they were sitting in the back of the room, but there they are, right up front.

Their rowdiness continued to interrupt the entertainment for the rest of the club and some of the Air Force people were becoming more than a little impatient with them. An Air Force major suddenly appeared beside Pete. His brightly polished name tag read Major Wells, not just his last name like everyone else.

You'd think people could look at the gold oak leaves on his shoulders and see he was a major. This guy is in full dress blues with ribbons and shiny brass. You'd think he just got off the plane from the States, but he's wearing a Vietnam Service and Vietnam Air Medal. Maybe he's on the edge of going nuts or going home. He's a real recruiting poster when compared to the rest of these guys. Pete gave the officer a smile and nod of recognition.

"Shore patrol!" Major Wells snapped. "I want you," he pointed his San Miguel Beer bottle at Pete's face, "to get your Navy out of ***MY*** club!" He drew closer. He smelled strongly of beer. "You sailors think you can come into any port and take over the entire base and all of its facilities. Well, this is one place you can't take over! This is ***MY*** club!" He reached up and patted the brightly painted, yellow, wing tank of an F-86 Super Sabre hanging from the ceiling in the shadows over the door. "This tank came off a plane that fought in Korea. This is our 'good luck' charm!"

The Major's face tightened like he had swallowed a lemon. He was almost yelling. "This is an Air Force Club! You sailors can't take it over!"

Out of military courtesy, Pete popped to attention and answered the officer. "Sir, I'll ask them to hold it down," he said. Turning, he scurried up the aisle to the table of rowdies. *I certainly wouldn't want this dingleberry to send the Air Police after my guys,* Pete thought. *There might be a fight, and my loudmouthed friends would wind up in the clink.*

There were six naval aviators in the group. Pete placed his left hand near the center of the small round table and leaned over toward Lt. James. "Sirs!" Pete said quietly, but as forcefully as he could. "One of the Air Force officers has asked that you please hold it down. You're getting a little out of hand."

Lt. Patric laughed very loud. "Pete! Sounds to me like Major Wells sent you over here. He's always on our case. I think he hates sailors as much as he hates the enemy."

Pete placed both hands on the table, and scowled at Lt. Patric. "Sir, if you don't want to get bounced, please be cool. I sure don't want to be the one to bounce you."

Lt. Patric looked at his watch. "What the hell, fellas!" he said, crushing a beer can with his left hand. "We might as well grab a couple of beers and head back to the boat." The entire group began to get up and move toward the bar.

A crash came from the left side of the stage. A table came sliding by Pete on the dance floor. He jerked upright and turned to see a fist fight in progress between an Army pilot and an Air Force pilot.

"What the. . . ?" Pete said.

Pete's guys were on their way, so he pulled his oak baton and moved toward the fray. There was already a Shore Patrol and an Air Policeman there, but they weren't having a lot of luck breaking up the fight.

Pete grabbed the soldier and pulled him off his opponent. "Come on, sir." Pete insisted, placing his night stick under the officer's chin to apply pressure to his throat. "This is one place where you can't win a fight." Pete's Shore Patrol counterpart was on one arm and the Air Policeman was on the other. They had the soldier headed for the exit.

Major Wells was practically jumping up and down near the door. "Take him outside and hold him for the hard hat APs. I've called them. They can take this trouble-making ground pounder to the stockade."

The Shore Patrolmen brushed by, knocking Major Wells back against the door jamb as they took the Army officer outside into the evening air. Pete handed the soldier his hat. "You had better hot-foot it, sir," Pete said, putting his baton away. "The Air Police will be here in a minute, and Major Wells will be more than happy to file charges."

"I didn't start it," the young officer argued. "I just happened to be there."

"That doesn't mean a thing, sir." Pete turned him toward his barracks area and gave him a gentle push. "I think you'll agree that an Army Second Lieutenant hasn't got a chance against a prophead Major on an Air Force base." The young officer made no more argument and kept walking.

As the soldier made the turn out of sight, an Air Police jeep skidded to a halt next to Pete. An Air Force "Hard Hat Patrol" Captain got out, his chrome helmet gleaming in the setting sun. "Where's the soldier we're supposed to pick up?"

"He seemed to be well under control, sir." Pete answered. "And besides, you wouldn't want a guy that was an innocent bystander."

"Come on, Lasky." The Captain said as he sat back in the jeep. He gave a wink as the jeep began to pull away. "Sounds like Wells is pulling another one of his tricks."

Pete turned to the Second Class Aviation Ordinanceman who was standing Shore Patrol with him. He was from the Naval Air Station on the base. "Who or what is this Major Wells?" Pete asked.

"That's kind of a hard story," the Petty Officer replied. "I don't think anybody knows it all. Wells is a hell of a pilot, one of the best in Vietnam. He was shot down about seven months ago and lost his navigator.

He went down at sea but wasn't picked up by Air-Sea Rescue, so he swam to shore and made it back to a friendly area on his own. I guess he went through quite a lot, and he blames the Navy for it. He could've been rotated home but wouldn't take the orders. He's got one screw loose by most people's estimate, but the doctors say he's fit to fly."

The Air Police Duty officer, a very sharply dressed Lieutenant Colonel drove up. "You fella's can pull out. We'll be closing this place down now and it seems pretty quiet. I did notice a large bunch of your guys down by the pier, so you'll probably be of more use down there."

Pete saluted, "Very well, sir. Thank you, sir."

As Pete walked toward the pier, he recalled what had happened when he was with K Company. He had placed his faith in a system and was almost let down. He hoped this Major Wells was not going to be another let down in his opinion of the efficiency and training of American fighting men.

When Pete got to the pier, he noticed there was a disturbance at the edge of the dock. The Shore Patrolman in charge of the pier was having an argument with some young aviation officers. "You're not going to take that thing aboard ship, sir." he said, as Pete got within earshot.

One of the officers jerked the object back to keep it from the hands of the sailor and in so doing, let it slip from his own hands and into the water. Pete rushed to the edge of the pier just in time to see the Air Force's good luck charm sink out of sight in Cam Ranh Bay.

"For crying outside!" Pete muttered as he rushed up to Lt. Patric.

"What in the world were you doing with that, sir?" he demanded. "Don't you know what that F-86 tank means to those prop heads? How would you like someone to steal your good luck charm out of the wardroom?" Pete put his finger in the middle of Lt.

Patric's chest. "When we get back to the ship, I'm going to ask our divers to get that tank back, and you'd better hope they find it. If they don't find it, your irresponsible actions may get the officers of every ship that calls here banned from the Air Force 'O' Club."

"Aw, come on, Pete!" he whined. "Don't be a hard ass. We're just playing a little joke. A college prank. It ain't no big deal!"

When Pete got back aboard, he contacted the UDT officer and a three-man diving team was dispatched immediately. The search team had been gone about two hours when Pete was called from the ET Shop by one of the Captain's orderlies.

"The Captain wants to see you in the wardroom, Pete." The young Seaman seemed in a hurry to get back into officer's country and get this assignment over with.

"The Captain is real upset. There's an Air Force light Colonel, a Major, and three APs in there with him. The Major keeps saying you were the cause of it all, Pete."

The messenger knocked on the wardroom door, turned the handle and stood aside. Pete stepped into the room.

The wardroom was spacious with a lounge area at one end, large overstuffed chairs, couches, coffee tables and a large color television set at the side. At the other end was the dining area, furnished with a long table and a chair for each officer. At the head of the table was a large chair with arms for the Captain when he chose to dine with the officers.

At the other end was the Executive Officer's chair, large, but it didn't have armrests. Only the Captain's chair had armrests.

The wardroom was clear of all personnel except the Captain, Lt. Patric, two of his flight officers and the detachment of Air Force who gave Pete the evil eye as he approached the table. Major Wells stood up. "This is the man," he charged, shaking a long finger at Pete. "He's the one!"

"Major Wells. If you would please calm down," said the Lieutenant Colonel.

"Pete." Captain O'Hara spoke and Pete came to attention at the end of the table near the XO's chair. "I understand you were on Shore Patrol at the Officer's Club at the time a certain wing tank was stolen by personnel from this ship. Is that true?"

"I'm afraid I was outside with a soldier at the time of the theft, sir," Pete replied, trying to be as honest and concise as possible.

"That's right!" The Lieutenant Colonel threw one of his dress white gloves into his hat on the table. "I remember seeing this man outside the club."

"I'm told Lt. Patric threw the tank into the bay," the Captain went on. "Were you there when that happened?"

"No, sir. I mean, yes, sir." Pete's face reddened with frustration. "I was there when Lt. Patric *dropped* the tank into the bay, but I am sure he didn't intend to. I think he thought of it as a captured enemy flag or a chess piece or something like that. I think he was just stealing it for the night to upset Major Wells, there." Pete pointed at the crisply dressed officer.

"Thank you, Pete. That will be all," said the Captain. Pete turned on his heel and left the wardroom.

Pete walked across the weather deck on the port side just in time to see the dive boat come alongside at the after-ladder. "Did you find the tank?" he shouted down to the Boatswain's Mate tying off the bow line of the boat. Another diver answered the question by holding a large yellow object over his head.

Pete rushed down the weather deck ladder to the main deck and back onto the hangar deck where he met the diver carrying the tank. It was clean and dry and in good condition. Pete grabbed it from him. "Thank you!" he said and headed for the wardroom.

Pete's knock on the wardroom door was answered by a Steward. He bounced past the Steward's Mate and stood by the Captain. Pete laid the tank on the table. "Here's the tank in question, sir." Pete clicked his heels together triumphantly. The Air Force was speechless as he left the room.

The next day's "Plan Of the Day" carried news of a Captain's Mast. Three officers would receive punishment: Lt. Patric, who had sunk an SP5B in Subic Bay, would be reprimanded and transferred to NAS Seward, Alaska for North Pole recon duty. LTJG Tims would receive a letter of reprimand in his record and be restricted to the ship for two weeks. LTJG Regan would get the same.

Pete felt bad for Lt. Patric, but he was a real wild man on the beach. He drank too much, started fights and was always trying to get something going. Of course, the crew owed him for the time he sank his flying boat and got the crew some time off in Hong Kong.

Air Force one, Navy zero.

Chapter 34

Getting Respect

Pete sat in the Electronics Supply Office a week after the "good luck charm" incident reading a letter from home when the phone rang. "Hey, Pete. It's Newstead." said the warm voice on the other end. "Would you like to come up to the Aerography Shack and listen to one of your friends who's out on a sortie right now?"

"Sure," Pete replied, and hung the receiver back in its place. It was fun to listen to fighter and bomber pilots as they went in on their runs. Sometimes it was like watching a John Wayne movie, and at other times it was like listening to truck drivers talk about delivering milk over a CB radio.

Pete's old friend from Treasure Island, Newstead, was now an AG1, a First Class Aerographer. He was Leading Petty Officer in his division, but he was still a good friend and Pete visited with him often.

As Pete entered the weather room, he looked up at the three large console speakers, each tuned to a different channel. The first one had a monitor on the Marine Weather Service out of Tokyo, the second was Air-Sea Rescue, and the third was set for the frequency of the three major military aircraft groups in the area.

Pete spoke to the Air Traffic Controllers and AGs as he came through the door. "I brought up a can of mixed nuts Moon gave me down in the galley. I thought you guys would like a snack." All five of the men crowded up against the AGs map table and began eating nuts and listening to the unfolding saga on the radio.

"Blue bird leader, this is Falcon leader. We'll be leaving you here. We'll meet you at point Xray for the ride home. We have to go down here and give this base a hotfoot." Pete recognized the voice. It was Major Wells, the best F4 jockey in the Air Force. "Roger, Falcon leader. Good hunting to you," said the other voice.

"Okay, chics." It was Wells again. "There it is, right there against the hill. Can you see it?"

"We're on you, Falcon leader," came another voice.

"Follow me in, boys. We'll make sure we don't get any more SAM's from this missile base," Wells said.

"Rockets away." It was Wells' navigator.

"Heads up, boys. They're shooting the real stuff at us today." There was a pause. Wells could be heard again. "What was that?"

"We took a hit, sir. We're losing fuel real fast. We'd best break off and head for the coast." The young navigator was obviously very anxious.

"I'm going to take her to the roof so we can jump off. You get a call into Air-Sea Rescue" said Wells.

The other radio crackled. "Air Sea Rescue, this is Falcon One, we're going into the drink at point Niner Twenty Xray. We should be about two miles out."

All of the men in the AG shack ran out onto the top of the ship's hangar and looked down as the crew of the HU16C rescue seaplane scrambled to get to their aircraft.

"Go get 'em!" Pete yelled down as he recognized Lt. James coming across the flight deck, his copilot already standing in the Plane Service Boat.

"Hey, Pete!" Lt. James looked up. "Get down here and grab a helmet. I think you're going to enjoy this one."

Pete had been on two other rescue flights with James. Lt. James was a squared away guy and quite a lot of fun, but at the same time, when it came to flying a rescue, he was the best. "Okay. Be right there." Pete waved and headed for the ladder and the Plane Service Boat.

Pete dropped into his seat still buckling his chin strap as the crew chief slammed the door and the seaplane lifted off. He plugged in his headset jack, and the radio conversation filled his ears.

"Oh no!" It was Wells. "There are red troops all along the beach. I sure hope they don't have boats, or you guys will find us in a POW compound somewhere. Would you Navy turkeys get off your back sides and answer me?"

"If you'll shut up a minute, sir," James said, trying to calm him down, "we'll be there within half an hour. The only real problem you have is the tide; it's coming in now, and your raft could easily be carried into shore. Pay close attention to your drift, and if you start going in, get out of the raft and swim out to sea. You've got to stay out of the range of their weapons."

"Thanks for the info. We're going out now," said Wells. The radio went dead.

Five very solemn minutes went by before the solid throb of the propeller blades was broken by the radio. "Navy Rescue, this is Falcon Two." It was Wells' wing man. "Rescue, we have finished our mission and we'll make a quick check run over where Falcon One went down."

"We'd appreciate that," said Lt. James, "we're still twenty minutes away. Any help you can give would be great. Thanks."

"Rescue, we're on the scene now. There's lots of enemy troops down there. They've spotted the raft, and are firing small arms and knee mortars at them. It looks like the tide is coming in, and Falcon One is getting closer to the beach." The voice of the wing man was showing stress.

"Falcon Two, this is Rescue. Is there anything you can do for us? Can you make a fire run at the beach and chase the enemy back into the jungle? Maybe you can break their concentration for a minute or two." Lt. James was willing to try anything.

"Can do, Rescue, but we only have ammo for one pass, and then it's back to base for us." The wing man finished, and the radio went dead for less than a minute. "Rescue, this is Falcon Two. We chased 'em back into the trees, but you can bet they won't stay there more than five minutes once they figure out we've gone. Good luck!"

The wing man signed off and went back to his flight channel as he headed back to base. Rescue One was still seven minutes away from the downed flyers when the three remaining F-4s of Falcon group zoomed past.

Lt. James' voice came over the in-house line. "Those guys will be on the ground back at Camrahn before we get to Wells. We're still six minutes away, but we should be able to see them any minute now."

The in-house chatter was suddenly broken up by an incoming message from another flight that had come up the line with the Falcon group. "Rescue One, this is Blue Bird Leader. We'll be passing over Falcon One's position in two minutes. If you're close, stay back a minute, and we'll rake the beach for you one time on our way home."

"Thank you, Blue Bird Leader," Lt. James responded. "We should have visual with Falcon One in about one minute."

"Rescue One, this is Blue Bird Leader. We just raked the beach and sent those rats packing, but they'll be back I'm sure. It appears Major Wells has had to abandon his raft and swim to avoid going on the beach. The raft is pretty close to the beach now and nearly sunk. You had better scamper if you're going to get in and out without taking some lead."

The fighter jets now appeared and disappeared in a loud scream, headed for home.

"There they are, boys!" yelled James over the in-house system. "We'll come around shallow and shield them from the fire from the beach while we pick them up. Pete, help Marris get that door open. The instant you get those guys clear of the water, let me know because I'm going to gun it out of here."

Marris and Pete pulled the door back as soon as the HU16C settled next to the flyers. Both of their faces were washed with happiness, and at the same time, Pete could see pain in the face of the navigator. He had blood showing on the left shoulder of his orange flight suit. The rescuers grabbed both men and wrestled them into the aircraft. "Clear! We're clear!" Marris shouted, as he slammed the large door shut and dogged it tight. The corpsman had already started working on the navigator who had passed out from exhaustion.

Wells was able to tell the corpsman what had happened to the navigator "Max was shot from the beach while we were trying to paddle the raft out of small arms range. I knew I couldn't paddle the raft alone, so I took the tie straps of Max's life preserver in my mouth and swam toward the open sea."

When Rescue One got back aboard the "Blue Goose," the injured pilot was taken to sick bay. Major Wells was examined and released.

Pete was standing near the afterbrow as Major Wells boarded a launch for the beach. He stopped suddenly and shook Pete's hand. "Pete. You tell your officers, all of your officers, they're welcome at the Air Force 'O' Club anytime they want to come ashore. Thanks. Thanks to all of you." His smile was genuine, and he seemed looser, more pleasant than at anytime since Pete had known him.

An Air Force Sergeant walking behind Major Wells stopped and spoke one last word as he departed. "It seems your Air-Rescue boys found the *old* Major Wells for us. Thanks."

Pete turned to Cagney who had joined him on the hangar deck. Cagney smiled. "Well, Pete. It looks like we've earned the respect of the Air Force."

Chapter 35

Relief at Last

The ship's company was really getting into this seadrome operation. There were plenty of things happening. The ship was serving in the combat zone. The SP5B squadron was flying missions, but at the same time there was liberty every night to go over to the Enlisted Men's Club or the Officer's Club at the base in Cam Rahn Bay. The entire crew was adjusting very nicely. They worked all day and drank warm beer all evening. Getting drunk was not hard. A beer only cost a nickel. Five pennies in Vietnam for what cost fifty cents back home. Still, a person could only drink so much. After a while, that got to be old hat. Most of the guys started staying aboard and just went over to the beach now and then. The ship had been overseas so long the crew no longer appreciated the novelty of new ports or the excitement of *Blue Island Sound* planes blockading enemy troops or boats.

It was during the fifth week in Cam Rahn that Admiral Moore called Pete into his office. "Pete, I want you to know how much I've appreciated your help while I've been aboard the *Blue Island Sound,"* he said as he extended his right hand.

Pete took his hand. "You sound like you're saying good-bye or something, sir,"

"I am, Pete." He smiled. "My section of the Naval Air Force Pacific Fleet, is being dissolved, and I'm being reassigned to Commander Seventh Fleet in Pearl Harbor.

"The day of the seaplane in naval patrol and blockade work is ending, and you and I are witnessing it. It was a proud force while it served."

Pete could see this command meant a lot to the Admiral, and he was about to get a little misty. "Yes, sir. I have been proud to serve with you," Pete spoke up.

The Admiral's mood became upbeat as quickly as it had fallen, saying, "Pete, your ship will be relieved in a few days by the United States Coast Guard. The *USS Blue Island Sound* will be rotated home for decommissioning."

So the ship will finally be allowed to return to the States. Pete's heart raced.

Pete shook the Admiral's hand and left his office. An empty uncertainty shook him. *The Coast Guard is going to bring its cutters and do the same job the "Blue Goose" has been doing with seaplanes for sixteen months. What a kick in the head!*

Later that day, an LST pulled into the harbor and anchored next to the *Blue Island Sound*. This LST would be the tender or mother ship for the ten shiny white Coast Guard cutters that arrived later in the afternoon and tied up in two rows, five abreast on the port side of the LST. This little flotilla would relieve COMPATFORPAC, Commander of Patrol Forces Pacific Fleet. The crew of the LST was about a hundred and sixty. The crew of each cutter was seven men. These two-hundred and thirty men would be relieving eight-hundred and sixty-four men, the crew of the *Blue Island Sound* and her VP squadron of SP5B aircraft.

Pete looked down at the young men tying off the lines on the cutters. *How young and fresh they look! How wide-eyed they are! Their eyes not yet blasted half shut by the flash of fear or terror. Their skins are light, not yet baked by the sun of the Orient. I'm glad to see them, yet sad to see how happy they are to be here and how proud they are to serve.*

The Boatswain's pipe blared in Pete's ear from a weather deck speaker. "Now all today's Shore Patrol report to the afterbrow at sixteen hundred hours for assignment."

Pete looked at his watch. He had the duty, and he was one of the people who had Shore Patrol. He drew his gear from the ship's armory and reported to the afterbrow.

Twenty minutes later, he was standing on the main pier at Cam Rahn Station. His responsibility was to see that all hands who reported to the pier would be kept under control and transported back to the ship without falling into the bay and drowning. His partner was Mitchell RM2, and there wasn't much going on. Most of the guys coming back drank very little. They were just having one for the road so to speak. The difference between here and Okinawa was here it took the shuttle boat fifteen minutes to make the run to the ship instead of five.

The sun was going down. Pete's pier was on a dirt road in an unprotected area. The base, on the other hand, was well protected. Flat wound barbed wire was strung all around the large base, rows and rows of it. Huge round tangles of wire were laced with claymore mines about every four feet and behind them were foxholes with armed sentries to ensure the base was alerted to any intruder.

Pete stood at the outer edge of the pier, right on the road waiting for more *Blue Island Sound* sailors to pass the checkpoint gate two-hundred yards to the north. As he looked around, he caught movement in the corner of his eye and turned to the south to see what it was. Two men dressed in dungarees were coming up from the south, an area strictly forbidden because of the extremely heavy barbed wire entanglements and the great number of mines. It was obvious they were sailors, and they were very drunk. One was leaning on the other and both were laughing like they were at a fun house. Pete looked hard as they approached. It was Howell and Racozad, the young trouble-finders from his division. They had lost all the stripes they could afford to lose in Hong Kong.

Pete rushed down to them and started hurrying them to the pier. Both men had cuts and bruises all over their bodies, and their clothing was torn to shreds. Howell was missing a patch of hair off the right side of his head, and both men had dried blood all over them.

"What in the world has happened to you two?" Pete demanded. "Where have you been?" He pushed them to the back of the crowd on the pier to ensure they would be the first to board the motor launch when it returned.

"Well, Pete," began Howell. "I'm not going to listen to this guy anymore. He claimed he could drive a jeep, and he couldn't. I don't think he knows the first thing about a stick shift. He is a terrible driver."

"I don't want to hear anymore!" Pete snapped as the forty-two foot motor launch pulled up next to the pier. "We'll go over this later. Now, both of you get back to the ship and have Doc Vesper look at those cuts and bruises." With the help of a couple of sailors in the launch, Pete forced them down in their seats.

Pete turned to the boat coxswain. "Would you please see these two get to sick bay?" he asked, as another thirty-five sailors found their seats. Pete waved his hand like a conductor and the boat pulled out with a full load of passengers.

"No sweat, Pete," called the Coxswain. "We'll hand 'em over to the duty corpsman."

Pete returned to the road and looked for more men to come down from the checkpoint, but instead, a military police jeep and a small bus appeared. The jeep screeched to a halt right beside Pete. A Texas-sized Sergeant Major with military creases in his uniform stepped from the passenger side of the jeep.

Not another one of those guys, Pete thought, remembering the Marine Sergeant who had wound up in Antarctica after his extreme actions in Yokosuka. The bus came to a halt behind the jeep and six hard hat MPs with automatic weapons jumped out and stood at attention in front of the jeep, awaiting orders.

The Sergeant wasted no time getting right into Pete's face. "Who's in charge here?" he demanded in a harsh tone. He had a Navy white hat rolled up in his clinched right hand, and was tapping the end in his left hand like one might tap a rolled magazine or newspaper.

"I'm in charge," Pete answered. "What can I do for you?" Pete tried to be as calm and cool as he could.

"I'm looking for the man that belongs to this hat! He and a buddy stole my jeep while I was inspecting the EM Club. They took the jeep for a joy ride and crashed it over a cliff about a mile south of here. Those idiots knocked out eighty-seven feet of triple-laid barbed wire exploding thirty-nine Claymore antipersonnel mines and destroying my jeep." His face was riddled with anger and frustration.

"It sounds to me like you should be bringing me a couple of dead sailors instead of looking for live ones," Pete smirked. It sounded just like one of Howell and Racozad's tricks.

"If you'll open the inside of that hat," Pete pointed to the Sergeant's right hand, "we can read the name, and we can check the IDs of all the men here. If your men are here, you can certainly have them."

The Sergeant looked out in the bay at the launch going away at full speed. "For all I know, you've already put these guys back aboard ship."

"Oh, no!" Pete insisted. "We are regular Navy here. We always say first come, first served. If those guys are here, you can have them." Pete pulled the hat from the sergeant's hand and turned it wrong side out to expose the name.

Pete looked hard. *Now, isn't that just like those dummies?* He thought. *Here is a brand new white hat, and he, whichever one he was, has forgotten to put his name in it in ink. How can he expect to get it back on laundry day?*

"I'm sorry, Sarge." Pete turned the hat inside out under the sergeant's nose. "There's no name inside this cover."

"I don't care!" The Sergeant was steamed. "I demand the right to inspect this body of men, and it's my right to arrest anyone who looks like they've been in an accident."

"By all means." Pete turned to the assembly of sailors looking on. "Company, form ranks for inspection!" he snapped. The sailors moved quickly into formation. "Be my guest, Sarge," Pete offered, pointing to the formation.

The Sergeant moved up and down the ranks of men, inspecting clothing and looking close at anyone who had lost his hat or traded it to a ground pounder for a fatigue hat.

By the time the boat returned to pick up the last thirty men on the pier, the Sergeant had satisfied himself the people he was looking for were not among the men on the pier and left. *Thank goodness!*

Pete did not see Howell and Racozad until the next day at Quarters For Muster. Each one had an arm in a sling, broken no less, and Howell had a large white bandage around his head. They had spent the night in sickbay under observation. The duty corpsman was sure they had both suffered major blood loss, but they seemed just fine. They just looked a little funny with their black eyes and swollen faces.

That afternoon the Aviation Boatswain's Mates pulled the last seadrome buoy and watched the last plane take off with the Admiral aboard.

Operation Market Time was over. The *USS Blue Island Sound's* patrol of the waterways leading into the Mekong Delta and blockading the enemy's source of supply had lasted for sixteen long months. The SP5B seaplane had flown its last mission in Viet Nam.

The special sea and anchor detail was set, and the ship got underway at seventeen-thirty hours. The Admiral's last orders had been for the ship to steam to Pearl Harbor, Hawaii. The ship was underway for home! The *USS Blue Island Sound* had been relieved.

Chapter 36

Orders from Pearl

The *USS Blue Island Sound* was underway for Hawaii. The ship would be there in just five days. The entire crew was excited. The ship had left the war zone and was steaming under very relaxed conditions.

Pete sat at a table on the mess deck enjoying a fine lunch with Chip, Cagney and Pooh when AG1 Newstead came up and set his tray down. Right away, the newcomer was assailed by the men already at the table.

"Hey!" Chip exclaimed. "If it isn't our local weather guesser. Got any weather tips for us today, Newstead?"

Newstead did not flinch, but lowered himself calmly to his seat. "Only that we're about to come into some very heavy weather," he said.

"That's bunk!" Pooh retorted. "I was just up on watch on the bridge, and the ocean is as smooth as glass. There's not a cloud in the sky, and the air speed indicator shows sixteen knots, which is the current speed of the ship."

"Give the bear a cracker," Newstead said, crumbling his crackers into his soup bowl. "We're ahead of a very large typhoon, gentlemen," he said, picking up his spoon and dipping into his soup. "That isn't too bad. She won't catch up for two days. The real problem is the fact that by sundown, I'd guess about twenty-hundred hours, we'll pick up the tail end of a real big typhoon that's running out ahead of us."

"So what does that mean to us?" Cagney asked.

"What it means is..." Newstead took a bite of his roast beef. "This will be our last good meal for several days. We'll probably be chasing our breakfast all over the table in the morning."

As the men finished their meal, the 1MC came alive with an announcement from the bridge. "Now rig for heavy seas. All hands will remain off the weather decks until further notice. All officer's country passageways aft of the midships frame are open for internal passage. All hands are reminded to stay clear of the weather decks."

"Wow!" Chip said. "This must be a big one. Let's go up and see if we can pick up anything on the radar in the Combat Information Center."

The group left the galley and went up the three flights of stairs to the combat information center where they were greeted by friendly radarmen. RD3 Hanley pointed at the storm on his sweeping console. The men left CIC feeling confident that anything that could be seen and tracked would not bother them.

Such a thought on Pete's part was wrong! By nine o'clock that evening, he was in his bunk feeling the ship pitch and yaw in heavy seas. He didn't feel like spilling his last meal, but he was nauseous and dizzy. It was worse than trying to recover from a hangover. He lay in his bunk and prayed for sleep, which finally overtook him.

At zero four thirty the following morning, the Messenger Of the Watch was at the edge of his bunk, pulling at his arm. "Pete," he spoke softly so as not to wake any other crew members.

Pete opened his eyes to see the man's shining belt buckle moving up and down. "Can you come to the bridge and finish a watch for your man, Racozad? He's awfully sick, and the OOD doesn't want him on the bridge. He threw up twice already."

"I'll be right there," Pete managed. The messenger disappeared from sight in the red night light.

Pete dressed and found his way to the bridge. Racozad was already gone, and his mess had been cleaned up. The OOD had ordered him off the bridge, and the Quartermaster Of the Watch had taken over the sound-powered head set. Pete assumed the watch, and it turned into a long hard night. The ship pitched and yawed and rolled and yawed some more. There was fifty feet between the bow and the water line, and there was water awash on the forward weather deck against the forward gun mount. Sea spray was even covering the 04 level windows of the bridge. The sea was running heavy, seventy-foot swells.

I saw a destroyer on escort duty with the Kingston during a storm. Everything but the smoke stack of the tin can would go under water from time to time, Pete remembered.

Daylight broke shortly after zero five hundred, making the watch a lot easier because being tossed around in the dark made a person feel totally disoriented. At zero eight hundred, Cagney reported to the bridge to relieve Pete. "Boy! Am I glad to see you," Pete said.

He went down to breakfast and found most of the galley personnel had stayed in their bunks, and that was advised for all hands since the sea was so rough.

After Pete ate an orange for breakfast, he stopped by the Supply Office to tell whoever was there that he wasn't going to work today.

He opened the office door and found Howell and Vickers at their desks, and to his surprise, Commander Hatchfield at his desk. He was not working. He had his feet up on his desk and his chair leaned back against the bulkhead right under an open porthole.

"I don't think having a porthole open is a good idea in this blow, sir." Pete said as he pointed to the open window.

Commander Hatchfield never raised his chair nor moved. "It's too hot to not have it open, Pete," he responded.

At that moment, a wave ran the weather deck and crashed in through the open window. Water poured in like it was coming through an eighteen inch-pipe. The Commander, his desk and SK1 Lee's desk were all covered with water. Pete took that as his signal to vamoose. He headed for his bunk.

On his way, he stopped at the Fox G and W head. What a mistake! The bathroom reeked of today's breakfast, and before Pete got out of there, he donated his orange to the collection. Pete now felt sicker than ever and crawled into his bunk, clothes and all.

The next three days passed quickly. Pete spent most of them in his bunk. He would have moments when he felt good. He would get up and go to chow or try to play some Canasta with other Storekeepers in the office, but before long he would be right back in his bunk.

One day out of Pearl, the storm broke. Pete answered reveille, ate a hearty breakfast and reported to work as though nothing had happened.

Something had happened, however. Pete had been missed by the men in OE Division. When he opened the door to ESO, he found a gallon jar filled with green colored sugar wafers. A handwritten sign on the front of the jar in bold letters read, "Pete's Sea Sick Pills."

Shortly after sundown, the ship neared to within twenty miles of Pearl Harbor. Since ships are not allowed to enter or leave that port after dark, the ship simply steamed in a four-mile circle all night and pulled into port at zero five hundred.

Everywhere the *Blue Island Sound* had gone on this cruise had been ports with many years of Navy history, and Pearl was the ultimate. The narrow harbor entrance and shallow water had been a boon to the Japanese in their devastating raid of 1941, and Pete noticed the monument in the harbor over the hulk of the battleship, *Arizona*, as the *Blue Island Sound* passed slowly by. All hands on deck popped tall and rendered a reverent salute to the brave men of the USS *Arizona*. Also, there were the beautiful but solemn white crosses lining the low hills in the Veteran's Cemetery known as the Punch Bowl.

The gangways had just been set to the pier when a white car and van pulled up next to the Quarterdeck brow. An officer and five hard hat shore patrol came aboard at the forward brow. They were all wearing dress whites and looked very businesslike with their shiny helmets, leggings and duty belts complete with .45 pistols and night sticks.

They went straight away to the MAA's Office and departed the ship as quickly and quietly as they had arrived. Pete watched from the Supply Office window as they loaded two men from his ship into their van. They had picked up Bagzendel and Smoot, the ship's two vice kings. Bagzendel was in charge of loan sharking, and Smoot was in charge of gambling. Pete strained his eyes at the small letters on the rear bumper of the van as it pulled away behind the car. It read simply, "NI-7."

At Quarters For Muster, all hands were given a three-by-five card which asked some very simple questions about the two men that had been taken away. The members of the S-1 Division filled out their cards and returned them to the Supply Officer. The cards were then given to the Legal Officer at Officer's Call.

After quarters, the Captain declared holiday routine and personally called away "liberty" for all hands except selected volunteers. This was kind of a split liberty situation. Since the ship would be in port for only one night, part of the crew would have day liberty and part would have night liberty. Pete's liberty would start at eight in the evening. In the meantime, he had a lot of work to do at the Naval Supply Center. A base operations car and driver had been assigned to Pete for on-base travel since he had so many parts to pick up for the ship's electronics equipment.

Pete was just about to the bottom of the afterbrow when a voice on the forward Quarterdeck got his attention. It was Commander Larkin of the Operations Department.

"Pete," he called, motioning for Pete to meet him at the bottom of the forward brow. "Do me a favor, and give this to the officer in charge over at NI-7," he said, holding up a small white envelope.

Pete met the officer on the pier, took the envelope and rendered a salute. "I'd be happy to, sir," he replied with a smile. "I'll be just a block away, so I'll stop there on my way in to the Naval Supply Center." Pete turned and stepped into the waiting car.

A few minutes later, Pete was standing in the outer office at NI-7. He looked at the pretty young woman at the desk across from him, a Petty Officer, but pretty nonetheless. He rubbed his hand in the lush carpet on the floor and eyed the drapes on the windows. The office was small but plush. *One thing about Intelligence, they always seem to know the secret of having the nicest offices in the fleet,* Pete thought.

"The Commander will see you, now," the young woman said with a large smile. "Just go right through that door." She pointed to a large hardwood door to the left of her desk.

"Thank you," Pete said as he pecked the small envelope on the thumb of his left hand and started through the door. *What could be so important about such a small envelope that I just couldn't deliver it to a secretary and be on my way?* Pete wondered.

Pete entered a larger, plush office with deep carpet, potted plants and two overstuffed chairs across from a huge wooden desk. The occupant of the high-backed swivel recliner on the other side of the desk had his back to Pete. Pete could see nothing but a whisp of smoke rising from a cigar held in an exposed right hand. A large signet ring from the Naval College sparkled from the third finger.

"Open the envelope and read the card aloud," said the officer in the chair.

"Yes, sir," Pete responded and began to tear the small envelope open. Pete held the card up and read aloud, "Happy family reunion. Your pal, Jim Larkin."

The chair suddenly spun around. The drama was over. The Commander, the officer in charge of NI-7 for the Pacific Fleet was Pete's brother, Bill. Pete almost fainted! He just stood there in total shock with his eyes wide open, and his chin nearly on the floor. The lump in his throat felt the thumping of his heart, and tears of joy wanted to flood from his eyes.

"How you doing, buddy?" Bill came around the desk and gave Pete a big hug. Another officer came into the office and extended his hand to Pete. "I'm Mike Walls. I've been with your brother since you helped us break up that "X" Division scam on Treasure Island."

Pete spent the entire morning with Bill, sending his driver away to be recalled later. Bill explained all of the things that Pete had thought were not exactly true, but Pete had been allowed to think them for security reasons. Bill explained he had graduated with a special group of people ahead of his class with the specific purpose of being assigned to the underground network of NI-7. He had been in the field until he actually did fall and hurt himself last year aboard the *USS Caliente*. The big shock for Pete was that their mother had been aware of the situation the entire time. *What a deal!*

Pete was still walking on air when he got back to the ship at eighteen hundred and delivered his parts to the ET Shop. The duty ET's immediately went to work to get the ship's electronic gear up, and Pete went to the Supply Office to see who was ready to go on the beach.

Pete found Howell, Racozad, Cagney and Chief Anderson in the office. Chief Anderson was an Aviation Storekeeper from the VP Squadron. He had elected to stay aboard because of illness when the squadron pulled out, and he had adopted the S-1 division as his own.

"Anybody going on the beach, tonight?" Pete asked as he dropped into his chair.

Chief Anderson turned, nodding his head up and down as he spoke. "I was just talking about going over to a real nice night spot I know at the International Market Place. Would you like to join us? Their food is excellent, and their drinks aren't so bad either."

"I don't want to go to a place like that," piped up Howell, "unless I can wear my civilian clothes."

"Listen, fellas," The Chief spoke, raising his right hand to get everyone's attention before an argument broke out. "We are just coming home from WESTPAC. The Navy owns Hawaii. If we wear our uniforms, it will look like we are the only sailors on the beach because in any Navy town everyone thinks like Howell. You can be surrounded by lots of sailors, but they'll all be wearing civies. Wearing our uniforms will simply say we're special. We're not locals. We're not just boys from the base."

That was all he had to say. The men put on their dress whites, and within the hour a car dropped them at the International Market Place. They entered a nightclub and were shown to a table on a higher level in the back. There was a show being presented on stage. The key entertainer on stage was a young singer named Don Ho. It was a very entertaining show with Hawaiian sword and fire baton dancers performing between his sets.

The men sat down, and each of them ate a large steak dinner. After dinner, they sat back to enjoy the show and more drinks. They all had plenty of money so the tab of three dollars and fifty cents per drink didn't bother them.

Don Ho asked the audience if there was anyone who had a birthday this week, and lots of young women in the crowd stuck up their hands. Chief Anderson had turned twenty-eight two days before. He was now over the hill, or so the younger men thought.

Cagney pointed him out, and a young woman from the show's cast came and took the chief to the stage. Through the good humor of all the people involved on stage, a very entertaining show was provided, and the Chief came back happy. He got to dance real close with all of the young women on the stage.

When it was time to leave, Pete pointed out that they should get their check paid and be on their way. Howell laid his wallet and a fifty cent piece on the table. "Let's play odd man out," he said as he took another sip from his drink. "Whoever loses has to pay!"

Reluctantly, the rest of the group pulled a coin from their blouse pockets. The Chief got out on the first toss. With each toss of the coin, someone else got out until only Howell and Pete remained. *It would serve him right to pick up the entire tab,* Pete thought, since this was his idea. "You going to be like me or different?" Pete demanded, placing his left wrist with the coin on it covered by his right hand next to Howell's left wrist.

"I'll be like you," Howell winked, removing his right hand to expose a heads up fifty cent-piece.

Pete pulled his hand away, and there lay his fifty-cent piece with the head showing.

While the boys finished their drinks, Pete quietly slid his chair back and walked to the head waiter's stand where the man was observing the customers and directing his elite group of service personnel. "May I have the check for our table?" Pete asked, pointing back to where he had been sitting.

The man flipped a couple of pages in a small book and said, "Your check was two hundred forty-seven dollars and thirty-one cents, sir."

Pete tried not to gasp. "I'd like to pay it." He said. The amount was a hundred dollars more than he had expected. The men must have been thirstier than Pete had anticipated.

"No need, sir," the head waiter replied. "Your check has been paid by the gentleman in the blue suit right over there." He pointed across the room to a large man in a blue business suit, seated at a table with two other business suits. As Pete looked, the man's eyes met his, and the gray haired gentleman raised his glass as if to make a toast. Pete walked to the man's table and extended his right hand. "I'd like to thank you very much, sir," Pete said.

"Happy to, my boy," he replied. "My name is James Odam. I work for Jack Daniels of Kentucky." The man was very distinguished looking and probably beyond the age of normal retirement. "I see you are wearing ribbons on your chest. What are they for? Are you boys coming or going?"

Pete reached up and touched the ribbons over his left shirt pocket. "Oh, we're on our way home, sir." Pete answered as he released the clasp on the ribbons and laid them on the table. Pete pointed to each one. "This is a Presidential Unit Citation, a National Defense Service, a Vietnam Service with three stars, one for each tour of combat duty I have served." Pete handed the ribbons to the man for a better look.

"I lost a son in Korea. They called it a police action. You boys are serving in what they are calling a conflict or war against local insurrectionists. Well, my son didn't come home, so when I see a man in uniform, I think of how I would have liked people to treat my little Bobby." It was obvious Pete was stirring long dead memories in the man.

Pete pushed the man's hand closed on the ribbons. "Why don't you keep these as a souvenir of your trip and my way of saying 'Thanks' from all of us?" Pete pointed to the men at his table who were now leaving. "Thank you," Pete said patting the man's shoulder.

If this man is one of the people I'm serving by wearing my country's uniform, then I'm more than proud to serve, thought Pete.

The next morning as the crew stood Quarters For Leaving Port, Captain O'Hara read the orders he had picked up while the ship was in Pearl Harbor. "You are to proceed to the continental United

States, reporting to North Island Naval Air Station for the transfer of personnel and further preparations for the decommissioning of the *USS Blue Island Sound.*"

As fate would have it, Pete would be completing his four year enlistment at the same time the *Blue Island Sound* would be completing her tour of service.

Chapter 37

Going Home

The ten days to the *USS Blue Island Sound's* stateside home port of San Diego passed very slowly. It was like Chief Wilks said one morning at Quarters For Muster. "It seems like we've spent a month at sea this week."

The last two days were particularly trying. The crew was staying up all night, every night, unable to sleep. Pete was among those who could not sleep for looking forward to being stateside. Doctor Vesper called it 'channel fever.' The entire crew had it, some worse than others.

The ship's last night at sea, the horizon seemed to have a corona around the earth. The lights of the cities on the coast could be seen from far out at sea. Pete remembered the false sense of closeness one could get while standing in the desert looking at the far away mountains of home and thinking what a short distance it must be. In reality, it was probably fifty to seventy miles.

The night before the ship pulled into port, Pete watched the ship's movie, an Elvis rerun, for the fourth time. Later, he sat at his desk in ESO reading when he fell asleep. "Now all hands to Quarters For Entering Port," was the call that woke him.

Pete turned from his desk. His neck was stiff, and his head ached. He had not planned to go to sleep at his desk, but exhaustion had crept up on him and even his raging channel fever could not keep him awake forever. Pete dashed out the door of his office and down to the weather decks. The ship was crossing the breakwater at Point Loma and Naval Air Station, North Island was off the starboard beam. In a half an hour, the ship would be against the pier. The crew would be home!

Pete raced down the three flights of stairs to his berthing compartment, jerked open his locker and started changing into his dress blues as fast as he could.

"I'll tell the Chief you'll be along," said Cagney, tapping Pete's shoulder as he passed in full dress uniform.

"Thanks a lot," Pete grumped as he pulled out his dress shoes and kicked off his flight deck safety shoes.

Pete joined his division at Quarters For Entering Port just as the first rope was cast to the line handling party on the dock. Pete looked out across the pier. He had missed some of the action, the marching of the fifty-one flags, the performance of the rifle drill team and the flyby of four F-4 Phantom jets from the base. However, the Navy band on the pier was still playing marshal music that brought patriotic tears to the eyes of anyone who was listening.

There were people of all kinds on the pier, lots of loved ones. There were banners all over, being held by mothers and children. Each banner had a family's personal welcome home sentiment on it. Sixteen months on this tour had been a long time for everyone involved. Pete studied the crowds of people for a face that stood out, for someone that he knew, but he could see no one. The after gangway was just being attached to the ship and then... "Secure from quarters. Liberty call! Liberty call!" came the word over the 1MC.

The crew had been reassigned to six duty sections. Pete had drawn the duty, and would stay aboard until zero eight hundred tomorrow when his section would be free to go on the beach.

The mail truck was on the pier, already loading mail on the ship. The crew would have mail call within the hour. While the ship was in Yokosuka, Pete had written to his brother-in-law in Salt Lake and asked him if he could see about getting Pete's '56 Ford ready for his return home, and Pete was sure looking forward to hearing from him. Pete had applied to Weber State College in Ogden for admission summer term, and he was anticipating that piece of mail, too.

Pete sat in the Supply Office drinking a cup of coffee, waiting for mail call. He was the only person in the office. The door opened, and Howell walked in. He smiled and motioned for Pete to follow. "Hey, Pete. You have a visitor on the seaplane deck."

Pete followed the smaller man to the seaplane deck where he pointed to a young blonde woman talking to the Petty Officer Of The Watch. "That gal right there was asking for you, Pete," Howell said.

Pete's mind raced as he mentally paged his high school yearbook for the face of the young woman. *Ah, yes. A cheerleader, pep club member, and honor student, Lindy Pearl, Miss Popularity herself. Why is she here? It must be a coincidence.* She turned toward Pete.

"Beauford Peterson," she called as her face lit up with a smile. She extended her arms to give Pete a hug. Pete felt the hair on the back of his neck stand up, and the sides of his face flush red as he heard his given name for the first time in almost two years. All the men in close proximity turned to look and Pete could hear his name repeated as if it were a muffled question, "Beauford?"

Pete took the young woman's extended right arm under his left and half carried her to a quiet area of the fantail where he was sure no one could hear their conversation.

"Please," Pete pleaded, regaining control of his fluster. "Do me a favor while you're on the ship. Call me Pete. Okay?"

"I'm sorry if I embarrassed you." Lindy smiled. "It's just that I haven't seen you in such a long time. I was happy to see you." She opened her purse and took out a set of shiny silver car keys. Pete recognized the big 'Ford' key chain right away. *The keys to my '56 Crown Victoria hardtop!*

"I'm here to drop off your car to you," she explained, placing the keys in Pete's hand. "I'm studying at San Diego State. When I was home for Easter, your mother asked me if I'd bring your car to you. I'll graduate soon, and I hope to see you when I get home."

The couple walked down the gangway and Lindy showed Pete where his car was parked. She had waxed it, and it was just as great looking as ever. Lindy waited for Pete while he went to get special permission from the Duty Officer to drive her home. It was great to have his little car back again.

When Pete got back from taking Lindy home, there were several letters on his desk. It looked as though he had a very good mail call. Right on top was a letter from Weber State. Pete had been accepted by their School of Business to start Summer Quarter in June. Easter vacation had just passed, and Spring Quarter would end soon, so Pete had better be getting things done in preparation for attending college.

The next day, Pete went right away to the Executive Officer with a chit requesting he be granted a sixty-day early separation at the convenience of the government for the purpose of attending school. Pete did not expect it to be so promptly granted, but a couple of days later the XO's office informed him he had been granted his request for early separation. Even though the war was still on and would get even more fierce, consuming more men and materiel, the Navy felt it could let Pete out early rather than assign him temporarily for another two months to another ship. Pete could hardly believe his good fortune.

By the end of the week, Pete had his DD-214 in his hand, his seabag on his shoulder and was on his way down the afterbrow for the last time. He had just saluted the Ensign and taken his first steps on the after brow when a voice came from behind.

"Hey, Pete." it was Chip Dale. He was holding something extended in his right hand. He had tears in his eyes. Pete could see the small item wadded in his hand was a pennant, a red, white and blue pennant. Pete looked at the highest point on the ship's main mast. The ship's commissioning pennant was gone. When a ship is taken out of service this pennant is given to the Admiral of the Fleet. This is a very special little flag.

A tear rolled down the side of Chip's face as he stuffed the pennant into Pete's jumper pocket. "A few of the ET's decided since the ship is going out of service, you deserve to get her colors," he said softly. He turned, hiding his face, and walked away.

Pete had been happy and excited to leave the ship. Now, as he stepped out onto the pier for the last time, it struck him that he was leaving his family. The *Blue Island Sound* had been his home and he was leaving people who were closer than family. For a moment his heart was heavy, or was it his seabag? Chip had been reassigned to the *USS Bon Homme Richard* and would be reporting there in a couple of days. By the end of the week, all of the crew would be reassigned to active ships and their beloved *Blue Island Sound* would be moved by tug to the 34th Street Navy Yard for decommissioning.

The old "Blue Goose," as they called her, had seen duty during the Second World War. Because of the lack of manpower, the ship had been operated with a skeleton crew of 130-180 sailors. In one island invasion in the South Pacific in 1945, a kamikaze attack had claimed the lives of half of those men. Decommissioned after the war, she had been recalled to service during the Korean conflict . Then later in 1961 when the seaplane once again became valuable as eyes to watch an enemy coastline and enforce our country's embargo, she had been called again. She and the crew on her last sixteen-month cruise had carried out the longest period of seaplane operations in US Navy history off the coast of Vietnam, effectively slowing to a tiny trickle the infiltration of Viet Cong strategic materiel by sea. Now, she would go into mothballs as it is called and await the next time she would be needed.

After Pete had changed out of his uniform and got on the road back to Utah, he had time to think past the excitement of the return to the States and his discharge. He had the honor, during the past four years, of serving with some very fine men on two ships that had long and distinguished histories of service in the Seventh Fleet. When Pete had come from boot camp, facing the challenges of those years, he had been a carefree, unorganized teenager. The Navy had offered him excellent training, which he had taken.

There had been some bad times and shocks to his youthful philosophies. Seeing a whole company of his fellow marines wiped out in one afternoon is a scene he would never forget. He would never forget the fine young marine riflemen of Company K, Company L and the leaders he had, Sergeant Perkins, Sergeant Walters, and Lieutenant Baxter.

After the unpleasantness of his experiences at Treasure Island, Pete had more companions. The crew of the *Blue Island Sound* had been a special, closely knit team of 800 men, working with pride to accomplish their mission.

Pete knew even with the challenges of the future, the frightening thought of facing college after being a marginal high school student, he could depend on the confidence and self-reliance he had gained from those years.

Pete guessed he had been fortunate to come out of the service with a positive experience overall, when so many Vietnam vets had to struggle with moving from the combat zone back to a seemingly uncaring, veteran-despising society. But Pete knew in his heart that he had served with honor and was proud to be an American serviceman.

As Pete made the turn east at Cove Fort, Utah and started the last leg of his sixteen-hour drive, he continued to mull over his four years, less a sixty-day cut, of service in the Navy. He had gone into the Navy to find a job, a job that did not require him to go underground. He had not had to go underground, that was true, and his job was never boring.

Pete had been to a lot of places and had met a lot of interesting people. He had enjoyed his work and had enjoyed his tour of duty.

Good old Chip, bringing me the Commissioning Pennant. Pete felt a little chuckle creep up his throat. *He doesn't realize the Blue Island Sound has several new pennants in the flag stockroom and the Signalmen will order a new one from Supply as soon as they realize it's gone.*

A few hours later, Pete stopped at the top of the hill next to the entrance to the magnificent Arches National Monument and looked down at his home town of Moab. The sun was just setting, and the beautiful corals, reds, pinks, and white sandstone sentries blended with the azure sky, smiling a welcome home to him. For awhile, Pete drank of the glorious beauty and shed a tear or two of joy. The street lights seemed to call to him as they were just coming on. They winked and twinkled and then stood bright as the sun paled against the rims of the beautiful red canyon walls and the darkness of evening drew down.

Pete remembered his love of hiking through the red rock country and looking down at the green valley and the wandering Colorado River. He thought then, there could be no place on the earth more beautiful. Pete knew for sure that this was the most beautiful spot God had created.

Pete's family would be waiting for him. His heart thumped. At last, he was coming home from his first real job. He had run away from home because he had not understood the accident that took the lives of some very good men. He was a boy then. Now he could handle the realities of life a little better. He had served and lived. His service, his work, his job for four years had been more than a job, it had been an adventure.

A Note About the Author

Meredith "Ike" Anderson was born in Osceola, Missouri, but did most of his growing up in the deserts of Southeastern Utah near Moab. While on active duty with the Navy, Ike served aboard the USS CURRITUCK (AV7), leaving active duty as an SK2. After graduating from Weber State University, Ike has spent the last thirty years writing outdoor articles about hunting, fishing, camping, cooking and survival to entertain the outdoor enthusiasts of Utah. He is a member of the League of Utah Writers and served as 2007 President of the statewide organization. He lives with his family in Elk Ridge, Utah, where he co-writes with both his wife, Linda and youngest daughter, Kristi Sandgren.

About the Type

The text of this book was set in Palatino Linotype. The fonts were originally designed by Hermann Zapf in 1948. The foundry version was cut in steel by August Rosenberger at the Stempel Foundry in Frankfurt. Zapf then adapted it for the Linotype machine. In photo and digital form, it has become the most widely used of all the neohumanist faces. It is popular among typographic professionals because in its authentic incarnations, Palatino is a superbly balanced, powerful and graceful contribution to typography.

Interior Designed by Mill Creek Press
Salt Lake City, Utah
Cover by Meredith I. Anderson
Elk Ridge, Utah
Printed and bound by BookSurge, LLC,
Charleston, South Carolina

1235955

Made in the USA